About the Author

Susan Griffin's talent for prose was discovered when at school her long descriptive essays won her high praise sparking her passion for writing. For many years Susan dabbled in the art of writing for her own pleasure, it was only when her children had grown up she decided to write a novel. 'Bird in a Gilded Cage' is Susan's first novel and she is currently writing her second book.

Susan Griffin lives in a small East Sussex town with her husband Shaun.

Find Susan at her website:

www.susangriffinauthor.co.uk

ISBN-13 978-1493605231

ISBN – 10 1493605232

Copyright © Susan Griffin 2013

ISBN-13 978-1493605231

ISBN – 10 1493605232

Copyright © Susan Griffin 2013

BIRD IN A GILDED CAGE

SUSAN GRIFFIN

Prologue

21st June 1908

The air was charged with excitement. Beth lifted her head and stood tall at the front of a long line of women waiting to begin what had been predicted to be a 'Monster Rally'. There was an array of ladies, all wearing white dresses with purple, white and green sashes around their waists, or hats and scarves in the same hues. Mrs Pankhurst's words had clearly been heeded. She'd urged her supporters to wear the colours for the first time in public, to show solidarity for their cause. They were joined in their unity by men; who all wore the shades on their ties or badges and either assisted the stewards, or waited to play in the band. Standing amidst the spectacular scene that surrounded her; the deafening buzz of female noise that filled the air, Beth felt both proud and privileged to be part of such a momentous day.

As soon as they stepped off the omnibus at London Bridge station, Alice had taken charge and was now flitting from person to person making sure everything was in order. Beth felt the familiar admiration for her friend as she watched Alice find order in the midst of chaos, relieved that their recent differences seemed forgotten.

At last Alice returned to Beth, satisfied it seemed, that everyone was ready to begin. She looked magnificent the emerald green in her silk scarf exactly matched her eyes, and her hair hung down her back in a mass of red curls. Looking across at Beth she raised her banner high into the air, as every woman in the march took her lead and lifted theirs. A sea of words filled the landscape: 'VOTES FOR WOMEN, DEEDS NOT WORDS or HOPE IS STRONG' were emblazoned across the material, embroidered by women devoted to their cause. For a moment, silence filled the air as everyone waited for the command. Then Alice turned towards them and shouted at the top of her voice: "Ladies, advance forwards!" A loud cheer went up, the band began playing 'Land of Hope and Glory' and the parade began.

The first faltering steps gave way to a determined march, as everyone put one foot in front of the other, keeping time with the band as its music swept above their heads. To be part of such an event filled Beth with a feeling of euphoria such as she had never felt before. For an instant she thought of her mother and wished that she too could be marching beside her and standing up for womanhood across the country.

All along the route crowds lined the streets. Many of the women were cheering at the tops of their voices as they walked past them. But Beth noticed a more mixed reaction from the men, some were jeering or just watching the procession, shaking their heads and frowning at such boldness. She tried to look at the horizon ahead, but sometimes felt compelled to regard the people around her, where occasionally a hostile gaze met her eyes. On the edge of the pavements there stood many female flower sellers, who were out in abundance today. They were a familiar sight in London's streets, selling their wares of small bouquets of pansies, lily-of-the-valley and fern. The obvious poverty they suffered showed in the threadbare shawls that barely covered their bony shoulders. Sad looks were etched onto their lined faces.

After what seemed hours, the procession made its way past Green Park and Beth was relieved to see Marble Arch coming into view. Her arms were aching from holding up the banner and her feet had begun to protest in their laced up boots. The crowd started to squeeze through the arch and Beth felt herself panic at the sheer number of people heading in the same direction. Alice caught her hand and they managed to stay together amidst the jostling of the masses. Beth noticed a woman who'd been carrying a bouquet of flowers drop them onto the ground, where their pretty petals were soon crushed underfoot.

Beyond the arch all order was dispelled as the marchers, mixed with spectators, swarmed like ants towards the park. The area had been transformed to accommodate processions from seven different locations across London. Twenty temporary platforms had been erected in a circle to enable the speakers to address the crowds.

"Beth!" Alice's voice interrupted her thoughts. "Keep hold of my arm, I hope they all remember we're meeting at stage Number Four."

"Yes, I'm sure they will, it's what we agreed." Beth was surprised her voice sounded steady because her heart was leaping about wildly in her chest. Looking around, she couldn't see any of the ladies with whom they'd marched. But as they approached the stand, familiar faces began to appear.

Alice, Beth and a few others fought their way through the hordes of people and clambered up onto the platform, where there was space to breathe again. Beth looked down at the activity beneath her. People were pushing towards the front and there didn't seem to be a square inch between them. The noise was deafening. Alice took her place on the platform, Beth could see the anguish on her face as she fought to get their attention. Then a bugle call sounded loud across the park.

A hush fell over the audience as everyone turned their attention to Mrs Pankhurst, who was standing on a stage nearby. Her voice resounded above their heads.

"Ladies and Gentlemen! Prime Minister Asquith has asked for proof that women truly want the vote!" She spread her arms wide spanning the expanse in front of her. "Surely he could not possibly need more confirmation than the multitude of people standing before me, and the enormous amount of support that both men and women are offering our cause. This is a day which will go down in history! I cannot thank you all enough and so without further ado I pass you over to our host of speakers waiting eagerly for your undivided attention."

A loud roar filled the air. Mrs Pankhurst stepped aside as all attention focused on the spokeswomen. Alice pulled herself upright, glanced down at her notes and began her speech.

Chapter *One*

November 1907

REALISATION

Through the hum of a retiring audience, a woman's whispered tones reached Beth's ears. She was sitting in the first row of the dress circle at the Queens Theatre with her eyes fixed on the now empty stage.

"That was Hugo Somerfield, wasn't it?"

Hugo had just gone off to the saloon bar, after voicing his discontent that Beth would rather stay seated in the interval than accompany him. It hadn't taken more than a moment or two, however, for him to get over his disappointment. Before he had even reached the bar he was consoling himself with the nearest attractive female. Beth's brows creased in a frown as she heard him laugh uproariously. Turning her head she watched him whisper into the woman's ear.

Beth racked her brains trying to fathom why she had thought that Hugo's offer of marriage was acceptable. At first she shunned him, for Hugo was like the others and he certainly had nothing except money to tempt her. He was overweight and did not have a handsome face, his nose was too long, his moustache hid thin lips. His dark unkempt hair was already greying at the temples, for he was ten, nearly eleven years her senior. His complexion was florid she thought, where he overindulged too much in drink. Thoughts distracted Beth's head as they had done last night when sleep had eluded her far into the night and she wrestled with herself over the truthfulness of Hugo's promises. Now she knew it was time to face the truth and move on with her life, she could no longer push the doubts away. She had turned down every other suitor her parents' had presented her with so why had she agreed to marry Hugo? It had come; she attempted to justify, at a vulnerable time in her life. At a time, her beloved grandmother had just died. Beth ached now as she thought how intensely she missed her.

Rubbing her fingers across her forehead where she could feel the beginnings of a headache, Beth looked down at the programme in her hand. She hadn't really taken in what the play 'Beau Brocade' was all about. The programme merely provided the convenience of avoiding the gaze of some of her mother's circle of socialites, and allowed her thoughts to be far away. Having already sat through the first act which had seemed interminably long to Beth, she was not enthusiastic about the next. It would no doubt be accompanied by more instances of Hugo sidling up to her, attempting to touch her in one way or another and making her feel sick with revulsion.

Her thoughts returned to Florence. Her grandmother had definitely been an influence in Beth's life with the stories she used to tell Beth of when she was a young girl. Of course it was even harder then, when Florence was young, to have a say in anything. But she was a woman of spirit and was known as a formidable force to be reckoned with. She was a woman used to speaking up for herself and getting her own way. It was just a few weeks after her death and at her parents' instigation that Hugo had approached Beth to begin their courtship.

It was his expressive eyes that had charmed Beth into thinking she could marry him. Hugo's one redeeming feature, they were dark brown almost black, with long eyelashes. They seemed to hold the promise that Beth sought, which was to still maintain a certain amount of independence in marriage. This was something she valued above everything else. She had long ago given up on fairy tale dreams of marrying for love, and knew the choices left to her amounted to little more than making the best of what was on offer.

Beth's thoughts returned to the day Hugo proposed. They had sat in the morning room. He'd stroked her hand and gazed with those large eyes into her face.

"I know," he said softly, "that you want more from marriage than mere companionship, and I am willing to offer you that."

Beth had stifled the desire to laugh, wondering what he could possibly mean. Then he told her all about the printing business he was running for his stepfather. He hinted that she could play a valuable part in it if she were to marry him. Beth could hardly believe her ears. "How," she had asked him, "How would that be possible?" His reply had been that he knew she needed more in her life than just socialising and that she could help him, not run the production floor or anything like that, but perhaps play a part in maintaining the business's success. Beth said she'd think about it, but next he'd offered to take her to the printing works to show her around. Beth began to feel excited by the prospect of helping Hugo with the apparently successful business, where books - the one love of her life since childhood, were printed. She had begun to think she would have a purpose to her life if she married Hugo, now though she could see he was not all he seemed.

His flirting with other women was the first thing she noticed. Whenever they went out Beth was often left alone and unattended, while he made a beeline for the prettiest woman in the room. She had often heard him lie or stretch the truth while they were out with other people. Hugo's charm was easily turned on. Beth would try to reassure herself by asking Hugo questions about how their lives would be once they were married. Hugo had taken to ignoring her pleas to tell her more about what exactly she would be doing, barely answering her and telling her not to worry her head about the business yet. She was being lied to she could see that now, and the realisation that her life would probably not be much different from her mother's had dawned. Beth could see now that Hugo would have used her as decoration at social functions and still carry on with other women; even the gossips could see that. He would have excluded her from helping with the business despite his promises.

"I see Mr Somerfield has his young lady with him tonight."

"What do you think of her? I don't know how he does it myself, apparently he's going to marry this one!"

Beth could hardly believe that the two women had the audacity to talk about her when it was obvious she could hear every word. Every instinct told her to turn round and confront them, but she also felt compelled to listen to their ramblings for a moment longer.

"Well, he can certainly lay on the charm when he wants to."

"I think that fools the young ladies into thinking he's genuine. But mark my words, a leopard doesn't change its spots."

"No, not if the way he treated his wife is anything to go by..."

"I know. Look what he was up to the other night..."

"And at the musical evening with that woman..."

"And drunk as a lord too!"

Beth had heard enough. She swung round to face the two gossips sitting just a few seats behind her. But she only glared at them, for any words she wished to say were drowned out by the audience acknowledging the orchestra entering the pit beneath the stage.

The women did have the good grace to look quite embarrassed, one of them going quite red in her over-made-up face. They obviously hadn't realised just how loud they had been talking and that the object of their conversation could hear their gossiping.

Beth turned her back on them and focused her eyes on the stage where a woman had just walked on and begun singing. The words of the gossips behind still rang in her ears and she knew they were right.

The singer's voice rang loud and clear across the theatre interrupting Beth's reverie. All at once she sat upright and took notice of the familiar words of the popular song being sung.

She's only a bird in a gilded cage

A beautiful sight to see

You may think she's happy and free from care

She's not though she seems to be

Beth's spine tingled as she sat riveted to the young woman, who was singing as if her life depended on it. For a brief moment, hot silent tears slid down Beth's cheeks.

Tis sad when you think of her wasted life

For youth cannot mate with age

And her beauty was sold for an old man's gold

She's a bird in a gilded cage

Beth quickly brushed the tears from her cheeks and straightened her back. The singer, in her sparkling gown seemed to be looking straight at Beth from her position on the stage. It seemed it was a warning to change things now before it's too late. Beth knew that she was that bird in her own gilded cage and that her life would always be that way if she married Hugo Somerfield. A new determination filled Beth to change her destiny. She thought of the recent pressure from her parents to name the day and knew what she had to do. Beth would end her engagement to Hugo as soon as was humanly possible.

The song finished just as Hugo returned to his seat, he sat down and leaned towards her, the smell of alcohol strong on his breath. "Were you enjoying the singing, my dear?" He said in a patronising tone, his hand running up and down her thigh and his eyes focused on her slightly protruding bosom.

Beth smiled at Hugo swallowing her anger. Now that she had made her decision to end their engagement she would soon be rid of him for good she reminded herself. She so wanted to tell him here and now, wanted to see the shock on his face. Instead she bit back the words that threatened to spill. This was not the time. Taking hold of his hand she lifted it up and placed it back in his lap. She was rewarded with a beaming look from Hugo, who had taken her smile as encouragement. Fixing her with his large dark eyes he mouthed the word 'later' to her. It took all her determination to keep from showing the disgust on her face as Hugo slowly ran his tongue over his lower lip while lifting his eyebrows suggestively. Over my dead body she thought, turning her head to watch the next act of the play.

During the rest of the performance, Beth worked out in her mind how soon she could displace Hugo from her life. The play had been given good reviews and was being described as 'a captivating romance of a chivalrous highwayman,' but Beth barely heard a word being said. The chorus of the song kept ringing in her ears and she knew in her heart it was the sign she had been waiting for.

At last the four acts had all been played out and it was finished. As Beth made her way down the handsome marble staircase, she found herself behind the two gossips she had confronted earlier. Leaving Hugo loitering on the stairs, Beth swept past the two older ladies with her head held high. An unfamiliar feeling of sympathy and kinship filled Beth for the two women, for despite all their finery they too were living in a gilded cage devoid of any kind of freedom and personal choice.

,

Chapter *Two*

FINN

Finn McGuiness was indeed an intoxicating sight as he gazed out to sea. His broad shoulders were covered by workingman's clothes; his flaxen curls lifted gently in the sea breeze. Two women walked in a leisurely fashion on the deck of the cargo ship the 'SS Golden Eagle,' turning their heads they brazenly stared at this lone man who stood on the lower deck. Their female attention went unnoticed, which was unusual for Finn; a man with copious amounts of Irish charm and a certain fondness for a pretty face.

The ship was destined to arrive at the Royal Albert Docks in London having set sail from the U.S. state of Virginia laden with a cargo of spices and tea. Finn had embarked at Cork where the ship had stopped to pick up passengers and stock up with the final few days' food supplies.

It was now the last day of the voyage and Finn's amber eyes were fixed on the horizon. Inhaling deeply, he filled his nostrils with the exotic smells that wafted over from the cargo hold. Whilst watching the swell of the waves, a shrill voice jolted him out of his daydream.

"Good afternoon there, Mr McGuiness."

Finn swung round to see Mrs Lane, an American woman he'd met at dinner the night before, standing behind him. Remembering how she'd not stopped talking, Finn had been surprised she'd managed to consume any food at all.

"Gee, it's a lovely afternoon for March, wouldn't you say, if a little chilly out on deck?" Mrs Lane pulled her shawl closer around her shoulders. She graced Finn with a toothy grin from beneath the large brimmed hat that she clutched firmly against the wind.

"It sure is a beautiful day," Finn agreed, lifting his face towards the spring sunshine. Before he had time to say another word the woman's husband came rushing up to her.

"There you are, Millicent!" He gasped, clasping her arm. "I've been looking everywhere for you."

Millicent seemed none too pleased to see her short stocky husband interrupt their conversation. "Oh for heavens sake, Howard, how far away can I be on a ship of this size?" she scolded, snapping at him like a crocodile.

It was only then the other man noticed Finn standing next to his wife. A dark look appeared on his face and straightening his back he looked Finn up and down rudely. "Good day, Mr McGuiness." He said curtly.

Finn couldn't help smiling at the poor man's demeanour, which seemed to make matters worse. "Good afternoon, Mr Lane. Your lovely wife and I were just passing the time of day." Finn's eyes sparkled with mischief and Mrs Lane beamed at him.

Mr Lane huffed loudly. Pulling on his wife's arm, he began leading her away in the opposite direction away from Finn McGuiness.

Finn turned back to his view of the horizon and anticipated the next day's arrival in London. How would he find the city he wondered? He knew it would be very different from Dublin, his hometown for these past twelve years. A part of him was already homesick for his native country as Dublin was a great place to live. But he wouldn't be sorry to say goodbye to the vastly growing unrest of the last few years. Strikes were now commonplace across the country. The worst so far had been this very year, nineteen hundred and seven. Now the middle of November, since January Dublin had seen over five hundred dockers out on strike.

Finn sighed as he remembered the general atmosphere rippling through the country. Despite all this his decision to leave Ireland and come to London hadn't been an easy one and on the day of his departure he heard again his friend Patrick's parting words. "Are you sure you're doing the right thing, Finn? After all the English are our sworn enemy." Finn had shrugged off Patrick's observation, knowing that Patrick was very different to him and would never leave Ireland. Besides it was too late now he'd made his decision and he was sticking to it. But Finn hadn't been able to shake off the feeling that he was betraying his roots by moving to England, leaving behind his own people for a big city full of danger, inhabited by unfriendly hostile people.

Focusing on the calm waves, an image came into his head of Aisling, the woman he'd left behind. It would have been so easy to stay, especially with the memory of her long chestnut curls, curvaceous figure and soft skin constantly forcing him to doubt whether he'd made the right decision. But something inside Finn told him she wasn't the woman for him. Despite this, guilt was Finn's constant companion on this trip. No stranger to guilt, he'd never stopped fighting against its heavy weight. Ever since that terrible day, the summer he'd turned fourteen, it had clung to him like an octopus's tentacle curled around its prey.

Suddenly the sound of the ship's bell rang high into the air. For a brief moment all those passengers enjoying the spring sunlight stopped to listen. They were trying to ascertain the reason for its sound for it was too early for the dinner bell. Finn's experience of working in the Dublin docklands stood him in good stead however. He immediately realised the significance of the five second ring, followed by one more ring.

"Fire!" Finn shouted as loudly as he could to the passengers. They were all standing agog watching him run towards the ladder. He began climbing the bridge deck. "There's a fire at the front of the ship!"

Everyone immediately scattered and panic broke out among the women. Mr Lane's white shocked face twitched repeatedly at the terrifying revelation that the SS Golden Eagle was now on fire. He did his best to calm his wife who clung to her husband crying. "We are all going to die!"

Chapter *Three*

MARY

Mary Davis slowly entered the darkened bedroom. The hour was early so there was a good chance Master James would be sleeping off his folly from the night before. Glancing nervously towards the bed, she could see his tousled head of dark hair protruding from the mound of covers as the soft sound of his snoring filled the room.

Heaving a sigh of relief Mary crept across the room, knelt before the fireplace and with shaking hands began hastily sweeping ashes from the night before. Behind her James slept soundly, but the young maid shivered as she remembered times past when his unwelcome advances had haunted her dreams.

As Mary toiled at her early morning chore her hands blackened with soot, her mind returned to her first day at Richmund House. Mrs Stokes had given her the instructions needed for her duties to be carried out and Mary had vowed to work hard every single day. She had made a promise to herself when she'd left her overcrowded and impoverished home just a few short months ago. A promise that she would make something of herself and already that promise was being fulfilled. Pride filled Mary as she thought back to the day before. Mrs Stokes had drawn her aside and told her that due to her hard work she had been promoted from scullery maid to housemaid.

As Mary dipped her head to concentrate on cleaning the fireplace she felt her white cap slip down across her eyes, momentarily blinding her and causing her to drop the dustpan with a clatter. The sound echoed across the room and Mary's heart almost stopped. She froze then glancing across at the bed she was relieved to see that the master's deep sleep hadn't been disturbed and so continued her work.

A moment later and without warning Mary was pulled violently backwards and pinned to the carpet beneath her feet. The dustpan with its retrieved contents was knocked flying and Mary felt herself choking uncontrollably on the dust from the ashes caught in her throat. James tugged at her corset and forced one hand down her chemise. His other hand had hold of her hair. Despite the pain being inflicted on her scalp, Mary was trying in vain to escape. Kicking up her legs, she attempted to ram her knees into his groin. But to no avail. Now devoid of their cap her blonde curls were in disarray on the floor and her face was a mask of horror.

James's quiet strength held her down as the room swirled around her. "Stop fighting. You know you want this, I've seen the way you look at me." His breath reeked of stale alcohol, his steady voice cutting through her panic. His eyes glowed like hot coals in the dark, his face was only an inch from hers. "You don't need to pretend now my comely maid. Give into the pleasure I'll give you."

Mary felt him looking deep into her soul as terror gripped her.

"Help, please...!" At last a sound had managed to find its way out of Mary's mouth.

James's lips touched Mary's ear. "Come on, Mary, it's only a bit of fun," he cajoled. Tears of frustration streamed down Mary's face as thoughts spun through her head of times past, when she had to resist this man's advances. James took advantage of her brief moment of hesitation and pulling her bloomers aside, he pushed himself deep between her thighs. Pain tore through Mary's unwilling body at this violation and an agonised scream escaped her lips. As James slumped forward, Mary truly thought the end of her days had come, for his partially clothed body was a dead weight on hers. As air was once again forced from her body, she felt a black void sucking her deep within its depths. Into that vacuum came an image of the door opening. The formidable Mrs. Stokes was standing in the doorway staring at Mary sprawled on the floor, her legs locked in fear and entwined with those of the young master.

"So, is it more pleasure you want, my fair maiden?" James taunted as the housekeeper's shocked face disappeared from the half open door.

Mary fought to breathe as the realisation that she might lose her position forced her into fighting for her life. With what little strength there was left she began pummelling and punching James for all she was worth.

James raised himself up, still holding onto her flailing arms. A look of amusement played around his lips. "Hey. Enough! It's too late for that my 'not so fresh-faced,' little maid." You're a dark horse aren't you?" he quipped. "I think you enjoyed that as much as me. Maybe another time, when I have you in my grasp, we can enjoy these pleasures again."

"No...It weren't like that!" Mary declared between ragged breaths as James let go of her arms and sat back laughing. She struggled clumsily to her feet, trying desperately to pull her chemise back into place. Glancing towards the door at the space where Mrs Stokes had stood only a few moments earlier, Mary was filled with mortification that the older woman had witnessed her shame. Hanging her head she turned her back on James and began doing up the few buttons that hadn't been broken. Behind her she sensed him walking back towards the bed.

Anger filled Mary like molten lava and her face burned as she pulled up her bloomers and dabbed at a trickle of blood running down her leg. She felt sick to her stomach as bile rose in her throat mixing with the taste of dust that had earlier made her choke. She remembered how months earlier James had cornered her in an upstairs room, his words once again rang in her ears. "You know you want this; I've seen the way you look at me."

Now he had carried out the threats he'd made that day and Mary knew for sure that what had just happened was all her own fault. Even though, for the life of her, she couldn't recall ever looking properly at his face before today.

The fastenings on the back of Elizabeth Hamilton-Green's moss-green gown were proving difficult to do up. Determined not to call a maid to help her with this most menial of tasks Beth wondered why her fire hadn't been made up, usually the room was warm even at this hour. Restless and unable to sleep Beth had risen early. The house was deathly quiet, but as she opened the bedroom door a muffled sound reached her ears, causing her to hesitate in the doorway. Silence once again reigned. Beth decided the noise must have been imagined and so continued on her way.

With her foot on the top step of the stairway, she heard it again, penetrating the early morning stillness. Stopping to listen, Beth's eye caught a movement in the shadows at the far end of the corridor. A huddled figure was hiding in the doorway. Beth recognised Mary, the young servant girl who was rarely seen by the family as she crept about the house carrying out her duties. Beth found it hard to accept the rule that the lower servants were not worthy to look upon their superiors, and whenever she saw members of staff she continually tried to acknowledge their presence. Beth approached the young maid with caution. "Mary? It is, Mary, isn't it? What's the matter... are you ill?"

Mary slowly twisted round to face her mistress and Beth was shocked by her appearance. A river of tears ran down her pale cheeks, dishevelled hair sat in ugly clumps around her head and shoulders, her eyes were red and swollen and her white housemaids cap was missing. The front of Mary's dress was partly undone, revealing the soft white flesh of her bosom. Beth saw that the girl was holding her cap in sore and grazed hands, staring down at the head covering as if her life depended on it.

Beth tenderly reached out a hand towards Mary's shoulder knowing that something terrible had befallen her. "Good Lord, Mary, what on earth has happened to you?"

Mary visibly flinched. Pushing herself further back into the doorway, she fixed her wide fearful eyes on Beth's concerned face.

"Sorry...M...Miss...E...Elizabeth."

Waving away her apologies, Beth took matters into her own hands. Gently; but firmly, she took hold of the girl, who was shaking uncontrollably. At the same time she glanced around the expanse of corridor to check they were alone, before quickly steering Mary away from her hiding place and into Beth's own bedroom.

Beth quietly shut the door behind them and led Mary over to the bed. She pushed Mary's pliable body down onto the edge of the mattress and took a step back. A fear clutched at Beth's stomach as she assessed Mary's vacant expression. "If the eyes are the window to the soul," Beth thought, "then Mary is surely already dead."

Chapter *Four*

ACCOUNTABILITY

Beth walked quickly over to her dressing table and sat down in front of the mirror, the face that looked back at her was flushed with suppressed rage. Without thinking she picked up a glass pot and threw it across the room. But it wasn't the sound of glass breaking, as it smashed into tiny pieces which echoed in Beth's head, it was the sound of Mary's distraught voice.

"It weren't the young master's fault though. I know. I know that Miss Elizabeth..." Mary had sobbed.

"Now, Mary, you know that's not true." Beth had replied, aghast at the young girl's perception of the situation. "Of course it was his fault." Beth knew that Mary was trying to take the blame, attempting to show her mistress that she understood her place in the hierarchy of the household. "And all for what?" Beth fought with herself. "A few shillings a week and a cold room in the loft with barely any daylight. Is that why? Is that what her wretched life is like in this tainted household?" Mary's words kept coming back into Beth's head round and round like a spinning top.

"It was because I give 'im the eye, Miss. Elizabeth, it's what he told me. He said I asked for it."

"No..." Beth cried aloud to the unhearing world, attempting to stop the repetition of Mary's words hammering in her head. Tears of pity, rage and torment filled her eyes. "No," she whispered as she saw herself again kneeling in front of the poor servant girl and looking into her face.

Now, peering almost fearfully into her mirror on the polished dressing table, Beth felt as if she were daring to look back, to relive Mary's account. Searching the mirror and her own reflection, she knew she wanted a reaction in her own face, her window to the soul.

Beth squeezed her eyes shut and exhaled slowly attempting to still the boiling rage still racing in her veins. The image of Mary rocking from side to side, her arms clasped around her body, spun in Beth's head. She felt an overwhelming desire to be sick, as she saw again the pain etched on the young girl's face, and heard the loud shrieking noise coming from her wide open mouth.

Beth was afraid that Mary's hysteria would bring the other servants running to the room. Without thinking she had raised a hand to Mary. The sting on the palm of her hand, and the noise as it made impact with Mary's cheekbone all came back in amazing clarity. Beth opened her eyes and looked down at her hands as if they alone were guilty of this terrible misconduct not her.

Afterwards there had followed an immediate silence.

The strike had the desired effect, for as soon as it was done, Mary had folded in on herself, and sliding from the bed she had collapsed onto the floor. Beth had not attempted to help Mary up, fearful that any tenderness might put her back in shock. Instead she'd waited until her crying had ceased. Beth had needed all the patience she possessed, to sit and gently coax the story from Mary, for the young maid kept apologising for looking such a state and not having her cap on. At first Mary had tried to imply that she'd fallen down the stairs, but she'd soon realised that Beth was more astute, and as Beth herself had said: "they would sit here all day if needs be, until the truth is out." Mary had faltered, until eventually Beth had promised not to tell a soul, only then did Mary allow the whole story involving Beth's brother to be revealed.

Calmer now, Beth tried to give herself a moment from re-living her encounter with Mary. Her respite was brief however.

Pulling out her perfectly-ironed, white laced handkerchief from the silken sleeve of her dress, Beth was reminded how Mary had, just a short while ago, fumbled in her apron pocket, and finding it bare of cloth or rag had dabbed at her nose with a sleeve. Mary had bitten down on her lower lip and looked at Beth, imploring her to understand. Now, Beth believed she was learning more about the household, and the people that lived under the rule of her parents' than, poor sweet Mary's eyes had ever intended. Of course she had seen servants dismissed from the household in the past, it was usually under the guise of some misdemeanour or other.

Some of the girls had obviously been pregnant, and Beth had judged them to have the morals of an alley cat. It had never occurred to her, in her naivety, that her own brother could be responsible for the fate of some of these young girls. How many other times had this happened before? Beth asked herself.

Ashamed of her ignorance of the injustices going on right under her nose, Beth closed her mind to the past and concentrated on helping Mary.

"Exactly when had James come across her?" Beth had questioned Mary. "Was James entering her room?" Beth was aware of the regulation that the female staff were not allowed to lock their rooms at night. Although now, she couldn't help asking herself, why she hadn't tried in the past to change this rule; which was a blatant disregard for their privacy.

"No, Miss, 'e finds me alone cleaning in one of the bedrooms, or when I'm going up the back staircase on me own. He says 'ell come and find me. But, Miss Elizabeth, I'm clever mostly." Pride had flickered briefly across Mary's face as she spoke. "I manage to get away from him, you see?"

At Mary's words Beth realised that the girl measured her cleverness against the ability to avoid being trapped and caught. Beth remembered then how she had felt wholly inadequate looking at the young maid, feeling as she did every-day, trapped and desperate to escape. It occurred to Beth that despite Mary and herself being on opposite sides of the fence, they were both playing the same dangerous game, where the ultimate prize was survival.

For a moment Beth had been struck dumb, unable to find words of comfort to offer Mary. The young girl had taken this as a sign that she needed to further explain herself, and repeat her earlier confession. "I give 'im the eye, Miss, and he says I asks for it." Mary hung her head and Beth had seen ' fresh tears fall onto her cheeks. Guilt had stabbed at Beth's heart at the red hand mark visible across Mary's right cheek. In taking her hand to a servant, Beth wondered whether she had, without meaning to, also violated this young girl. She pushed this thought away knowing that regardless of rank or social position, a swift slap across the face was known to be the most effective remedy for hysteria.

Beth had known she had asked more than she'd dare: knowing the poor girl had been fragile and vulnerable. But still she felt she needed more clarification of what exactly happened. Mary's voice had risen hysterically again as she'd revealed, in basic detail, what James had done when he had finally caught up with her. Beth had felt a ridiculous desire to laugh, Mary didn't have the nuances and subtlety of phrase to cushion such an account for ladies ears. She couldn't protect Beth with educated words and etiquette, and allow her to remain naive to his stalking by simply glossing over the incident. Beth's mind turned to her beloved books, and she likened Mary's account of what happened to a recently read novel. In her pursuit of good reading material, Beth had found one such author who wrote in a way that at times made her blush, the story was told leaving little to the imagination.

Beth had been heartily ashamed of James's misconduct and her own words echoed in her ears. "I'm sorry, Mary, for my brother's behaviour. I really am." Stripped of her own eloquences and aware of the unfairness of what had happened to Mary, all she could say was. "I'm sorry, I'm so sorry. I will make sure he doesn't come near you again."

James would need to be dealt with. Beth knew the girls dilemma would not go away without intervention, she could only hope that she would be able to keep her promise to Mary. The girl had been ensnared in her brother's disgusting web but would not remain imprisoned if she had her way. Beth stood up, lifted her skirts, and began stepping carefully over the shards of glass scattered across the carpet, then walked briskly out into the corridor.

The chill in the air hit Beth as she flung open James's bedroom door, her eyes blazing with anger. The heavy velvet curtains were still drawn, and in the half-darkness Beth glanced towards the fireplace at the fire banked up ready to be lit. Mary's pain reeled in Beth's head, and in her mind's eye she could see the girl fighting for her virtue. She willed the disturbing image to leave her head, it was justice Mary needed from Beth now, not more sympathy.

The sound of James's soft snoring drew Beth's eyes to the bed, where he lay sprawled amongst the bedclothes. His breakfast lay cold and congealed on a tray, and a cup of tea next to the untouched plate had grown a skin. There was nothing in Beth's soul but contempt for this person who was her blood brother, this man, whose days were spent gambling or shooting and his nights drinking and womanising. Despite this as she approached the bed, Beth found her anger turning momentarily to wry amusement, for part of his anatomy had fallen out of his nightshirt and lay exposed for all to see. Well, she wasn't going to cover him up. Let him feel ashamed that she'd seen that private part of him she shouldn't have - for he more than deserved a little humiliation.

"James!" she shouted wildly. When this prompted no response Beth stooped towards the still form, and taking him by the shoulders shook him roughly.

His eyes flicked open in surprise as he attempted to focus on her face.

"W... what is it, Bunty, old girl?" James croaked. He looked disorientated and stared at Beth standing to one side of the bed. Then following her line of vision he looked down and realisation dawned. But, instead of being embarrassed James took this opportunity, as he so often did, to tease his younger sister. So, making no attempt to cover up he simply hoisted himself to an upright position in the four poster bed and stared at her intently. "Why, Bunty, you had better have a good look - it may be the only opportunity for you to see some manhood," he jested, then threw back his head and howled with laughter.

"Don't be so vile, you evil creature!" Disgusted at her brother's behaviour Beth turned on her heel and strode away. "I will speak to you downstairs within the hour. Or, I will report to Father your dealings with the maids!" She said, glaring back at James from the doorway.

Beth sat in the small library waiting for James and had almost given up on him when at last he appeared. His hair was standing on end and his clothes were crumpled. He obviously hadn't bothered to summon a valet to help him dress.

"You were almost too late," Beth scowled, as James sat down shooting her an arrogant look. "Tell me. What do you think you are doing?"

"I'm doing anything I choose to do, Bunty, and you can't stop me." James gazed at Beth from under half-closed lids still full of slumber. In his face was reflected the confidence that Beth had no way of stopping him doing exactly as he pleased. Whatever it was she was mad about was of little concern to him.

Faltering slightly Beth repeated. "Tell me, what do you think you are doing?" As a flicker of confusion passed across his face, Beth realised that James was bewildered as to which particular dirty deed she was referring.

"Bunty, I don't know what you are talking about."

"Stop calling me by that ridiculous nickname." She forced her voice to sound calm. "James. Mary is a young servant girl. You have no need to take your pleasure from her, as I'm sure you have plenty of choice in other directions."

"Oh yes. Our little encounter this morning." A slow smirk spread itself across James's handsome features and he shook his head and sighed.

"I would hardly call it an encounter!" Beth's temper flared at James's flippant way of describing what he had done to Mary that morning. "You took away the girls virtue, you animal!"

"Look, Sis, she's pretty and she's forbidden; that makes her more exciting than the others." James leaned towards Beth and looked into her narrowed eyes. "Anyway, I've had my fun with her now, she got what she wanted from her young master. I won't be touching her again."

"James! How could you?" Beth could hardly believe how her brother was justifying his appalling behaviour. Standing up she began to pace the room, the red-hot rage had returned and was racing in her veins, making her feel like lashing out at him. But common sense prevailed. Violence would achieve nothing. Leaning against a bookshelf to the side of the fireplace, she glared across at her brother slouched in the leather armchair. He was mocking her with his eyes and enjoying her discomfort. In that moment Beth found it hard to believe that this was the same young boy she had idolised as a child, and looked up to during their growing years.

James's expression softened at the dispirited look on Beth's face and sitting upright he attempted to placate her. "Look, Bunty, old girl, calm down, there's no harm done surely? If she doesn't spill the beans then I certainly won't. Mother and Father don't worry about the odd incident here and there." He stood up turning to go. Beth was speechless as she watched him walk towards the door.

"And...What if she's with child?" Beth hissed at James's retreating back.

James hesitated for a moment in the doorway and then turned to look back at his sister. With a half smile and as if offering advice, he tapped the side of his nose and added in a confidential half whisper. "If she is, then it's her millstone and nothing to do with me."

Chapter *Five*

ESCAPE

Being a spectator to her brother's ridiculous antics did not seem a worthwhile pastime to Beth Hamilton-Green. She was however inexplicably drawn to the bedroom window to watch enviously at the freedom he enjoyed.

The sound of the car arriving in the drive had not initially prompted her to rise from the buff wicker chair where she sat working on her embroidery. It had been the driver tooting the horn, followed by loud whooping from both men which had caused the muscles to tighten in her pretty face, and the blood to boil in her veins. With fists clenched by her sides Beth watched as James quickly deposited something in the boot of the car, then drove off at speed; leaving behind a trail of dust in the air.

The driveway now empty Beth inhaled deeply and turning from the window walked over to pick up her work. Attempting to resume the task in hand, she found her efforts were being hampered by the violent thumping of her heart, and the intensity of the anger raging in her body. Images filled Beth's head of the escaping car and she heard again the sound of screeching tyres on gravel. Struggling with the tiny stitches, a sharp pain penetrated her finger. No longer able to hold in a torrent of frustration, she let out a loud piercing wail that ricocheted off the bedroom walls. Torment etched itself across Beth's features and her raven hair clung in wisps around her forehead.

For a brief moment, only the crackling of the fire in the grate broke the silence, then as she expected there was a loud rapping on her bedroom door.

"Miss Elizabeth! Miss Elizabeth. Are you unwell?"

Beth glared at the closed door and spoke sharply to the unfortunate servant. "I am perfectly well. Please go away." Sitting on the edge of the bed Beth felt the walls were closing in on her. The ever present sense of being suffocated returned with a vengeance. As a lone tear began snaking its way down her cheek, the red flame of rage loosened its grip. Sighing deeply, Beth rubbed furiously at her eyes. Retracing her steps she unfastened the catch and swung open the window.

The rush of cold air on Beth's reddened face began cooling her cheeks. Glancing across the driveway into the garden beyond, she could see old Ned tending to the greenery. Just at that moment he stood up and stretched, catching sight of her at the open window, and the lines on his weathered face creased into a smile. A memory flashed through her mind of a day gone by, when she had whiled away the time with him. Having little else to do and longing to escape from the house, she'd come upon him sweeping debris from the pond. Beth had stood watching Ned with his hands in the water skirting around the huddle of fish, and made an observation that the small black one was often alone and separated from the others.

"It's as if 'e don't fit in, Miss." Ned explained. "The other fish shun him, you see?"

"A square peg in a round hole." Beth had replied thoughtfully.

"Be a bit like someone else I knows..." Ned's pale eyes twinkled at her knowingly.

Beth had smiled back at the kindly old man whom she'd known since childhood. He seemed to see through her so easily, despite her attempts at hiding her feelings.

Now, in the distance she could see a glimpse of winter sunshine peeping through the clouds, making everything appear brighter. Suddenly the need to escape came upon her so fiercely that she could barely still her hands to close the window.

Feeling quite desperate now to abscond and already miles away in her thoughts, Beth was jolted out of her reverie by a soft knock on the bedroom door. Impatiently she opened it to find Helen standing in the doorway looking back at her intently. Clearly Beth's mother had sent her own ladies maid to soothe 'the rebellious daughter.'

"Is everything in order, Miss?" Helen glanced at the red and orange flames in the fireplace, before her eyes fell on Beth shivering from a distinct chill in the air.

"Yes, Helen." Defiance, Beth's constant companion struck urgently as she glared at the other woman. "What is it you want?"

"Your Mother sent me, Miss Elizabeth, to help you with your hair."

"Not now, Helen." Beth's tone was sharper than she'd intended which showed in the dismayed expression on the maid's face. "Very well then, but I don't have much time." There was nothing for it but to let the woman in. Helen nodded then on entering the room made her way towards the dressing table.

Beth hesitantly sat on the cushioned stool, her eyes darkening as she stared at her reflection in the mirror. Helen took up her position, brushes in hand, and began slowly untangling the knots, pulling gently at Beth's dark hair which hung down her back in an unruly mane.

While this ritual was taking place the two women were silent and Beth could feel the red wave of anger begin its fight for freedom once more. She pursed her lips together in order to stem the flow of words threatening to spill out, and reminded herself that Helen had no time for her confidences. Once before, when desperate to talk to another female, she'd attempted to explain her feelings to Helen, mainly highlighting how her need to escape was at times overwhelming. It had been a huge mistake. Her mother's maid had not understood. Having only ever experienced a life of hard work, Helen had failed to see how Beth could possibly be unhappy in this beautiful house, where her every whim was taken care of without needing to lift a finger.

Now, as Helen concentrated hard on the task in hand avoiding eye contact with her mistress's daughter, her face held a closed look. The atmosphere between them hung heavily in the air and it was more than Beth could bear.

"That will be enough for today," she announced loudly, standing up abruptly and overturning the stool. Helen's brushes went flying out of her hands as she was forced to take a step back.

"But, Miss, your hair. I need to finish it..."

"No! I'll do it myself." Beth's agitated fingers pulled at the strands of dark hair that hung around her face. Helen was used to Beth's outbursts, which had become more frequent of late. She bent to the floor to pick up the brushes, which were scattered around the heavily patterned carpet. As Beth watched the other woman crawling around the floor on all fours, she became aware that she had acted rather harshly. After all, Helen was only trying to do her job.

"Don't worry about the brushes," she said. Helen stood up and straightened her back, but before she could utter a word Beth had opened the bedroom door and stood with her hand on the knob, waiting for her to leave.

"Are you sure, Miss?"

"Perhaps later. I can't bear the brushing at the moment, my head is full of pain and I need to lie down on my bed to recover." The fictional headache seemed to appease Helen who gave Beth a half smile as she left, silently closing the door behind her.

Beth waited until Helen's footsteps could no longer be heard on the stairs, and then opened the door glancing around her furtively. All was quiet once again. Beth hurried back into the bedroom to pick up a letter lying on her bedside table. She took a book from a pile stacked on the floor by her bed. Then she hastily made her way out into the silent corridor and was about to descend the long stairwell, when her eye was caught by her grandmother's portrait at the top of the stairs. The solemn face stared at her from its gilt edged frame. Beth took in the steely glare, taking strength from her grandmother's fiery spirit, before continuing on her way with her head held high.

Passing the mirror at the bottom of the stairs Beth's reflection startled her, a woman she hardly recognised stared back at her. The eyes, red from recent tears and the tangle of knots in her hair made her look like a common woman of the street. This was despite her purple velvet dress with the silk ivory sash which accentuated her hourglass figure. Shrugging she realised her desire to flee was more desperate than the need to sort out any changes to her outward appearance.

The door to the morning room was open and Beth caught sight of her mother sitting at her desk, her greying head bent over spectacles perched on the end of her nose. Beth crept past quickly not wanting to draw attention to herself, when a 'tell-tale' creak in the floorboards caused Sarah Hamilton-Green's head to swivel upwards, diverting her attention away from her work.

Beth stopped in the doorway and returned her mother's intense gaze, feeling like a rabbit caught in the full glare of a car's headlamp, exposed and vulnerable.

"Mother, I have decided to go into town," she announced defiantly. "I have some errands to run." Beth pushed the letter between the pages of the book and tucked it under her arm, then turned on her heels to walk away.

"Elizabeth!"

Beth swung round to face the reprimand she knew to be imminent. Sarah was looking at her intently, her gaze lingering on her daughter's dishevelled hair.

"Has Helen neglected to do her duty and help you dress your hair this morning? What a state you look, girl!"

Beth's free hand flew to her head instinctively. "Mother! Why can't you see there is more to life than tidy hair?"

Sarah heaved a heavy sigh and sat down, pulling the spectacles from her nose and rubbing furiously at the sore patch on her neck, that only seemed to appear when her daughter was being particularly difficult.

Beth observed her mother, taking in the stiff collar of the high necked blouse. She knew this would be one of many outfits she'd be required to wear during the course of the day. For a moment her defiance gave way to a slither of sympathy for this woman who had brought her into the world.

"I like my hair this way, Mother," she lied, dipping her head so that her mother could not read the sympathy in her eyes.

"That may be the case, Elizabeth, but it looks *such* a sight." Sarah's hands were still, the red patch on her neck spreading to her face which now held a resigned look.

"Mother, can't you address me as Beth? I do much prefer it, as you well know."

"I need to buy some lace and could do with the fresh air," Sarah said, choosing to ignore her daughter's request.

Beth's heart sank. But for once she decided not to argue with her mother, knowing there was nothing to be done if she had made up her mind. She took a step into the room and watched her mother's hands flying over the paperwork, as she tidied it into a neat pile.

Sarah stopped her activity to address the questioning look in her daughter's eyes. "What is it? I am going with you whether you like it or not."

"I know, it's not that. Tell me, Mother, do you know where James is today?"

As if she knew what was coming, Sarah exhaled loudly then held her daughter's gaze. "You know as well as I do I have no idea where James is." Beth's mouth opened then closed again, as her mother continued her explanation. "Let's not go over old ground, Elizabeth, your brother can do as he pleases."

Beth's rage boiled over into a child-like retort. "Well, I saw him earlier getting into Alfred's car, he had his golf clubs with him. It's not fair! He has so much more freedom than me!"

Sarah shrugged having heard this particular argument many times before. "Perchance, he may have, but there is nothing to be done about it."

Their first port of call was the home of the wealthy Middleton family. Here Beth handed her borrowed book to the butler to pass onto her friend Emma. Emma's mother and father knew her parents well and were often at Beth's home on social occasions. Beth would have liked to stop and pass the time of day with Emma, but this was impossible, the subjects the two young women liked to discuss were not for her mother's ears.

On their arrival in town Sarah headed towards the haberdashery. As Beth watched her emerging from the shop clutching the paper bag, she remembered her mother's drawers at home bulging with lace, and knew it hadn't been needed at all. Resentment at her mother's controlling ways rose in Beth's chest, forcing her to stifle the desire to confront Sarah with the knowledge of her lies. This would undoubtedly lead to a disagreement in public, and that would never do, Beth told herself. For now, she would have to let her mother think she had won this small battle.

After a quick visit to the post office to obtain postage for her letter, Beth went in search of a post box with her mother ever present and close behind her. As she pushed the envelope through the slot, an image entered her head of her friend Victoria's wedding day. Frowning, Beth remembered the man standing by Victoria's side, he was almost a head shorter than his young bride and his ugly face was filled with lines. Beside him Victoria shone with alarming beauty, her auburn hair perfectly complimenting her peaches and cream complexion. Having been forced to marry a wealthy man old enough to be her father, Victoria was now living with the consequences. She wrote often to Beth from her new Oxfordshire Manor House, of the days stretching ahead of her, as she waited for the heir to her husband's fortune to be born. Beth replied as often as she could in an attempt to brighten her lonely existence and keep her spirits up, determined that she would not share Victoria's fate.

With the errands done, there didn't seem much to do but amble along the quiet streets and peer aimlessly into the shop windows. Beth missed the sense of freedom that going out alone brought her and felt stifled by her mother's presence.

As they walked along their way, Beth's eyes were drawn to a cluster of women on the other side of the road. She stopped to look with interest at their activities and the women began shouting loudly. Their voices carried high above the noises of the street. Other passers-by stopped to see what the commotion was and her mother tugged at her elbow, sensing trouble not far away.

Beth gazed across at the group, and her eye was caught by a particularly striking looking woman marching furiously along the pavement. She was tall with a head of flaming red hair, which stood out against the greyness of the chilly February morning. Beth thought she looked similar in age to herself and couldn't help noticing how her commanding presence made her look different from the others. Straining to hear the words they were chanting, Beth noticed that all the women were wearing billboards with the words: **VOTES FOR WOMEN & WOMEN HAVE THE RIGHT TO VOTE** on the front in big black letters.

Never having seen such a spectacle before, Beth felt excited and exhilarated just watching these inspiring women. She had heard about the Suffragette movement, but to actually see them demonstrating with such energy and strength, was an extraordinary experience.

The red-haired woman had noticed Beth's gaze from across the street and was now waving furiously at her to join them.

Without thinking Beth began crossing the road. As she dodged the oncoming carriages and motor cars the sound of a car horn honking loudly, echoed through the air. Sarah still had hold of Beth's arm but was unable to halt her daughter. 'Red hair' stopped shouting as the others took over, holding out her hands as Beth approached. As they clasped hands Beth's breath caught in her throat. In that moment they were complete strangers, but she felt a bond forge between them.

"Join us, sister." 'Red hair's' voice was rising once again.

Beth nodded as her horrified mother looked on. By now the others had stopped reciting and were turning their attention towards the two fixated women.

"Stop it, you, charlatan!" Sarah's resounding voice echoed in Beth's ears as she felt herself being roughly pulled away. But before Beth released her grip something was pushed into her hand.

As she walked away, Beth looked back at the small group and noted they had started chanting again. A few people were gathering around. 'Red hair' still stood where she had left her. A smile was exchanged between them, Beth felt the world shift beneath her feet.

"Elizabeth! What were you thinking of, my girl?" snapped her mother as she marched her daughter towards the motor car. Beth slipped the tiny piece of card into her coat pocket, making a mental note to look at it later in the privacy of her own room.

"Well?" Sarah wanted an answer from her headstrong daughter.

Beth glanced overtly at her mother as they walked side by side. Inwardly she cursed her for stopping her from joining those exciting women. Despite this, she knew deep down that her mother's short temper was due to Beth's own rebelliousness. She realised with a jolt, that things would never improve between them. Beth knew she could never agree to live the quiet, boring life her mother wanted for her.

Later, when an excited Beth eventually got to read the secretly smuggled, now crumpled note, given to her in town, she found it was a business card.

It was hard, after that eventful day to contain her excitement and be patient. Beth tried to appear normal to her mother, who kept questioning her whenever she went out. In the end it was barely a week after meeting 'Red Hair' that she managed to escape and go in search of the address on the card.

Hesitating outside the front gate with the card clutched securely in her hand, Beth felt her courage desert her. The noise levels coming from the house indicated there was a meeting going on inside, and therefore dashing any hopes Beth had of avoiding too many prying eyes and finding out more about *'Alice Sparks – Seamstress at your service'*.

Chapter *Six*

VIOLET'S LODGING HOUSE

Violet Williams genuinely liked her sister in law Millicent. She never ceased to wonder however, how she could actually be related to Violet's late husband Fred. The two certainly looked alike but in character they were as different as chalk and cheese. The woman sitting across the kitchen table from Violet was loud and brash, whereas Fred had been the dark brooding type.

"Well, it's good to see yer, Milli, after so many years." Violet declared through red painted lips. " You must tell me how the boat trip from America was, my dear."

Millicent's mouth curved into a wide smile revealing two protruding eye teeth. "It must be twenty four years since the last time we met, Vi. I have to say that you look just as good now as you did on your wedding day."

Violet sighed, patted her coiffured hair and visibly puffed up her chest causing her bust-line to protrude further out of her low-cut tightly fitting dress. So engrossed was she in her own vanity, that she missed the look of contempt on Howard's face. "Why thanks for your kind words, Milli," she said, her eyes brightening at the compliment.

"It must be so hard without Fred though?" Millicent frowned at Howard's downcast expression as he sat drinking his tea. "Tell me, how have you managed these past four years?"

"Silence is golden," said Violet following Millicent's line of vision and ignoring the other woman's question. 'What was the matter with Howard?' She mouthed the words silently to Millicent who lifted her eyebrows and shrugged. Violet hadn't seen Howard since her wedding but couldn't remember him being this quiet even then, in fact he'd talked constantly, almost as much as Millicent had. It was true there had never been any love lost between herself and Howard. She had always considered him to be far too boastful, what with the way he constantly bragged about his investments and moneymaking skills.

"I know you said Fred didn't suffer when he died..." Millicent ploughed on ignoring Violet's puzzled looks in Howard's direction. But I do hope you weren't just trying to spare my feelings."

It seemed to Violet there was a note of envy in Milli's voice, and she didn't wonder at it, for Milli would be a very rich widow if Howard died. "Oh. No. It was a terrible accident but thankfully it was instantaneous." Violet was philosophical about her husbands tragic death, having had plenty of time to get used to it. Fred had been a Stevedore at the West India Docks. On the day he died a large crate of cargo had come loose from a crane and crashed down on top of him. "It were a crying shame though that you and Howard couldn't come to the funeral."

Violet couldn't resist this tiny jibe at Milli, who had plenty of money but had made no attempt to attend her only brother's funeral. She secretly suspected that it was because brother and sister had never seen eye to eye.

Milli was immediately defensive. "I'm truly sorry about that, Vi. As I said at the time business was such that it would not allow Howard to have any time off to attend Fred's funeral. I was hardly going to travel all this way alone was I? I mean there's just no knowing, how a lady, vulnerable in grief, could be taken advantage in that situation."

Violet nodded, unconvinced that this was the truth.

"You seem to have done very well for yourself though, I can see that..."

Millicent's words cut through Violet's thoughts, making her bristle with annoyance. What a cheek she thought, as she watched the other woman's eyes roam the comfortable kitchen, where they sat sipping their tea and eating Violet's homemade biscuits. "Hard work never did anyone any harm!" she retorted, reciting an age old proverb as she was often prone to do and thinking how different Milli's life was to hers. "I had no choice but to make a living. In the end me and Fred's small house wasn't big enough for me to run a lodging house proper like."

"Oh I know that, Vi, but how do you make enough now? It must be such hard work."

Millicent ploughed on with her tactless words being true to how Violet remembered her, Violet knew however, that the other woman was not malicious in nature. While listening to Millicent's endless questions, she soon realised that she needed to clarify a couple of things, if her sister-in-law and husband were going to stay in her house. "You might as well know," she said standing up to clear away the table, "I'm sure it won't take you both long to notice, especially 'im!" She jabbed a finger towards Howard. "That I have some women staying here. Some working women if you get my drift. "Instantly Howard looked up, his eyes wide with astonishment. "I thought that might make you sit up and pay attention." Violet's head lolled back and her loud cackle of laughter filled the kitchen.

Millicent also found something to laugh about in Violet's revelation and put her hand over her mouth to stifle her mirth. "Well...there's a thing," she said, turning to her husband.

Violet had expected Milli to show disgust at her words but she should have realised that her reaction would be very different from that of her brother's, if he had still lived. Fred would never have allowed such a thing to go on under his roof, but then he was no longer here and she was the one making the decisions now. She remembered her good fortune the day a desperate young prostitute had knocked on her door looking for somewhere to live. Now she had three of them working for her. "They are good girls." Violet said affectionately, seeing out of the corner of her eye how Howard's eyebrows raised at this contradiction. "It gives 'em a base, much safer than them working from street corners."

"You mean you have some of your own kind living with you now eh?" Howard's words dropped like a lead balloon into the room, bringing the two women's amusement to an abrupt end. There was a stunned silence as both women stared at him.

Millicent was the first to speak, her face reddening as she turned to confront her husband. "Howard! How dare you be so rude to Vi?"

"Of course, you must be making *lots* of money from them too." Howard ignored Millicent's anger and fixed Violet with a penetrating stare. His face was taut with anger and Violet could see his eyes were full of loathing for her.

'Well what was all that about, thought Violet, What on earth had she done to warrant that?' She knew Howard had no time for her, but it was a shock to hear him likening her to a woman of the street. "That's nice ain't it?" she said sarcastically. "Dunno who's upset you, Howard, but don't take it out on me." Knowing that she was being unfairly judged by Howard, Violet felt the need to justify her actions in the face of his anger. "Course, I get me share that's only fair - it helps me get by."

"Violet, there's no need for you to explain anything to us, it's your business." Millicent's lips pursed together and she shot her husband an angry glance. "And I sure don't know what's got into Howard today!"

For a moment no-one spoke then Violet, who was anxious to stop discussing her financial situation with these two, remembered the young man who was asleep upstairs. "What 'appened onboard the ship yesterday, Milli?" She suddenly found herself curious about the tall, good-looking Irishman who had arrived late the night before, with Millicent and Howard.

"Oh, Vi, I'm so glad you had a spare room for him." Millicent enthused, her face lit up as all anger at Howard seemed to vanish. "He had no lodgings to go to and he was so exhausted, after being such a hero onboard ship."

Howard looked up from where he had been studying his fingernails. "Oh, for goodness sake, Millicent! Stop exaggerating."

"Surely you can't deny, Howard, how that young man worked hard at putting out that fire," Millicent argued.

Howard straightened his back, his expression was thunderous. "Huh! He wasn't the only man fighting the fire. There were five firemen on-board and they all worked hard to control the flames."

So that was it, thought Violet. The reason for Howard's foul mood was that he was jealous. Green eyed over the young and handsome Irishman Millicent had obviously taken a shine. Surely though, even Howard could see that this Finn would never look at the likes of Millicent, who looked like a female version of the long departed plain and ordinary Fred. Violet inwardly glowed at the good fortune that her relatives from America had by chance met Finn on the journey to England. She couldn't wait for her girls to set eyes on that muscular body and go to work.

The Lane's argument however wasn't over yet. "If that fire had reached the cargo hold the whole ship would have gone up. Finn fought alongside the firemen." Millicent was now explaining as much for Violet's benefit as Howard's. "Also, he was a great comfort to the female passengers." Millicent's mouth was set in a firm line daring her husband to argue with her.

"Finn McGuiness was all over the women like bees round a honey pot," Howard retorted, his face reddening by the minute.

Violet liked what she was hearing, but decided to quickly change the subject before the pair began screaming at each other. "Tell me, what made you choose to travel to England on a cargo ship, surely you could afford one of them there luxury liners?"

Suddenly the room was charged with unspoken words. Both Millicent and Howard stared intently back at Violet. Then slowly and deliberately Howard pushed back his chair and walked from the room, slamming the door behind him.

"Milli, what have I said?" Violet was confused and felt as if somehow, with her innocent question, she'd opened a huge can of worms. Millicent put her head in her trembling hands and began to cry, great wracking sobs that shook her body. Immediately Violet tried her best to comfort the other woman, but in the end could only sit and wait for the wailing, which she believed to be so uncharacteristic for Milli, to subside.

Millicent lifted her head, took the hanky Violet was handing her, and dabbed at her wet cheeks. Hiccoughing between retreating sobs she attempted to explain the situation to Violet. "Howard lost all his investments on the stock market a few months ago," she said, staring into Violet's pale blue eyes. "We are virtually penniless."

So that was the reason for their interest in her financial affairs.

Violet was shocked at Millicent's declaration, although a tiny part of her couldn't help feeling slightly smug at the Lane's misfortune. Violet found it hard to believe that she, after all the struggles since Fred's death, was now wealthier than Millicent and Howard. Furthermore, upstairs lay a handsome lad who would surely bring more work to her three working girls, making more money to line her pockets. Life certainly had a funny way of turning out, she pondered inwardly, while outwardly fixing the distraught Millicent with a sympathetic look.

Chapter *Seven*

EXCITEMENT

Beth woke smiling and instead of the heavy feeling of dread weighing her down, excitement lightened her heart. Lying in the cold, darkened room, for the first time in a long while she felt optimistic at the day ahead. Despite feeling chilled, a warm glow was creeping slowly from her toes to her head. Yesterday, she had managed to deceive her parents and investigate further the business of Alice Sparks.

It was still early, too early even for the fire in her room to have been lit, which meant hours before contemplating getting up. As Beth slid under the covers, one of her toes accidently touched the hot water bottle put there by a servant the night before. The bottle, which now resembled a block of ice, sent a cold shiver spiralling up her leg. Pulling her foot quickly away and back up into the cosy cocoon of her long nightdress, Beth lay there contentedly, endeavouring to remember every precious detail of the evening before.

Beth's heart raced uncontrollably and her woollen skirt grasped her thighs, as she purposefully approached Alice's small Victorian terraced house. Walking up the pathway butterflies danced in her stomach. Looking through the large bay window Beth could see the room was almost full to bursting and her first instinct was to turn and run.

Stirring in the comforting embrace of her bed Beth saw herself walking Alice's path once again. Feeling the excitement fluttering in her chest she rested between the sheets content in her reminiscence.

A smile played around Beth's lips as she recalled herself knocking on the brightly painted front door, and the realisation that with the noise levels coming from inside, this was futile. Leaning against the door wondering what to do Beth felt it yield beneath her body inviting her into the narrow hallway, crammed with coats of all descriptions.

Was she intruding, Beth asked herself? But ignoring her inner doubts she stepped over the coats then made her way towards an open doorway.

It was in this room, ahead of her that everyone was gathered. The noise was deafening and in a room devoid of furniture every spare inch of space was occupied. Beth pushed herself forwards, into an area filled with women of all descriptions and class. They were all jostling for space and talking animatedly to each other. Beth found herself aware of the strong smell of lavender mixed with a wall of warmth, the result of so many female bodies gathered together. Beads of perspiration clung to

Beth's breasts beneath her tight corset; they trickled down the front of her dress, causing her to shudder with anticipation. Despite squeezing herself to the back of the room in an attempt to hide, she began feeling exposed amidst the crowd. Someone was watching her. Beth scanned the room, her chest rising with her quickened breath until her gaze rested on a familiar face. Smiling across at Beth was unmistakably the lady with the head of flaming red hair.

Hurrying through the throng of females towards Beth was Alice, and within the space of a heartbeat she clasped hold of Beth's hand. Alice's eyes lingered on Beth's face as she squeezed Beth's hand tightly and leaned towards her. "Don't look so nervous, I'll look after you," she whispered. Beth remembered their cheeks brushing before Alice turned away to lead her to the front of the room. "Welcome to my home," Alice added.

Beth was inspired by their enthusiasm. With the other women's bodies pressing up against hers, excitement coursed through the air like an electrical current. Loud clapping echoed across the room as all eyes turned to Alice. They watched as Alice stepped up onto a makeshift stage, which was a wooden box turned upside down. For a moment there was silence, immediately followed by Alice's powerful voice filling the room.

Afterwards Beth held back as everyone filtered out of the door. She was uncaring of the consequences of her late return home. When at last

Alice's guests were gone she walked slowly back into the now empty room and faced Beth, who felt a sudden shyness in the presence of this courageous woman.

"Beth, I'm so pleased you could make it to the meeting," Alice's emerald eyes were fixed on Beth's face. "Tell me about yourself, would you?"

Beth let out a long held-in breath and felt the tension leave her body. As the two of them found a seat on the small sofa, which had been pushed into the corner of the room, Beth explained everything to Alice. She told Alice about sneaking past her mother to come out today, and how trapped she always felt by having to abide by the rules and regulations of the privileged household in which she lived.

For a moment after Beth had finished her story Alice looked thoughtful. The un-asked question shone in Alice's eyes, why hadn't Beth left this stifling household before now? Perhaps Alice had not voiced this question because she didn't want to judge Beth and knew what the answer would be. Courage would be needed on a vast scale to face that kind of change, to alter the way you have always lived, to a frightening arena of a whole different world. This other world where rules leant since a child are no longer relevant, would be an exciting but daunting place with a whole set of new values.

Alice offered no advice to Beth after hearing her story, but proceeded to explain all about the movement and what the group were planning. Beth felt this was the answer Alice was offering, an escape from her unhappy life. If Beth were to join their fight for freedom Alice explained, she would feel differently about her life and could perhaps begin to make changes. Beth listened to Alice, watching her animated expression as she told of the suffragette activities, and felt a kinship with this woman she barely knew. The spark between them lifted Beth's heart. Into her closeted, dismal world appeared a bright beam of light that shone deep within her.

Some time later she left Alice's house, determined that this was the path her life would now take. Beth had always believed she would one day change her life, but the mystery was in what shape or form her escape would manifest itself. Now she knew that at last her opportunity was staring her in the face, demanding that she find the courage to tread its path. There was, however, one area of her life that needed addressing before she could proceed, which was her engagement to Hugo. Filled with a new and deep courage never felt before, Beth was not daunted by dealing with her betrothed. Her future was now brighter than ever before and she was determined to keep it that way.

Chapter *Eight*

ALICE

Alice began washing the mountain of cups that lay stacked on the draining board next to the small sink, her eyes focused on the water as it ran in rivulets over the finely patterned china. Once again her young maid had been called away, leaving Alice to do the chores herself. The girl's mother had given birth to yet another sibling, and Nancy being the oldest had been summoned to help. When Nancy asked to be free of her duties for a few days Alice reluctantly agreed, stopping herself from voicing disgust at the girl's mother for bringing this child into the world to a life of poverty. Nancy's father being nothing more than a drunken layabout was of little help to the family.

Now, as Alice attempted to cope with the upheaval caused by the previous evenings meeting, she began to regret her generosity. Her backlog of needlework sat on a chair in the far corner of the room. The bright colours of the Suffragette flags and banners waited their turn to be sewn in preparation for the next big meeting. On a small table next to them was the work she'd undertaken to earn her living, the silks and fine fabrics were folded neatly by the idle sewing machine. Turning from the sink, Alice stumbled over the small furry animal weaving furiously in and out of her legs, seemingly determined to trip her up. She picked up Mrs.P's warm body and cuddled the soft fur into her neck, but without being fed the feline tabby wasn't happy and wriggled desperately to be free. A knock at the door caused the cat to meow loudly in protest as her owner went to answer it.

Mrs Weston, one of Alice's best customers stood in the doorway dressed in a canary yellow gown and holding a scarlet coloured cape tightly around her against the cold chill of the March morning. On her head she wore a large hat, its gaudy flowers piled high upon her head. Alice wondered how, after all this time of making the woman's garments for her, she couldn't somehow find her way to matching the colours together.

"Mrs Weston, what a surprise. How are you this fine morning?" Alice forced a smile onto her face wishing she had got up a little earlier to tidy the debris left from the night before.

"Good morning, Alice." Mrs Weston was clearly waiting to be invited in as she stared meaningfully at her seamstress.

"Please come through." Alice opened the door wider for her client to enter. "Would you like a cup of tea?"

Mrs Weston followed her into the back parlour. "No thank you, Alice." She loosened her cape then sat down hurriedly on the sofa. "Pray tell me. How did last Saturday's meeting go? I couldn't get away at the last minute and had to miss it!" Leaning towards Alice she peered out from beneath the enormous hat her angular face now looking decidedly animated.

Alice knew that, despite numerous unfulfilled promises to attend one of the suffragette meetings Mrs Weston was unlikely ever to do so, for it was well known that she would never dare to defy her husband.

"It was excellent, we had a full house." Alice's eyes lit up as she told how everyone was full of plans for the mass meeting soon to be held at the Albert Hall. Mrs Weston sat listening eager for something exciting in her mundane existence.

"We also had a new member join the cause." Alice enthused.

"Oh really, who was that? Anyone I know?"

"No. At least I don't think so. Her name's Beth Hamilton–Green." It was only after the words were spoken that Alice realised her mistake. Beth had told her at the meeting, that for the moment anyway, she was keeping her involvement in the movement from her parents.

"Elizabeth Hamilton-Green, of Richmund House? Why, I do know her, we have visited her parents on several social occasions." Mrs Weston would liked to have known the Hamilton-Green's more intimately, but had actually only ever been invited to Richmund House once. She had a habit of stretching the truth when it suited her, making life more colourful.

"You must be mistaken..." Alice tried hard to retract her hastily spoken words but

Mrs Weston was having none of it. She gave Alice a look of disdain and glared back at her.

"Alice dear, there can't be two Elizabeth Hamilton-Greens of Richmund House!"

"No, of course not." Alice became aware of the collar of her blouse digging painfully into her neck and shifted uneasily in her chair. "I must have got the name wrong." Mrs Weston continued to frown at her, and they were both saved from further embarrassment when the cat's loud meows could be heard from the doorway.

"Oh. The cat. Sorry about the noise, Mrs Weston, I haven't fed her yet. Is there something you need to discuss with me about the dress? I'll have it ready for you as soon as I can."

"No, I know my garments will be well made in your capable hands, you're always my first choice of seamstress. It's not easy to find someone who is as well qualified as you. Mrs Weston raised her eyebrows at Alice as she stood up gathering the red cape around her shoulders.

Alice nodded at the other woman knowing that she spoke the truth. Her father had paid for her to learn her trade at the famous 'Lady Brooke's' establishment, so she had been extremely fortunate. Glancing across the room at her parent's photograph which stood on the mantelpiece above the fire she felt tears spring to her eyes.

"Oh, my dear..." Mrs Weston was instantly contrite although she wasn't sure what for. "I'm so sorry if I've upset you."

Alice was horrified at showing her emotions in front of her visitor and began dabbing furiously at one eye with a handkerchief. "No, its all right, Mrs. Weston. I think I have something in my eye."

Alice's glance towards the mantelpiece had not gone un-noticed. "You must miss them both." Mrs Weston said tactlessly.

Alice lifted her head, looked at the pile of work waiting to be done and gave Mrs Weston a determined look. "Naturally I do, Mrs Weston. Now, if there's nothing else you need?"

"Not at the moment, my dear." Mrs Weston hastily made her way towards the door, having clearly read her dismissal in Alice's expression. Before leaving however she turned towards the younger woman obviously feeling the need to clarify things. "I only called to enquire about the meeting. I like to keep abreast of what's going on, you understand?"

That was certainly true, thought Alice as she bade her visitor goodbye, watching from the window as she hurried up the street.

Alice stood in the kitchen feeding Mrs. P, her mind buzzing from Mrs Weston's unexpected visit and her thoughts constantly straying to her recently departed mother. She put down the cat's bowl then walked through to the front parlour and picked up the framed photograph. Focusing on her mother's smiling face Alice found it hard to imagine how she had coped during those long months of her illness, and the conversation they shared before she died echoed in her head.

"I have always longed for the freedom to fight for a better life but I never had the opportunity. You have - so if that's what you want, Alice, you must do it." Megan had taken hold of her daughter's hand and held it tightly between her own, lifting her head from the pillow of her sick bed as she did so. Alice was aware that her mother knew of her involvement with the movement, though they had never discussed it.

"Mother. Please . You must rest."

"No. Let me explain. While your father was alive I owed it to him to be a good and dutiful wife, I could never pursue my own ambitions, it would have been selfish." Megan lay back against the pillows, her laboured breathing echoed across the darkened room. Alice waited patiently for her to continue, knowing that since her father's death only the year before her mother had enjoyed greater freedom.

Now it had all been taken away as Megan's own health deteriorated.

"Father wouldn't have protested, he would have understood, surely?" Alice felt positive her kind and generous father would have been sympathetic to his wife's desire for change. For a moment Megan didn't reply as Alice looked down at the familiar features and felt her heart contract. Her question hung unanswered within the confines of the bedroom. She rose from the bedside to open a window, pulling back the heavy curtains as she did so.

"I had no choice but to marry," her mother struggled to explain. "When I was only twenty years old my father told me that if I failed to choose a man for myself he would do it for me." Megan stared intently at her daughter as two spots of colour appeared on her ashen cheeks. "Your father was dependable and reliable and he clearly loved me, that was enough for me. I saw what happened to other women once married, there was no escape from their cruel husbands." Alice nodded and dabbed at her mother's forehead with a damp cloth.

"Mother, you don't have to tell me all this, there's no need."

"Yes, there is, Alice. I saw you looking at me at the funeral and I know what you were thinking."

Alice hung her head. It was true she'd been shocked at the lack of grief her mother had shown for her father. Her dry eyes had been devoid of emotion and this had led Alice to experience the unsettling sensation that she didn't really know her mother at all.

"I did love him, you know...although it was more a love akin to friendship."

Alice had witnessed an easy going relationship with never a cross word and knew this was the truth. But something else hung in the air, something her mother wasn't telling her. The two women's eyes locked as Alice took hold of Megan's hand in an attempt to soothe her anguish.

"I was in love once, but it was a forbidden love." Her mother's voice was barely more than a whisper.

Alice leaned closer and held her breath waiting to hear more. But Megan closed her eyes and sank back into the pillows. Suddenly everything fitted, her mother's relationship with her father, which was more a friendship than a passion and the words 'forbidden love.' Alice desperately wanted her mother to know that she understood. "Mother, it's all right I understand," she murmured into Megan's ear, but it was no use she had slipped into another world and was unable to answer.

Megan died the next day and Alice had never felt more alone in her life. A few weeks later, forcing herself to face the future, she began sorting through her mother's belongings. It was then she found the letters. They were scented with rose perfume, tied up with a red ribbon and signed only with the letter 'R.' As Alice's eyes skimmed the pages her tears blurred the words of love and devotion declared on the hand-written pages. Her sorrow was not self-pity, but more of regret that Megan had been unable to confide in her this love she had kept hidden.

Now, as Alice replaced the picture back onto the shelf she inhaled deeply and looked across at her pile of work. The vibrant greens and purples of the Suffragette colours called out to her. So today she would concentrate on them, leaving the likes of Mrs Weston's garments until another day. Her mood lifted as she picked up a half finished banner and began to sew, grateful for a little respite from the aching loss that had become her constant companion.

The following day dawned with a thick fog and a drizzle of rain had just appeared as Alice placed the tulips on the grave. Their scarlet petals stood out proud and bright adding a blaze of colour to the dull background.

Staring at the two graves which stood side by side the earth sodden from recent rain, Alice fought against the desire to cry. Weeping was pointless and didn't change anything. But fighting this agonising pain however, was almost impossible. In a desperate attempt to find comfort Alice wrapped her arms tightly around her chilled body and squeezed her eyes shut.

After a time the vice-like grip of Alice's grief loosened its grip. Lifting her head and focusing once again on her surroundings her eye was immediately caught by a movement in the distance.

A shiver ran down Alice's spine and her eyes narrowed as she gazed intently across the graveyard. A quick flash of the colour blue had suddenly appeared in the grey fog but had now disappeared. The last time she had been here she had seen someone hiding in those trees. Curious to find out who and why someone was watching her again, Alice began following the winding path to the other side of the graveyard. In the next moment as her foot caught a loose branch, she found herself tumbling to the ground.

Rain clung in droplets to Alice's hair and eyelashes as she stared dismally into the distance. Then, deciding that today was not the day to investigate further this second sighting of being obviously spied on, she lifted herself up and smoothed down her damp crumpled dress.

As Alice turned to walk away, a pair of bright blue eyes watched intently from beneath the dark twisted branches of the trees.

Chapter *Nine*

THE OTHER WOMAN

The statuesque figure of Beth's father leaned towards the woman, whose face was turned upwards looking into his eyes. She was smiling and Beth could hear her soft laughter above the low hum of the street noise. The cream muslin dress showed a tiny waist accentuated by a black velvet band. A biscuit coloured straw hat sat atop her fair hair. Charles Hamilton-Green wore a black bowler hat which was drawn down across his face and Beth could see the collar of his favourite blue-grey shirt protruding from his suit.

For a moment Beth felt a flicker of pride at this handsome man who was her father. Even from this restricted view he looked for all to see a very desirable man.

But then anger surged through Beth's body at the unfairness of what was going on in public. Her cheeks burnt at the thought of her mother's humiliation. Unable to move she watched them turn away and look into Harrods magnificent window display, his companion pointing animatedly towards the glass. As the world went about its business, Charles took hold of the woman's waist; pulled her towards him *and kissed her on the lips,* before disappearing into the store. Beth suddenly became aware of her position on the edge of the pavement at the sound of a motor car beeping loudly, as it passed within inches of her feet. She stepped back quickly, put a hand across her eyes and let out a long sigh. Standing this way for a second or two she became aware that her name was being called.

"Elizabeth... Are you alright you look rather pale?"

"I'm fine, Mother. Just feeling a little faint."

"Has Helen tied your corset up too tightly again? She often does that with mine and after a while I find it hard to breathe..."

Her mother's voice droned on as Beth tried hard to focus on what she was saying. With her heart beating wildly she longed to run after her father, scream at him to stop and drag him away from that wicked woman. There was no doubt that her mother would have to be told of her father's infidelity. She would wait for the right moment.

As they walked in the direction of the motor car Beth once again felt grateful to James for teaching her how to drive. It had taken her a long time to persuade her older brother to help out in this way, but eventually he'd given in.

They drove in silence through the leafy suburbs and Beth glanced across at her mother and the familiar sight of her sitting bolt upright in the car with her lips pursed. Sarah had made her view known that the motor car was a mode of transport not to be trusted, saying she much preferred the security of the horse and carriage. She heartily disapproved when her husband had allowed Beth to occasionally drive the vehicle, fearing for her daughter's safety in one of those *'new fangled machines.'*

Beth's mind was running in circles and she longed to tell her mother what she'd seen, well aware that once home her courage was likely to desert her. As they approached the village of Barnes and the magnificent bridge came into view she could bear it no longer.

"Mother, I saw Father in town today and he was with another woman!" The words tumbled out and her tone was more abrupt than she'd intended. Her mother's sharp intake of breath forced her to apologise for her outburst. "I'm sorry..."

Beth's words hung heavily in the air, overhead the clouds had begun to disperse giving rise to a clear afternoon. Out of the corner of her eye she could see Sarah fiddling with the bow on her white frilled hat tying and untying its ribbon, then staring intently down at her fingers. Without thinking Beth pulled over and stopped the car.

"Mother." She turned to face the other woman. "Are you listening to me?" She took hold of Sarah's hands in an attempt to stop their incessant fidgeting.

"There's no need for you to shout, Elizabeth. What you're implying is nothing new to me." Her lips were set in a firm line but the hurt showed in her blue eyes.

Beth looked at her mother and thought she must have been a beauty once with her round face and dark curls, but time and a sour expression had robbed her of any looks she'd had a long time ago. "So you already know?"

"Of course, how could I not? It's normal for a man to take a mistress."

Beth's eyes widened. Of course she knew it happened but surely her mother was virtually encouraging it with her subservient attitude.

"He is usually more discreet, his mistress's are hidden away. Not paraded on the streets for all to see."

"But, Mother, why do you tolerate such behaviour?" Beth couldn't contain her anger. "You don't have to put up with it, surely?"

"Oh for goodness sake, Elizabeth!" She snatched her hand from Beth's. "You do not understand these things."

Sarah lifted her chin and turned towards her daughter, for a brief moment Beth thought she saw a fleeting expression of envy pass across her mother's face.

"One day when you are married you will know to what I am referring."

"Never!" retorted Beth. Sarah shot her a resigned look then waited patiently for her daughter to begin the short drive home.

"I cannot marry you, Hugo!" Beth stood, hands on hips anger blazing in her eyes. The sound of her rage reverberated off the walls of the library. While the man she confronted seemed unconcerned by her outburst and sat with a passive expression on his face.

"Why not? Tell me *again*, Elizabeth." Hugo caressed his moustache and waited for Beth's episode' to be over, women could be so tiresome at times. He hoped this particular tantrum wouldn't go on too long. He had an appointment with a certain lady of the night in less than an hour, so he had no intention of listening to this spoilt madam for much longer. His eyes slid down Beth's body from his position on the leather settee, gazing at the line of her full skirt and imagining the shapely legs beneath it. Beth was a fine looking woman, even more so when she was angry. Her face was flushed and he could see her bosom heaving under the high necked blouse. With his legs sprawled out in front of him and the buttons on his silk waistcoat straining against his bulging stomach, Hugo observed Beth's attempts to control her temper.

"Look, Hugo. We both know there is no love between us and that this is a marriage my parents instigated… I realise now it's not what I want." Beth sat down next to him putting her hand upon his arm.

Hugo's face changed as he at last grasped what Beth was trying to tell him. His dark eyes turned black as he sat upright glaring back at her and his normally florid complexion had turned puce. "If you are serious you are making a terrible mistake, Elizabeth!" Hugo suddenly had the feeling he was losing control of the situation.

"Of course I am serious." Beth's voice quivered as she moved slowly away from him and Hugo noticed she was biting nervously on her lower lip.

"What an ungrateful bitch you are!" All attempts at smoothing over the situation had gone from Hugo's mind as angry words gushed from his mouth. "I am prepared to marry you even though you are well past the ripe age for matrimony." Hugo got to his feet and towered over Beth obstructing her attempts to rise from her seated position on the settee. The fear in her eyes was evident as she lifted an arm to shield her face.

"Tell me. Why? What's the real reason? I demand to know!" The words were spat out with a voice full of venom.

Beth, regaining her courage in the face of Hugo's bullying abruptly got up and with all her strength pushed him roughly out of her way. She watched his heavy body sway with the force of her blow as he fell backwards, narrowly missing the edge of the hearth and the unguarded flames in the grate.

As he struggled to get up from his position on the floor, Hugo's white hot anger consumed his body, as Beth stood in front of him with her chin in the air and that damned determined look on her face. Hatred forced itself into his mind along with an image of taking hold of this woman and shaking the very life from her body. Hauling himself to his feet he held his hands close to his body in an attempt to resist committing murder.

If Beth meant what she said he was in deep trouble, for there would be no funds to replace what he had been frittering away from the business. It wouldn't be long then before his thieving was noticed. Hugo had no intention of spending time at 'His Majesty's Pleasure' because of Beth's refusal to marry him. He would have to find another gullible rich woman. The thought of starting his search all over again filled him with dismay and Beth mistook his downcast expression for a broken heart.

"I need my freedom, without that I am nothing." Her voice was firm as she tried to explain. "I am only just beginning to realise that myself. I've joined a movement to help women fight for their rights."

Hugo ignored Beth's plea for understanding and his anger flared once again. "Freedom! Is that what you want?" Throwing back his head he let out a cruel mocking laugh which echoed around the room. "Don't you realise that women are nothing without men?"

Beth did not reply but exhaled loudly her blue eyes gazing brazenly into his. For a moment Hugo's anger disappeared and desire for this rebellious woman re-kindled itself in his chest. He stifled the urge to rip the clothes from her body and take her there and then. The realization that he had mistakenly thought he would be able to tame Elizabeth hit him, for he knew now it would have been an impossible task. He could do no more to persuade her to marry him and his own conceit prevented him from begging for her hand. Forcing his way past her he stood in the doorway glaring back at her upright figure.

"Well it's your loss, Elizabeth Hamilton-Green! You'll spend the rest of your life as a dried up old spinster disowned by everyone, including your family. No-one else will marry you!" As he slammed the door behind him causing the flames to flare in the grate, Beth slumped into the nearest chair then covered her face with her hands and wept.

Chapter *Ten*

LADY MIDDLETON

Beth stepped off the omnibus at Greenwich Park and began the ten minute walk to Alice's house. Not wanting to draw attention to herself, she'd dressed in a plain grey gown in an attempt to blend into her surroundings. She knew that if her parents found out where her journey was leading there would be more confrontation and this was best avoided.

Walking slowly alongside the park, Beth took in the touch of spring in the air enjoying the February weather which was improving. At last the cold chill of past days seemed to be diminishing, causing her to loosen her coat as she looked across at the expanse of green. People were sitting on benches dotted here and there, or walking up towards the observatory, its impressive golden ball was balanced high on the roof signalling the time to the world beyond.

Taking a deep intake of breath, excitement fluttered featherlike in Beth's chest at her surroundings. She found herself involuntarily smiling as she walked along her way. She was struck by the contrast of the stifling atmosphere at home and this new and growing sense of freedom.

Beth's smile however was soon chased away to be replaced by a concerned frown as she turned the corner and Alice's house came into view. A young woman and what appeared to be her Lady's maid were clearly in disagreement about something. They were standing just outside the front gate inadvertently drawing the attention of passers-by. Beth's first thought was to turn around and go back the way she'd come, but an affinity with the young woman and her own situation made her hesitate.

As she approached, Beth noticed an older lady waiting in a motor car parked outside the house. Her butler sat rigid in the front seat with the engine running and his eyes set firmly on the steering wheel. She immediately recognised the woman as a friend of her mother's, who often attended their house for entertainment. Her name was Lady Middleton, she was the wife of the wealthy landowner John Middleton and Beth realised the girl in front of her was their daughter, Beth's friend, Emma.

Beth paused for a moment to observe unfolding events. The Lady's maid had one hand on Emma's arm whilst the other firmly held the gate. The maid's long thin face was pink with frustration. She was obviously reluctant to let go of her charge. Emma had a look of defiance etched across her features and she stood firmly resisting the woman's demands.

Not a word was being spoken as the silent tussle was taking place.

Beth straightened her back and marched towards the waiting car. "Good day to you, Lady Middleton." Beth kept her voice light and addressed the woman through an open window. "How are you today?" Narrowing her eyes Lady Middleton stared back at Beth. "Don't you remember me? I'm, Elizabeth Hamilton-Green."

Suddenly a smile lit up the woman's face. "Hello, Elizabeth. How are your dear Mother and Father?" Beth noticed the look of relief on Lady Middleton's face and realised she saw Beth as her saviour in this situation.

"They're very well. Thank you, Lady Middleton." Beth looked back at the scene still being played out behind her. "But what seems to be the trouble here?" Before Lady Middleton could answer Beth offered her help. "I am myself visiting Miss. Sparks' house," she announced with confidence. "Would you like me to accompany Emma?"

Lady Middleton's face turned quite red and beneath the elaborate hat her chin wobbled. Beth had to inwardly chuckle to herself as they both pretended that this would be perfectly fine.

"Why thank you, Miss Hamilton-Green. That is really most kind of you." She then wound down the window further and summoned her frustrated servant. "Wilson, Wilson!" The maid immediately turned around at the sound of her mistress's voice and hurried towards the car. "Miss Hamilton-Green will now escort Emma into Miss Sparks' house." She told her.

As Wilson got into the back of the car Beth promised Lady Middleton that she would make sure that the younger girl got home safely after her visit. As they were driven away Lady Middleton's frown was clearly visible on her face.

Emma took hold of Beth's hands, obviously relieved to be free of her burden. "Thank you so much, Beth. Mother found out where I was going today and sent Wilson after me."

"So I see, perhaps you need to be more secretive about your whereabouts, Emma." Beth had been friends with Emma, who was several years younger than her, for some years and felt that Emma often looked up to her for advice. "Since joining the movement I have to constantly evade my mother's eagle eye, which isn't always easy."

"I know. My mother didn't want to refuse you though did she? She trusts you to make sure I'm a good girl." Emma giggled at this observation.

"I probably shouldn't have done it, but the look on her face and that maid..." Beth caught Emma's infectious laugh.

"And! You're the naughtiest girl of all!" They were both overcome with laughter and clutched at their sides leaning on the gate.

"Don't worry. Mother deserved it." Emma said after she'd regained control of herself. "Things haven't been going too well lately." Emma's smile had now gone and her eyes looked troubled.

Beth stared intently at her friend. "Your mother has been boasting to mine about your forthcoming wedding. I was surprised to hear you are engaged? Is it really what you want, Emma?"

"Oh God, has she? Honestly. I am so confused about what to do, but there's no telling her that. She just won't listen."

"I know, they are out of the same mould." Beth placed a hand on Emma's arm. "We mustn't allow them to get away with it though, Emma. As we have discussed many times before it's up to us how we live our lives." Beth knew how hard Emma found it to stand up to her domineering mother.

Emma visibly brightened at Beth's words. "Of course not! I intend to fight for what I want. I will be at the front of the Suffragette gatherings holding high my flag of freedom." Emma lifted her arm high into the air to demonstrate how she would look standing amongst all the other women. "along with you of course," she added smiling.

"That's my girl. Now let's get on with the business in hand shall we? By the way how did you know about the meeting today? I haven't seen you for so long you couldn't have known I would be here."

"I picked up a flyer in the street advertising the movement and was immediately interested in finding out more." Emma explained. "I'm glad I did now." She added.

Beth felt a moment of pride that the flyer Emma had come across might well have been one that she had distributed. "I'm sure you won't regret it, Emma," she said opening the gate.

"Beth! There you are at last, I thought you weren't coming." Alice stood in the front doorway looking fabulous. Her face was flushed with excitement and her eyes sparkled.

Beth waved at Alice and then pushed Emma gently ahead of her. "Come on, Emma, mothers will be mothers. Let's go in and enjoy ourselves."

As Alice held open the door for them Beth introduced the new recruit. "Alice, this is, Emma Middleton and she's a very determined young lady indeed."

"Good, that's the kind of members we need." Alice graced her visitors with a wide smile and held the door open for them to join her.

At the breakfast table the next day Beth became aware of an uneasy atmosphere in the air, which was reflected on the servant's tense faces as they waited on the family. Her mother's head was dipped as she murmured 'Good Morning' and her father only spoke after he'd finished his meal and rose from the table.

"Elizabeth. There are things we need to discuss, please come to the drawing room after breakfast."

"Of course, Father." She answered, looking up at his surly expression. "Is there anything wrong?" Ignoring her question he stared back at her blankly then turned and strode from the room. Her mother got up and quickly followed him. Beth fought against the feeling of being a child again, when her parents had found out she had committed some misdemeanour or other and were about to punish her.

For a while Beth sat picking at her food. She'd noticed the house seemed quieter than usual this morning, it was as if a hush had fallen on the entire household. News certainly travels fast, and she could only conclude that this summons was about the events of the day before. 'May as well get the confrontation out of the way she thought,' as she rose from her chair leaving her unfinished breakfast, and made her way towards the drawing room.

Holding her breath she knocked gently on the door. "Come in!" Her father's voice resounded from beyond the door.

The scene that met her was one of stillness and formality. As was usual the room was tidy with not a cushion out of place, the fire burned brightly its flames casting a flicker across the room. Her mother sat bolt upright in a chair by the window, her back was ramrod straight as she stared at the landscape beyond. She made no attempt to look round as her daughter entered the room. Pacing up and down impatiently, her father turned towards her his face contorted in anger. She stood in the doorway reluctant to enter the lions den.

"Hello, Elizabeth." It was more a statement than a greeting." Please sit down."

His tone was aggressive it must be worse than she'd first thought."Yes, Father." Beth murmured.

For once her voice showed no rebellion and her father latched on to this, for his fiery daughter rarely obeyed his commands. And so he began his tirade.

"Young lady, what do you think you're doing? The question was purely rhetorical and gave no pause for answer. "Our friends are disgusted at your antics!" He began to pace the room again his arms flailing around him. "Don't you realise we could lose our social circle? We will be outcasts if you continue to be associated with such goings-on! Don't you care about your family?" His voice got louder with each question and as he stopped to face her, she noticed a tiny speck of saliva clinging to his bottom lip. "Well, what have you to say for yourself?"

"Father, I don't know to what you are referring. I'm not aware of doing anything wrong."

"Nothing wrong? You've been seen going into a suffragette house." There was a pause as if she had blasphemed or committed some gross act of murder.

"Not only that," he continued, "I am told you are misguiding another girl, younger than yourself, who I believe needs no encouragement to join these intolerable activities."

Beth let out a long sigh and straightened her back. "Father, I'm just trying to find some justice in the world for women. So that we can make changes to the way we live our lives." The feeling returned of being that child again and she had to remind herself she was a grown woman who had a right to stand up for what she believed in. Waiting for his response, she could feel her mother's eyes on her from her position by the window. As usual she was saying nothing in the presence of her father.

For a moment the room fell silent. Into that void came a scuffling noise from the doorway which made all three of them turn their heads in that direction. Beth's mind flew to the servants who could probably hear her father's every word. He must have had the same thought, for he lunged towards the door and flung it open, staring into the empty space beyond.

Beth attempted to bring calm to the storm. "Father." She spoke tenderly, her hands gesturing towards him. "Surely you can see there should be more choices available to women?" She was trying to appeal to his better nature but this threw him into an even bigger frenzy.

"What! What are you trying to say? There is only one place for a woman and that's by her husband's side. Certainly not on the streets of London parading that sort of nonsense. Those women are not natural, just frustrated spinsters. That will be you if you don't hurry up and marry that man of yours."

Beth could hear the disdain in her father's voice for her fellow women and she could no longer contain her anger. "Father!" She shouted, her eyes flashing with rage. "That's not fair!" Standing up to face him Beth watched as he turned from her and leaned on the piano, taking long deep breaths. The clock ticked loudly in the space of time that seemed endless. He looked old as he stood before her, old in a way she hadn't seen before and he took his time to speak. But the words uttered didn't come from his lips.

"Elizabeth, we forbid you to have anything to do with those women!" It was her mother's voice that carried across the room from where she now stood by the fireplace, it came with a look of disgust that etched and aged her face. Beth was unsure whether fear or anger shook her mother's body as she spoke. "Think of us if you don't care about yourself, Lady Middleton is threatening to cut us out of her social circle and then where would that leave us?"

"But, Mother..."

"And, Hugo, what will he say when he hears about what you've been up to?" Sarah said with a sneer.

Beth gulped at the air as she reached for the words she needed to free her thoughts and feelings. "I've called off the wedding. I'm not being pushed into marrying Hugo. I don't love him and I've already told him." She faltered slightly. "Yesterday... actually." Beth could feel the tension in the room reach its peak. Her heart beat wildly as her father slowly turned from his position by the piano and her mother stared at her speechless. But before they could react to her confession Beth spoke again. This time she had no control over the words that spilled from her mouth, words that tumbled forth seeing an escape for her thoughts. Sentences barely formed in her mind before being spoken loud and clear across the room.

"How can you be such a hypocrite?" Beth was pacing the room now. "You, who has a loose woman in your bed by night whom you choose to parade on the streets by day," she looked straight into her father's eyes and saw the shock her words brought.

Her father looked accusingly at her mother then back to her. He seemed confused as to how she would know his intimate business. But ignoring her shocking accusation he took a step towards her. His hands were clenched into tight fists by his side as his voice echoed around the room. A voice as cold as steel replaced his anger as he issued her with an ultimatum.

"If you choose to live your life as an old spinster that's up to you. Persist in your activities with the suffragette women and you'll no longer have a place in this house."

The impact of her father's words on her mother was evident. She swung her head in his direction and clasped her body as if reacting to his fist. Her eyes were pleading with him to undo the terrible thing he'd just said. But he stood tall and straight looking at Beth, daring her to argue with him.

Beth glared back at him with defiance dancing in her blue eyes. Beneath her skirt and unseen her knees shook but her heart and mind were strong. She turned and strode from the room her chin held high closing the door quietly behind her.

Chapter *Eleven*

THE EVICTION

The bedroom door was slightly ajar and Beth, who was in a frenzy of activity, suddenly sensed someone in the doorway. She turned to see her mother standing rigid, a hand clamped across her mouth and a look of horror on her face.

"Elizabeth, *what are you doing?*" She demanded.

"Hello, Mother. I'm leaving." For a moment their eyes locked and the atmosphere in the room was laden with tension. Beth could almost see the invisible sparks crackling between them. But no-one, least of all her mother was going to stop her now. Exhaling loudly she dropped her eyes and began throwing the garments into her suitcase at an alarming rate. Sarah stepped forward grabbing hold of the hands, which seemed at that moment unstoppable.

"You can't prevent me from going..." Beth struggled violently with Sarah's grip, determined not be manhandled in this way. A polite cough from behind them made the two women swivel round to see Helen standing to one side of the bed with her head bowed.

Sarah let go of Beth and stood upright. "You can go now, Helen." She ordered. "Elizabeth will ring for you if you're needed again." Helen scuttled from the room like a frightened rabbit.

"You don't think he meant what he said do you?" Sarah said after the door had clicked shut behind Helen. "He was threatening you, warning you to kerb your ways and put a stop to this silliness."

Beth sat down on the edge of the bed and rubbed furiously at her sore eyes. "Of course he meant what he said. You heard him say it, that I must stop my activities or leave. How is that fair, Mother, how?" Beth's anguished face held a question she knew her mother could never answer.

Sarah reached out her arms towards her. But Beth would not be comforted and pulled herself abruptly away from her mother's intended embrace. "There's no other way, I must leave." She said standing up.

"But, Elizabeth. All you need to do is stop the suffragette activities and all will be well. You don't even have to marry Hugo if you don't want to, we'll find you someone more suitable." To Sarah the solution seemed very simple.

Beth stifled her frustration and turned to face the window, she would miss looking at the scene below where all was still and tranquil. "I'm sorry." Her voice was controlled and low. "I will not give up the fight, now or ever." She heard her mother's deep intake of breath followed by soft footsteps, as she walked from the room closing the door softly behind her.

It was an hour later when Beth had finished packing that she realised she had nowhere to go. Sitting down next to her case she gazed around. She had grown up in this room and leaving it was not easy. In the corner of the room stood her dressing table, its cream-painted wood was decorated with lilac moulding which matched her quilt; and familiar objects cluttered its top. Hat pins, boxes and china sat on its surface and the swing mirror reflected an image back to her. The sight that met her eyes almost made her waiver in the face of her own defiance. A young woman on the edge of the biggest change in her life looked back, her face flushed and fear showing plainly in her blue eyes.

She would go to Alice. Beth knew she was the only person who would be able to help. Lifting the case from the bed her eyes fell upon the car keys that lay on the bedside table, she quickly picked them up and slid them into her coat pocket. Just as she was about to open the door a loud knock penetrated the silence. Her mother stood on the threshold with a defeated look upon her face.

"Elizabeth, my dear."

"Oh, Mother." Spontaneously they hugged and for a moment the women clung to each other. Then they stood apart on different sides of the fence once again.

"Where will you go? What will you do?" The concern for her firstborn and the fate that awaited her showed on Sarah's face.

"I have a good friend. Her name's Alice."

"No! Please listen, Elizabeth. Why don't you go to the cottage?"

"The cottage, but isn't Ned living there?"

"No he's moved out. He decided a while ago to move into town nearer to Billy and the grandchildren now that Grace has left. It's been empty for a few months and will need airing.

Sarah's eyes were full of hope that her daughter would agree to this and her kindness touched Beth's heart. She reached out and touched her mother's arm. "I'm sorry this is just something I have to do, you understand don't you?"

But this was an area that Sarah knew nothing about and she refused to let herself be led. "I don't understand that you seem to want to give up everything, or how you can walk away from a potentially good marriage and a secure future."

Beth lifted her head and turned the car keys in her pocket whilst staring at a point just behind her mother as she spoke.

"But I do see that you will do it whatever I say, that's why I'm asking you to live in the cottage. Give me a few days to get it aired for you."

Beth was doubtful this was the right course of action. "But, Mother. I know Father will not be happy with this arrangement? Would it not be better that I move away properly?"

"For once, I don't care what your father says. I'll insist!" Two spots of colour appeared on Sarah's powdered cheeks as she spoke.

Beth knew her mother wouldn't dictate anything to her father, who made all the decisions. But at least for now she had a place to stay. If the truth be told she was relieved she wouldn't have to ask Alice for help. "I'm not sure but maybe as a temporary measure."

Sarah turned away satisfied it seemed that at least she'd won one battle. "I'll tell Helen to organise clean sheets and towels for the cottage." Her hand was on the door handle but she hesitated in the doorway.

"What is it?" Beth asked, aware there was something else on her mother's mind.

"The car keys," seeing the dismay on Beth's face Sarah attempted to explain, "It's your father. I told him you were leaving and he demanded you handed them to me before you left."

Beth took a step towards her mother, reached into her pocket and reluctantly drew out the keys. Sarah took them from Beth's outstretched hand. Beth stared intently into her mother's eyes, there was a tiny beat as they held each other's gaze. It was Beth who broke the silence. "I told you he meant what he said." She said quietly. "Was there something else, Mother? Did father say anything about our argument?"

"Nothing at all." Sarah dropped her eyes and stared silently at the floor. Just...take care of yourself, Elizabeth." She murmured and was gone.

Approaching the sixteenth century cottage with its thatched roof and white washed walls Beth's hopes were high that this lodge, half hidden behind a cluster of trees would be her cosy retreat. Upon entering the front door she realised it might be quaint, but old Ned had been gone several months and the air was heavy with abandonment. The cottage had died without the care and attention of its inhabitants.

Beth walked from room to room trying to ignore the grubby walls and the strong musty smell that filled the air. It seemed as if the cottage had been empty for years. Beth realised then how lonely Ned must have been, for he had obviously not looked after the cottage for some time before he left. Her mother's insistence that she should get the maid to give the place a good clean resounded in her ears. For once Beth realised Sarah had been right, the stark contrast of the cottage to the elaborate and highly polished home she'd come from, was almost too much. But pride would not allow her to turn back.

Despite her misgivings she found aspects of the cottage she could warm to. In the sitting room with its fireplace flanked by a gaslight on either side, she noticed a small carriage clock which reminded her of the one in the small library at home. The bedrooms although sparsely furnished were a delight with chintz curtains and low beams, but she was dismayed to find the kitchen just beyond the sitting room was so tiny. It housed a range, a small wooden table and two chairs, a tin bath hung from a hook on the wall.

At home she'd spent many happy hours as a child in Cook's spacious and well organised kitchen, this one was barely bigger than one of the walk-in larders in the big house. The hunger pains gnawed at Beth's stomach. She began to unpack the basket of provisions she'd brought from the house and fill the small larder. Outside the light was beginning to fade and her apprehension grew at the long night ahead. She occupied herself with her chores trying desperately to push any fears to the back of her mind.

Where are all the candles and the oil for the lamps? Helen had assured her they would be found under the stairs. Tonight they were nowhere to be found.

In the pitch darkness Beth felt the panic rise in the pit of her stomach and slowly come up to choke her.

She stifled the urge to get up and run back to the safety of the house. This was what she'd wanted she reminded herself, freedom. But freedom had its price and tonight the price was high. She lay still, her body stiff under the covers and swallowed the self-pity that threatened to consume her. The lamp lay unlit on the table by her bed. Tomorrow she would purchase oil and make sure there were plenty of candles. With that thought in mind came a glimmer of hope that somehow she would get used to this small abode and her unwelcome solitude.

Burrowing under the sheets, which smelled clean and fresh, Beth remembered Helen and the look on her face as she entered the cottage with a pile of bed linen. 'Are you out of your mind?' was the question written in her hazel eyes. Perhaps she was, tonight even she doubted what had motivated her to leave her luxurious home for this sparsely furnished dark cottage.

The hours ticked by as sleep eluded her. Thoughts of Mary, the young maid dismissed from the house filled her mind. Where was she tonight? What happened to her on the streets of London? Beth was ashamed that her family could treat the girl in such a manner. Although, she reminded herself, Mary had not been the first. She squeezed her eyes shut in an attempt to erase the maid's face from her mind and tried hard to focus on the meeting with Alice the next day.

As the first light of dawn peeped through the curtains Beth at last fell into a deep sleep. Rest however was replaced by vivid dreams, where a man with no face forced his way into the cottage and attacked her in bed. A loud crash penetrated her head, as she awoke with a start, muzzy from sleep. Sitting bolt upright with her whole body shaking, she forced herself to focus on the room. At first she was confused by her surroundings. Then the reality of the situation hit her. She was alone in the cottage and someone was trying to break in! Lowering her legs and hardly noticing the coldness of the wooden floor underfoot she went to the window. All was quiet again. Had the noise been in her dream? This notion was soon discounted however at the sound of footsteps and in the half light below she saw the figure of a man running away from the cottage.

Chapter *Twelve*

THE ROYAL ALBERT HALL

Excitement filled the air as the high pitched sound of female voices flowed up and down, echoing off the elaborate walls of the Royal Albert Hall.

Beth held her breath. Feeling her corset dig into her ribs she tried to remember where the exits were. How had they got into the building? Thoughts jumped about in her head. There suddenly seemed no escape from the closed-in atmosphere or the bodies pressed up against hers. Her heart contracted in protest as she gulped instinctively for air, the sounds around her receded as her head began to spin.

Someone touched her arm. She turned to see Alice, her face full of concern and indicating for her to look upwards. Beth followed her line of vision and gazed towards the high ceiling, noticing for the first time the natural light that streamed in through an oasis of different coloured glass. For a moment or two Beth was mesmerised, as she watched the light dancing merrily with the colours. How she longed to be outside in the spring sunshine on this 19th day of March 1908.

Taking a deep breath she glanced back at Alice and mimed the words 'thank you.' Her heart returned to normal and Beth was able once again, to view all that was going on around her.

It had taken the two women several hours to arrive at the Albert Hall. With thousands of others heading in the same direction, the train had been full to bursting. Beth was so excited at this, her first real 'Mass Meeting.' The crowd swarmed like ants through the back entrance, all pushing their way in and then coming to a standstill on the steps. Looking up at the monument of Prince Albert standing straight and proud against the blue sky, Beth had asked herself what it would have been like to be his wife, Queen Victoria? How much easier it would have been for women throughout the country, if the lady had supported their cause. Instead their monarch had seen the Suffragette activities as the *'mad wicked folly that her poor sex was bent on.'*

Once inside the building Alice and Beth forced their way through the crowd. Their intention was to get as far to the front as they could.

"I don't want to miss a single word," Alice had admitted the day before. They had headed for the arena, but the nearest they could get was a few rows back in the stalls. It seemed that a world of women were in front of them that day. The air was filled with the perfumed aura of their scent.

Now, waiting patiently for the speeches to begin, Beth observed the scene surrounding them. "Next time we'll be wearing white dresses with purple and green scarves." She mouthed the words at her friend knowing that her voice couldn't be heard above the noise. Alice understood and smiled as they both remembered the mountain of brightly coloured material waiting to be sewn together, ready for the next mass meeting in Hyde Park.

In front of the women behind the stage, loomed the magnificent organ illuminated against a background of deep vibrant reds and golds. Only a year before Hugo had brought Beth to this beautiful hall for a concert, if only he could see her now. Beth lifted her head amused by her own thoughts. At that moment as she looked towards the arena she was distracted by the feeling of being watched, a man was looking behind him in her direction. What struck her as unusual was not that he was a man, although they were in a minority here, but that he too looked as if he wanted to escape just as she had a moment ago. Across the numerous heads Beth felt an invisible thread bind them together. But, in the beat of a heart, he had turned away merging into the audience once again.

The stage was now a hive of activity with a line of seats placed across it, they were slowly being filled up with the women speakers shuffling papers or chattering. A woman appeared whom Beth recognised as the treasurer Mrs Lawrence. She walked towards a large armchair, which had been left empty at the end of the row of chairs. Here she placed a large notice for all to see before making her way back to her own seat. Alice peered through her binoculars at the words and handed them over to Beth.

'To Our Absent Leader, Mrs Pankhurst.' She read.

Everyone knew that Mrs Pankhurst wasn't able to attend this important meeting due to her imprisonment, so her chair was left ceremonially empty on stage. This gesture was to remind them all of her absence and to encourage donations for the cause, hopefully attracting large contributions, with Mrs Pankhurst's suffering seen as a sacrifice for all women of the world.

A hush fell upon the crowd as Mrs Lawrence asked everyone to quieten down as she took her place at the front of the microphone. "My fellow women and of course men, I am overwhelmed by the sheer number of you standing in front of me today..." Before she could utter another word, one of her colleagues appeared on stage, dashed over to the treasurer and whispered something in her ear. The pair of comrades were so close to the microphone that the audience caught a few of the words exchanged. A ripple ran through the crowd. Mrs Pankhurst's name could clearly be heard and Beth's first thought was that something had befallen their pioneering leader.

Mrs Lawrence's next words were to bring joy to all those waiting in anticipation, as she declared at the top of her voice, "Mrs Pankhurst has been freed!" No sooner had the words been spoken, than the lady herself strode onto the stage to a deafening standing ovation from the crowd.

Beth felt the hairs on the back of her neck prickle, finding herself caught up in the same sheer excitement and abandon that took over the audience. Everyone cheered, raised their arms in the air and shouted words of encouragement at the top of their voices. Beth had never before felt so at one with her fellow gender as she did at that moment. In the few seconds that followed she knew the right decision had been made to abandon her cushioned life and support the suffragette cause.

As the noise died down all eyes were upon Mrs Pankhurst who stood upright on the stage waiting for order to be restored. As her words rang out loud and clear across the hall, Beth was reminded of Alice. It was the way that Alice, like this woman, addressed an audience with her commanding presence. Inspiring all who listened to stand up and fight.

"Welcome Women of the World to this Suffragette Meeting where we will all Stand up and be Counted! It's important for women to have the vote so that, in the government of the country, the woman's point of view can be put forward. Very little has been done for women by legislation for many years. Everywhere you hear and read details of social reform. You hear about legalisation to decide what kind of homes people are to live in. That surely is a question for women!"

Mrs Pankhurst's words were drowned out as the applause that followed shook the walls around them, causing the floor to vibrate beneath their feet. She had to pause until silence once again reigned before she could continue.

"No woman who joins this campaign will need to give up a single duty in her home. It is just the opposite, for a woman will learn to give a larger meaning to her traditional duties."

All too soon the speeches were over and the throng of women began to file out of the hall, excitement still buzzed amidst a high pitched chatter. Beth heard Alice talking to her as they pushed their way forwards, but found it hard to focus on what she was saying. At last out in the fresh air Beth stood with everyone else but not a word could be uttered from her lips.

"Don't worry." Alice said, leaning forwards and brushing her face against Beth's flushed cheek. "I felt the same way at my first big meeting. You'll come down to earth again soon."

Beth nodded, feeling tears of emotion prick her eyes as Alice turned away to take part in the conversations going on around them. A feeling of separation came upon Beth as she stood alone and she felt distant from those standing close by, as if she were an actor taking part in a play. For want of something to distract herself she glanced up at the magnificent red brick of the building behind her and read the foot high letters above the frieze.

'Thine, O Lord is the greatest and the power and the glory and the victory...'

Whispering the words to herself Beth began to feel more at ease. Then once again she had the feeling of being watched. Scanning the sea of faces she saw the man again, his fine-looking features were set in a smile and he blatantly stared in her direction.

For a moment as their eyes met, that invisible thread returned, binding them together once again. For a brief, insecure moment, Beth dropped her gaze and when she looked up the handsome stranger had gone leaving her feeling alone once more.

Chapter *Thirteen*

TEMPTATION

Finn stirred in his state of semi-sleep and turned over staring up at the ceiling. He had been dreaming of a young woman with wide blue eyes and long raven hair and her image refused to leave him. If only he'd approached her the day before outside the Albert Hall, but it hadn't been easy to find the courage. For once his reliable Irish charm had deserted him.

Finn had never had a problem with the lasses back home, but this woman was different - she was gentry. Of course he had only seen her from a distance. Despite this he could still gauge how striking her features were. He could see the determination etched on her face to fit in with those around her. It was obvious to Finn that it was her first time at a suffragette meeting and the vulnerability showed in her expression.

He watched her from a distance as she lifted her head to study the words carved above the frieze on the building behind her, then before he could avert his eyes she'd turned and met his gaze. Finn felt the hairs on the back of his neck prickle and in the pit of his stomach he knew this woman was special. She'd shifted her gaze and broken the spell, reminding Finn that he was but a working class man. To approach a lady such as her would have been madness indeed. Common sense may have prevailed as he disappeared into the crowd, but regret stabbed relentlessly at his heart. Thoughts crowded his head that now she was lost to him forever.

A raucous laugh reached his ears from the landing outside his room and he sighed to himself. He was now used to 'Violet's girls' who occupied three bedrooms of the lodging house in which he was staying. He remembered back to the first morning he'd woken to find them going about the business of greeting their clients, before disappearing behind their own bedroom doors.

Finn had been annoyed at first, and it had taken several weeks to get used to the grunts, groans and high pitched giggles frequently overheard when they were entertaining. Of course he was no stranger to these types of women himself. In the past in Ireland he had occasionally frequented their houses, when the fancy had taken him. Finn had known back then, that many a man had been left with more than a warm glow after being with a prostitute. He had barely given this a thought until one of his close friends in Ireland had contracted a terrible infection from such an encounter. The doctors had named the disease syphilis and his friend had died an agonising death as a result.

Finn had taken a while getting used to being on dry land again. At first he would wake up in the morning, still feeling the sway of the ship and hear the lapping of the waves beneath him. The fire onboard had also featured in his dreams for weeks afterwards. At the time he had done what was necessary, but thinking about it afterwards made him shudder. Thankfully the flames had been contained and the ship had been saved just in time.

Now, as Finn became aware of how parched his throat was and rubbed at his aching head, a result of too drinking the night before, he began to long for one of Violet's morning cuppas. Swinging his legs over the side of the bed, Finn stretched and put his feet down onto the bare floorboards. Instantly a cold chill chased its way up his body. He shivered, then grabbing his clothes from the chair to the side of the bed he began dressing hurriedly.

A low murmur of voices was coming from the dining room below, competing with the sound of the girls' chatter, which could still be heard coming from the landing. 'I must have overlaid again' Finn thought, 'how rude I must seem to Violet and the Lanes.' Having no reason to rise early, Finn had sometimes laid in bed longer than he should. At those times, Violet, anxious to please him, had cooked his breakfast later. This was done when the lanes had already gone about their day.

In a way he preferred to eat late, as the Lanes were not easy people to tolerate first thing in the morning. What with Millicent's constant over-cheerfulness and watchful eyes, she was almost as bad as the call girls. And Howard was forever glaring at him and frowning constantly. God alone knew why the silly man had taken such a dislike to him but he had. With these two factors combined, there always seemed to be an atmosphere at the meal table that even Violets meaningless gossip couldn't camouflage.

Now dressed, Finn ran his fingers through his hair and opened the bedroom door. Two familiar heads turned in his direction and their laughter, which had been irritating a moment before, seeped into Finn's morning fug and he graced them with a smile.

"Hello, my lovely," drawled the one he knew to be Mimi. She took a step in his direction, her heavily made-up eyes wearing a come-on expression. Finn took in the gaudy dyed red hair piled up into a loose knot on the top of her head, the black strappy dress and expanse of thigh on show. Against his will he found himself being drawn to the long black stockings and red frilly drawers nestling at the top of her leg. Mimi leaned towards him and jiggled two white bosoms in their barely contained neckline.

Finn ignored his manly desires. Determined not to be tempted by this scarlet woman he pushed her away, perhaps a little too roughly. "Not this morning, Mimi." He declared through ragged breath. 'How was a man supposed to resist?' Finn asked himself, doing up a couple of buttons on his shirt which he'd missed in his hurry to get dressed. He had no intentions of succumbing to Mimi's wiles this particular morning, nor would he rush to share in his departed friend's fate.

"Not so fast, my handsome one," Mimi persisted, draping her half naked body across his chest.

Once again Finn shook her off. "Mimi! Don't you ever give up?" Mimi reeled back at Finn's angry tone and heaving a loud sigh shrugged her shoulders. "Please yerself then, Finn." Despite the glint of temptation in Finn's eyes Mimi knew when she was beaten. "Although...pleasing yerself will never be as good as feeling a good woman between your thighs." She jibed.

Roxy suddenly appeared from behind Mimi where she had been watching her friend attempt to seduce the burly Irishman. "Why, Finn, its me you want ain't it, darling? Get out of me way, Mimi, its Roxy's turn." Fixing her small grey eyes on the area of Finn's crotch, which was showing signs of his reluctant arousal, Roxy ran her tongue slowly over her brightly painted lips.

Finn had to stop himself from making a sarcastic comment at Roxy's revelation. She was the last one of the three girls he would pick if he were in the choosing mood. There was something about Roxy that repelled him. She was older than the other two girls for a start. Her body was flabbier, well used and looked it. However much she tried with make-up and clothes, she just looked to him like an old worn-out woman. Finn had no idea how she got any clients at all.

Stifling the desire to laugh in Roxy's face, for even Finn recognised the cruelty of this, he took one last look at their painted faces and walked towards the stairs. On passing the door in which the third prostitute Candy slept, he could hear she was already hard at work. That was if the sounds of a man's deep moans coming from within were anything to go by.

With his foot on the top step Finn couldn't resist teasing the girls and turned back to confront their disappointed faces. "Well girls, maybe a man needs his sustenance first, a hearty breakfast, before committing himself to the *sexual act* so early in the day." Finn found that using a bit of banter with the women often helped him defuse their anger at being continually refused. Loud laughter echoed around the landing once again as both women, taking Finn's rejection in good humour, disappeared with a swish of their frilled dresses into their respective rooms.

Finn paused on the stairs for a brief moment, then taking a deep breath felt his racing heart return to normal. A man could only take so much temptation before he caved in. Finn wondered how long it would be before Mimi, or perhaps Lola got their wicked way with him. Hearing his stomach growling loudly however, beneath his hastily put-on clothes drove everything else from Finn's mind. He hurried down the stairs towards the dining room and one of Violet's wonderful breakfasts.

On opening the dining room door Finn was surprised to see that Millicent and Howard were still there. He was hoping that at this late hour they would already have gone, leaving him in peace in which to nurse his headache and enjoy his breakfast. Immediately he showed his face however, he was assailed by Millicent.

"Good morning to you, Finn." She greeted him ' warmly and leaned across the table for a hug. Finn tried not to wrinkle his nostrils at the heavy, sickly scent of Jasmine Millicent favoured wearing and ducked out of her way, aware of Howard watching their every move.

"Oh, there you are, Finn." Violet appeared by his side and begun clearing away Millicent and Howard's dirty crocks. "How are you this morning?" She stopped what she was doing when Finn didn't immediately answer and peered into his face. "My, you do look a little peaky this morning, dear. Have you been playing with my girls up there?" She looked towards the ceiling and let out a loud cackle of laughter.

Finn smiled weakly at Violet's humour. "I'm fine, Violet. Just a headache that's all. Nothing a fine cup of tea and one of your hearty breakfasts won't fix." He often found that flattery worked well with Violet.

Violet visibly brightened. "On its way, Finn," she said rushing away and cheerfully, "on its way," she reiterated.

Finn studied the pattern on the tablecloth as Violet bustled out of the room. Out of the corner of his eye he could see Howard nudging Millicent, then to his relief they both stood up.

"Well, I hope you have a nice day." Millicent gushed as she was ushered from the room by the still silent Howard. "See you later then," she called over her shoulder.

Once they were gone and while waiting for his breakfast Finn focused on the day ahead. His relentless search for work since he had been in London had been futile. That was until yesterday when he'd called into the Thames Ironworks to ask after employment. He had been told he should go along at midday today and make himself known to the foreman, a man by the name of George. He hoped he would get a job as a carpenter as the money he'd brought from Ireland was rapidly diminishing. Finn always felt sorry for the simple labourers who were two a penny and had to queue endlessly every day to get their work. At least he had had the foresight and good fortune to get a trade.

Just then Violet came back into the room, she was carrying a tray which was laden with breakfast. Finn's much longed for cup of tea arrived too, amid the heavenly smell of bacon and eggs.

Chapter *Fourteen*

THE CONFESSION

The sound of Alice's sewing machine as it whirred into life interrupted the silence as the two women worked studiously at the small wooden table. Outside the light was beginning to fade as late afternoon turned to early evening dusk. Beth raised her head, stretched out her neck and rubbed furiously at a place just between her shoulder blades. She'd finished the banner she was working on and passed it to Alice, who began folding the work they had completed.

"Cup of tea?" Alice asked as she folded.

"That would be nice," said Beth, who had begun to move her neck in small circles in an effort to get rid of some of the stiffness that had accumulated there. Suddenly Alice's hands were on Beth's neck and her fingers were massaging it back to life. Beth wasn't sure why, but a part of her felt uncomfortable with the situation and she raised her head abruptly. Alice's fingers dropped away and she resumed her unfinished task.

"Thank you, Alice. That feels much better." Beth heard her own voice waiver as her words echoed in the silence. Alice seemed not to hear her and carried on sorting the finished work into two separate piles as if her life depended on it. "Did I tell you about that handsome man who caught my eye the other week, at the Albert Hall?" Beth had no idea why she desperately wanted to tell Alice this information right at that moment, but somehow it seemed imperative. "I don't expect I'll see him again but he certainly was good-looking..." Beth's voice trailed off as she realised she was being ignored. "Is everything alright, Alice?"

"Of course why do you ask that?" replied Alice curtly, looking thoughtfully at Beth. "I'll make the tea," she added leaving the room in a rush, her skirts swirling behind her. Beth pondered on the situation that appeared to be developing. She'd become aware of late how close the two of them had become. They were spending a lot of time on preparations for the meetings coming up; even so in the last two weeks she'd noticed a change in Alice, which at times made her feel ill at ease with her friend.

"I'm sorry, Beth. It must be the grief," said Alice as she carried the tea on a tray and laid it down on the table. "Sometimes it catches up with me and that woman in the graveyard...I've been dreaming about her. I need to know who she is. None of it makes sense."

Beth nodded then watched as Alice sat in a nearby chair and put her head in her hands sighing deeply.

Beth's sympathy was immediately aroused for her friend who was so downcast. "Oh, Alice," she said sitting on the arm of the chair. "Of course. I'm so thoughtless you've suffered such tremendous loss you must miss your mother and father. Don't worry please we'll confront 'the woman in blue' and find out what she wants." Beth soothed. "You're not alone you know that don't you?" The question was as much for Beth's reassurance as for Alice.

Alice stood up hastily and smoothed down her skirt. Her eyes now held a different look that Beth found hard to identify. "Thanks, Beth. But I'll be fine."

Alice's hands moved swiftly as she hurried around the kitchen preparing dinner. It was usually Nancy who cooked the evening meal but today was her day off.

"Is there anything I can do to help?" Beth asked, standing the doorway. But Alice's back was all that she could see and her abrupt change of mood puzzled her. Beth longed for her friend to be her usual happy self again. "Perhaps, I had better go home?" she suggested sadly.

Alice, who must have heard the unhappiness in the other woman's voice stopped what she was doing and turned to face Beth. "You can't go home at this late hour the cottage will be freezing with no fire alight. By the way I meant to ask you, have you had any more warning notes pushed through your door?" Alice's tone had softened and Beth was relieved to see the awkward moment seemed to have passed.

Beth's forehead creased into a frown. "No I haven't and I'm trying to forget what happened that first night. The note was disturbing and as you know I did tell the police but there was little they could do."

"It was the bit about you facing the consequences if you don't leave the cottage that worries me. You know you're always welcome here if you don't want to live on your own?"

"Yes I realise that, Alice. I appreciate the offer. But I refuse to be driven away by someone playing pranks which is all it can be."

"Well, if you're sure. Thank you for all your help today. Tomorrow when Mrs. Weston comes for her dress I can say it's ready for her." Alice walked through to the back parlour and began laying the table as she spoke.

Beth, suddenly feeling weary, sat down. Immediately Mrs. P jumped on her lap meowing loudly, as she stroked her small furry body the two of them watched Alice darting about the room.

"Beth, you look tired. Dinner will be a while why don't you go and have a bath," suggested Alice, as she opened a drawer then handed Beth a sprig of lavender. "Here take this and put it in the hot water, it'll help you to relax."

"Thanks Alice." Beth stifled a yawn. "Are you sure you don't need any more help?"

"No. You've done enough for one day, go on." She gently pushed Beth in the direction of the door.

Beth dropped the lavender into the bath and its scent filled the room as it floated in the steamy water. Her eyes drooped as she lay back letting the steam-filled aroma take over her body, soothing the aches and pains that resided there. Suddenly she was jolted out of her reverie as the bathroom door, which was left unlocked, slid open causing her to sit up in surprise. Alice stood there, a towel draped across her arms, her green eyes riveted to Beth, who suddenly felt exposed and aware of her body in the cold air.

For a moment Alice said nothing as a whirl of emotions chased themselves across her face, like autumn leaves blown up in a storm. "I'm sorry, Beth...I"

"It's all right, Alice." Beth looked down and fiddled with the sprig of lavender, unable to move but desperate to cover up. Understanding dawned then confusion reigned, as she realised all at once, that Alice loved her, she'd seen the desire in her eyes. The moment passed and Beth slipped down into the water as Alice hurriedly put the towel down on the chair and left the room.

Beth's face was burning and her whole body felt alive with something she'd never experienced before. It was a sensation extremely pleasant and with a sigh she lay back in the bath and closed her eyes.

Later, as she dried her body her mind was racing in all directions. It was hard to understand how Alice, had fired up in her a wanting, a pleasure, she'd not known existed before. Something needed to come out in the open but Beth wasn't sure what it was. She found Alice in the front parlour standing by the window looking out at the passing traffic.

"Alice. I think we need to talk." Not a muscle moved in the other woman's body and she appeared not to hear Beth, then a muffled reply rippled through the air. "What was that I didn't hear you?"

"I said you are very beautiful, my love." Alice turned around, her mane of red hair hung down her back as she gazed intently at Beth. "You must know I love you." She said the words evenly and without faltering, and it came to Beth that she must have rehearsed this particular sentence many times before.

Beth was at a loss to answer her friend and dipped her head, breaking the eye contact between them.

"Do you love me?" Alice persisted.

Wringing her hands Beth let out a long sigh. She moved away from Alice towards the fireplace her reflection in the mirror above it showed a face full of confusion. "I don't know Alice. Well...of course I do. You're my dear friend and mentor, without you I would still be living at home. Feeling like a bird trapped in a cage."

Alice moved towards Beth then laid a hand upon her arm and for a moment silence hung heavily in the air as the fire crackled in its grate.

"Please, let me explain. Alice, I didn't love Hugo. But you tonight, something's changed." A smile teetered on the edge of Alice's lips as she listened to Beth. "I never want our friendship to end because you mean everything to me." Taking hold of Alice's hands Beth tried to explain. "Hugo's kisses meant nothing whatsoever, I never welcomed them and could never have..." she hesitated at the words she was about to utter, "bedded with him. You helped me to find the strength to escape all that."

"So what's altered tonight?" Alice's expression was full of hope as she whispered the words.

"I don't know, tonight I experienced something I hadn't felt before. You aroused a passion in me, now I feel bewildered. How could this happen and what does it mean? Surely it's unnatural?"

Alice's hands flew to her face and tears filled her eyes. "Oh, Beth. This is nothing new to me just something I have to live with." Alice wiped her eyes with the back of her hand. "At first I felt I'd never find anyone to love, but since joining the movement I've learnt I'm not alone in feeling this way. Then you appeared." She went to a drawer took out a large white hankie then blew her nose hard into it.

"But, Alice..."

"No! Let me finish, Beth. I need to tell you how it is. There are women in the movement..." She returned to the window and stood for a second gathering her thoughts, while Beth waited for her to continue. "They are like me, but not entirely. These women have the same feelings, 'unnatural' as you call them, but they're playing a game, obviously not looking for love as I am. Promiscuity is not my way and although I haven't had much experience in that direction, I know when I do it will be because I'm in love."

Beth's mind was racing as she tried hard to make sense of what Alice was saying, beginning to feel as if she wanted to escape. Before she could move away Alice was by her side with her face close to hers.

"Beth, I love you and from what you've just told me you could love me too."

"No, Alice. Please, I don't know." Beth tried to turn away unsure of her feelings, Alice took hold of her chin and lifted it up till their eyes met.

"You've just said I've aroused a passion in you. We can start from there surely. I won't rush you, Beth." Alice's voice was soft and liquid desire filled her face.

"Yes, I did say that but I don't know." Something wasn't right and Beth knew she had to make this stop. She needed time to think before it went any further. "I'm sorry, Alice. I'm confused and don't know what I feel anymore." She pulled away from the other woman and sat down unable to meet Alice's gaze.

A crashing noise followed by Mrs. P's loud meowing came from the direction of the kitchen interrupting the heavy silence. Alice cursed the cat loudly then rushed away, leaving Beth alone with her thoughts.

Later, as the two women ate in silence, all that had been said that evening hung in the air between them. Beth fervently wished that she was back at the cottage on her own. That night she lay awake well into the night, her mind mulling over what Alice had said and no matter how much she went over it she still felt confused.

The next morning it was well past nine when she awoke. She felt groggy and lethargic as she made her way downstairs. She found Alice in the back parlour sewing, her head bent towards the machine, her face creased in concentration. As she stopped what she was doing and looked up, Beth realised that she too had not slept well.

"Morning, Beth, there's still porridge on the stove," she said flatly, looking in the direction of the kitchen.

"Thank you," replied Beth, who didn't feel like eating. She sat in the kitchen sipping at her tea, trying not to think of the atmosphere that now existed between them. Mrs.P, having used up one of her nine lives the night before when she'd knocked over a vase in the kitchen, sending chards of glass over the floor, lay on a chair fast asleep. Her furry body was curled up into a neat circle.

The two women seemed to have nothing to say to each other. Beth left earlier than usual promising to see Alice the next day for the planned meeting. She met Nancy on her way out. "Hello, Nancy. How's your mother?" Beth enquired.

"She ain't too bad, Miss. Thanks for asking," replied Nancy. Her step was light and it was pleasing to see that for once, the young girl's family troubles were not weighing too heavily on her shoulders.

Beth decided to buy some provisions before she started her journey home and tried to think of things she needed. Her head felt befuddled from lack of sleep and the streets were busy that day, as she found herself struggling not to bump into passers-by. Afterwards, she was to think it happened so fast that she could not have seen it coming. It was as she stepped off the kerb to cross the road, that she felt someone take hold of her arms and haul her roughly backwards, pulling her clean off her feet. She landed on the pavement with a thud and for a moment was unaware of where she was, or what had befallen her. Dazed, she looked up and a man's face swam into view, just as a memory flashed through her mind of another time not so long ago that these features belonged to.

"Jaysus! Is there anything broken?" exclaimed the concerned face, holding out his hands to help her up from her place on the pavement. Passers by had begun to stop and stare.

"What do you think you are doing?" Beth hissed accusingly, grabbing hold of his outstretched hands and feeling herself being propelled upwards.

"Attempting to save your life I would say." Despite the concern in his voice Beth detected amusement beneath those sparkling amber eyes. She tried to contain her irritation, feeling desperate to remember where she'd seen this handsome stranger before.

It seemed he read her thoughts. "The Albert Hall?" he said as she scrambled to her feet.

"What? Oh, yes." it came back to her then and she felt her face flush with embarrassment.

"My names, Finn McGuiness. And to be sure you were about to step under a motor car." His expression was now serious as he held her gaze, pushing back a flaxen curl from his forehead.

Beth felt ashamed and knew he was probably · telling the truth. Her thoughts had been far away and she hadn't been paying attention to where she was going.

"Yes, well... thank you, Mr McGuiness for saving me ... I am most grateful." Abruptly turning on her heel Beth began to walk away.

"Miss. Miss!" Finn raced after her and then stood blocking her way. "I don't even know your name."

Beth pushed back her shoulders straightened her spine and faced him. "Hamilton-Green," she informed him quite formally. "My names, Miss Hamilton-Green."

"Miss. Hamilton–Green. Now there's a mouthful. Don't you have a Christian name?" He hurried on before she could answer. "Are you certain you're all right? See, you've had a nasty shock, so you have."

"I'm perfectly fine, Mr McGuiness. Really I am. Now if you'll just move out of my way."

"Why you are in such a hurry, Miss. Can I make your acquaintance again?"

Despite herself Beth couldn't help smiling, but she was shocked at the audacity of this attractive but cheeky young man and began walking away. He was following her closely and she did her best to ignore him and his unwanted attention.

"I just want to be sure you're all right," he said breathlessly, trying to keep up with Beth as she weaved her way in and out of the way of the crowded street.

Suddenly Beth stopped and spun around to face Finn. Later she was to wonder what on earth brought the words to her lips. "I will be in Hyde Park tomorrow at ten," she announced and before he could utter another word she'd disappeared into the crowd.

Chapter Fifteen

HYDE PARK

Marble Arch stood out high in all its splendour against the blue sky overhead, beckoning those making their way towards Hyde Park to walk beneath the magnificent structure. The tall flaxen haired man stood admiring its beauty and the work that had gone into the elaborate architecture. Running his fingers along its cold surface he pondered on how it would feel to carve her smooth exterior instead of the uneven texture of wood. He constantly found things to appreciate in London town. Even the weather was better, being particularly good for April which was a welcome change from the constant rain his homeland had suffered recently.

As Finn headed for Speakers Corner he realised he had no idea where Miss

Hamilton-Green would be in the vast grassland of the park. Or indeed whether she would turn up at all, the meeting had been arranged in such a hurry. He remembered the expression on her face the day before, after he'd manhandled her away from the path of the oncoming car. He had to smile to himself. She was so angry that she'd failed to realise he'd saved her from almost certain death, but at least when he'd attempted to explain his actions her look had been contrite if a little shaken. Her hot temper had then disintegrated into embarrassment and it seemed she couldn't get away from him quick enough. Finn felt himself even more attracted to her strong character and incredible beauty and knew he had to see her again.

Several people were milling around the corner of Hyde Park as he approached, where those with an opinion to air could do so if others were willing to listen. Finn marvelled at this freedom of speech and reflected that in Ireland where tensions were building and unrest was always in the air, it would more than likely cause a riot. As he came closer he noticed a small cluster of women chatting amicably to one side, he watched as they parted to allow one of their members to withdraw from the group. It was then he saw her.

Even though she was half turned away from him, he recognised her immediately from the way she held herself, her back was straight and her head held high. Dressed in a dark blue skirt, which accentuated her magnificent figure and matching cape, she wore a violet coloured hat on her head her dark tresses were swept up away from her face. Observing her from a distance, he took in her striking appearance, noticing that all her attention was centred on the person about to stand on the upturned box. Following her line of vision he watched a woman with vibrant red hair, begin an impassioned speech on the rights of women. She was obviously someone who knew how to capture her audience and a hush fell over the small crowd as she spoke. But it was the raven haired beauty that held Finn's attention.

"Good day to you, Miss Hamilton-Green," tipping his hat Finn stood boldly in front of the young woman, who for a moment looked at him blankly. As recognition dawned on her fine features she smiled lighting up her vivid blue eyes.

"Good morning, Mr...? I'm so sorry I've forgotten your name"

"McGuiness, Finn. I hope you're feeling better today, Miss Hamilton-Green."

"I am, Mr McGuiness. Thank you for helping me yesterday." She turned around as a woman behind her declared that she was listening to the speech, so 'please be quiet.' Half smiling at Finn she obliged by moving to one side.

Finn followed her to a quieter spot away from the gathering crowd and noticed she kept glancing constantly over her shoulder at her red-haired friend.

"Mr McGuiness. I'm aware that I could quite likely have been killed yesterday and am grateful for your help. However, our agreement to meet...I'm sorry but I have other things to do today." Again her eyes followed the woman on the soapbox, now in full flow. "My friend, Alice she's such a good public speaker." She added almost to herself.

"I'm pleased to have been of help," Finn's eyes never left her face, "wouldn't you like to walk awhile? We wouldn't venture far and it's such a fine day." Finn looked up at the sun as if to emphasise that she mustn't miss this opportunity to enjoy its warm rays.

"Maybe just for a few moments then, Mr McGuiness."

"Please call me, Finn," he said, as they fell into step beside each other and began following a footpath. "I don't even know what your Christian name is, *Miss Hamilton- Green*."

"It's, Beth. Pleased to meet you," she held out her hand and he grasped it tightly in his own, reluctant to let it go and feeling its warmth fill his body. Beth recovered first removing her hand from his and dipping her head. Her face had gone quite pink and her eyes were averted as they walked together in silence.

The gravel path crunched underfoot and a small sparrow hopped alongside them and they both watched as it perched on a nearby bench, its short tail bobbing up and down. "Shall we sit down?" Finn looked over his shoulder. "You can still see your friend from here," he reassured, dropping his head to one side and winking cheekily at her.

Beth couldn't help laughing. She sat down on the opposite end of the bench to him and the sparrow sprang across and hopped around between them. "Sorry, we don't have anything for you today," she told the bird as it looked at her expectantly, its brown-grey feathers standing proud and its stubby beak moving up and down in protest.

"You were in a tearing hurry yesterday, Beth." Finn said into the silence, as they watched the small creature bobbing up and then hop to the ground searching for worms.

"I was on my way home having just had a very busy day. Unfortunately when I stepped into the road my mind was full of other distractions." Beth explained, sitting up then stretching out her arms and stifling a yawn as she did so. "I'm so sorry, that was very rude of me," she said, "sleep was elusive last night."

"Did you enjoy the Albert Hall the other day?" Finn tried desperately to keep Beth's attention. This had never happened to him before, he must be losing his touch he told himself.

"Yes, I certainly did, although it was a new experience for me." Beth shifted uneasily on the bench and looked intently at Finn. "I know this is a strange question to ask as we have only just met but...from a man's point of view tell me, what was it like being surrounded by so many women, with men in the minority?"

A smile played around Beth's lips as she spoke and Finn realised she was teasing him. He also knew instinctively that beneath the mirth, she obviously took this suffragette business very seriously. "There was a lot of the fairer sex there," he observed, "but the speeches were well put together it must be said," he hesitated, trying hard to say something she would approve of. "Of course it's always good to see another's point of view, so it is."

"That was the intention, to show men we should be treated more fairly." Beth's smile had now gone and there was a determined look in her eyes.

Finn was lost for words for a moment feeling somehow under pressure to defend the role of man.

Beth arched her eyebrows at Finn. "It's good our message came across and there was a mixed audience. Some would only have been there out of curiosity." As she spoke she looked down at her skirt and began smoothing out a non-existent crease.

"I'm not sure all men need to be shown how a woman should be treated." Finn said trying not to sound peeved at her observation. "I have to admit it was curiosity that drew me to the Albert Hall." Finn tried to choose his words wisely, this woman intrigued him and he didn't want to scare her off. "I've seen so many women shouting at the top of their voices in the streets that I decided to see for myself what this 'suffragette business' was all about."

Beth nodded and stared out across the park, once again Finn felt her attention begin to wander. "Do you often come to Speaker's Corner on a Sunday?" He could have kicked himself for his ill-chosen words and had merely wished to change the subject.

Beth regarded him and he saw that some of the tension had left her body as her smile returned. "No, at least I haven't up until now. I think I will want to come back again."

"I hope you don't think, Miss Hamilton-Green, that by coming here today I'm being presumptuous. It was just that after our encounter yesterday I knew I had to see you again."

Beth's face coloured at his words. "Of course not, Mr McGuiness...Finn. After all it was my suggestion we meet today." Beth's blue eyes danced as she spoke and he was entranced by her beauty.

"Whereabouts in London do you come from?" he ventured tentatively.

"I come from Richmond." She said. "And you?"

Finn could see that Beth wasn't giving much away, but then they had only just met. "I'm in lodgings in Whitechapel I've only lived in London for a year. I expect you can tell I originate from Ireland."

"I did notice the accent. How are you finding our fine city?" Beth leaned closer to Finn as she spoke and he instantly became aware of the softness of her skin and a faint smell of lavender. Just at that moment a shadow fell across them and they both lifted their heads squinting into the bright sunlight.

"Beth!" At the sound of her name being spoken in such a manner Beth stood up abruptly. Finn recognised the young woman standing in front of them with her hands on her hips, as Beth's 'red-haired' friend, Alice. She was striking in appearance with the combination of vibrant hair and emerald eyes, which were now filled with anger.

Beth looked concerned at the urgency in the other woman's voice. "Alice, what on earth is the matter? What's happened?"

"Where have you been? Everyone is waiting and you're missing the agenda!" Alice said angrily, her fine features contorted with rage.

Finn didn't care for the woman's tone of voice and felt uncomfortable with the turn of events. He stood up from his place on the bench and held out his hand to Alice. "I'm sorry if I've kept Beth from the meeting, it was entirely my fault so it was. I was just about to go on my way."

Alice ignored Finn's gesture and threw him a disdainful look. Then swinging round on her heels she walked back towards the gathering of women with her skirts swishing behind her.

"Alice!" Beth shouted after her. But Alice appeared not to hear and kept walking. Beth began to follow her friend, until it seemed she remembered

Finn. "I'm sorry." She said walking back towards him. "I don't know what the matter is. She's acting out of character speaking to me like that." Beth's brows were creased in a frown as she addressed Finn. "I apologise for her bad manners, I really must go and have words. It was nice seeing you again."

Finn took her hand as she held it out towards him, feeling the delicate fingers beneath his own and becoming aware once again of the electricity between them. "No worries sure enough, but can I see you again?"

Beth lifted her chin then glanced over her shoulder towards the small crowd. "Yes, I think that would be very pleasant."

"How about next Sunday by the boating house, at the Serpentine Lake?" Finn proposed. Beth nodded quickly at him then began to hurry away. "About this time?" he added at her retreating back.

The little sparrow sat chirping by Finn's feet as he watched Beth walking over to join her friends. Her back was ramrod straight and her head held high. A woman of spirit she certainly was he thought and already he was longing to see her again.

Chapter *Sixteen*

THE LADY IN BLUE

Alice heard the key in the front door and was surprised to see Beth standing in the doorway. Her eyes flashed with anger and her hair hung down her back in disarray. Alice's eyebrows lifted in a silent 'not now please' look.

"Hello, Elizabeth. As you can see I have a visitor. I believe the two of you are already acquainted?"

Beth's face went quite pink as a woman dressed in an emerald green skirt and a mismatched purple jacket stepped out from behind Alice. "Good morning to you, Miss Hamilton-Green." The lady offered, "pray tell me, how are your dear parents?"

Beth pursed her lips together and attempted to smile. "They are very well thanking you, Mrs Weston."

Beth's reply sounded convincing, but Alice knew that in truth she hadn't seen them for several months. "Thank you for coming to see me, Mrs

Weston." Alice ushered her client to the door moving quickly past Beth.

"My, the tulips are looking good," announced Mrs Weston, whilst straining her neck in a desperate bid to look behind her at Elizabeth, who had now disappeared from the hallway.

"Yes, they certainly are. Goodbye, Mrs Weston see you next time." Alice began closing the door forcing the other woman to retreat to the pathway beyond. She found Beth sitting on the sofa her face looking mutinous and began to regret her actions the day before. "Why don't you come into the kitchen, "she said hurrying out of the room, the swish of Beth's skirts followed behind her. "Cup of tea?" Alice didn't wait for a reply but filled the black kettle with water and put it on the burner, then reached up for cups and saucers.

Beth's eyes flashed with rage. "Stop that now and look at me!" "Why are you behaving as if nothing's happened?"

Alice put down the cups and sighed then sat down at the table and looked at Beth. "Sit down and let's talk," she suggested.

Beth frowned, then reluctantly did as Alice told her and sat down opposite her friend. The air was heavy with unspoken words.

Alice knew she would have to apologise but this didn't come easy. She laid her hands flat on the table and studied her fingernails not trusting herself to look at Beth. "I'm sorry, it was wrong of me to act that way yesterday..." Her words tumbled out quickly as Beth interjected.

"It certainly was! I can't believe you embarrassed me in that way. Then afterwards, the way you refused to discuss it. Well, it made things seem much worse. You owe me an explanation."

Alice put a trembling hand up to halt Beth's tirade. "Stop. Let me speak." Beth glared back at her with narrowed eyes. "How can you not understand? I thought I had made my feelings for you clear." Alice's eyes searched Beth's face. "Sometimes I can't help my behaviour towards you." Alice intended to stay calm and explain to Beth how she felt but her eyes began to water.

"Please. Don't do this, Alice." Pausing briefly Beth sat back in the chair and folded her arms across her chest defensively.

"Do what?" Alice sobbed, "do what, Beth. Love you!" Alice heard her words come out as a shriek. Shocked by her own passion she watched the sympathy form itself on her friend's face. "Oh, for goodness sake," Alice dabbed at her eyes and took a deep breath, "don't pity me." She so wanted Beth to understand how it was. Beth stared at Alice obviously at a loss as to how to put things right between them. "It annoyed me," Alice began, "that you left my speech half way through to go off with that 'man'." She winced as she heard her own voice come out as a whine.

Beth tried to explain and began picking at a loose thread on her blouse as she spoke. "It slipped my mind that I'd agreed to meet Finn. It was only arranged the day before and I only went for a short walk - I wasn't abandoning you."

Alice felt a stab of pain at the mention of 'his' name and once again sensed the powerful black emotion that had been evoked by seeing Beth yesterday with 'the Irishman.' "Will you be meeting him again?" She said quietly. When silence was the only answer, she could help herself no longer. "What about me, Beth. What about us?" Alice's stomach tightened and her brow furrowed in confusion as she spoke. Her longing to hear Beth's answer was interwoven with dread that her heart was about to be broken.

Beth dipped her head and stared sightlessly down at her hands. "I'm sorry, Alice. There is no 'us.' I just don't feel that way about you." There was a tiny beat as the hope in Alice's eyes died.

Alice calmed her jittery nerves and told herself she was relieved, at least now she knew for sure that Beth could never love her. Rubbing her hand across her forehead she attempted a watery smile. "At least we know where we stand. It obviously wasn't meant to be," she said sadly getting up to make the tea.

"Alice, I should have told you before and now regret that I didn't." Beth lifted her head looking anguished at her friend's sad acceptance of what could have been.

"No more apologies, Beth." Alice said focusing on the teapot. "We must move on now." Avoiding her friend's gaze, she sat back down and began pouring milk into the teacups determined to push away the feeling of loss threatening to overwhelm her.

"You know, don't you, that you are my dearest and most valuable friend?" Beth looked up and leaned towards Alice willing her to look up. "I owe you so much. What would I have been without you?"

"Of course." Alice's voice waivered but she dare not meet Beth's eyes. She pushed a steaming cup and saucer towards her, "there is something else, Beth. It's not you it's me, you see..." As she spoke Alice reached down to stroke Mrs. P who'd appeared beside her, winding her body around the table leg and meowing loudly. "I've not been feeling quite myself lately."

Beth reached for her tea and took a sip. "Tell me about it. Maybe I can help?" She said thoughtfully.

Alice wrung her hands and raised her head. Mrs. P meowed loudly as the attention she was receiving stopped abruptly. "Well, you know we had the conversation about the woman I see when I visit the graves?"

Beth nodded and sat up straighter in her chair, eager to help Alice in any way she could. "The strange woman always dressed in blue?"

Alice nodded. "It's driving me mad. I see her standing on the edge of the graveyard watching me." Alice struggled with the words and repeated herself. "Constantly watching me, Beth. I think...." She looked stricken with anxiety as she attempted to explain to Beth how she was feeling and stared down at her fidgeting hands.

"What on earth is it, Alice?" Beth's face was creased in confusion at her friend's discomfort. "Tell me, what is the matter?"

Alice looked up with eyes full of sadness. "Beth, I think it's my mother." She said quietly.

Beth looked alarmed at her friend's suggestion that her recently departed mother could be stalking her in the graveyard. "Your mother, of course not. Now, Alice, you know that can't be true."

Alice didn't hear Beth's words. She gazed into the middle distance with tears coursing down her cheeks. "She's in my dreams too, Beth, dressed in blue just the same." Grief for her mother, intermingled with an aching loss that the woman sitting opposite would never return her feelings, cut deep into her soul. She let out an animal-like howl, covered her face with her hands and sobbed uncontrollably.

Beth could only reach towards Alice as her own face crumpled in distress at her friend's suffering. "Alice," she murmured. "I'm so sorry." She was at a loss to know how to comfort Alice, knowing that some of the hurt she was feeling was because of her own rejection. She put her arms around Alice softly and waited.

It was some time later that Alice lifted her head and faced Beth, who sat quietly stroking Mrs. P. while watching her friend. Alice's eyes were red and swollen and her face looked blotchy as she shakily lifted her handkerchief and blew her nose noisily. "I'm sorry, I lost control." She eventually said.

Beth nodded sympathetically. "Alice, why do you think your mother is the lady in the graveyard? Tell me." She spoke softly, hoping not to open the floodgates of grief once again.

"Because my mother died without telling me how things really were." Alice spoke logically while she rubbed at her sore eyes. She said the words as if it were natural that her mother's spirit had come back to haunt her. "Mother is trying to reach me, do you see? In my dreams, in the graveyard." She explained.

Beth was suddenly frightened for Alice and knew her friend needed proof that what she suspected was not true. "It's the grief, Alice." She said calmly. "The grief of your loss is distorting everything."

Alice shook her head violently. "I'm not sure what you mean. Maybe you need to go home now."

Beth pushed a reluctant Mrs. P. from her lap and reached out to touch Alice's hand. Alice snatched herself away quickly, physical contact was too painful. "Alice, don't push me away." Beth leaned back in her chair and regarded Alice. "You must see that it is only a manifestation of your grief, this feeling that your mother is haunting you."

Alice dipped her head but made no further attempt to argue with Beth.

"It's because you feel there is unfinished business with your mother." Alice had told Beth about the last conversation she'd had with her mother and about finding the letters after her death. "You wanted her to know you understood how she felt didn't you?" Alice kept her head low and nodded slowly at Beth's words. "It's not the case, Alice and I will prove it to you." Beth inhaled deeply hoping that her words would not be in vain. By helping Alice to reveal the true identity of the woman at the graveyard, Beth hoped Alice would be able to move on with her life and deal with the grief clearly overwhelming her.

Leaving Alice to digest her words Beth made another cup of tea. When she returned to the table with the fresh brew Alice had a framed photo in her hand, she was staring at it intently. "I miss her so much." She said her voice barely audible, as she gazed at the image of herself and her mother standing close together.

"You look like her you know." Beth said, trying to offer comfort as she placed fresh cups on the table. "Your mother was beautiful, like you. Tall, maybe not as curved." She smiled as she said this, attempting a positive slant on the comparison. Anxiety was quick to stab at her though, reminding her that her words could easily be misconstrued by Alice.

The look on Alice's face soon laid this to rest however for her eyes were narrowed as she lifted her head to meet Beth's gaze. "I've never been short of men followers." She half laughed, firmly lifting her chin defiantly. "It never worked and I'm not interested as you now know."

"I'm sorry it can never be, Alice. But I hope our friendship will still survive?" Beth implored Alice to understand. "For I value it above all else."

Alice looked away leaving Beth's question unanswered. Picking up her tea she sipped at it, then putting her elbows on the table she rested her head in her hands.

Beth was filled with regret that her rejection of Alice had hurt her so much. Maybe she could make up for it by helping her identify the woman Alice believed to be her mother. Beth got up and began pouring water into the sink to wash up her cup. "I will always be here for you, Alice." She said soothingly.

Alice looked longingly at Beth's back, and for a brief moment the mask slipped again as desire and longing were reflected naked and intense in her emerald green eyes.

The tulips were in full bloom around the gravestones that morning and Alice inwardly smiled at the abundance of colour. Briefly she glanced across at Beth who was hiding in a cluster of trees the other side of the graveyard.

The 'blue lady' always appeared at the same time and Alice's hands shook as she tended the flowers, fiddling with their stems as she did so. There was really nothing to be done but somehow she had to pass the time. The sun was shining and she felt its heat on her skin, as she forced herself to draw back from her parents resting place to sit on a nearby bench. She sat motionless, convinced that now Beth was here 'her mother' would not appear as a noise overhead caused her to glance upwards. A blue tit was flying freely in and out of the overhead branches feeding its young. She watched the bird flapping its wings wildly as it nurtured its fledglings and a keen sense of loneliness filled her body.

As Alice looked across the graveyard she saw Beth waving her arms furiously at her. She leapt to her feet. In the distance she saw 'the blue lady' and Beth standing together. Hurrying over to them, her feet raced beneath her and she had to concentrate hard not to fall over. Beth smiled as she approached and Alice turned her attention to the other woman, who was dressed in different shades of blue from head to toe.

"Good afternoon, Alice." The words were so softly spoken that they seemed to be carried on the gentle breeze that blew around their feet. The eyes that looked back at her were large, a dazzling bright blue colour, full of apprehension and framed in an angular face. She wasn't young, perhaps fifteen years older than Alice and the colours she wore complimented her smooth skin and complexion.

"Alice, meet Rose." Beth reached out and put a hand on her arm.

"Rose...?" Alice's long awaited questions tumbled from her mouth and she was suddenly aware of the perfume of sweet roses in the air, which inexplicably brought forth an image of her mother's letters. Confused she tried to make sense of her thoughts. "You're not... then who are you?"

"She was your mother's friend, Alice." Beth explained quietly. "Very close to your mother." She reiterated.

"I apologise..." began Rose, "I've heard so much about you and couldn't help watching you on your visits to Megan's grave." Her eyes were now moist and imploring Alice to understand. "Somehow, I didn't feel able to approach you."

Alice's heart lurched with realisation. This was the woman who'd written letters to her mother, letters which Alice had found after her mother's death. Of course they had been filled with the same rose perfume. Alice felt her knees wanting to give way beneath her. But where was her mother? She knew it was her mother who'd been watching her, now she was no-where to be seen. Megan had vanished and this other woman now stood in her place. This 'other person' was her mother's secret lover, secret lover...the words echoed in Alice's mind. Suddenly the strength was being drained from her body and she felt herself sinking towards the ground.

The last thing Alice remembered was Beth's hands taking hold of her arms and propelling her back towards the bench. As they sat down she could hear the bird, having now finished the frenzied feeding of her young, twittering contentedly above their heads. To Alice the world seemed out of kilter and also blissfully unaware that her dear mother was not where Alice had believed her to be.

Chapter *Seventeen*

ROSE

Rose rapped hard on the door knocker then had a sudden urge to run down the path past the array of spring flowers and out through the garden gate. Stifling the desire, she waited patiently for Alice to answer the door. A week had passed now since they'd met for the first time. Rose couldn't help but speculate on whether her arrival would be welcome. She was about to follow her instincts and turn around when the brightly painted front door swung open. But instead of Alice appearing before her, a young lady whom she recognised as Beth stood in the doorway.

"Good afternoon, Rose. Do come in," she said opening the door wide. "I don't think Alice was expecting you. I'm afraid she's not in."

Rose stepped over the threshold into the hallway and followed Beth into the front parlour. "I called round because we need to talk. Can I wait for her?"

"Of course, she's just gone to get material for a client. Please sit down. Can I offer you a cup of tea?"

Rose loosened her coat and sat down on the sofa. "No thank you...to be truthful I'm not sure that Alice will want to see me."

Beth's dark hair cascaded around her shoulders and her blue eyes looked intently back at Rose. Not for first time, Rose wondered if this beauty was Alice's lover. The way she helped Alice at the graveyard certainly pointed in that direction, if not there was a very strong bond between the two women. She blinked and forced herself to focus on what Beth was saying.

"Alice's feeling a bit mixed up at the moment. It was a shock finding out who you were. She always felt her mother should have been able to tell her, especially towards the end."

"I understand completely that she probably needs more time." Rose pulled her coat around her shoulders and stood up to go, both women turned at the sound of the key being turned in the front door.

"Beth, I couldn't get the colour I needed, oh...."

Alice stepped into the front parlour taking Rose's breath away. The likeness to Megan was incredible. Of course there would be a similarity. Although they'd only met for the first time last week, Rose hadn't taken in those startling green eyes, or how much she resembled her lost love. "Alice. How are you?"

"What do you want, Rose?" Alice's icy tone conveyed her dislike for the other woman as she hovered in the doorway.

Rose faced Alice's hostile gaze. "I wanted to see you, but I can see the feeling is not mutual."

"Alice, won't you spare Rose a few moments?" Beth implored her friend to reconsider. "Surely there are things you want to ask her?"

Alice shrugged, then moved past Rose and sat down brushing a non-existent speck of dust from her sleeve. "Yes, there is something." Alice's voice was thick with emotion. "I want to know why you always ran from me?"

Rose felt the chill in the air begin to evaporate and out of the corner of her eye she saw Beth quietly leaving the room. "I'm sorry, that was unforgivable of me." She said to Alice's bent head. "I knew you were Megan's daughter, but I wanted to keep my identity secret. There was the risk you might hate me."

Alice looked up. "Hate you? Why would I do that? I don't know anything about you. It was only after my mother died I learned of your existence."

"So I understand but...how?"

Alice's eyes were two liquid pools of sadness. She hesitated, then turned away from Rose and disappeared into the back parlour. Rose could hear her opening and closing a drawer.

Rose gasped, feeling a tightness form in her chest as Alice reappeared. She was now standing in front her clasping a small pile of letters tied up with red ribbon.

Alice's hands were trembling and her eyes were full of accusation. "I found these. You must have sent them to mother... behind my father's back."

Rose tried to keep her composure in the face of Alice's obvious hostility. She exhaled slowly. Megan's daughter was now holding out the letters for her to take. Endeavouring not to stare at her own familiar, long spidery handwriting, she took the letters and laid them gently down on the sofa by her side.

Despite Rose's best efforts her calmed breathing could not stop the flow of tears from tumbling down her cheeks. Keeping her head bowed she fumbled for her handkerchief, dabbed at her eyes and blew her nose softly. Then lifting her head she addressed Alice who was now sitting in the armchair opposite her. "Your father didn't know," she said falteringly, "oh no, she wouldn't allow that." Rose attempted, for Alice's sake, to unravel the layers that lay hidden.

Alice leaned slowly back in the armchair and studied Rose, her expression still looked anguished but had softened. "I'm glad to hear that, because it would surely have broken his heart in two."

Guilt stabbed relentlessly at Rose as she looked intently back at Alice's face. She would have to be careful to choose her words wisely.

"Tell me why did you only ever sign the letters with the initial R?" Alice asked before Rose had a chance to speak.

The sound of Beth moving around the back parlour echoed in the room. Rose felt the tightness in her chest begin to subside, and in its place she felt the fragile thread of understanding growing stronger between them. "I couldn't sign them properly. Your mother made me promise never to write my name, in case they were ever found. I wasn't afraid of being discovered, but I had less to lose than her." Rose looked intently at Alice as she spoke. "And... you could say I have what some would call a rebellious nature."

Alice's brows lifted slightly and the corners of her mouth twitched into the beginnings of a smile at Rose's words. "You remind me of someone else I know," she said quietly, glancing briefly towards the front parlour as the sound of a sewing machine whirred into life. Getting up she went to the fireplace and placed a log in its midst. Then taking a moment she gazed at the small red and orange flames as they began to flicker around the wood. Mrs. P appeared from no-where and flopped down in front of the growing heat.

"Beth helps me with my sewing," Alice explained stroking Mrs. P along her soft back then taking her seat in the armchair again.

"She seems like a good friend." Rose observed, her heart feeling lighter, for the atmosphere in the room had now settled into a new hesitant peace.

"Yes she is but..." A frown passed over Alice's face and Rose regarded her steadily.

"Are you two lovers?" Rose instantly regretted being so outspoken at Alice's despondent expression. She watched Alice dip her head and stare down at her hands. "I'm sorry it's none of my business." She countered.

"No. It isn't." Alice said abruptly, then lifted her head and fixed Rose with her green eyes. "Are you married? Do you have you any children?"

"I'm widowed. My husband's name was Gerard. He was a military man, hard and at times cruel. My only solace was that he was frequently away fighting."

"Why did you marry him then, if he was cruel?"

"Well. He didn't seem bad at first. He changed, especially once I couldn't become pregnant. He constantly took it out on me saying it was my fault he didn't have a son." Rose's face contorted in pain as she recalled her past but struggled on as the tightness returned in her chest. "Then... after several years I gave birth to a child and things improved for a while. He left me alone." Rose stared down at the floor and Alice waited for her to go on. "Then at two years old, little Billy died. It was pneumonia."

"Oh, Rose. How awful for you." Alice looked distraught at the other woman's misfortune, "did you have any more children?"

Rose lifted her head and pushed a wisp of fair hair back from her face. "A short while after that Gerard was sent to fight in the Boer war. He never came home and was killed in December 1899; during the battle at Magersfontein. I met Megan about six months after he died." Rose looked intently back at Alice. "Do you want me to go on?"

Alice nodded. "I want to know more about my mother and the life I knew nothing about. I remember her visits to the church to arrange the flowers or help out at Sunday school, but I never guessed..."

Rose wanted to be clear about her relationship with Megan. "We were just friends at first. I mean, I knew straight away that I loved her and one day I confessed. She constantly denied she felt the same. Until one day when we were alone at my house." Rose stopped for a moment reluctant to go on. She looked up to see Alice's eyes full of sympathy.

"It only happened once." When there was no answer from Alice she forced herself to continue. "Just the once," she reiterated. "After that, she made sure we were never alone together again. We remained amicable and I had to be content with that." Alice's expression looked troubled and Rose could see she was finding it hard to hear about the sacrifice's her mother had been forced to make.

"Megan loved you and in her own way she loved your father too. She did love me, she told me so. She could never think of leaving your father or cause social disgrace to fall upon your heads." Alice nodded in agreement.

"Megan distanced herself from me after that. That's when I began to write to her. I never received any replies. When we did bump into each other at the church she urged me to keep writing. She told me how she loved to read my letters. I never knew she'd kept them all. That was a surprise." Rose's heart lifted knowing that Megan had treasured her letters. "I'm sorry it must be hard for you to understand."

"I do understand." A sudden loud crackle from the grate drew Alice's gaze towards the flames now leaping high into the chimney. The sounds from the other room had now ceased and her words fell softly into the stillness of the room. "I'm so in love with Beth."

Rose impulsively lifted herself from the sofa walked over to the armchair and crouched in front of Alice. "Look at me, Alice." She said softly. Alice obeyed and Rose stared into the emerald green eyes that were so like Megan's. "I know," she whispered. "I can see the way things are."

"Is it that obvious?"

Rose nodded and laid a hand upon Alice's arm.

"There's no hope though. My feelings are not reciprocated." Alice said sadly.

"I'm sorry to hear that." Rose now understood how much Alice was really like her mother. "Unfortunately history seems to be repeating itself." Rose stood up and smoothed down her skirt. "I think I should go now. I'm sorry if I've caused you pain."

"You haven't. Not really. I just wish it could have been different for you both and yet...I loved my father and wouldn't have wanted to see him hurt."

"I know. But times are beginning to change, Alice. I'm sure you'll find love one day. Maybe not with Beth, but one day that person will come along."

Alice afforded Rose a brief smile as Rose buttoned up her coat ready to leave.

"Thank you for explaining things to me." Alice opened the front door for Rose her eyes lingering on the other woman's attire. "I've just realised why you always wear blue." She said suddenly her eyes brightening.

Rose nodded at Alice's perception. "Yes, she always loved that colour didn't she?"

"Wait. There's something I should give you." Rose was about to step outside the door, when Alice quickly disappeared back inside the house leaving her hovering on the step.

Within a moment Alice was back and in her hand she held Megan's letters. Once again she held them out to Rose. "You must... you should have these,

Rose." She said firmly. "Mother would have wanted you to."

"Thank you, Alice." Rose hesitated, unsure about the emotion that seeing these letters again would evoke. "I'm not sure..." She began, but the pleading in Alice's eyes overrode any reservations she had personally. So she took them from the younger woman and slipped them into her coat pocket. "I will treasure them." She said quietly. In truth she was uncertain she could ever look at them properly again for at the time of their writing her heart had been breaking.

As Rose walked down the pathway towards the gate, the rays of sunshine were warm upon her skin. It was early May and for the first time in a long time her spirits were lifted and she was looking forward to the days of summer that lay ahead. She turned, waved goodbye to Alice who was standing on the doorstep and walked down the street with a spring in her step.

Chapter *Eighteen*

THE BOATHOUSE

Beth's hands trembled slightly as she struggled with the fastenings on her white lace blouse. For the first time ever, she wished that Helen was here to help her dress. With her back to the mirror and stretching her fingers; she at last managed to reach the tiny buttons which kept sliding from her grasp. Turning to look at her reflection, the young woman who returned her gaze was filled with exhilaration and apprehension. Her eyes were bright and cheeks flushed revealing a turmoil of emotions in her face.

Beth's excitement over meeting Finn was however tinged with guilt, as she remembered Alice's reaction to her growing relationship with the handsome Irishman. Her friend's recent behaviour suggested she'd prefer Beth not to see Finn, but Beth knew she could never allow the other woman to dominate her life. She walked over to the window and peered out at the gloriously sunny day. Unfastening the catch she breathed in the mild air. It was time to go she told herself putting all thoughts of Alice from her mind.

Beth stepped off the omnibus at the park. Pleased to be out in the fresh air she   began the short walk to the boathouse, the sun was warm on her skin and so she stopped briefly to put up her parasol. The park was buzzing with everyone outside enjoying the sunshine. For many, it was the only day of the week they had to relax and forget about work for a few hours.

As she walked past the lake, a couple of young lads were splashing in and out of the water with their trouser legs rolled up. Her eyes followed a young couple feeding ducks nearby the sound of their laughter filled the air. Glancing at her watch Beth realised she was early for her meeting with Finn. Not wanting to appear too eager for his attentions, she paused to sit on a nearby bench. A nanny strolled past along the footpath pushing a perambulator and the sound of the child's crying carried itself to Beth's ears. She watched the young woman lean forward making soothing noises towards the infant.

The boathouse was busy, with several people milling around the area some waiting their turn to board and others disembarking from the small rowing vessels. As Beth approached she caught sight of Finn, who was peering into the lake where a swan and her cygnets were gliding along the water's edge. Stopping for a moment, she observed his appearance. He looked dashing in his straw boater and crisp white shirt and having removed his jacket it was slung carelessly over his arm. Just as she took a step forward he turned as if sensing her presence.

"Dia dhuit, Beth." He said removing his hat and performing an elaborate bow in front of her. She laughed at his theatricals and held out her hand. "It means 'Good Day' where I come," he explained dropping a light kiss into her palm.

Shivers pulsated up Beth's arm at Finn's touch. "Good afternoon, Finn." Beth's face was flushed as she tried hard to retain her composure. Finn's sparkling eyes took in her appearance and she was glad she'd dressed carefully that afternoon in a cream jacket and pink and white lace hat. "I see you've been watching the swan and her young family."

Finn looked back towards the birds as they weaved their way along the lake in a long line. The sun was glistening like diamonds on the surface of the water. "They surely make you feel as if spring is here," he said.

"How's about a good boat ride, Sir. For you and the lovely lady?" They both turned to see a burly looking man dressed in a striped jacket standing behind them.

Following the man towards the side of the jetty Beth was helped into the boat. Striving to keep her balance, as the little vessel bobbed up and down beneath her feet, Beth managed to sit down. Looking across the lake a fleeting image of her mother came into her mind. Beth mused at what Sarah would think of her daughter on the Serpentine Lake, un-chaperoned and with an Irishman no less. She lifted her face to the sun and inwardly smiled.

"Are you sitting comfortably?" Finn's flaxen hair fell across his forehead as he rolled up his shirt sleeves and took hold of the oars. Beth nodded, hardly able to tear her gaze from the rippling muscles on his strong arms as he began to row. Finding herself in such close proximity to this good-looking man caused her an unfamiliar feeling of shyness. She glanced over the side of the boat dipping her fingers into the cold water.

"Tell me about where you live in Richmond, Beth?" Finn enquired, "I want to know more about the beautiful woman with whom I'm spending my Sunday afternoon."

Beth looked up from under the shade of her parasol and met his eyes. "I recently moved out of my parents' home and now live in a tied cottage."

Lifting one eyebrow Finn was clearly surprised but said nothing, waiting for Beth to continue as he rowed.

Swallowing hard Beth attempted to find her voice which seemed to be eluding her. Why had she told this man her situation so quickly? The words had been out of her mouth before she could stop them. However, it was too late now she may as well tell him the whole story. "It was the only way to escape from what they'd planned for me, which was to marry a man I did not love." She said firmly.

Finn's amber eyes clouded over as he paused in his rowing to look at her. "We all need our freedom," he said, as the low muffled sounds of the other boaters and the noise of the wildfowl swirled around them.

"You're so right." Beth felt immediately more at ease with Finn. Maybe it hadn't been such a mistake to reveal her background. "What about you?"

"Me?"

Beth laughed and pointed to the side of the lake to which they appeared to be drifting. "Watch the bank!" She warned.

"Oh, what an eejit I am!" Finn grinned back then began rowing furiously away from the edge. "I was born in a small fishing village in Southern Ireland," he said once they were safely back on track. "My father was a fisherman and expected my brother and me to join him when we left school. Shamus was happy to work alongside him, but I felt trapped and escaped as soon as I was old enough. It caused many family rows when I was in my teens." A frown appeared between Finn's brows as he spoke and his eyes darkened. "I moved to Dublin as soon as I could and took an apprenticeship as a carpenter."

Beth couldn't help being inquisitive and hadn't missed the painful expression on Finn's face as he mentioned how trapped he'd felt in his teens. "What made you move to London? I assume you were happy in Dublin once you'd left home."

For a moment Finn concentrated on steering beneath the bridge, once out the other side he paused and relaxed letting the boat drift for a moment on the open water.

"Things haven't improved in Dublin for a long time. The dock strike last year made everything much worse." Finn stared intently back at Beth. "The troops being drafted in didn't help causing the battles between Catholics and Protestants to worsen." All the muscles tightened in Finn's face as he spoke. "The suspicion and hatred caused a tension in the air which was intolerable. I chose not to live that way and wanted to try my luck in London."

"You didn't have any ties in Dublin then?" Beth couldn't resist asking the question. There was a tiny pause and the answer was on Finn's face as he took hold of the oars and began turning the boat around. So there had been a woman in his life.

"There was someone. Her name was, Aisling. For a while it was good but we wanted different things, she means nothing to me now." Finn stopped and reached across to touch Beth's hand. "Why don't we take the boat back and go for a stroll?" He suggested.

Back at the jetty Finn helped Beth from the boat. He took her hand and placed it on his arm and they walked along the pathway past the trees and benches. "So, are you enjoying living in the cottage?

174

It must be a vast change from the home you used to live in."

Beth bit down on her lower lip and frowned. "It's fine. Except for the first night, I had an intruder."

Finn was immediately concerned. "What happened?"

Beth's voice sounded strained as she began to explain. "It was very early in the morning. I heard a loud crash and looked out of the window to see a man running away. I told the police. But of course he was long gone by then."

"Was there anything missing or any damage to the cottage?"

"The only damage was where he tried to break in through the back door. He fled knocking over a watering can and other gardening equipment, which had been left behind in the long grass. I had to get the gardener to fix the lock on the door where it had been forced." Beth shivered in the afternoon sun. "The next day I found a scribbled note through my door warning me to leave the cottage."

Finn shook his head then put an arm around Beth's shoulders. Instinctively she leaned against him as he began steering her away from the pathway. "My poor, Beth," he murmured into her hair.

For a moment they walked in silence then she looked up to find herself in a more densely wooded area of the park. Finn was leading her towards a weeping willow tree and into the shade beneath its branches. In an instant they were in each other's arms, *"Tá cion agam ort,"* Finn whispered, as he looked deeply into Beth's blue eyes.

All resistance drained from Beth's body as Finn's lips met hers. The world around them fell away and at that moment she knew without a doubt, that she was deeply and madly in love with this incredible man.

Chapter *Nineteen*

HYDE PARK RALLY

Beth watched in awe, tingling with anticipation. She could hardly believe she was here in Hyde Park at this momentous occasion. A loud roar filled the air as Mrs Pankhurst stepped aside and all attention focused on the spokeswomen.

Alice pulled herself upright, glanced down at her notes and began her speech. "Welcome to everyone standing before me, who have taken the time today, to march alongside us through the streets of London to support women in their quest for the vote. I ask you one question: What is the vote? As our forefathers who fought before us knew, it is a symbol of Freedom, Liberty and Citizenship, and it seems to me something worth fighting for! If you believe in justice then I call on you all to..."

As Alice's even tones rang out loud and clear, Beth heard her name whispered along the crowd below her. Her eyes followed the direction in which she thought the voice had come. A multitude of faces greeted her gaze and she looked away thinking she'd imagined the sound. Then it came again.

"Beth, here!" said the voice.

This time the words were clearer. Beth looked again and saw a hand waving a red hankie at her. Then one face stood out among all the others and her stomach turned to jelly. As the familiar twinkle in Finn's eyes caught her attention, she returned his smile. All at once Beth longed to be in his arms again. Trying hard to focus on Alice's speech, she was constantly drawn back to this enigmatic man. Finn had edged his way forwards and now stood squashed up against numerous other people, a few rows back from the front.

"Beth! I don't suppose you heard a single word I said." Alice sneered. Gone was the happy exterior of an hour before, replaced now by the dark mood that had returned with a vengeance. Without Beth noticing Sybil had begun speaking and Alice now stood next to her.

"Of course I did, Alice..." murmured Beth attempting to disregard her friend's anger. She turned her attention to Sybil, but Alice wouldn't be ignored. Tension filled the air as she sidled up closer, pushing Beth further towards the edge of the stage.

Beth swivelled round to face Alice. "For goodness sake stop it, I don't know what's wrong with you!"

Alice looked across at Finn who was watching them, a frown etched across his forehead. "Yes you do! If it wasn't for me you'd still be stuck in that house like a caged bird."

"Yes that's true, but I can't be grateful forever or become your lover when I'm in love with someone else!" Beth's angry voice had risen and a loud 'shush' could be heard from behind her, she turned away, embarrassed at the spectacle they were making.

Alice, who seemed unaware that most of the front rows were watching them instead of poor Sybil, who was now struggling with her speech, took hold of Beth's arms and violently shook her.

Fighting to be free from Alice's hold, Beth stepped back without realising how close she was to the edge of the platform. As her left foot flew from beneath her, she felt herself suspended in mid-air. Then her whole body lunged backwards as she fell into the void below and blackness followed.

The world spun as Beth tried to open her eyes. An overpowering pain in her head forced them shut again. Then, struggling to breathe she felt someone behind catch her head in their hands. "It's alright, Beth. You're safe now," said a familiar voice.

Beth fought to remember what had happened and forced her eyes open to see Finn's worried face staring down at her, along with many others she didn't recognise.

Finn's tones boomed out loud above her. "Clear the area and give her some space!" He shouted, lifting Beth into his arms and carrying her through the crowd. She knew no more as the darkness claimed her once again.

As Beth slowly opened her eyes, the smell of disinfectant filled her nostrils and an intense pain made her head throb. Everything looked starkly white as she attempted to focus on the person sitting by her bed. Alice's concerned face stared back at her.

"Alice...? What happened?" She croaked.

"Beth. Oh, Beth..." Alice looked forlorn and desperation filled her green eyes. "How are you feeling now?"

"I don't know..." Beth rubbed at her forehead where the pain was at its worst and blinked quickly at Alice.

"You fell." Alice closed her eyes and dipped her head as tears rolled down her cheeks. "It was my fault. I've been so worried."

A memory of their argument began to unravel through the fug in Beth's brain and she attempted to lift her head as she remembered Finn. "Alice. Where's, Finn?"

Alice fiddled with her hankie, dabbing at her eyes then she met Beth's gaze. "He was here." she explained. "He'll be back later to see you, I'm sure. Beth...I'm so sorry."

"Oh, Alice." Beth sighed. For a moment the two women were silent. Both were aware that if Alice hadn't fought with her on the platform, Beth would never have fallen.

Just at that moment a nurse bustled into the room and began taking Beth's temperature. "How are we feeling now, Miss Hamilton-Green?" she said, as if she were addressing a child.

Beth had a sudden fear that the damage to her head was quite serious, after all she had lost consciousness for some time. "What's wrong with me, nurse?" She said urgently. "Why is my head so sore?"

"A bit of concussion that's all. Nothing a short rest won't cure." The nurse glanced across at Alice's tear stained face. "You women will cause friction and this is what you get for your trouble," she said rudely, removing the thermometer from Beth's mouth. "Five more minutes and then you must rest," she told Beth before adjusting the covers and briskly leaving the room.

"Finn got you out of that crowd." Alice said suddenly, then pausing for a moment she began to explain. "And...I'm grateful to him. I couldn't go with you, I had to stay with the other women and finish the speeches." Beth was surprised at Alice's words of praise. "I did help you when you were lying on the ground."

"You did?" Beth only remembered Finn helping her - the rest was oblivion.

Alice leaned forward and rested her arms on the edge of the bed. "I held your head as you lay on the ground. I reassured you that you would be fine."

181

Beth nodded numbly at Alice then needing to rest she laid her head back onto the pillows. The relief was immeasurable. Having no words of reassurance for Alice she suddenly felt completely drained of energy.

As Beth closed her eyes and drifted off to sleep Alice glanced briefly at her friend and quietly left the room.

Chapter *Twenty*

A SURPRISE VISITOR

After leaving hospital Beth had struggled for two days feeling confused and exhausted. It was now almost a week since the eventful Hyde Park Rally and she had at last noticed the dull ache in her head was beginning to ease. On the first night home, Beth had been grateful to Alice for staying overnight and constantly checking on her progress. Alice had shown herself to be an excellent nurse and Beth could see how sorry she was for what happened.

The sound of the cuckoo had awoken Beth early. Getting up, she looked out of the window at the fields beyond. A low mist covered the landscape. Recognising some of the wild flowers growing there she was enthralled by their beauty. She was thankful that part of her education had been to learn the names of these splendid plants and paint them in vivid watercolours.

It was now almost ten o'clock. The sun was beginning to break through the clouds as Beth made her way to relax on the bench beneath the old apple tree. Admiring the view and for a moment glancing away from the meadow, she spotted someone in the distance walking down the rough track towards the cottage. Alice was expected at any moment and at first Beth thought it must be her. Striding purposefully towards the gate the figure got closer. The masculine shape made her heart race and brought a flush to her cheeks.

Finn neared the cottage and Beth froze, afraid that if she took her eyes away he'd disappear from sight and she'd find it was just a dream. He was only a few steps from the gate when he noticed her sitting on the seat.

"Beth," he said breathlessly," looking down at her face, "how are you my love?" His hair flopped lazily across his forehead as he hurried towards her.

In an instant she was in Finn's arms, his lips on hers. They clung to each other for a moment or two and then he held her at arms length. His amber eyes focused on the bruise which covered the left side of her head and he stroked his fingers gently over the blue-black mark.

Beth pulled herself out of his arms. "Why haven't I seen you, Finn. Since the Rally? I know it's only been a week but I thought you might want to see me."

Finn's eyes flashed with anger. "Alice didn't tell you?"

"What do you mean, tell me?" A sliver of alarm filled Beth.

Finn sat down and put his head in his hands. "I came to see you while you were in hospital. I came twice. The first time you were asleep. Your friend was there, but they said you were only allowed one visitor. I waited until after visiting hours and saw her as she left." Finn lifted his head and looked intently at Beth. "I told her to tell you I would be back the next day to see you. But when I arrived she'd already taken you home."

Beth's heart sank at Finn's words. She'd been convinced Alice regretted her outburst at the rally and was trying hard to make amends. Perhaps she'd been too quick to believe that this was the case.

Finn took hold of Beth's hands. "That woman knew I tried to visit you and yet she didn't mention it. Listen to me, Beth. I'm worried about you. I really want you to leave the movement, stop all contact with Alice. I'm sorry, so I am but that's how I feel."

Beth pulled her hands away quickly and bit down onto her lower lip. The familiar feeling of suffocation began to threaten and the world was turning grey. To shake this off she got up abruptly and walked into the cottage. Heavy footsteps followed behind her. Sitting down on the sofa she touched the bruise which was making her head throb, then regarded Finn as he stood in the doorway. The sight of this handsome man, his large frame blocking out the light, almost made her waiver. Her heart melted at the expression on his face. As he held her gaze, she could see the naked passion reflected in his eyes. But she knew she had no choice except to disappoint him. "I can't do that, Finn. Not even for you." She lifted her chin defiantly. "I will *never* leave the movement."

The steely determination in Beth's voice only fuelled Finn's frustration. "Alice is risking your life so she is. Why can't you see that?" Finn looked agitated and began to pace up and down the room.

Beth immediately defended Alice. "She must have forgotten to tell me, that's all! I'm sure there's nothing more to it." Needing for a moment to put space between them and to stem the urge to throw herself into Finn's arms, she walked through to the kitchen. After filling up the kettle she placed it on the hob then walked back into the parlour. The room was empty and Finn was no-where to be seen.

Putting down the tea tray Beth looked out of the window. Finn's silhouette beneath the trees was disappearing into the distance. A deep sense of loss filled her body and she dipped her head whispering under her breath. "Finn, please come back for my heart is breaking."

Finn hurried along the crowded streets trying to avoid bumping into passers-by as he went. Why was Beth being so stubborn? He knew he shouldn't have left so abruptly but he had to get away from Beth, before he said something he might regret. He didn't want to lose her. Never had he felt so strongly about a woman before. Sure he was in love with her, so coming right out with ordering her to leave the movement was not what he'd intended. Even though he hadn't known her very long he could see she was strong willed. It was one of the things he already loved about her, but his concern lay more with the red haired woman's behaviour. The jealousy in her green eyes could clearly be seen whenever he was close to Beth. The incident at the Rally was alarming. Finn knew Beth's injuries could have been much more serious and this made him anxious for her safety.

"Lookin' for a good time are you, Sir?" A woman of the night stood barring Finn's way along the pavement. Her long matted hair hung down her bony shoulders and Finn's sympathy was aroused for the pathetic creature. He felt in his pocket for a half crown and pushed it into her grimy hand. He was rewarded with a toothless grin which looked more like a grimace. As he strode away he glanced back quickly to see her already accosting the next man walking towards her.

As he turned into 'Old Castle Street' he breathed a sigh of relief. It was quieter away from the main street, which was always busy on a Saturday morning and it was good to be beyond the jostling crowd. Arriving at Mrs Williams' terraced house, he began to unlock the front door. But before he could turn the key someone opened it from the inside, sending him reeling into the hallway and coming face to face with his landlady. Taking a step back to avoid a collision she righted herself staring at Finn with arched eyebrows. A gleam brightened her pale eyes. As was usual for her, she was dressed in a frilly piny with her white blonde hair immaculately coiffured.

Her voice was as smooth as syrup. "Hello, Finn." He had a fleeting thought that she looked like the cat who had just found the cream. "Happen there's a visitor waiting for you in the front parlour..." she purred.

Finn could tell that she'd hardly been able to wait to tell him this news a good gossip was something she often enjoyed.

"A lady visitor!" She elaborated opening the door to allow him to enter the hallway.

Finn nodded and stepped over the threshold just as her brightly painted lips added, "From Ireland no less." She circled his body like an attention seeking cat rubbing itself against the legs of an unyielding visitor.

"Thank you, Mrs Williams," he said wondering what his mother was doing visiting him in London unannounced.

"Call me, Violet," she insisted as she always did.

Try as he might Finn found it hard to address this older, somewhat kindly, but extremely nosy woman by her christian name. Somehow it didn't seem respectable. She led him through the dark hallway. Nodding his thanks he walked into the front parlour.

"Hello, Finn," said a voice from inside the room and he stared in disbelief at the woman sitting on the sofa.

"Aisling. What are you doing here?"

"Well! That's not a very nice welcome for someone that's travelled a long way to see you, Finn McGuiness." She laughed loudly, unfolded her long legs and stood up.

"Why are you here?" Finn persisted, unable to believe his eyes.

Aisling looked back at him her brown eyes looked hurt at his question. A full bosom peeped out from the bodice of her dress, but his eyes were drawn to the long curly hair he'd once found so attractive. She was indeed a striking woman he observed. But he remembered, it was Beth he loved now and this woman's looks barely touched his heart.

"I missed you so much, Finn." She turned her head away frowning. "After you'd gone I berated myself so I did, for not fighting for you. For just letting you leave like that. It was very remiss of me."

"Aisling, we weren't serious were we? We had a good time but..." Finn was clearly confused.

"But what?" Aisling's head came up and on her pale cheeks the tears trickled slowly. She wiped them away roughly with the back of her hand.

Finn took hold of her arms and held her firmly. "Aisling, you must have travelled all alone. How did you know where I lived?"

"I have to admit it wasn't the most comfortable few days of my life on that cargo ship." Aisling's voice was thick with emotion. "Although, I would have travelled for months in the same conditions to reach you. As for travelling alone, there was a man and his wife who looked out for me, so they did. Your mother gave me your address after I told her I had to find you. That I'd let you go without saying how I felt."

"Oh, Aisling." Finn groaned and shook his head. "So, my mother thinks we're in love?"

For a moment she said nothing. When Aisling did speak her voice was barely more than a whisper. "I do love you so, Finn. You have no idea how much."

Finn was lost for words. He saw the pleading in her eyes for him to return the sentiment. Silence clung to the air like a heavy blanket. Then there came a slight rustling at the door followed by a loud knock. "Come in." Finn answered despite the fact that Violet had already plunged uninvited into the room with a tray of tea.

"Refreshments for you both," she announced gaily putting it down on the small table.

"Thank you, Mrs...Violet," he said looking pointedly towards the door. For once she took the hint and left. He shut the door behind her and then lowered his voice. "Look, Aisling, I don't know what to say. I didn't ask you to come to London and I don't think it's the right place for you. Where will you stay for a start?"

"At Maud Prescott's house in the next street along. Violet recommended her to me."

Finn had the feeling that the two women were conspiring against him but seeing the look of anguish on Aisling's face felt he had to say something positive. "Well at least that's something. Maud is a friend of Violet's and runs a lodging house like this one so at least you'll be safe until we can get you back to Ireland. Although if Maud's house is the same as this one you need to be careful you are not drawn into anything..." Finn ran his fingers through his flaxen curls and seemed to be searching for the right word. "I'm sure you won't, you're a sensible girl, but..."

"If you mean prostitution, Finn. Don't worry there's no fear of that." Aisling laughed at Finn's discomfort. "I couldn't fail to notice, in the time I've been waiting for you to arrive, what's going on here."

Relief flooded through Finn. Of course Aisling wasn't that naive and was definitely not that kind of girl. Now that was sorted, Finn felt the need to escape from Aisling and think about this latest dilemma. "Now if you'll excuse me," he said turning towards the door.

Aisling stepped towards Finn and in a flash had grabbed hold of him roughly staring at him with a penetrating gaze. "There's someone else isn't there?" She questioned angrily. Finn sighed, pursed his lips together and quickly stepped away from her. Ignoring her accusation he backed out of the room and into the dark hallway.

Chapter *Twenty One*

BETH'S FIRST SPEECH

Beth adjusted her hat feeling the perspiration dripping down the back of her neck. It was a warm day. Her mouth felt dry and the words on the paper held in her hands, danced in front of her eyes. She was surrounded by women chatting amongst themselves as they waited for the meeting to begin. Speakers Corner was now familiar territory for Beth, but today was to be her first public speech. It all began that morning when on arrival at Alice's house her friend had answered the door in her dressing gown. Her face was deathly white and she looked at Beth through bloodshot eyes.

"I'm not feeling too well," she had croaked pulling the dressing gown further around her shivering body.

"Oh dear, Alice, then you must go back to bed," Beth said with concern, whilst steering Alice into the front parlour and onto the sofa. Alice began coughing and couldn't stop, her head bobbing up and down as she fought to get her breath. Beth had rushed into the kitchen to get her a drink. She watched as Alice gulped down the water and the coughing fit subsided. "What else can I get you to ease the coughing? I really think you should go back to bed before you get any worse."

Alice had managed to point Beth in the direction of some Owbridge's cough syrup in the kitchen cupboard. But her real concern had been with the day ahead and was clearly agitated at letting her fellow women down. "What am I to do about the meeting today? Everyone's relying on me."

Ignoring the look of anguish on Alice's face Beth returned to the kitchen to get the Owbridges. "Well, they'll just have to do without you today," she said, handing her the medicine. "I'm sure it won't matter just this once." Beth added. She could see Alice was in no fit state to attend the meeting. "Sybil will take over for you. She's been doing this kind of thing for a long time." Little did Beth realise where her words would lead.

Alice had taken the cough mixture then rested back on the sofa watching Beth as she flitted around the room tidying. "Sybil has her own speech to do. What about you? You could do mine for me." Alice's eyes had brightened and two spots of colour glowed on her pale cheeks.

Beth blinked at Alice in surprise. "I don't think so. I've never done a public speech before and I wouldn't know how."

Now, as Beth waited for everyone to arrive she tried her best to remain calm.

"You've watched me often enough...You're more than capable..." Alice's neat handwriting covered the pages. "Please, Beth." Alice's pleading words echoed in Beth's head. "It'll give you some experience in reading aloud." Her words in Beth's head were like a processional drum willing her on. "You know today's speech is all about the wearing of the colours... The colours, Beth." Beth heard herself repeating Alice's words as if fuelling a fire. "The colours and how important they are after the success of Hyde Park."

A woman dressed in an elaborate red hat appeared beside Beth. "Hello, Beth. Have you seen Alice? She appears to be late."

"Alice is not well today, Sybil. I'm doing her speech." Beth was surprised at how level her voice sounded despite the butterflies dancing in her stomach. Sybil looked surprised and leaned forwards, scarlet feathers from the other woman's hat fluttered against Beth's cheek.

"Well good for you," Sybil whispered. "Try not to be *too* nervous, my dear. You'll be fine."

"Oh, I'm not at all nervous." Beth, who'd always found this woman slightly patronising had the feeling that Sybil would love to see her make a fool of herself. Lifting her chin Beth decided that there was no time like the present. She stepped quickly up onto the small handcart that had been put there in readiness for the speeches. "Ladies and Gentlemen." She began. "Please may I have your attention?" She'd seen Alice do this many times before starting a speech. A hush fell over the gathering crowd as all heads turned her way.

"Purple, White and Green..." Beth took her time to say the words slowly and deliberately and could still hear Alice's words inside her head willing her to read on. Drawing courage from a new found source of strength, Beth smiled inwardly. The risk she was allowing herself to take was causing a ripple of confidence to grow inside. All at once Beth felt herself nurturing this unfamiliar feeling, and she began to enjoy the challenge that lay ahead.

"Purple, White and Green are very important colours in our fight for the vote. Wearing the colours showed solidarity for our cause, as we found on the 21st of June and it will continue to do so." Beth felt her voice waiver but continued regardless, raising it higher above the sea of heads in front of her. "We must never give up the fight." Beth was determined to get the message across. "We cannot give up the fight or fall by the wayside. In the face of opposition we must stand up and be counted!" As she paused to get her breath everyone began to clap. Her first ever public speech was going well. Proudly, she looked out into the crowd where her eyes fell upon a familiar face smiling back at her and clapping enthusiastically.

Beth hardly looked at Alice's handwritten notes throughout the rest of the speech, which passed in what seemed just a few seconds. She stepped down from the stage and smiled at a decidedly sour faced

Sybil as she walked towards the platform, to begin her own speech.

Eagerly, Beth hurried towards her admiring onlooker. Great warmth and compassion lifted her through the crowd, as Beth was drawn by excited eyes and outstretched arms waiting to greet her. "How are you? And what may I ask are you doing here, Miss Emma Middleton?" Beth playfully mocked. The two ladies fell against each other and laughed like naughty school children.

"I've defied Mother and decided not to get married!" Emma's fair hair danced beneath her white hat and her eyes sparkled as she spoke. "Oh, Beth. You were such an inspiration to me that day we met at Alice's house, I knew I couldn't go through with the wedding. I'm still living at home but I'm stronger now. The decision of who I will marry and what I want to do is now mine." Emma spun around like a carefree girl whirling in the fields. "And, I'm going to be a nurse!" Emma put her arms around a surprised Beth and hugged her tightly.

"That's really good news, Emma. I'm so glad I was able to help, but how are your parents taking all this?"

"Oh, them." Emma laughed out loud. "Well of course they are mortified." Talking of her parents as they were unruly adolescents she continued, "I just told them, it's something I've always wanted to do. And after reading about Florence Nightingale and her work…"

"I'm so very pleased for you." But Beth was concerned for Emma's financial welfare. "Will you be able to find the money to live while you're training?"

"Well, that's the thing, Beth. Things are changing like you said. My father's decided to still give me an allowance. He knows I won't change my mind and has no choice but to help me."

"That's such good news. Oh, Emma. I wish you luck with your nursing. At least you'll still be able to survive. My father cut me off without a penny when I left although he has allowed me to live in the cottage on the estate."

Emma looked horrified. "How do you manage when you need new gowns or have to buy food?"

Beth smiled and looked down at her grey dress. "I rarely have a new gown, Emma. Making do with old ones being repaired, or Alice makes one for me. I'm helping her with the business since her workload has almost doubled recently. Many people like the garments she makes for them. Also, there are always flags and banners to sew. Her young maid Nancy had to leave her employ recently. So I help out wherever I can. Alice pays me a small wage each month, enough to keep body and soul together anyway. So I'm lucky."

Suddenly, everyone behind them clapped and Emma and Beth's attention was drawn to Sybil, who was just stepping down from the platform. As they began walking away many of Beth's fellow suffragettes came up to congratulate her on such an inspiring and wonderful speech.

Chapter *Twenty Two*

BETRAYED

Finn knocked on the front door and waited. When it opened a tall angular woman dressed in a brown dress looked back at him. Her hair was grey her expression sombre and she seemed to merge into the dullness of the decor around her. Somehow he'd expected another 'Violet' to open the door. They might be friends but they were as different as chalk and cheese, he observed. He couldn't imagine this woman asking anyone to call her by her Christian name. Or heaven forbid, to allow prostitutes to frequent the house.

"Yes?" The woman said stonily.

"Good Day to you, Madam. Would you be, Mrs Prescott?"

"That's right. If you've come for a room we're all booked up at the moment." Mrs. Prescott began closing the door in Finn's face.

"No, I sure have not, Mrs Prescott." Finn smiled, desperate to inject some warmth into the woman's demeanour. But her eyes were unblinking and her face cold. "I've come to see Miss. O'Sullivan," he hurried on, "would she be in at all?"

"Who, shall I say is asking for the young lady?"

"Mr. McGuiness, she does know me."

Mrs Prescott shot Finn a look of disdain and hurried away leaving him waiting on the doorstep. He heard her calling to Aisling then a short while later Aisling's footsteps on the stairs.

"Hello, Finn. How are you?" Aisling appeared before him slightly breathless, looking striking in a cream figure-hugging dress. Her excitement at his unexpected visit was reflected in her brown eyes and wide smile.

Apprehension at Aisling's enthusiasm surged through Finn and he endeavoured to hide his misgivings. "I'm fine thank you, so I am." He sensed Mrs Prescott hovering in the background. Mrs Prescott and Violet may look completely different, but they obviously shared some traits. "Would you like to go for a walk, Aisling?"

"Sure, wait there. I'll get my shawl." Aisling's face glowed as she dashed back into the house and was back within a moment.

"Do you want to go into town?" Finn asked, as he shut Mrs Prescott's gate behind them. Aisling nodded then falling into step beside him put her arm through his. A fleeting wave of unease ran through Finn's body.

On the omnibus they sat in silence whilst others chatted around them. Finn knew he had to take Aisling somewhere more private before telling her about Beth. He tried to lighten the atmosphere with small talk. "That Mrs. Prescott is a sour faced woman indeed. How are you getting on with her?"

Aisling turned from where she'd been staring out of the window. "She's always a bit hostile to single men looking for lodgings after having a bad experience recently. A man booked in for one night then left in the early hours with some of her valuables. Now she only takes single women or couples and usually those recommended by Violet."

"That explains why she looked at me as if I was the devil himself." Finn lifted his hands up to mimic devil horns growing out of his hair and pulled his face into an ugly expression. Aisling laughed heartily at his banter.

Falling into an uncomfortable silence Finn and Aisling seemed strangely tongue tied with each other on the rest of the journey. At last they arrived at Oxford Street where they stepped off the Omnibus to make their way along the busy pavement. Finn couldn't help noticing other men looking their way obviously admiring Aisling's curvaceous figure. Glancing across at her, he began to realise how strongly she must feel about him. Strong enough to make her travel for days alone on a ship with all the risks that entailed. The sooner she knew he was in love with another woman the better. They could then sort out her safe and swift passage back to Ireland.

Finn couldn't wait a moment longer. He stopped abruptly, pulling Aisling into a shop doorway. "We need to talk," he said urgently looking into her face.

Aisling tried to avoid his gaze and fiddled with a stray curl. "What is it, Finn?" She asked. "What's the matter?"

"Let's find a cup of tea," he suggested, knowing that the busy street wasn't the place for their discussion. He began leading Aisling across the road dodging the horse drawn carriages and motor cars as they went.

Beth and Emma walked out of the park towards Oxford Street, eager to find the nearest tea shop.

"You should be proud of yourself, Beth. I thought you spoke up loud and clear and if that was your first ever public speech you did very well." Emma praised her friend.

Beth was about to thank Emma for her kind words when a figure in the distance caught her eye. She felt as if she'd been hit in the stomach as she recognised Finn and he was not alone. A shapely woman with dark hair walked beside him. Beth stood frozen to the pavement watching as arm in arm they darted in amongst the traffic and crossed the road, disappearing from view.

"Beth, what is it?" Emma's voice was full of concern for Beth who'd stopped abruptly in the street. Beth appeared not to hear and began hurrying away leaving Emma standing alone. "Do you know that man?" Emma persisted as she struggled to keep up with her.

Beth swivelled round and nodded. A frown covered her forehead and her eyes were wide with disbelief as she turned to cross the road.

"Be careful!" Emma shouted.

Beth didn't hear Emma and was distracted. Her eyes were set on the disappearing couple ahead. She couldn't help remembering the look on her mother's face after she'd told her of her father's infidelity. She'd appeared not to mind, but if Sarah felt a fraction of what Beth did now, Beth knew it must have been agony. The raging jealousy inside was like a wild tiger glimpsing its prey. She wanted to tear the shapely woman from limb to limb. A part of her was afraid she wouldn't be able to control the 'predator within' and she stopped abruptly, almost causing a collision with a man walking behind her.

"I apologise," Beth said breathlessly. The man raised his eyes heavenwards and continued on his journey. Beth took a long breath as she stood to one side of the pavement watching people walk past immersed in their own world, feeling as if her own life were crashing around her ears. She then noticed for the first time that Emma was still standing beside her, she turned towards her friend whose face was full of sympathy. Feeling a little foolish now she tried to smile. Finn was no longer in the distance and she began to think that perhaps she'd been mistaken and it was someone else she saw. "I need to stop for a moment." She told Emma.

"Yes you do!" gasped Emma as she also fought to steady her breath. "What on earth is the matter?"

"Sorry, for rushing ahead. I thought I saw..." Beth paused and pushed a strand of hair back into her hat, "a friend of mine. Shall we go for that much needed cup of tea?"

Emma looked confused by her friend's behaviour, but agreed that they should find a tea room. She took hold of Beth's arm and the two of them began walking at a more leisurely pace. Occasionally they stopped to look in shop windows and marvelled at the work in progress on the new department store, Selfridge's.

Beth tried to forget what she may have seen. It was, she told herself unlikely to have been Finn she'd sighted. Despite this, she was feeling a little ill at ease and found herself driven by an urge to constantly glance around at passers-by. She was fearful her eyes would rest upon Finn arm in arm with another woman.

The tea rooms were brimming over with customers that day. On entering Finn and Aisling were immediately approached by a waitress in a black uniform. They were shown to the only available table which was a window seat. They sat down amid the clatter of cups which echoed around the room. Finn began to wish he'd taken Aisling somewhere a little quieter. The waitress approached and directed her question at Finn.

"Tea and cakes, sir?" She enquired.

"Yes, please." He glanced across at Aisling. "I'm not sure about the lady."

"Me too. Thank you." Aisling smiled at the waitress whose response was a curt nod then a disappearing back.

For a moment they both sat immersed in their own thoughts avoiding one another's eyes as the conversation of other customers buzzed around them. It wasn't like Aisling to have nothing to say, so Finn decided she must have an inkling of what he was about to say.

"Aisling." He began. "You'll have to go back you know."

"Will I?" Aisling said petulantly.

Aisling's dark eyes were staring imploringly into his and Finn felt himself being drawn into their depths. He mentally shook himself. "Yes. Surely you can see it will be for the best. You don't belong here."

The clatter of the tea trolley being pushed towards them interrupted their conversation. They both watched as the waitress put a silver stand of assorted cakes and scones in the middle of the table. A teapot, milk and sugar bowl followed. As soon as this was done she was gone as quickly as she'd re-appeared. Finn watched Aisling focus on the steam drifting out of the teapot spout.

"Aisling. Please." Finn attempted to awaken her out of her dreamy state.

"I'm not ignoring you." She said with a voice as cold as steel. "I was just thinking about us." She looked up and met his eyes.

"Why did you come?" Finn asked a deep frown appearing on his forehead. "I don't understand."

Aisling let out a long sigh then sat back in her chair. "You know why I came, so you do. I've explained that already." She looked flirtatiously up at him from under her lashes. "You used to love me," she accused.

"I'm sorry, Aisling. That was a long time ago and things have changed." As she glared back at him he saw the glint of tears in her eyes.

"Now, don't take on so." He said softly, shifting uneasily in his chair. "It's not as simple as that. You can't stay in Whitechapel... it's rough." Finn attempted to explain the dangers she was obviously unaware of. "There are so many immigrants," he lowered his voice. "Violence erupts on the streets nearly every day. A man is not safe after dark from the gangs looking for trouble let alone a woman." Although he'd never truly loved Aisling, Finn knew he couldn't leave her to fend for herself. The consequences could be disastrous. "Whatever you decide to do you must be aware of the perils of living in London."

Doubt passed across Aisling's face at Finn's words. "I know," she said. "I'm used to Dublin though, I'm not from some little village somewhere. Besides, I can take care of myself." Pausing for a moment she picked up her tea and sipped slowly at the hot liquid. Then putting down the cup she fixed her eyes on his face and lifted one brow questioningly. "Tell me, Finn. What's changed in the year you've been in London?"

"Aisling, the truth is..." He watched as realisation dawned on her face. "I'm in love with someone else." Her whole body flinched at his words and guilt surged relentlessly through his body.

Aisling quickly dabbed at her moist eyes with a hankie. "I'm too late then? I should have come sooner." She was flustered now. "I thought about it. I just didn't have the courage at first. Then Patrick asked me to marry him."

"Patrick?" Finn's head lifted in surprise at the mention of the man he'd known since childhood.

"Sure, we became friends after you left. He told me you wouldn't be coming back he said he loved me. I had to tell you how I really felt just in case.

You know... in case you felt the same. I realised you looked on me as a good time girl. I was always in love with you though, Finn."

Finn looked intently at Aisling. "I'm sorry. I had no idea you felt so strongly. But what did you tell Patrick?" Finn felt sorry for his fellow Irishman. He obviously very much loved the woman sitting opposite him. To Finn's horror instead of answering his question Aisling put her head in her hands on the table and began silently weeping.

"That I'm in love with you of course," she said between sobs.

The background noise receded and only the sound of Aisling's soft crying could be heard between them. Finn could feel other people looking in their direction. He reached out towards Aisling and patted her arm not really knowing how to comfort her. Slightly embarrassed and at a loss he turned to the window and peered out as if for inspiration. His mind went back to a time when he'd first met Aisling. He'd been a lad of tender years and women were an enigma to him. In his local pub one evening with a few friends he'd made at the docks, she'd walked in. Aisling and her banjo were part of the Saturday night entertainment.

"What do you intend to do now?" Finn asked gently looking back at Aisling to see she'd stopped crying and her tear stained face now held a resigned look.

"I'm staying, at least for now as I can't face going back yet." She ran her fingers through her long ringlets of hair and sighed. "Maybe I could find a temporary job somewhere."

Finn nodded trying to understand how she was feeling. "I've asked Violet to keep an eye on you while you're here."

"Finn, there's no need. I can take care of myself." Aisling dropped her head and he barely heard the words. "I don't need Violet to look after me," she murmured.

"I'm really sorry, Aisling." He reached across the table and lifted her chin. "Can you promise me one thing if you decide to stay? That you won't go wandering around on your own at night as it's not safe. I'm sure you know you must be on your guard." As Aisling held his gaze he saw the flash of mischief dance in her eyes just before she leaned forward and unexpectedly kissed him firmly on the lips.

Finn pulled away so abruptly his chair almost overturned beneath him. It was a split second of contact, but the feel of her lips on his made the bile rise in his throat. "Aisling!" He admonished wiping the back of his hand across his mouth. "What are you doing?"

"For old time's sake," she declared and he saw the flame of desire burning in her eyes. What would it take to make Aisling understand he no longer cared? Finn despaired at the way she just wasn't listening to him. A feeling of dislike was growing inside him for the woman sitting opposite him, as her features became distorted, her brown eyes full of deviousness and her smiling face sly.

How he wished it were Beth with him in the tea shop and her lips he had felt on his. The need to see Beth struck him so urgently, that Aisling took the flush on his cheeks and the way his amber eyes looked so intently back at her, to mean Finn had definitely enjoyed their spontaneous kiss.

Beth chatted to Emma as they walked down the busy street. She felt calmer now and pondered on her behaviour a moment or two ago. Why was she so heartbroken to see Finn, if it was him, out with another woman? She no longer had any hold on him since the last time they'd met and he had given her that ultimatum. Beth didn't have any choice but to choose the movement. But it didn't stop her hoping that somehow he would see how much the suffragettes meant to her and most of all how much she was achieving.

Beth glanced across at Emma walking beside her and couldn't help wishing the praise she'd lavished on Beth after the speech, had also come from Finn. She wanted him to be proud of her, wanted him to see how much stronger she was with each passing day as part of the movement. Beth's choice to send Finn away had been painful, causing her to dream of him nightly and long for him daily. And now, she mentally kicked herself, she was even imagining that she saw him in the street with other women.

Emma nudged Beth out of her reverie as they came abreast of a tea shop. "Lyons tea rooms, Beth. This is just what we need," she announced.

The two women stopped to peer inside the shop to see if there were any spare seats, and shock waves shot through Beth at the scene before her. Sitting at a table in the window, just a few inches away from her was Finn. He was with the 'shapely woman' and their heads were bent together in an intimate tête-a-tête.

Red hot anger, like molten lava exploding from a volcano, surged through Beth's body. Clenching her fists she dug her nails into her palms in an effort to stem the churning, which had reached boiling point in her chest and was trying to explode through her mouth. Clamping her mouth shut and unable move, she watched the woman lean forward and kiss Finn firmly on the lips. Beth was riveted to the spot as she watched him sit back in his chair and speak to the woman, who was looking back at him with passion filled eyes. Finn glanced up and for a split second Beth held his gaze through the glass. Turning hastily away and almost knocking Emma over, Beth found herself running whilst hot burning tears flowed freely down her cheeks.

Alarmed by this turn of events Emma followed Beth closely urging her to stop, Beth kept running pushing her way through the afternoon shoppers.

Beth could feel the wild tiger behind her now, pursuing its prey. Eventually taking hold of her arm Emma pulled Beth into a shop doorway. "Beth, please! Tell me what's going on. Who was that man?"

"Emma. Oh, Emma. It is of no consequence!" Beth fought the sobs that threatened to overwhelm her. "I thought it was but it just isn't." She straightened her spine and looked evenly at Emma. "I wish you every success in your nursing career," she said rubbing the back of her hand across her tear stained face. "A woman can achieve anything, it's only men that hold us back. Please, never forget that." Beth hugged her confused friend and with the swish of her skirts walked purposefully away. A bewildered Emma stared after her.

Aisling had watched with interest as Finn stood up abruptly nearly overturning the table. "Beth!" he shouted at the top of his voice. All heads had turned in their direction as Finn rushed noisily out of the door and a hush fell over the tea rooms.

Finn disappeared quickly into the crowd but from her position at the table Aisling tried not to smile for life was good. The beautiful dark-haired woman had stared, eyes wild with jealousy, through the window at them. The naive woman's mouth had been set in shock. Aisling knew she must have witnessed her kissing Finn's lips and now she practiced a sympathetic look ready for Finn's return.

Crestfallen Finn soon reappeared. Aisling prepared herself to comfort him, watching as he sat down in his seat and covered his eyes with his hands. She waited a moment. The clatter of tea cups could once again be heard across the tea shop.

She then gently laid a hand on his arm."Finn." Aisling said quietly. To her surprise he pushed her hand forcibly away.

Finn's eyes held a look so full of contempt that Aisling reeled away from him. "What *do* you want from me, Aisling?" He yelled at the top of his voice, still oblivious it seemed that they were in a public place.

Maybe this wouldn't be as easy as she anticipated. "I'm just trying to comfort you, Finn. Don't take it out on me." Aisling dipped her head and blinked her long lashes at him.

Finn's look of hatred intensified as once again he stood up and pulling a pound note from his pocket slapped it down on the table. "For the love of Mary. Stop that!" He berated.

Aisling could see the rapidly approaching waitress out of the corner of her eye. She stood up quickly, eager to be out of this embarrassing situation and followed Finn out the door. All she needed to do was be alone with him, she told herself. He would then see it was her he had wanted all along. Aisling inwardly congratulated herself for timely expressing her affection for her man at the very moment that this 'Beth' woman had appeared.

Chapter *Twenty Three*

AISLING

Violet handed Aisling a cup of tea before sitting down at the wooden table and leaning towards the younger woman. "There's more than one way to skin a cat, dearie," she said. "Bide your time, love. What wiv' your womanly curves," she pointed a finger towards Aisling's protruding bust-line. "Finn won't be able to resist you."

A smile spread across Aisling's face lighting up her brown eyes. She sipped at the hot liquid then let out a long sigh. "Well, I hope you're right, Violet. You see I haven't come all this way to lose him again. We had something in Ireland, so we did."

"And, love. You can 'ave it again. Just play your cards right. Be here when he gets home from work." Violet glanced towards the closed door, "show him what a good girl you are and how loving you can be. Work them curves, dearie."

Aisling's expression darkened as she stared back at Violet. "You mean...cheapen myself?"

"I didn't say that now did I? Just a little attention wouldn't hurt." Violet poured more tea into her cup her scarlet painted nails clinking against the white teapot.

Aisling watched her, wondering how she managed to keep so immaculate with all the household duties to do. "Maybe you're right, Violet. But sometimes I think I should just return to Ireland and leave Finn to his new love. After all I can't seem to find a job and my savings will run out eventually."

"No!" Violet sprang quickly to her feet and towered over Aisling. "You mustn't do that, me dear. Men should be made to pay for their mistakes and honour their promises." She rubbed her hands together gleefully as she spoke. "Finn must 'ave taken advantage of you surely...a man like him, with all that Irish charm." Violet licked the tip of one of her fingers and ran it along a pencilled eyebrow. "From my experience most men need teaching a lesson. I may have been married once, but he wasn't the first." Violet hesitated then winked at Aisling who was looking back at her intently. "The man I truly loved abandoned me at the alter. The shame of it." Violet sat down and lowered her coiffured head.

"I'm sorry to hear that, Violet. It must have been terrible."

"It was a long time ago now. Before me safe secure husband, me poor sweet Albert came along. Albert who went and got himself killed." Violet spoke as if

Albert had died deliberately in order to inconvenience her.

Aisling wound a finger around a curl of brown hair and shot the other woman a sympathetic look. "Finn didn't make no promises. When we first met I was attracted by his looks. He was a few years younger than me and I was looking for an older man, someone to take care of me." She looked to Violet for understanding, who nodded her agreement. "As time went on I began to fall in love with him. Then he talked of his future which I soon realised didn't include me. The warning signs were there and I chose to ignore them."

Violet's eyes glinted with mischief as she lifted her head and regarded Aisling. "But 'e led you on, you see. Finn shouldn't have done that. You know, Aisling, he didn't think of your happiness. He should've told you the way things were." Violet was insistent that it must have been this way.

Aisling seemed to be re-living her and Finn's time together as she continued to explain. "He said he wanted to try new horizons and at times was restless. I just always hoped I was enough for him." She hesitated and the glint of a tear appeared in the corner of one eye.

"Oh, love. Don't take on so." Violet got up and wrapped her ample arms around Aisling, who felt strangely comforted by this motherly gesture. "Well, anyways, it happens he does still care for you. He's warned you enough about the dangers you face 'ere hasn't he?" Aisling nodded. "Well then, if Finn didn't care he wouldn't have done that."

Aisling looked thoughtful and the tightened muscles in her face began to relax. "Sure, he obviously feels responsible for me and keeps telling me not to walk the streets on my own at night. Maybe in time… he could love me again."

"That's the spirit." Violet got up and began clearing away the dirty crockery.

"Although, he did say he's in love with that other woman." Aisling dabbed at her face with a hankie. "The one I saw the other day."

Violet stopped what she was doing and turned from the sink. "I know from Maud that her name is Elizabeth and she's one of them there suffragette women."

"Really, how would Maud know that?" Aisling was curious as to how Violet's friend knew Beth.

Violet lowered her voice as if someone else was listening to their conversation. "One of Maud's lodgers is a suffragette too and knows of this 'Elizabeth woman.' Apparently she's the strong willed demanding type. Happen she'd be a handful for any man."

"It sure sounds as if she'd be trouble for Finn." Aisling answered as if in hope that her former lover would soon tire of this wilful woman.

"You know you're always welcome here, Aisling." Violet glanced up at the clock. "I really must get on now, me lodgers wouldn't like their evening meal to be late. I'm busy but will always find time to listen." She busied herself around the kitchen suddenly losing interest in the conversation.

Aisling pushed her chair under the table and gratefully thanked Violet for the tea. Often lonely in this unfamiliar land, she'd appreciated the other woman's company these past weeks.

Violet wiped her hands on her apron and saw her guest to the door. "Don't forget what I said now. It's hard at the moment, but men can be won round especially by women like you." Laughing loudly Violet looked Aisling up and down. "Keep that pretty chin up now, dearie," she cackled, patting Aisling lightly on her cheek.

Aisling left Violet's with a tiny feeling of hope inside her chest, before long she and Finn would be together again she told herself lifting her head to face the world.

Chapter *Twenty Four*

THE PROPOSAL

Beth shut the gate behind her. Glancing at her watch she looked up at the grey sky. The sun was trying to break through from behind a black cloud, promising some respite from the previous day's rain. Hurrying along the street, she considered the mountain of work Alice and her were about to tackle that day. The meetings were becoming larger and the preparation for them filled Beth's days and left little time for reflection upon what might have been.

The soft lilt of a familiar Irish accent startled Beth out of her reverie. "Hello, Beth." Swinging round she came face to face with Finn. Her eyes rested on his handsome face and his amber eyes sparkled as flaxen curls fell across his forehead. Momentarily speechless Beth stopped and regarded him. Trying to control her rising temper, she struggled to ignore the picture in her mind of Finn with the 'shapely woman.'

"I've been waiting around, so I have. Not really sure which is Alice's house..." He looked apprehensive as he leaned on a nearby lamppost and pushed the hair from his eyes. "Well, Beth, my love?" As he spoke Finn broke into a little jig. "Please don't be angry with me, dear Beth," He sang merrily, attempting to lighten the atmosphere between them. "I meant no harm."

"Meant no harm!" Beth hissed. "What do you want?"

Finn stopped dancing and a worried frown formed between his brows. "Beth. We need to talk, so we do." He said breathlessly taking a step towards her holding and out his hand.

"I have nothing to say to you." Beth answered coldly, turning her back on him to resume her journey. Out of the corner of her eye she could see he was following her.

"Please, Beth! It isn't what you think." Finn pleaded as he walked behind her.

Cursing her dress for its narrow hem preventing her from walking quicker, Beth stopped to lift her gown.

"Why did you run off? I could have introduced you." Finn immediately knew his words were making the situation worse. He searched his mind, wondering how to express reassurance to Beth. He knew she had misinterpreted the situation with Aisling, he had seen the look on her face that day. Beth had assumed that they were lovers but nothing could be further from the truth.

"Huh? Introduced me! To someone you were obviously having a rendezvous with?" Beth's cheeks were flushed with anger as she glared back at him.

"Please... to be sure, you must give me a chance to explain." Finn spoke quietly now feeling fear mushroom within him that Beth was lost to him forever. He reached out to her but she pulled away. Before he could speak again Beth interrupted.

"Is it because I won't give up the movement?" Her eyes flashed with fire. "Is that why you've found someone else so quickly? If so you never really loved me did you?"

"Beth... How could you think that?" The colour drained from Finn's face and he felt as if he'd been hit in the stomach at the sight of Beth standing there, so angry and disbelieving. "For the love of God will you let me explain, woman."

"Who was that harlot you were kissing?" Beth shouted the words into the air then clamped her hand over her mouth. Passers-by had begun to stare. Struggling to control the monster within, she had a sudden image of her brother James. The feeling of being suffocated that used to plague her daily was threatening its grim return at any moment.

Within Beth's expressive blue eyes Finn read her agony and it stabbed at his heart. "It was Aisling." He said quickly. At the look of shock on her face Finn hurried to explain. "After the last time I saw you I went home to find her in Mrs Williams's front parlour."

222

"Aisling? From Ireland? What's she doing here?" Beth felt the tight knot in her chest begin to loosen.

Finn paused in the middle of the pavement and glanced around. They'd reached the end of Heath Road and he looked across at the Park opposite. "Let's go for a walk in the park where we can talk *'mo mhuirnin'*," he said softly. Before Beth could stop him Finn had taken hold of her arm and steered her across the road.

"Aisling came to tell me she still loves me. She is refusing to go back to Ireland." Finn explained once they were seated on a bench. "I was trying to tell her I'm in love with you when you saw us."

"You have a funny way of showing how much you love *me,* by kissing Aisling." A whirl of emotions chased themselves across Beth's face like autumn leaves blown up in a storm.

"I called out to you but you'd disappeared so quickly and didn't hear me." Finn begged her to believe him as she sat on the edge of the bench next to him her eyes filled with doubt and disbelief.

"And… I didn't kiss her she kissed me." Finn ran his fingers through his hair clearly struggling to make Beth understand how it was. "I know how it looked but I took Aisling to the tea room to persuade her to return to Ireland. Beth, look at me." Finn took hold of Beth's hand then lifted it to his mouth where he began softly kissing each finger. "She means nothing to me," he said. "It's you I love and want to marry."

Beth gasped and took in a deep breath. "How can I believe you? Tell me, are you just playing a game? I know you've talked about Aisling before but...," she held his gaze imploring him to tell the truth.

"Beth, I wouldn't lie to you and if you still don't believe me I'll take you to meet her."

"I don't think there's any need for that." Beth said quietly leaning back and concentrating on brushing an imaginary speck from her skirts. "Is it true? Do you really want to marry me?"

Finn's eyes, which were full of love and desire held Beth's. As he pulled her into his arms his familiar masculine scent filled her nostrils and she could feel her heart racing against his chest.

"I love you, my darling. Desperately." He whispered. "I do want to marry you."

Finn's lips sought hers leaving Beth breathless. But there was one more question she had to ask him. She pulled slightly away and met his gaze. "Do you mean you want us to be married with no conditions attached?" Finn's body stiffened as she moved away from him.

"I wouldn't want my wife gallivanting around London standing on soap boxes and preaching to the masses." The look of tenderness had quickly vanished from Finn's face. "That goes without saying, so it does." He gave a wry smile as he looked back at her.

"But…Finn. This is something I have to do and you must understand that!" Beth couldn't help the passion in her voice. "Alice and I have come to an understanding. We've sorted out our problems, so there's no need for you to worry about her jealousy anymore."

Finn lifted one eyebrow and looked confused. "What about us and our future happiness? Don't you want to settle down with me and have a family?"

"I can still do that, Finn. Why must I choose? It means everything to me and millions of other women that we get the vote. It's the beginning of so many changes for women and their lives."

Finn refused to answer her. His face had taken on a hostile look shutting Beth out as he stared over at the observatory.

"I'm sorry you feel like that, Finn." Beth's spine straightened and she lifted her head gazing at his profile. "That's the way it is."

For a moment only the distant sound of children playing and the birds twittering in the trees above could be heard as they were both lost in their own thoughts.

"Do you love me, Beth?" Finn continued to study the observatory as he spoke.

"Yes, of course I do." She bit down on her lower lip and sighed. "But, you do have to love me for who

I am, not who you want me to be. That's the only way I will marry you."

Finn stood up and took a step away from the bench. He looked down at her with determination etched across his face. The chill of dread shivered through Beth's body and she knew what Finn was about to say before the words were spoken.

"Well I'm not sure where we go from here, *A grá*."

Struggling to stem the tears that threatened, Beth held his gaze waiting for him to go on. When he didn't she attempted to hide the anguish she felt and continued where he'd left off. "Are you saying we should cease our courtship?" Against her will the tears forced their way out. They slipped silently down her cheeks and she dipped her head quickly, dabbing furiously at her eyes.

In a heartbeat Finn was close to her again. "My love," he said softly, "I don't want that." Kneeling down he lifted her face to his. "Surely we should be able to work it out. Why not leave the decision about marriage. Carry on as we are?"

Feeling bewildered at the conflicting messages Finn seemed to be sending, Beth nodded. She was exhausted by emotion. At least for the moment the crisis was over. Holding out his hand he pulled her up into an embrace and they stood that way for several moments. Overhead the sun had broken through the dark clouds sending bright rays of light down onto the earth below.

Chapter *Twenty Five*

THE HOUSES OF PARLIAMENT

Darkness clung in long fingers to the elaborate Gothic building standing in all its splendour overlooking Parliament Square. Shafts of light from intricately patterned windows shone like stars in the night sky. Big Ben stood out high against the heavens, its hands pointing to seven o'clock. Far below, across the green anticipation mounted amongst the women gathered there.

After a day of demonstrating Beth's feet were sore and her head ached. She looked across the green at the dark uniforms of the police, with their silver buttons glistening in the dark. Ready to do battle, the men stood to attention, with their Black Maria's lined up behind them. Some were already involved in minor scuffles as people attempted to cross their lines. Beth had been told that five thousand Police constables were placed on special duty that evening. The square had been completely cordoned off. They were already anticipating many arrests following the publicity campaign lead by Mrs Pankhurst and her followers.

Beth looked at Alice and Sybil standing beside her. Their faces were animated with excitement with no trace of the fear clutching at her stomach.

Sybil squared her shoulders and made an observation. "It looks as if the weeks of publicity have paid off at last."

Beth tried to smile at Sybil's words but she only managed a nervous high pitched laugh. In the darkness she felt Alice's head turn in her direction. Leaning towards her Alice whispered softly into her ear. "Don't worry, stay close to me you'll be fine," she said reassuringly.

Beth silently berated herself for feeling concerned. This was after all what they'd worked towards for many weeks. Putting up the handbills had encouraged the public to help the suffragettes. *'To rush the House of Commons on this 13th day of October 1908.'* Through distributing flyers and explaining to all who would listen, their intention was to push their way through the doors of the House of Commons and confront the Prime Minister.

Suddenly, the noise around them changed from loud excitement to a low hum. Women lowered their heads and seemed to be whispering to each other.

Alice moved forwards and Beth saw her speak to someone nearby. Then she turned to all assembled with a wide smile across her face. "May I have your attention!" She commanded. "I have just heard that Mrs Pankhurst, Christabel and Mrs Drummond have been arrested!" A loud cheer resounded in the air. This was exactly according to the plan. Beth marvelled at the bravery of the three women and her feelings of apprehension evaporated into the cold night air. Beth was proud to be part of this attempt to show the public just how determined the suffragettes were to succeed.

"Come on everyone." Alice raised her arms above her head. "The time has come for battle!" She moved forward, her head high glancing back just once to ensure that Beth was following. Walking determinedly towards the front of the square, Alice's action galvanised others into motion. Not only their group, but others around them began to follow.

Dodging amongst the women Beth felt as if numerous bodies were closing in upon her. She dare not look behind, imagining that from the air they must all look like a pack of ants descending on a grain of sugar. Shortly the pushing began, slightly at first then harder and stronger. Beth's feet were propelled from beneath her and she was carried along by the crowd. A woman next to her coughed and Beth felt her breath touch her own cheek. Their eyes met and an unfamiliar face stared back at her in the darkness. Where were her friends? Shouting Alice's name, Beth's voice was lost in the loud noise around her. For a split second she spotted Sybil's hat bobbing up and down ahead.

Claws of panic seized Beth. Gasping she felt the air leaving her body as the pressure from others around began to squeeze the breath from her body. Struggling for oxygen, she realised they were already at the front of the square. In a flail of arms and amid shouts of protest Beth could see people were being bodily removed from the barriers by the police. Just as she felt on the point of collapse, she spotted a small gap in the gathering to one side of the green. In desperation she lunged towards it, tripping over in her attempt to break free. Finding herself sitting on the damp ground she gulped fresh air. Feeling dazed, she pushed herself up and quickly began to run. Her only thought was to get away as fast as possible from the stifling crowd.

Stopping to take deep breaths Beth found herself beside a bronze statue. By the light of a nearby lamppost she read the words engraved below the static figure, 'Viscount Palmerstone.' Beth's eyes roamed the statue as he stood proud and majestic with a coat slung carelessly over his arm. He seemed to be looking straight at the activity on the green and Beth fancied she saw the hint of a smile playing across his lips.

She paused for a moment letting her breath return to normal. Then she addressed the statue. "Well, Mr Palmerstone," she said out loud, placing her hands on her hips and staring into his face. "What do you, I wonder, think of us women fighting for justice? I have a feeling you would have approved." Beth smiled at herself then hearing loud noises coming from behind her decided she must re-join the protest.

Just as she was about to turn back a slight movement around her ankles caused her to hesitate. Glancing down she saw a pile of old rags stacked up against the statue. The 'rags' moved. Surprised Beth took a step back. From the pile there next came a small mewing sound. Instinctively she knelt down and pulling at the clothes she tried to free whatever unfortunate animal happened to be inside. A woman's thin face appeared from within the rags. Beth stared at the gaunt features and the familiar wide eyes that looked back at her. In a split second the woman had brought her legs up and lowered her face again, burrowing back into the dirty clothes layered around her body. She pulled a tiny bundle closer into her cocoon.

Beth got unsteadily to her feet and leaned towards the creature. "Can I help you in any way, Miss?" She asked the bedraggled female. The woman shook her head beneath the shawl which made the rags she was holding fall open. Beth caught a glimpse of the miniscule face of a baby and gasped. She stared at the poor mite. Her eyes shot to the mother, whose strands of dirty hair had escaped from beneath the filthy shawl that had previously been wrapped around her head. Immediately Beth realised who this woman was just as the infant began to let out low mewing sounds again.

"Mary! Oh, my God. You poor girl." Mary looked back at Beth with red rimmed eyes and gripped the baby protectively against her chest.

"It's me. Beth." Seeing the blank expression on Mary's face she tried again. "You remember me? I'm, Miss Elizabeth."

"Oh, gawd. Miss Elizabeth is it really you?" Mary held out one arm while clutching the baby in the other. Beth pulled her to her feet and the class divide fell away as both women embraced. Tears of joy fell down Mary's cheeks at finding her mistress again. Beth could hardly believe this was the same Mary, who'd once been such a bonny young girl. She now looked old beyond her years. Behind Beth sounds of the battle still in progress, raged on.

"Tell me, Mary, what's happened to you?" As she spoke Beth held out her hands to relieve the other woman of her tiny bundle. Mary allowed Beth to take the baby now that she recognised her rescuer. It was obvious to Beth her former maid had fallen on hard times since leaving the house as clearly the baby needed help.

"Oh, Miss, it's been awful. First I tried to go home to my mam. But it was the usual story, she's pregnant again and me Da was down the pub drinking his wages. There's no food or room for me and the babe." She looked up at Beth willing her to understand how it was. Beth nodded remembering Alice's young housemaid Nancy, who was looking after her siblings now her mother had died.

"I managed to get a job in a small household as I didn't show at all, you see, Miss." Mary gestured towards her stomach. "So no-one suspected anything. I had no references of course," she glanced at Beth who would obviously be aware of this. "They must 'ave been let down a few times and took me on without one. It was the man of the house who interviewed me. His wife had just died so in his confused state and desperate for help with a newborn and a young son, he took me on. It must have slipped his mind that I'd come empty handed." Mary stopped and looked across the green as a particularly loud shout reverberated through the air from across the square.

Beth cradled the tiny baby rocking it backwards and forwards until the mewling had stopped. "What happened next?" She asked ignoring the activity going on behind her.

"I got fat and began to show. I'd hoped the hard work would make me lose the babe." Mary held out her arms to take the child back and then held it protectively against her breast. "It wasn't to be. The housekeeper noticed me condition and told the master. He let me go, there an' then." Mary's face looked dismal at this memory and Beth at once felt guilty at her family's appalling treatment of this young girl.

"Tell me how on earth did you survive?" Beth's voice was low with sympathy as she studied Mary's haggard face.

"It was hard, but I managed to save a bit in the few months I was employed and moved into a rented room. It was dingy and full of cockroaches but it was somewhere to sleep. That's how I survived for the rest of the pregnancy until two weeks ago when I give birth. After that I couldn't pay the rent no more and 'ad no money. We bin living on the streets trying to make ends meet."

In her naivety Beth asked a question which seemed blatantly obvious when she recalled Mary's answer later. "But, Mary, how have you managed to earn any money at all?"

Mary's face took on a closed look and she bowed her head murmuring something under her breath.

"I'm sorry I can't hear what you're saying, Mary." Beth said firmly.

"I said there be only one way to earn money living on the streets." Mary's eyes filled with tears once again as she lifted her head and looked intently back at Beth.

In that moment Beth saw reflected in Mary's eyes the same haunted expression she'd worn the day she'd come upon her weeping in the corridor. A shiver of dread ran through Beth as she held Mary's gaze. "Mary, I'm so sorry." She bent towards Mary and enveloped her and the baby in her arms.

The sound of the baby's continued whimpering forced Beth to withdraw from Mary and take action. "Now, Mary." She said firmly. "What is done is done.

Tell me, what of the little one, is it ill? From what I can see it looks very tiny."

"The baby is hungry all the time and hardly has the strength to cry. I'm starving and I have no food for her." Mary stroked the tiny head as she spoke.

The noise from across the green intensified and both women turned to look at what was occurring. Beth was alarmed to see, in the distance, silhouettes of police officers dragging women into the prison vans. In the half light from the overhead lamps she could see the women fighting like wild cats to get into the House of Commons. All at once she had to know if Alice was all right.

Grabbing hold of Mary she steered her away from view and led her round the back of the statue. "Mary. Hide here until I get back." She saw the fear cross Mary's face. "Don't worry I will be back in a moment. I won't abandon you and the baby. It's just...I have to know whether my friend is safe. Please don't go anywhere. I promise I'll return." Then Beth ran as fast as she could towards the now immense gathering of people.

Beth pushed as hard as she could towards the front of the crowd struggling in the darkness to see someone familiar. As she got to the cordoned off area she saw Sybil standing on the edge of the crowd shouting at two policemen. Beth thrust her body forward and forced those in her way to move. Taking Sybil's arms she began shaking her hard forcing the other woman to stop her tirade and pay attention to her. "Sybil! Where is Alice? Please, have you seen Alice?"

Sybil's face bobbed up and down and was contorted in anger. "There she is!" She screamed pointing to the scene taking place about five feet away.

To Beth's absolute horror she saw Alice and two other women being bundled into a Black Maria. Sybil ran towards them and began fighting with one of the policemen. Next Sybil was swallowed up into the scuffle. Beth stood frozen watching this spectacle appear in slow motion. Powerless to help, and knowing that if she attempted to intervene she'd be arrested, Beth backed away. She couldn't leave Mary and her child alone and once again felt torn between divided loyalties. As the van door was banged shut and the vehicle began moving off, Sybil's face stared accusingly at her through the barred window.

As Beth turned to go back the way she'd come something made her glance towards the Houses of Parliament. She narrowed her eyes in the gloom and stared evenly towards the building. Was it the darkness playing tricks or could it have been wishful thinking that she thought she'd seen someone loitering in the doorway? She waited for a brief moment her heart racing. Then deciding it must have been nothing more than her imagination Beth continued on her way, eager to reach Mary and the baby.

Chapter *Twenty Six*

MARY'S BABY

Beth felt an awful clawing fear in the pit of her stomach as she approached the cottage. The front door was slightly ajar and alarm bells resounded in her head. The breath caught in her throat, making it difficult to breath, as a sudden image of a dark and furtive figure running from the cottage filled her head. What if he was still inside, if disturbing him instigated a violent reaction? Beth took a slow step backwards and almost fell over Mary who was standing behind her clutching the whimpering child to her breast. The immediate protection of her vulnerable charges forced her to move.

"What's the matter, Miss?" Mary's large brown eyes were like saucers in her head as she pulled the baby in closer and stared trustingly at Beth in alarm.

"Mary, don't you worry." Beth was surprised at how steady her voice sounded as she struggled to control the churning in her stomach. "I'm sure it's nothing. You and the baby wait here for a moment." Beth spoke firmly and gave Mary a gentle push backwards.

Mary nodded numbly and looked down at the baby. "But, Miss. We have to feed her...don't we? Or else...?"

"Yes we do, Mary, and we will in just a moment." Ripples of fear surged through Beth at what she'd find in the cottage and the imperative urgency of feeding the baby was momentarily forgotten.

Forcing herself to be brave Beth lifted one trembling hand and pushed hard on the wooden door which moved slightly. Beth pushed again. A loud crunch underfoot reverberated in the still night air as she put her boot through the gap in the doorway. She lifted her foot to reveal one of her small ornaments smashed beyond repair. Taking a sharp intake of breath she ignored the twisted fearful feeling in her stomach and entered the cottage.

Tears sprang to her eyes and she clamped a hand across her mouth to stifle a scream. Everything was in disarray, all her belongings were scattered on the floor and were either broken or chipped in some way. Cushions from the sofa lay ripped open, their insides revealed for the world to see. Beth's mirror lay cracked in the middle of the room her pale face reflected in its distorted image. She stared at the small carriage clock that usually sat on the mantelpiece above the fire. It was lying in the hearth the glass front had been smashed and its hands lay twisted and bent. Anger was now replacing the clinging fear in her stomach at this blatant invasion of her privacy and wanton destruction of her belongings. Why would someone do this to her?

"Miss Elizabeth?"

In her anguish Beth had temporarily forgotten Mary. The more pressing matter of feeding the child forced her breath into a slow rhythm.

"Wait there, Mary. I need to do something." Beth shouted over her shoulder. Her anger was now giving her courage and she knew she had to check over the whole cottage in case someone was hiding. Stepping over the broken items, she forced her way through into the kitchen and made her way upstairs.

Having quickly inspected the two small bedrooms Beth arrived back downstairs and ushered Mary through the door and into the cottage.

"What happened?" Mary's face was stricken as she hovered in the doorway staring at the floor. The baby's whimpering echoed around the room.

"Quick, Mary, come in. We must feed the baby at once." Beth said breathlessly and began leading her former maid over the scattered items into the kitchen. Beth felt her heart rate return to normal and the clawing sickness abate, as she reassured herself they were indeed alone in the cottage.

Mary sat on the kitchen chair and watched impassively as Beth made up the formula. Beth's hands were shaking as she measured out the milk then poured the boiling water into the bottle. Now they knew they were not at risk of attack from whoever had ransacked the cottage, they were at last free to get on with the business of feeding the baby.

Earlier Beth and Mary had been hammering on the door of Westminster Hospital for what seemed hours until finally a sympathetic nurse had appeared. She had taken one look at the baby and had hurried them through to see the Doctor. After his examination he'd ordered the nurse to feed the baby immediately and had taken them aside. His prognosis was what they had both feared, that the child was near to death.

Mary had wept and begged for his help. The doctor advised that the child was to be fed little and often if she was to have any chance of survival. Beth had looked at Mary's face, seeing again the terror in her face she'd witnessed the day she'd found the young maid in the corridor. An image of James and his mocking, uncaring face had then filled Beth with a determination to do her selfish brother's duty. To help this young girl and her unfortunate baby survive. Leaving the distraught Mary, Beth had stepped forward and asked the nurse to instruct her on how to make up the baby's food.

"It's what the Doctor recommended, Mary." Beth reassured Mary now who was beginning to look concerned at the stillness of the baby lying in her arms. "Nestlé is the alternative to a wet nurse." She added, trying to get a response from Mary who seemed to have gone into a trance.

Beth tested the temperature on her wrist and turned back to Mary. "The bottle's ready at last. Try and wake her." Mary lifted her head then took the bottle from Beth. Her eyes were staring intently at the soft rubber teat. Mary put the teat to the baby's tiny lips. There was no response. Then to Beth's horror, large tears began to slide down Mary's cheeks and her head came down onto the infant's face where she began to sob noisily.

"Mary, stop that!" Beth pushed Mary aside and grabbed the baby. Taking her into her own arms she admonished, "she's not dead! We must try again." Beth then began pushing the teat firmly into the infant's mouth. "Come on, sweetheart," she cajoled softly, as the child's mother silently wept beside them, "come on you can do it."

Beth fought against the black thoughts crowding her head. This tiny baby cannot die now. Not here in this cramped and messy cottage. Not now when her and Mary, she realised with a jolt, could have such high hopes for her future. A life for this child filled with freedom would be what Beth wished for her, without feeling trapped in an existence from which she could never escape. To be snatched away from Mary now, after the trauma of her conception and the struggles endured since her birth, would be the worst possible outcome for the young maid.

The child's little dove eyelids fluttered. Her tiny eyes opened and she fixed Beth with a penetrating stare. Gripping the teat, she began to suck furiously. To both women it was the most wonderful sound in the world. Heaving a sigh of relief Beth passed the baby back to her mother.

"I'm so sorry, Miss. I don't know what came over me." Mary spluttered. "I thought she was gone."

"It was fear that came over you, Mary, fear. Oh, Mary, it was like having your hands tied and unable to help. But we can help her, you and I. We can make a difference. We have to believe that, Mary. We will be strong for her and she will be stronger than the two of us one day, it doesn't matter now, she's feeding."

Beth sat for a moment watching mother and baby. Letting out a long sigh she stood up. She was aware that while one crisis had been averted another awaited her in the front parlour. The shock of seeing her belongings smashed and scattered everywhere had knocked her off balance and her mind whirled with unanswered questions. Mary's voice penetrated her thoughts.

"She looks a bit betta now, Miss." The baby's deathly white pallor had begun to turn pink and at last the heart rending mewing noise ceased. Mary seemed visibly relaxed for a moment before suddenly remembering the debris next door. "Who do you think did all this 'ere damage, Miss?"

Beth turned towards the doorway and the parlour. "I don't know who would do this to me? As far as I know I have no enemies. Not everyone agrees with the suffragette movement, but would someone be so against my involvement to do this?" Beth ignored the reoccurring thought in her head that her mother may be behind the destruction in the cottage. Could she be trying to frighten her into returning home to be forgiven by her father?

Stepping into the parlour Beth perched on the edge of the sofa and lifted her spine. Mary followed her into the room carrying the child and sat down beside her, adjusting the shawl around the baby's body. For a while only the noise of the baby feeding could be heard. When the bottle was empty Mary lay her little girl down on the sofa between them.

"Have you thought of a name for her?" Beth said trying to focus on something other than the state of the room and the whirling emotions she was experiencing.

Mary tore her eyes from the child. A half smile played around her lips as she looked up at Beth. "I've thought of a few, Miss Elizabeth."

"You can call me Beth now, Mary. We don't live in my parents' house anymore."

Mary looked doubtful but tried anyway. "Well...Beth, one name keeps coming back to me time and time again, it's your name, Miss... I mean, Elizabeth."

"Well, I'm honoured." Warmth filled Beth at Mary's words, bringing a smile to her face. "You could always shorten it to, Lizzie. That might suit her don't you think?" Beth stroked the baby's tiny cheek causing little Lizzie to stir briefly and in her brief gesture she caught the flicker of an expression on the child's face that reminded Beth of her brother James.

"Oh, I like that, Miss really I do. Lizzie, it is then." Mary's eyes sparkled as she returned Beth's smile.

Ignoring the thoughts swirling in her head that James should be taking some responsibility for his baby daughter, Beth got up and focused on the surrounding chaos. As she began clearing up she knew she had to find out who was responsible.

"It must be someone trying to get their own back on you," Mary observed. "Could it be anyone from your old life up at the house?"

"I don't think so. I always got on well with everyone there except for Helen, my mother's maid. It wasn't anything she ever said, it was more the way she used to look at me sometimes."

"I knows something about her, Miss." Mary eyes looked guarded as if she wasn't sure she should tell Beth what was on her mind.

Beth's brows rose and she studied Mary's face. When Mary avoided eye contact with her she was suddenly suspicious about what the girl knew. "Well, Mary? What do you know? Tell me."

"I shouldn't have said that, Miss, you won't like it if I tell you."

Beth was curious as to what Mary could be keeping from her. "What do you know, Mary?" She repeated.

"It were me friend Ethel what told me. She still works at the house and I happened to see her one day in town not so long after I was dismissed."

"Go on, Mary." Beth coaxed.

"It's Hugo and Helen. They is carrying on."

"How do you mean carrying on?" Beth felt apprehensive about what Mary was about to tell her and sat down on the sofa careful not to disturb Lizzie.

"Ethel's a good girl really, Miss. She told me cos she's never liked that ladies maid and the way she always talks badly about you. We all know you're the kind one in the family." Beth smiled at Mary's compliment and waited for her to continue.

"Hugo likes Helen. He was already moving in on her before the engagement was broke." Beth's face had gone white, but Mary was in full flow now and hadn't noticed. "Ethel reckons that they're stealing from the house. I told her not to be silly but maybe she's right."

"I don't know, Mary, do you think Ethel's telling the truth?" Beth knew how the staff used to gossip about those above stairs.

"I think she is, Miss, although Ethel does see things differently from other people sometimes. Bit more colourful like."

Beth put her head in her hands and let out a long sigh. "Maybe there's an answer there somewhere, Mary." Could there be a connection with what Mary had just told her and the state of the cottage? Beth asked herself. Her thoughts were in turmoil again.

"Whoever has done all this," Beth spread her arms wide taking in the expanse of the room, "Will be brought to task," she said firmly.

Mary wasn't sure what her former mistress meant by 'brought to task.' So she picked up Lizzie and holding her tiny body close to her chest answered her the best way she could. "Happen you're right, Miss." She said quietly. "Happen you're right."

Chapter *Twenty Seven*

ALICE IN PRISON

The door slammed shut behind the women. For a moment in the dark airless prison van no-one spoke. The vehicle was set in motion as outside the battle with police continued to rage. Like everyone in that confined space, Alice could hardly move. It was of little wonder that this appalling vehicle had been nicknamed the 'Black Maria' thought Alice as she observed her surroundings. The women were all in individual 'human cages;' not dissimilar to upright coffins with an iron grating on each one just big enough through which to poke your face.

"I feel like an animal." Alice whispered defiantly to Sybil who was in the cage next to her.

Sybil nodded her lips set in a firm line. She opened her mouth and said in a loud voice, "I think we should sing now, what do you think?"

"I think you're right!" returned Alice forcefully. Some of the other women nodded enthusiastically. Their plan if they were arrested, was to sing loudly in the prison van. The intention was both to keep their spirits up on the way to jail and to antagonise the police. So with gusto and defiance they began.

Alice's voice rang out leading the others into the song. 'Sing a song of Christabel's clever little plan.'

'Four and twenty Suffragettes packed into a van,' chorused her followers.

'When the van was opened, they to the Commons ran'

'Wasn't that a dainty dish for Campbell Bannerman'

'Asquith was in the Treasury, counting out the money,' the women's voices rang out loud and clear filling the tiny van with noise. Alice's voice was the loudest as she looked around at her fellow suffragettes, feeling animated by their support.

'Lloyd George among the Liberal women speaking words of honey'

'And then there came a bright idea to all these little men'

'Let's give the women Votes they cried, and all be friends again'

Alice had read in the Daily Mail in February of that year, how a suffragette had written the song during her prison sentence. The woman had smuggled in a pencil despite the rigorous stripping and searching by the wardens. Alice had then had the idea to sing in the event of being arrested to show their resistance to the police and honour the courage of the woman.

Repeatedly they sang their song. Eventually the van lurched to a halt and the doors were flung open. Alice faced her captors as they were all manhandled out of the van, feeling her spirits had been lifted and her courage returned to her. What lay ahead promised to be an unpleasant experience, but was a necessary part of their fight. Bracing herself Alice and her comrades were marshalled into line outside Holloway Prison.

In a tiny cell not unlike the size of a small pantry, Alice sat with the other women and waited for the next step in the process of imprisonment. Earlier, one by one their personal details had been taken by a prison wardress and these had been entered into a ledger.

The sound of keys jangling echoed through the air. "Right. Everyone out!" The same large 'wide faced' wardress who had taken their details began unlocking the cell. Her man-like features held a half smile, as if she were taking pleasure in dealing with these rebellious women. Women clustered around, some had fear in their eyes at the unknown and others who had walked this road before looked unconcerned by the process.

"Queue up!" Ordered 'wide face' and handed them each a bundle of old clothes. The group were herded into a room where a fire burned in the grate. This was the only warmth in the cold and empty space. Alice dreaded what was about to happen.

"Stand in line and strip off," 'wide face' barked at the women. She seemed to be giving the orders while another equally stern looking wardress stood by. Slowly, the women began taking off their clothes, only to be prompted to get a move on. The searching began when the lady at the front of the line had got down to her chemise. She'd obviously had past experience of prison and stood calmly, her face averted while the wardress's hands felt her body up and down several times.

Alice watched in her under garments at the way everyone was being manhandled. She felt repulsed by the wardress's actions and great admiration for the woman at the front, who was undergoing this most private of searches with great dignity. When it came to her turn Alice defiantly looked 'wide face' in her hard and steely eyes.

"Turn around!" Shouted the wardress, into Alice's face, spraying her with spittle.

Alice gritted her teeth refusing to wipe the invading sliver of saliva from her cheek. Glaring back at this man-woman with the square body and bloated face, she refused to move.

The woman immediately grabbed hold of Alice's hair and roughly yanked it loose, causing it to cascade in a red mane down her back. "Ouch! Bloody stop that now!" Alice shouted angrily, bracing herself for the inevitable, her hair to be cut off.

"Give me your combs," demanded the woman, holding out her hand to Alice.

Alice considered rebelling but was jabbed in the back by Sybil.

"It might be best to do as you're told for now, Alice." Sybil hissed, as she waited behind Alice in the queue.

Alice conceded, delving into her pocket to retrieve her comb. This might be the best solution for the present. The wardress watched Alice retrieving her comb then stared regretfully at the waiting women behind her. Snatching the comb from Alice's hands she replaced it with an old and dirty one, ordering Alice to put her hair back up. Alice sighed with relief that her hair would for now, stay intact.

Alice felt sick as the wardress's hands roamed her body. Lifting her head she tried to pretend she hadn't noticed when 'wide face' fingers touched her most private of parts. The urge to slap the woman came upon her so strongly, that she had to pin her arms rigidly to her sides. Thankfully it was soon over but not before 'wide face' shot her a knowing wink and a sly scheming smile. Alice returned the look with one of steely determination. The woman shrugged dismissively and pushed Alice roughly into the line of 'done' women.

A stale body smell filled the air as Alice shivered in her undergarments in the chilled room. Waiting for the searching to finish she stood watching the rest of the women, most were defiant but some of the weaker ones had begun to look tearful. She tried to catch their eye to offer encouragement wherever she could. The wardress's were truly despicable women who all seemed to be taking a perverse pleasure in what they were doing. Alice could see it took a certain type of woman to treat people in this degrading way.

"Right!" shouted the chief wardress at the now searched group of women, "you are all going to have a bath." She smirked as a sigh of apprehension filled the room.

Alice's heart sank for their ordeal was not over yet. All the women were then marched out of the room down a long dark corridor and into a filthy bathroom. With no choice but to obey, they took it in turns to bathe in the grimy bath. At least the water was hot thought Alice as she stepped into the steaming water feeling herself being watched from the corner of the room by a grinning 'wide face.'

Arriving in the cell Alice had been shocked at how small the dingy room was. Slightly wider that the width of the bed, it had only one blanket with which to keep warm at night. A bucket with a toilet seat attached stood in the corner, which would they'd been told, have to be slopped out everyday. The compartment was completely enclosed, tiled in white from floor to ceiling, with a thick metal door complete with a sliding hatch in the middle. It was through this hatch she found herself constantly peered and jeered at by 'wide face' or one of her colleagues. Feeling totally lost she folded and unfolded the programme that had been shoved into her hands earlier, as she was pushed into this wretched room. It told of numerous punishments but otherwise gave no instructions on when they would be free.

As she lay on the lumpy mattress feeling the concrete bed beneath digging into her aching back, Alice longed for someone, anyone, to come with a kind word to ease the loneliness gripping her by the throat. Long fingers of isolation wrapped around her neck and threatened to suffocate her in this tiny airless space. She tried to ignore the smell of carbolic soap and the unclean smell, coming from the old clothes she'd been forced to wear.

Rubbing at the skin on her arms, reddened by her own scrubbing, Alice yearned for home. She wondered if Beth would feed poor Mrs. P, then smiled in the darkness as she remembered she was too good a hunter to starve. Mrs.P was a born survivor not unlike her owner.

Having no idea what time it was, the pitch darkness could only allow Alice to guess it must be around three o'clock in the morning. Hunger pains gnawed at her stomach. Low weeping sounds were coming from another cell, piercing the silence. She hankered after joining the distressed woman, who was obviously finding the conditions as gloomy as she was.

In her naivety, Alice had imagined herself sharing a cell with another woman. Loneliness clutched at her heart and she was finding the desire to join the weeping woman interspersed with her forbidden yearning for Beth. In this dark and desolate place, thoughts of Beth and the false hope that one day she would return Alice's feelings, ran through her mind. She soon gave up fighting this fantasy, when she realised it was better than the feeling of dread at what tomorrow might bring, so closing her eyes she fell into a deep and fitful sleep.

Chapter *Twenty Eight*

HELEN

Helen's hand shook slightly and hovered over the large open jewellery box sitting on the dressing table top. Winter sun glinted low through the window reflecting the sparkling gems on the mirror above. Which piece to take this time? She asked herself, resting her hand on the side of the dressing table. Slowly she began to count the pieces of jewellery in her head. Only six pieces left, their numbers were now much depleted. So far she'd managed to avoid the mistress seeing exactly how much was missing, with Helen having to frequently steer Beth's mother away from choosing the stolen pieces.

It wouldn't be long though, Helen observed, before it would become impossible to hide the fact that a fair proportion of the jewellery was gone. Probably not even in Hugo's possession anymore. Even though initially he hid them in the cottage, it didn't take him long to find a buyer and quickly turn the mistress's jewellery into cash.

The thought of Hugo brought a smile to Helen's lips and she glanced at her reflection in the dressing table mirror, her hazel eyes sparkled with excitement. She wanted Hugo for herself. It was as simple as that. Their affair had started long before his attempts at marrying the young miss. Then when he'd been jilted by the selfish and spoilt Miss Elizabeth, Helen had indulged him with her attention making sure he hadn't forgotten her charms.

Hugo had told her about the printing business he ran with his stepfather, revealing that the company was slowly going out of business, after he'd paid his gambling debts out of the profits. He desperately needed money to replace what he'd taken. This was the reason why he was so keen to marry Miss Elizabeth. Once the engagement had been called off however he no longer cared about the business. His intention was to dismiss his responsibilities and run away to make a new life. Helen was under no illusions, as she listened to Hugo, that he was a selfish man who was making use of her. He groaned and murmured words of love into her ear, while using her body for his own pleasure.

He was her ticket to a new life she told herself. As his plan was to extort money from the house in vengeance, to be paid what he was owed from the Hamilton-Greens. Helen did not think for one moment that Hugo loved her. He loved only himself, for even though his body was slack and his eyes dull from too much drinking, he thought himself to be a wonderful catch. She decided that very first night when she gave in to his sexual demands that she would use this to her own advantage. Turn it around to suit herself and to escape from her life of drudgery.

Helen knew that as Ladies maid she possibly had the best position in the hierarchy of the staff. Despite this she was fed up with seeing those around her living in luxury, while her meagre wage didn't stretch further than the necessities of life. Hugo, although soft with words when he wanted her to steal for him; or while they lay together after making love, wasn't to be trusted. Given half the chance Helen knew that he would disappear regardless of the fact that she'd risked her job for him and much more besides. So she'd kept a trump card up her sleeve.

There was one piece of jewellery her mistress owned which was extremely rare. It was left to the mistress by her grandfather, who had acquired it on a trip to India. One day her mistress asked Helen to fetch it for her. She wanted to show a visiting cousin. Helen remembered that day well. She'd lifted it out carefully and her eyes widened in wonder at the sheer size of the sapphire set in the middle of the butterfly shaped brooch. She knew instantly it was very valuable and worth many hundreds of pounds. Helen had told Hugo about the piece deliberately, smiling to herself at his reaction and for once feeling as if she were the one in control. She told him how it was kept separate from all the rest of the jewellery in another compartment of the box under lock and key. Greed lit up his face, and his eyebrows lifted as he licked his lips and looked at her. She waited for him to ask and it wasn't long in coming.

"I want that brooch, Helen," he had demanded.

Helen smiled and promised to take it for him as soon as she could. She'd seen her opportunity immediately, this was different from the other jewellery. This piece was worth more. It was some time later that Hugo asked her if she'd had the opportunity to take it. "I stole it weeks ago, Hugo," she'd teased. "I've hidden it in a safe place."

Unable to contain himself Hugo demanded to know where it was hidden so that he could sell it and add it to their collection of money. Helen fixed him with a penetrating stare. The muscles in Hugo's face tightened and he leaned towards her his cheeks red with rage.

"Well! Where is it?" He'd shouted.

"It's in a place where it can't be found until we're ready to leave. When that time comes I will fetch it." Helen had stood firm holding onto to what she looked of as her insurance, refusing to tell him anything more than that it was hidden in the cottage.

Hugo's eyes lit up and he assumed it was hidden in the usual place where the other pieces had been stowed away until they were sold. "Is it in the kitchen?" He was referring to one of the cupboards where he'd put in a false back.

Helen had pursed her lips together and said nothing. Hugo's temper had risen, and he'd left the room before Helen had a chance to tell him the cottage was now occupied by the spoilt Miss Elizabeth. Even so she knew he would never find it without her help.

Helen was aware that the time was getting near for her and Hugo to leave. It was getting increasingly hard to keep Hugo calm. He was becoming obsessed with finding the brooch and now she was regretting that she'd told him it was in the cottage. Yesterday he had told her he'd searched for it again. Turning the whole place upside down and still he hadn't found it.

Hugo's anger had frightened her this time. He'd grabbed her by the neck and she'd gasped, feeling the breath being torn from her body as he held her in a tight grip. Still she'd refused to tell him. Begging him to trust her, she'd calmed him by saying she had another gift to bring him first. She'd described another piece of jewellery which was an emerald green necklace and was almost as valuable as the brooch. Hugo finally let go realising that he would never know where it was if he harmed her.

Just another week or two and then they would be ready to go she thought, as she lay naked and spent in his bed. Helen knew she was playing with fire. A man like Hugo would stop at nothing to get what he wanted. Now, still feeling his hands around her neck she shuddered, wondering what the outcome would have been if he had not let her go.

Suddenly there was a knock at the door interrupting her macabre thoughts. Automatically

Helen grabbed the emerald necklace from the open box, slipped it into her pocket and closed the lid. When she answered the door she was surprised to find Mr Bowler the butler, standing there as 'stiff as you please' with a sour expression on his face.

"Helen." His tone was sharp. "You must come downstairs with me now."

"Of course, Mr Bowler. Just give me a moment." Helen curled her fingers around the necklace in her skirt pocket.

"No, you must come now. The mistress needs to see you urgently." He stepped inside the room towards her. She didn't like his tone, but there was nothing for it but to follow him down the long staircase towards the drawing room. He knocked loudly in response to the master's voice and pushed open the door. Helen entered the room, Mr Bowler followed. Alarm bells began to ring in her head.

"Good morning, Helen." Mrs Hamilton-Green addressed her from the couch and after bobbing a curtsy Helen stood before her. She couldn't help glancing nervously around the room. It seemed to be full of people and she looked from face to face trying to quell the panic that was building in the pit of her stomach. The master stood with his hands clasped together and his dark eyes bore into hers. Miss Elizabeth was standing on the other side of the mistress with her hand on the couch. The young mistress stared at Helen her expression full of anger. Then Helen saw something dark move out of the corner of her eye. A police constable was watching her from the corner of the room notebook in hand, waiting it seemed for proceedings to begin.

"Helen. You've been brought here because you're suspected of theft." Charles Hamilton-Green's voice boomed out across the now silent room, in his usual disciplinarian way of addressing the staff. Helen thought she might at any moment be sick. She fought the rising nausea and tried to stay calm. Tightening her lips her expression was that of a coiled spring.

"We've been told, about your association with Hugo and the plot you've both hatched to steal from this house." The master stepped forward and leaned towards her leaving a long dramatic pause. Helen focused on the tiny bit of spittle which had attached itself to his lower lip. She was unable to speak.

"What have you got to say for yourself, woman?" He boomed.

The coil sprang to life as Helen glared back at the master. Having regained some of her composure she decided that denial was the best option. "What a thing to accuse me of. After all this time serving Mrs Hamilton-Green and the many years of loyal service to this household."

"Then you won't mind if we search you, Miss?" The police constable appeared by her side.

"I most certainly will mind! What evidence have any of you got against me that I'm being accused of such scandalous goings-on." Helen held her mistress's eye and watched as she rose from her seated position on the couch.

"Helen," Mrs Hamilton-Green's voice was low and her face held a resigned look. "Over half of my jewellery is missing and you're the only person to have access to it. The only one I trust with it and you've been seen with Hugo."

"As I see it, Helen, you have one of two options."

Helen's head lifted in defiance at the sound of the cosseted Miss Elizabeth speaking and glared at the mistress's daughter.

"Confess all now and tell us exactly where you and Hugo have stored everything. If this were the case we could ask the strong arm of the law..." she looked at the waiting police constable, "to be slightly more lenient with your sentence. Or you could say nothing, deny everything and get whatever's coming to you."

White hot hatred for Miss Elizabeth blinded Helen's reaction, to what she only realised later was a bluff on the young mistress's part. Making the biggest mistake of her life she opened her mouth, and instead of giving herself time to form the words that would render her blameless, she raised her voice and declared, "it was all Hugo's idea, he forced me into it!" As soon as the words were spoken, Helen's face turned beetroot red and she clamped a hand tightly across her mouth.

Mrs Hamilton-Green let out a long sigh then signalled to the police constable to move forward. He took hold of Helen, drawing her to one side of the room where he proceeded to search her person. It didn't take long to retrieve the necklace. Getting out the handcuffs he attached them to his prisoner.

Helen hung her head as she was marched outside towards the prison van. A small cluster of servants watched from the side of the building. It was only the young scullery maid Ethel who noticed Hugo's crouched figure hiding in the nearby bushes, watching the former ladies maid's sad departure.

Hugo's back ached and his legs were beginning to go numb. From his vantage point he had seen the lower members of the staff emerge from their doorway. Clustering together and whispering loudly to each other they took turns to peer around the side of the house. Hugo hardly dared to breathe. They had been within a few feet of where he was hidden. Crouching in the bush, he tried not to move and was frustrated he couldn't see what was occurring. Hugo imagined the servants were watching a spectacle of some kind unfolding and impatiently he edged his way out of the foliage, craning his neck as curiosity got the better of him.

Helen was being led, handcuffed to a police constable, down the steps of the house. A hush had fallen over the staff and Helen's loud sobs filled the air. Hugo coldly watched this woman who had stolen for him, given him her body willingly and was now making the ultimate sacrifice, with no feelings of remorse or sympathy to hinder his conscience. She had known what she was doing and had been well aware of the risks she took.

Hugo caught a glimpse of Elizabeth standing in the doorway with her family and his heart missed a beat. Now there was a beauty. Hugo would have had such fun taming her. Her looks and money aside, Elizabeth's rebellious nature was what had attracted Hugo. He had never had a woman like her, and still dreamed of ripping the clothes from her body while she lay helpless beneath him. She didn't know what she was missing he mused, for it was certainly her loss and not his.

As he watched he saw that Elizabeth had begun glancing around her. Alarm bells rang in Hugo's head and he slid quickly back into the bushes grateful that earlier he had seen the Black Maria parked at the front of the Hamilton-Green's house. It appeared this was his little stroke of luck, forewarning him of a police presence and therefore giving him time to run to the side of the building and hide in the greenery opposite the servant's quarters.

It was from his hideaway that Hugo was now bitterly regretting his decision to come back for Helen. Telling himself he should have gone without her as he intended to do from the outset, he thought back to yesterday's confrontation with his stepfather. Suspicious that there was an imbalance in finance, this substitute parent had begun looking into the loss of the profits from the business. Hugo feared it wouldn't be long before his thieving was discovered and knowing this had forced him to consider leaving earlier than he'd intended. It was only the '*Sapphire Brooch*' that drove him here to find Helen before he fled the country. He cursed her for still having his bounty in her possession.

Despite ransacking every nook and cranny of the wretched cottage he couldn't find where Helen had secreted his ticket to a new life. He imagined her mocking laugh as she declared he would never discover it without her help, knowing that it was her insurance against him abandoning her.

Hugo shuddered at the sound of the van disappearing down the drive, sweeping dust under the bush and fouling the air. Like a frightened rabbit he jumped at the sound of the servants' footsteps as they hurried back to their duties.

The butler scolded them. "Hurry along there the show is over." He reprimanded, his tongue matching the bite of the cold wind that caused the servants to tightly wrap their shawls around their shoulders as they scurried away.

Hugo waited until all was quiet. Slowly, stiff from squatting, he got up from his haunches and put out his hands parting the thick branches of shrubbery. At that moment the door to the servant's quarters opened bringing Hugo face to face with a young maid. For a spilt second time stood still as their eyes met. Then he quickly pushed his way out of the bushes and ran as fast as his stiff legs would allow.

Behind him he could hear the young girl shouting as he felt his body protesting at this forced and unexpected activity.

Weighed down with the bag on his back full of unsold jewellery, cash and other stolen goods, Hugo gasped for breath from his exertions as he stood on the edge of the pavement waving furiously. "Taxi!" He'd run the two miles into Richmond town without stopping and now clutched at his side in agony as a stitch sent shooting pains through his body.

"Where to, Sir?" Asked the taxi driver, as he swivelled round to address the rather red-faced gent, who seemed to be having trouble breathing.

Hugo clambered into the back of the cab huffing and puffing as he slumped into the seat slamming the door behind him. ""East India Docks, quickly!" He ordered, looking out of the back window anxiously as the car began moving out into the traffic. The dark clouds overhead had burst. The heavens opened with a downpour of hailstones. Pushing his body deep into the back seat Hugo kept a firm hold of the bulging bag by his side as the car weaved in and out of the traffic.

"Sailing off to somewhere nice then, sir?" The cab driver attempted to engage his client in conversation, as he watched Hugo in his mirror nervously running his fingers through his hair in an agitated fashion. No answer was forthcoming so he tried again. "Looks like there's a storm brewing happen it'll be a bad one."

Hugo ignored the driver's incessant chatter, willing the car to go faster. The journey seemed to be taking forever. Finally they pulled up outside the dock and leaping out of the cab, Hugo hastily threw the driver a note, uninterested in any change or etiquette involving a tip.

Driving rain had replaced the hailstones and Hugo was immediately soaked to the skin. A strong wind like two burly constables threatened to lift him off his feet and despatch him in a heap in the gutter. Despite the filthy weather he took a moment to compose himself. Pulling himself upright and adjusting the bag on his back he strode purposefully towards the closed steel gates. A cluster of men loitered at the entrance, their backs were arched against the atrocious weather; they were looking at him with pinched hungry faces that wore a glimmer of hope, that a ganger may return and have need of their labours. Hugo pushed roughly past them and headed straight up to a member of the Dock police standing guard just inside the gate.

"Can you let me in? I've a ship leaving in an hour and I need to do a check before it goes, which will be difficult in this atrocious weather." Hugo kept his voice level as he addressed the officer and forced his face into a friendly smile as he did so.

"Good day to you, Mr Wright," said the constable who was used to seeing Hugo around the dock ironing out any problems arising from his printing exports. "How's business these days?" He undid the gates as he spoke allowing Hugo immediate access before shutting them quickly lest one of the ragged looking men outside should chance his luck and try to sidle through.

Although every instinct told him to run, Hugo forced himself to answer the man. He told himself it wouldn't be good to raise any doubts about his visit to the dock. "Going well thanks," he answered backing away. The policeman nodded then distracted he turned away to deal with one of the ruffians who had begun rattling the dock gates in desperation.

Dodging the frenzied activity, Hugo hurried into the dark port. The strong odour of tea filled his nostrils. Steam cranes clanged overhead, whirling, dragging and swinging huge bales from the ships hold. Men rushed to and fro carrying packages and bales into sheds and warehouses. As he approached the quay Hugo's eyes fell upon a cargo ship, The 'SS Ghost.' She was already loaded up and a crew member was standing on deck signing off the men's names as they boarded. Joining the back of the queue, Hugo waited casually in line acutely aware that he looked different from the others in their well-worn working clothes.

Chapter *Twenty Nine*

EVENTS UNFOLD

Having just finished the washing up and reaching for a towel to dry the lunchtime crockery Alice enquired. "The police haven't found him yet then?"

Beth sighed. "There's been no trace of him. After Helen's arrest he just disappeared. Poor Helen, she deserves to pay for her crime but he should have gone down with her."

Alice's forehead creased into a frown and her green eyes held a puzzled look as she stared at her friend. "What! How can you say that, poor Helen? She was a thief and a liar and she hated you." She dried her hands then began untying her apron. "You're too generous by half you know."

"Maybe you're right but I can't help feeling sorry for the woman." Beth turned around and leaned against the sink pushing a strand of hair away from her face. "She was taken in by Hugo. He must have told her a pack of lies. I think Helen must have seen Hugo as an escape from the life she was living, what other explanation can there be for her behaviour?"

Feeling that Beth's sympathy was misguided and that Helen deserved all she got Alice answered her friend. "Yes, but wasn't it just pure greed that drove her to steal your mother's jewellery and then pass it onto Hugo the way she did? Don't forget they were carrying on even when you were engaged to him."

Beth dipped her head and for a moment neither woman spoke. The silence was eased by the sound of Lizzie sucking gustily on her bottle.

Slightly embarrassed Alice regarded her friend. "Sorry, Beth, that was cruel of me."

Beth laughed out loud but to Alice it sounded hollow and forced. "That means nothing to me I wanted Hugo off my hands." She sat down next to Mary and leaned on her elbows causing the baby to stop drinking and turn her downy head in her direction.

"Come on, darlin," Mary coaxed gently wriggling the bottle in the child's mouth.

Alice's eyes were full of sympathy for her friend who suddenly looked troubled. "Is there something else on your mind, Beth?"

Beth lifted her head. "Sometimes I'm confused, Alice. Finn's asked me to leave the movement. Of course I refused, but it's causing tension between us. Then there's Aisling."

Alice fought against the multitude of emotions that threatened to be unearthed by the green-eyed monster often rearing its ugly head at the mention of Finn's name. "Where does Aisling come into it? Didn't he explain all that to you?"

A lone tear snaked its way down the side of Beth's face as she spoke. "I can't help doubting him."

Mary who'd been listening intently to the conversation blinked quickly. She looked down at the child in her arms who was now the picture of health, with rosy cheeks and chubby limbs. She could hold her tongue no longer. "You must have nothing to do with him, Miss Elizabeth!" Her face was clouded with anger and her fair curls bounced around her head as she spoke. "He's making you so unhappy, it ain't fair."

Many years in service made Mary feel she had spoken out of turn. Alice and Beth looked in surprise at Mary just as Lizzie, feeling the tension in the air, began to whimper. Against her natural instinct to apologise and bow out of the discussion Mary continued. "I mean it. Me and Lizzie here owe you everything and that Finn bloke is just no good for you."

Beth forced a watery smile. "Thank you, Mary. But you mustn't worry. I can handle Finn. And, Mary, you underestimate what you have achieved. Lizzie's health is down to your efforts, not mine."

Mary fixed Beth with her large brown eyes. "Yeah but,… we couldn't have done it without you. Don't you see? You took Lizzie and me off the streets. We was living in the gutter, Miss...Beth." She stared at Lizzie and stroked the baby's fair curls. "Every day it was a struggle. Since that terrible day...when the young master..."

Mary stifled a sob and Alice could see that Beth wanted to reach out to the young girl. The two women's eyes met across the small kitchen and Alice indicated to Beth to let Mary speak. She knew instinctively that the words being torn from Mary's body had to be told.

Mary lifted her head again and her eyes held a determined look. "You made me feel better," she said to Beth, struggling to find the right words to explain herself. "You helped me see I was worth something. No-one's ever believed in me before, Miss. You looked after us and I owe you everything."

"Oh, Mary. There's no need to upset yourself." Beth leaned forward and hugged Mary tightly. Then wiping away a tear she sat back and observed both women. "I know what I want and I won't let anyone tell me otherwise."Her eyes sparkled with enthusiasm as she spoke. "As women we all have a right to choice, whatever our social standing. If that choice is denied to us then we must fight." Beth held Alice's gaze. "When I met Alice I was weak." Alice held up her hand to stop Beth. "No, Alice, let me explain to Mary," she continued. "I was trapped with no way of escaping the unhappy, stifled future mapped out for me by my parents. Alice showed me how to believe in myself. That belief has carried me through the changes I've had to make in my life and helped make me feel stronger." Beth looked intently at Mary. "So you see, Mary, we as women can help each other to overcome the difficulties we face in life, no matter what our background we can always support each other."

Mary beamed at Beth emboldened by her words and feeling for the first time that maybe she could address her ex-mistress by her first name. "Beth, I know you are right. We are all the same underneath it all and we need each others help."

"That's right, Mary." Beth's eyes moved to Alice as she spoke who had turned from them and was placing the kettle on the hob.

Alice felt Beth's eyes boring into her back but she knew she needed a moment to compose herself. She inhaled deeply and attempted to still her shaking hands. Beth's words had brought a lump to her throat, causing her to recall the ups and downs of their relationship. She had loved Beth from the moment she set eyes on her that day in London. That love had been unrequited and was often so painful Alice wondered if she could possibly bear it a moment longer. Just as Alice felt she could no longer be with Beth without loving her as she so longed to do, Beth would show her another type of love. The love of true friends.

Beth was constantly there for Alice whenever she was needed with wise words or practical help. She never let Alice down. Despite Beth knowing that Alice desperately wanted to be her lover, Beth had never judged her. Their friendship had survived

Beth had made sure of this and Alice would be eternally grateful. One day she would tell Beth all this but not now, not today, while Mary was present. Her words would be for Beth's ears only.

"It's strange how one problem in life can lead to the solving of another." Beth observed as Alice turned back to the two women and began laying cups and saucers on the table.

Alice lifted one brow and regarded her friend, hoping she wasn't showing any of the emotion she was feeling. "Meaning?"

"Meaning that my relationship with my parents has improved a great deal since Hugo and Helen's misdeeds were discovered and dealt with. Somehow a truce has emerged out of it all."

Alice spooned tea leaves into the teapot trying to keep her expression neutral. She didn't think Beth would appreciate being reminded of Alice's advice on this subject. "Well, it's nice to hear some good news for once."

"Alice, I know you've told me to make it up with my parents before. But I was looking at it from a different perspective. They were so difficult and set in their ways that I had no way of communicating with them. They refused to listen to anything I had to say before I left home and could only see their own beliefs and views. Since the Hugo and Helen affair, I have come to realise that it's too late to make it up with my parents when they are no longer here. Also if there is any way possible

274

to do it, bridges should be built in families and any past grievances laid to rest." Beth smiled at Alice. "You were right as usual."

Alice felt the emotional turmoil begin to lift as a feeling of warmth replaced it. She was proud that Beth had listened to and appreciated her advice on the subject of her parents. She nodded her understanding at Beth's words just as the high pitched whistle of the kettle boiling penetrated the room.

"Well done, Beth. I'm glad you were able to see things from my point of view for once." Alice jested and the two women's laughter echoed across the small kitchen.

Mary re-appeared in the doorway having just put Lizzie to sleep in her pram, her skills from being a maid and at leaving the room un-noticed were well refined. "I will make the tea for you." She offered, seeing Alice's eyes go to the clock on the wall and wanting to appear useful.

"That's kind of you, Mary. I do have a mountain of work waiting." Alice pushed her chair beneath the table. "With next months event to plan and my backlog of needlework the pile of work is never ending."

"I'll help you catch up." Beth said and then glanced across at Mary where she was pouring boiling water into the teapot. "Did Lizzie stay asleep when you put her down?"

"No. She's wide awake, I need to take her for a walk in the fresh air."

"Could you buy me a newspaper while you're out?"

Mary nodded as Alice handed her some coins, "and this week's Suffragette News for me please?" Alice said.

Mary's face lit up as she placed the steaming teapot on the table. "Need any flyers put through doors?" She asked eagerly, anxious to be included in anything to do with the movement.

Alice went to the cupboard where she pulled out a pile of leaflets and handed them to the younger woman. "Good idea thanks so much, Mary."

After Mary had gone the other two women poured themselves tea and settled into a routine. Working alongside each other in the back parlour, their needlework was spread out on the table in front of them. Beth asked Alice what needed to be done for next month's meeting at the Albert Hall where it was planned to heckle Government Ministers.

"Mainly, we need to make people around the capital aware of what's happening that day. Mary's flyers will help."

"It's good that she's helping, we certainly need as much help as we can get. She's always so enthusiastic and persistently asks me what she can do for the cause." Beth placed a piece of material into the sewing machine. "I've told her though there's Lizzie to consider."

Alice sat back in her chair and wound a ringlet of fiery red hair around her fingers. "I've been thinking about that. What would you think if I asked Rose to look after Lizzie from time to time?"

Beth paused from her work and looked thoughtfully at Alice. "Well, Rose is constantly calling round interrupting us which is becoming a problem."

"I think she's holding us back. We cant' get on when she's visiting and quite frankly I don't know how to tell her to go home. She's lonely I suppose." Alice observed.

"I think it's a good idea. It would give her something to do and make her feel more useful maybe?"

So the problem of Rose's loneliness and Mary's desperation to help the movement was settled. Alice would ask Rose about helping out with Lizzie the next time she called round. Which they both knew wouldn't be long in coming.

Mary returned a short while later and laid the newspaper on the table. "That did the trick, Lizzie's sleeping now."

"Thank you, Mary." Alice said. "Now, Mary. Beth and I have been talking about asking Rose to look after Lizzie from time to time. What do you think?"

Mary looked puzzled. "Why would we want to do that?" she questioned, suddenly looking insecure and vulnerable.

"Oh, Mary. Not to take Lizzie away. No. Just occasionally, so that you could help us," she indicated towards Beth, "you know, with the movement as you have today with delivering the leaflets."

Excitement danced in Mary's eyes at Alice's words and she did a little jump into the air like the young girl she was. "Oh, Alice, Beth, that's made me so happy." She enthused then as Lizzie's loud wails filled the air she added. "Not that I don't love her or nothing. She's my little angel, she is." Mary's face was a picture of guilt.

Alice took Mary by the arms and looked into her brown eyes. "Don't be silly, Mary, we know you love her. It's just that we desperately need your help."

Mary's face broke into a broad smile which lit up her features. "My, that's just... I'm so happy. She repeated as she left the room to attend to her tiny daughter.

Alice and Beth exchanged a pleased look then turned back to their work with only the tick of the grandfather clock echoing around them. Glancing towards the window Beth saw a petite figure with fair hair walking up the garden path.

"Rose's here now." She declared to Alice just as a loud knock on the front door caused Lizzie's wails to once again fill the air.

Alice shrugged. "No time like the present." She said over her shoulder as she went to answer the door.

Chapter *Thirty*

HUGO'S DEMISE

An extremely tall, thin figure, that of the chief officer towered over Hugo as he stood in line on The SS Ghost. Looking him up and down with suspicion and noticing his drowned-rat appearance he said, "Name, sir?" He raised one eyebrow and lifted his pen while holding Hugo's gaze.

"It doesn't matter what my name is." Hugo growled, pushing his dripping hair back from his face and wondering how a man could get to be that skinny. Obviously the food was pretty bad on this vessel. "Wherever this ship is headed I intend to get on!" He put a hand into his pocket and pulled out a wad of money.

The officer's eyes narrowed. "We're sailing to Calcutta with a cargo of steel and stopping off in Spain for supplies, anyway what's your hurry?" He jabbed a bony finger into Hugo's chest and a smirk snaked itself across his angular face. "Someone after you is there?"

"Of course not, do you have a cabin or not?" A nerve twitched under Hugo's left eye as he shifted from one foot to the other.

"You're in luck. We have a spare cabin but it's a double so you'll have to pay the extra."

"Fine, just get on with it, man."

The officer shot Hugo a warning look and took the notes from his outstretched hand, then doing a quick count handed Hugo some of the money back. "There's too much here, sir."

"Keep it. What time do we sail?"

The officer quickly pocketed the money and handed Hugo a printed leaflet. "That's a list of onboard rules, make sure you stick to them, you're in cabin two. We sail within the next half an hour." He then turned away and began shouting orders to the crew nearby.

"Hey! Which way?"

Hugo's voice went unheard amongst the sudden rush of activity and he turned back to grab hold of the officer's sleeve, trying desperately to keep his footing under the swaying deck. "Where's my cabin?"

The officer turned towards him and gestured across the ship. "Down those steps, follow that man."

Hugo looked around to see a well-dressed man descending a stairwell and followed him until they came to a line of steel doors. The man disappeared through the first door and Hugo noticed that the door to the second cabin was ajar. Pushing it open and seeing it was empty he stepped over the bulkhead and into the cabin. Its cramped space held a bunk bed with a small table to one side of it and a wooden chair in the corner of the room. Hugo walked over to the porthole and looked out at the busy dock.

It wouldn't be for long he told himself, intending only to go as far as Spain. Putting down his heavy bag he sat wearily on the hard mattress of the bottom bunk. Deciding there and then to keep himself to himself until they arrived at the Spanish port, he told himself this would avoid having to make any tricky explanations about why he was on board.

Feeling desperately tired he wound the strap of his precious cargo around his wrist before laying his head on the pillow, lest someone should try to rob him while he slept. Soon, despite the lurching of the ship he was unable to keep his eyes open any longer. His last thought before he fell asleep was how lady luck had looked down upon him that day, in escaping the police who were surely after him now, and in avoiding sharing Helen's unfortunate fate.

Hugo yelped with pain as he fell out of his bunk with a loud thud jolting him out of a deep sleep. For a moment he struggled to remember where he was, then opening his eyes he attempted to focus in the darkness. A heavy weight was pressing on his chest. Realising it was his bounty self-preservation took over, so in order to breathe freely he quickly untied his bag and pushed it roughly onto the floor. Rubbing at the skin where the strap had left a deep red welt, Hugo attempted to bring the circulation back to his numb hand whilst at the same time lifting himself up to peer out of the porthole.

Sensing something was dreadfully amiss the blackness that met Hugo's eyes did nothing to reassure him. He found himself being flung back onto the bed as the floor lurched heavily from side to side beneath him.

The sound of the ship's siren tore through the air, its shrill sound piercing Hugo's eardrums as he hauled himself back onto his feet. Slinging the bag around his shoulders, he staggered towards the cabin door. Desperately trying to stop himself from losing his footing, Hugo flung open the cabin door to see the corridor full with people emerging blearily from their cabins. They were all making their way carefully along the dimly lit passage.

"What's going on?" He asked a man who had appeared beside him and was now struggling to stand upright.

"Don't know, but I think we should get up on the deck." The man disappeared back into his cabin for a moment, then reappeared holding a woman by the hand. "Come on, dear. We must go and see what's happening." He said to the woman. They were both clad in dressing gowns covering nightwear and the woman's eyes were wide with fear.

Hugo followed the others out of the doorway and onto the wooden deck where the wind tore at his breath. Within seconds he was soaked to the skin. Under the direction of a crew member, they all began to climb the steel stairs leading up onto the bridge deck. The ship was listing badly as giant waves lashed up against her sides and torrential rain battered her body.

From the bottom of the steps the climb had looked easy to Hugo. But suddenly it had become a marathon feat. Hugo was clinging on to railing as tightly as he could in a desperate bid to avoid being swept off the ship and swallowed beneath the hungry waves. Glancing down he could see his neighbour's wife weeping profusely and refusing to attempt the climb. He didn't care. It was of no consequence to him that she may perish as it was every man for himself. Helen's face flashed through his mind and he was grateful he hadn't been saddled with her on this nightmare journey.

The bridge deck was teeming with men all rushing around in the ferocious gale. In the middle of the chaos Hugo recognised the chief officer who'd let him on the ship just a few hours before. The man was attempting to direct people towards the lifeboats and organising everyone into an orderly queue, having to shout to make sure he could be heard above the noise of the roaring sea. Hugo put an arm across his face to shield himself from the driving rain and launched himself towards the queue. The ship was leaning heavily to one side and ahead members of the crew were lowering the lifeboats into position.

As Hugo waited along with the other passengers he grabbed hold of a crewman as he rushed past. "What's happened? Is the ship sinking?"

"Afraid so, mate." The sailor pointed towards the boats. "Get yourself into a lifeboat quickly." Then he was gone, swallowed up in the frenzy of activity.

"Attention, everyone!" The chief officer shouted into a foghorn. "Don't take any luggage onto the boats as we can't take any extra weight. Women on-board first."

"There are no women here!" Hugo shouted angrily, trying desperately to be one of the first to board. "Now let me on!" Suddenly he felt himself being pushed roughly backwards.

"Here!" Shouted one of the crew, pulling the wife of Hugo's neighbour forward where she'd just emerged from the ladder sobbing loudly and clinging to her husband's arm.

The officer took hold of the woman and hauled her onto the boat ignoring her pleas to stay with her husband. He turned back towards the men. "Are there any more women?" He persisted loudly.

A scuffle followed and they all looked around to see a young man pushing a female passenger towards the officer. She stepped forward meekly saying nothing as she climbed into the lifeboat her wide blue eyes fixed on her companions face.

At last it was Hugo's turn. As he began to climb into the boat one of the crew noticed his bag. "Ere you!" He hollered, pulling at his sleeve, "you can't take that on board!"

Hugo fell backwards, then pulling himself up he pushed his face into the man's. "I'm not getting on this boat without it!" He shouted angrily, holding on to the bag with both hands.

"You'll just 'ave to stay behind then won't ya..." The crewman shoved him to one side and helped the next person.

Hugo stood for a moment wondering what to do as the ship continued to sway uncontrollably beneath his feet. He knew the ship was going down quickly and it wouldn't be long before she was beneath the waves. Despite this, his greed would not allow him to leave his precious cargo behind. They were only telling him to leave it he thought, so that they could steal his treasures for themselves once he was in a lifeboat. He wasn't going to let that happen. Attempting to push his way towards a lifeboat he was immediately restrained by one of the men.

"I told yer, mate!" The crewman's face was inches from Hugo's, "no luggage on board the boats."

Hugo scowled at the man and let his hands fall to his sides, as the crewman turned away Hugo saw his chance. Launching himself forwards he lunged towards the small lifeboat just as an enormous wave hit, engulfing the vessel and causing it to swing precariously away from the side of the ship. Amid the screams of frightened passengers Hugo felt time stand still. Oxygen was wrenched from his lungs and he plummeted towards the angry sea.

As Hugo hit the freezing water he felt its force sucking him downwards to the ocean bed. Weighed down by his heavy load he at last realised, too late, he should've let go of the bag. His struggles were futile as he was enveloped by the waves. The strap of Hugo's bag had been wound around his back and shoulders so many times, there was little chance of it being unravelled. In a vain attempt to stop himself sinking, he emptied his pockets. It made no difference the load on his back was drowning him.

As consciousness left him, Hugo saw Helen swimming in the water alongside him her face full of accusation. "It serves you right, Hugo!" She said, her laughter ringing in his ears as she swam towards the surface. "Now you have your just deserts and they are nothing less than you deserve."

Chapter *Thirty One*

REJECTION

Finn fought desperately against the crowd who were pushing, shoving and screaming at the tops of their voices. He had walked for what seemed like hours around the red brick building, looking for Beth amongst the thousands of women. He'd at last sighted her in the distance. Finn had come to the meeting today, knowing Beth wouldn't have missed Lloyd George's speech. To the suffragettes this was another occasion to fight the establishment refusing to listen to their voice.

Now in the mayhem that surrounded him, Finn could see Beth hardly ten feet away, struggling with a police constable on the steps outside the Albert Hall. His overriding concern for Beth's safety surfaced as he launched himself at her attacker.

Finn's anger took control of his senses so that he became its slave. Blurring his vision fury drove him forward punching his fist into the police constable's face. Blood spurted from the man's nose covering Finn's grey working man's shirt in spots of scarlet colour.

"Finn!" Beth's voice rang out above the noise.

Finn wrestled with not one but two policeman who had hold of both his arms. Despite his muscular body, it was hard to move at all. All around him people were being pulled, pushed and led towards the waiting prison vans. Women were being as roughly handled as the men as they lashed out at those struggling to restrain them.

At the sound of his name being called Finn stopped struggling. The two men's fingers dug deep into the soft flesh of his arms. Beth stood facing him her face flushed and her blue eyes flashed with rage. Finn noticed her lilac dress was ripped down one sleeve revealing her bare flesh. 'What was the matter with her, hadn't he tried to save her from harm?'

"What do you think you're doing, it's not your fight?" She said struggling to be heard amid the turmoil that surrounded them.

"It is now, Miss," announced one of the uniformed officers who had blood streaming from his nose.

"Beth! Why are you so angry with me? I'm vexed for your safety so I am, worried that these here, dirty pigs..." Finn shook his head in the direction of one of his assailants, "should lay a hand on you," to his surprise Beth turned her back on him violently pushing those in conflict out of the way. He watched as she disappeared into the angry crowd. Staring after her with empty eyes Finn felt the fight leave his body, as he allowed the police officers to drag him roughly away towards the waiting 'Black Maria' along with countless others suffering the same fate

Dodging the demonstrators as she went, Beth walked slowly away from the fighting. Her anger at Finn was now turning to remorse. She realised she'd lost her temper at him knowing that all he was trying to do was protect her. Finn's confused face spun in her head leaving her feeling drained of energy and close to tears. Finding a quieter spot, she sat down and leaned on the wall for support. Her body felt limp as she put her head in her hands in an attempt to shut out the surrounding noise.

"Beth..? Are you hurt?" She felt a hand on her arm and looked up to see Alice.

Alice exhaled loudly and sat down beside Beth. Alice's dress was torn and her hat knocked off her head, leaving her hair a tangled mane of red curls.

"I thought for a moment you were injured and was worried." Concern for Beth clouded Alice's eyes as she spoke. "I lost sight of you as we filtered out of the hall. You obviously aren't hurt so what's wrong? Look… I know it was disappointing and sometimes I feel as if we're never going to win but that doesn't mean we'll give up the fight. Lloyd George is a stubborn man but we can be more so..."

"Alice. It's not that," Beth interrupted, "Finn was here." Beth touched Alice's arm. "Do you know you're gown is torn?"

Alice gave a wry smile at her friend's observation and pointed a finger towards Beth. "Well, Miss Hamilton-Green, you're not looking so lardy-dar yourself, my lady." Alice's fingers gently brushed Beth's revealed arm.

Looking down Beth noticed for the first time that not only did she look worse than Alice, but she also had a few cuts and bruises on her arms that were bleeding. For a moment they both laughed fixing each other's gaze with warmth.

Alice broke the eye contact for a moment and continued. "What's Finn done now?" Her obvious dislike of Beth's beau was making her voice sound harsher than she'd meant. Beth raised her head in defence of the man she loved. "He was trying to help me and ended up getting arrested himself. To make matters worse, in my anger I acted as if I couldn't care less."

Beth's tears poured down her cheeks and Alice's face softened. Although it pained her to say it she wanted to put things in perspective for Beth. "You know that he was only showing concern for you, don't you?"

"Yes. But I don't want him to watch over me or try to protect me. If he had his way I wouldn't have anything to do with the cause and..." Beth's voice was low with emotion. "I can't be tied up in chains again."

Alice stood up and held out her hands to help the other woman to her feet. "Let's go home now and think about Finn later I think we've both had enough for one day."

Beth nodded and let herself be led away from the crowds of women, who were now beginning to disperse, leaving the magnificent building in peace once again.

Chapter *Thirty Two*

CONFRONTATION

As Finn's lips came down onto hers Beth was lost in a world where their love was impenetrable. They were immune to the outside world and all its problems. This instant reaction on seeing each other could neither be stopped nor halted in any way. As all barriers tumbled down they clung together, their bodies moulded as one. After a time they pulled apart each taking a step backwards lest they fall into each other's arms again.

"Beth. How I've missed you." Finn's breath was short and his voice husky as he looked into her eyes, his arms were held firmly by his sides and his large frame filled the tiny hallway.

Beth reached up one hand and smoothed a flaxen curl away from his face which in their passionate embrace had come astray. "Oh, Finn," she said softly stepping into the front parlour. The warmth of the fire sent an orange glow across the room.

It had been many weeks since events at the Albert Hall and now at last, Finn was here in the cottage, looking tired but as handsome as ever. Beth's heart was racing and her lips stung from the force of his kiss. His presence filled her with hope that somehow this time, they could resolve their differences. She would explain everything today and Finn would understand, she was certain. Too many hours she'd spent agonising over whether she should've followed her heart and visited him while he served his time at 'His Majesties Pleasure.' In the end she'd decided against it because they needed to discuss their problems. For that they needed privacy.

Imagining life without Finn was unthinkable. She'd held back spending week after week waiting for news that he'd been released, hoping that he'd come back to her. Now here he was, waiting for her to speak. Beth couldn't look at him, but found herself staring out of the window at the dull mist that clung in silver threads to the meadow beyond.

"I'm sorry I lost my temper that day. I never meant to hurt you." Beth's voice was low and she felt the words tumbling from her mouth. This was a script she'd rehearsed many times over during the past weeks. But no answer came from Finn and she turned to face him.

"Beth, you know how much I love you." Finn took a step towards her.

Beth held up a hand to stop him aware that for the moment words needed to be spoken. "Yes I do, Finn. More than you realise and I love you too. But we have to talk about what's happening to us. Please sit down and listen."

Finn nodded slowly then sat down on the settee while she perched on a stool to the side of the fire. Tension filled the air as they looked at each other.

Beth had forced this distance between them lest she was tempted by her longing to taste his sweet lips again, or be enticed by the musky scent of his body back into his arms. She couldn't be weakened by her own desires lest she unconsciously let go of the ribbons that tied her to the suffragettes cause.

"I want to marry you, Beth." Finn's firm declaration echoed around the room bringing Beth back to her senses. His amber eyes were full of passion and his hands clasped tightly together.

"Surely, marriage is not the answer right now, don't you see?" Beth struggled to keep the frustration from her voice. Free from the nectar of his touch she continued, "I won't leave the movement, you have to understand that. If you still want to marry me then..."

"Of course I do. But I'm worried for your safety and confused as to why you were so angry with me that day." Finn leaned back on the sofa and ran a hand through his hair staring back at her intently. "I know I shouldn't have acted the way I did and I have paid a price for that, Beth. You could have got seriously hurt that day. Why can you not see that in loving you I can't bear to see you injured or, for the love of Mary, be killed fighting for this fruitless cause?"

Beth's hackles rose at the words 'fruitless cause' but she took a deep breath and tried to choose her words carefully. This conversation wasn't going as smoothly as she'd hoped. "I was angry because I didn't want you to interfere with what we were trying to achieve that day. I didn't mean to lose my temper and guilt has dogged me ever since. I do realise you were only trying to protect me." Beth's chin came up in defiance. "You have to realise, that I am perfectly capable of looking after myself."

Finn let out a long sigh then sat forward dropping his head into his hands and staying this way for a moment or two.

"Some men support their women in their quest for change." Beth ventured uneasily. "Could you not find it in your heart to at least try to understand why and what we're fighting for?"

"The cause is becoming too rough." Finn's head jolted up at Beth's words. "It's changing and is so much more risky. How could I cope with knowing you're in the middle of all that and I'm not there to help you?"

Finn's pained expression cut into Beth's heart. She knew there was truth in what he said and that the rallies and meetings were becoming more violent. It seemed the only way in which to make themselves heard.

"Is it because I'm not rich," Finn stood up and towered above her, his face flushed with anger, "is that the *real* reason you won't marry me?"

"What on earth do you mean? Money has nothing to do with this." Beth was thrown from her rehearsed speech this wasn't part of the scenario. She faltered, confused for a moment by Finn's question.

"Are you sure, Beth?" Finn moved to stand in front of the fireplace and she saw his vexed expression in the mirror above. "For sure, I can give you love and devotion, a man never loved a woman more than I love you. But I cannot give you riches as you could've had if you'd married Hugo." He turned and looked down at her and she saw the raw emotion reflected in his eyes. "Maybe, this has more to do with money than your precious fight for the vote. Perhaps you are only dallying with me, as James did with Mary making you as bad as him. Perhaps now you've finished pulling these Irish strings you are ready to let me go as I'm no further use to you."

For a moment Beth was speechless, her face had gone very red and she suddenly had the awful feeling she couldn't put this right. There was so much she wanted to tell him. She'd wanted to explain about the victory the suffragettes had at the rally on the day she'd found Mary. In her minds eye she saw Finn understanding at last and rejoicing with her that the determined Suffragette Mrs Symons, had entered the House of Commons, which had been the sole purpose of the demonstration.

Beth wanted him to understand that they were winning the fight, but only through hard work and solid action. Now she floundered for he seemed past understanding. How could he misread her and their situation so badly? His words made her sound shallow and greedy and to liken her to James and the way he behaved with Mary. Beth couldn't fathom out the words that would put things right between them. What on earth could she say that would make him believe she really loved him? In the end she could only tell the truth.

"I didn't love Hugo," she began. "It's always been you I love." She stood up and took hold of his arm. Finn flung it off and pushed roughly past her. "I threw away my chance of riches because it wasn't what I wanted," she continued at his retreating back feeling a need to finish explaining even though he wasn't listening. Before she knew what was happening Finn was gone. "Where are you going? Please come back," she pleaded to the empty room. Panic made her voice wobble and she began to run after him, how could it all have gone so disastrously wrong?

Finn stopped at the gate and momentarily glanced back at her standing in the doorway. "Miss Hamilton-Green, I love you and always will. But I won't be at the rallies and meetings anymore looking for you. And, you know where to find me if you change your mind." Backing through the gateway and bowing slightly he was gone.

Beth stood still for a moment wanting desperately to turn back the clock so that she could somehow explain things to Finn more clearly. Instead she lifted her head and smoothed down her dark hair. As she walked slowly towards the bench beneath the sycamore tree, she remembered how she'd read about this tree symbolising strength and endurance. The irony of it struck her as she stared forlornly at the empty landscape beyond, for right at this moment all the strength seemed to have been sapped from her body. A while later when the light began to fade, Beth lifted herself from the bench. Her eyes were moist with tears as she slowly shut the gate.

Chapter *Thirty Three*

NEW YEARS EVE

"The boy I love is up in the gallery."

Watching through glazed eyes from the gallery above, Finn listened as Marie Lloyd's husky voice and cockney accent rang out loud across the music hall. She danced across the stage with her lace umbrella in one hand and lifted her skirts with the other. Her hat wobbled on her head and she winked and gestured to the captivated audience as she sang her first ever hit song. Petite and fair haired she held her audience enthralled, as she whirled and twirled her way through the performance. Finishing the song she gave an elaborate bow to a standing ovation from a crowd who never tired of her enthusiastic act. "Happy New Year to You All!" she shouted before leaving the stage.

Finn pushed his way hurriedly through the crowds flocking from the theatre. The shock of the cold night air hit him and through a haze of alcohol he felt slightly dazed almost losing his footing in the throng of people. The pre music hall drinks in the 'Prince of Denmark' were as much as he could take in one night, not being a heavy drinker. His friends from earlier had somehow vanished and he found himself alone on the walk home. He'd been persuaded to go to the performance tonight this being the last night of the year. Despite his heart not being in it he'd tried desperately to enjoy himself. No doubt if he hadn't been separated from his friends, he would be downing more beer as they were very likely doing at this moment.

As Finn staggered along the pavement towards his lodgings, it wasn't the enigmatic Marie that filled his mind but his lost love Beth. Emerging from the shadows a figure joined Finn's stride and a hand clutched his arm.

"Lookin' for a good time, sir?" Surprised by her boldness Finn found himself looking into the eyes of a woman of the night. Her matted hair and gaunt face gave her a witch-like appearance. Even in his drunken state, Finn had cause to wonder what man would be desperate enough to take a poor creature like this. Pulling out of her grasp, he reached deep into a pocket and extracted a couple of coppers, throwing them in her direction. Gratitude lit up her face and she smiled revealing in her eagerness that she wasn't old but merely a young girl who'd fallen on misfortune. Glancing back as he strode past her, Finn saw her bend down to pick up the money from the pavement before lifting her head to shout her thanks.

The walk home seemed endless and it seemed to Finn that everyone was out enjoying themselves. His thoughts turned to Beth and the row they'd had only a few weeks before. He longed to see her again, regretting his harsh words, for he knew well enough that it wasn't lack of money making her refuse his proposal. There would be no point in seeing her though he told himself as the problems still remained between them. Until they were resolved they would only hurt each other again. This didn't stop him longing for Beth in the middle of the night.

He saw Beth in his dreams her beautiful wide blue eyes looking into his face as she lay naked beside him. Her skin was silky beneath his fingers as he explored her body. He would lie awake filled with regret that their relationship had ended before they had a chance to discover how much happiness they could bring each other. Left with a desperate yearning in the cold light of day, Finn could only find solace in his work.

Finn's work at the Thames Ironworks was hard allowing him to forget Beth for a few hours while he toiled away the day. He often worked late fooling himself he needed the money, but knowing he was really avoiding going home to his lodgings and Violet's eagle eye. Despite being downhearted Finn considered his position and tried to console himself with thoughts that he was lucky he'd managed to come out of prison to find he still had his job. They didn't want to lose a good worker they had told him, on his return and even sympathised saying, 'those bloody suffragettes' to a mute Finn, who wouldn't be drawn on the subject.

"Finn. Is that you?"

A feminine voice cut into Finn's thoughts and he half expected another prostitute to grab him by the arm. Instead as a woman stepped out in front of him, he was suddenly convinced that thinking of his lost love had conjured her up before his eyes.

"Beth!" He flung his arms around her and held her close. In the darkness he clung to his sweetheart repeating her name over and over again. Beth pulled apart from him abruptly holding him at arms length.

"Finn, it's me, Aisling," she said letting go of him and walking a few feet to a lamp post before turning back towards him. Finn blindly followed her and under the illumination of the lamp he attempted to focus on her face. The brown eyes that looked back at him were not Beth's. The curly hair and full bosom did indeed belong to Aisling, but in his befuddled state it was as if his mind refused to acknowledge the truth. Once again he uttered Beth's name. This seemed to catapult Aisling into action and she took hold of his arm and began to lead him towards Whitechapel High Street. "Let's get you home, my love," she said softly.

Aisling took the front door key from Finn, who seemed to be having trouble putting it in the lock and gently knocked.

Violet appeared in the doorway smiling broadly at her young friend. "Come in the two of you. Come out of the cold and share a drink with us tonight, to see in the New Year," she trilled, winking at Aisling as the two of them stepped into the hallway.

Instead of walking into the front parlour, where the clinking of glasses and the low murmur of voices echoed around the house, Aisling headed straight for the stairs. Taking hold of Finn's hand she led him towards the bedrooms.

As they disappeared from view Finn's landlady paused at the bottom of the stairs, straining to hear what was being said and just catching the words 'Beth, I've missed you so.' Violet went back into the front parlour to join her guests. Silently she congratulated the younger woman for listening to her advice.

Aisling was in heaven. Kissing her passionately as he used to do, Finn undid the buttons on her blouse. Her heart raced as she let go of all inhibitions. It didn't matter that he was saying Beth's name over and over again, it didn't matter that he thought he was with another woman. After tonight he would be hers again and they could go back to Ireland and get married.

Aisling knew that what she was doing was wrong, but she justified it by telling herself that Beth didn't want him anymore. Violet had told her so. She wanted Finn, more than anything in the world. That was the reason she'd stayed in Whitechapel all these months hoping to win him back, spending her days working in the hospital cleaning the wards, hoping and waiting for him to notice her again.

Aisling had ignored Patrick's pleas for her to go home. Knowing that all the time there was a chance for her and Finn she couldn't settle for second best. After Violet had told her Finn was going to the Majestic Music Hall on Grace's Alley, she'd gone looking for him even though she was risking her own safety by going out alone late at night.

"Oh, Beth, I love you so...much." Finn whispered in her ear as he pulled Aisling's clothes from her body in the darkened room. The street light shone through the bedroom window onto his handsome face and Aisling returned his words of love feeling his fingers tugging at her chemise. She pulled him towards the bed, making sure she didn't let go of him lest it should break the spell he was under. His passion was as she'd never known it before and she revelled in the marvel of this man she loved so dearly.

As they spread themselves across the bed in a frenzy of lovemaking, Aisling felt herself caught up in Finn's fervour as she was lifted to new heights. This was her fatal mistake. As he called Beth's name she could bear it no longer, in her passionate state she whispered to him to call her Aisling.

Finn heard her echoing across the dim room piercing the intensity and entering his conscience. Pulling himself away from her, he stood up. His hair was ruffled and his clothes were in disarray and he blinked furiously as Aisling waited for him to resume their lovemaking.

"Finn, come back to me, please," even as she spoke Aisling knew it was too late. The spell had been broken.

Finn was confused and stared searchingly around the room then glared accusingly at the wanton woman lying on his bed. "Aisling, what are you doing here?"

"You asked me up here. You insisted I came up to the bedroom." Aisling tried to pull her clothes around her now almost naked body and attempted to smooth her hair back into place.

Finn slumped down onto the side of the bed and buried his face in his hands.

Aisling quickly put on her chemise and stood up. She lit the oil lamp by the bed then waited for him to speak. When he remained motionless she began her lies once again. "Finn, do you not remember what happened? How you begged me to come home with you..."

Finn looked miserably up at her and shook his head. "I must have mistaken you for Beth." His voice was low and controlled as he glared at Aisling's state of undress. "But you aren't Beth are you?" Finn's face was contorted in pain and his words slurred as he clenched his fists menacingly.

Suddenly Aisling was frightened for Finn seemed to have recovered from his drunkenness and looked as if he might attack her. Refusing to answer him she concentrated on hurriedly putting on her blouse and skirt. Her hands shook and her heart raced as she could feel his rage sucking the oxygen from the air.

"Well! What have you to say, tricking me in that way?" Finn stood up and stepping towards her lifted he lifted his fist. Alcohol made him slow however and Aisling quickly dodged out of his way and headed towards the door.

With her hand on the door handle she couldn't resist torturing him one more time. "No, Finn, I'm not Beth. She doesn't want you anymore, remember?" With that she walked through the door slamming it hard behind her.

Finn made a low guttural sound, then picked up the oil lamp and threw it after her causing a loud crash as it smashed to smithereens on the wooden floor. Slumping back onto the bed Finn's eyes closed just as a flash of flames shot into life in the now spreading puddle of hot oil.

Chapter *Thirty Four*

ROSE'S JOY

"My life's changed so much. I can't imagine being without them now." Rose pulled Lizzie's arms out of the small pink coat to reveal a beautiful white lace dress underneath. She then laid the baby onto the settee covering her with a tartan blanket. Lizzie waved her arms in the air making a high pitched gurgling sound.

"Goodness she's so bonny, looks so like Mary with her blonde curls and big brown eyes and hasn't she grown?" Alice looked with interest at the way Rose handled the child, and marvelled at the change in Lizzie who'd not so long ago been nothing but skin and bone.

"Filled my house with love they have and Mary is like the daughter I never had." Rose's angular face broke into a smile. "I have you to thank for suggesting that I look after Lizzie for Mary. After that it seemed only natural that they should make their home with me. It certainly was the best thing I could have done."

"I'm glad it's worked out well." Alice stroked the baby's soft face as she spoke, remembering how things used to be for Rose. Asking her to look after the baby while Mary helped out with suffragette duties, had solved several problems in one go. It had also helped Beth with the problem of space in the cottage. Lizzie was now growing so fast the cottage had become too small to house all three of them.

The whistle of the kettle boiling interrupted the women's conversation and Alice went into the kitchen to make the tea. Rose followed her and sat down at the wooden table making sure the door was ajar so that she could still see the now slumbering baby. When the tea was made Alice reached up to get the cups and saucers out of the cupboard. "How is Mary's job at the grocery store going?" She asked, placing some 'nice' biscuits on a plate next to the steaming teapot.

"Mary's doing well working in the store two days a week and enjoys the company of the other women."

Alice nodded at Rose as she listened and pushed the plate of biscuits towards her before pouring the tea into cups. It was hard to believe the change in her mother's friend since Mary and Lizzie went to live with her. Rose's whole demeanour was different and her azure eyes sparkled with contentment. Gone was the pinched look of loneliness.

"How are things progressing in the movement? I haven't been to many meetings for a while." Rose glanced towards the sleeping child as she spoke.

"Mary asked me to tell you she will be along to help out for a few hours tomorrow."

"It's going well, thank you. Tell Mary that's fine whenever she can spare the time. My workload has doubled with the alterations to garments in the suffragette colours needed constantly." Alice picked up the weekly newspaper and handed it to Rose. "We get new members every week. Take the latest 'Votes for women' it will update you on the news up and down the country."

Rose reached across the table to take the newspaper when her eyes fell on another paper lying on a nearby chair. The headlines read: **SHIP SINKS AMID STORM - NO SURVIVORS.** "Oh my, Alice, that sounds awful. I haven't heard about this tragedy."

Alice picked up the paper and stared at the front page. "I know it's terrible and with so many people dead. Listen to this," she began to read aloud, "The 'SS Ghost' a cargo ship bound for Calcutta sank just a few hours into the voyage off the north sea, taking with it the crew of seventy five and twelve passengers."

Rose glanced towards the back parlour to check on Lizzie then turned back towards Alice.

"The ship was caught in a bad storm." Alice continued to read, "lifeboats were launched but were lost in the ferocious bad weather and by the time a nearby ship reached them there were no survivors."

"They all perished?" Rose could hardly believe that no-one had survived the sinking of the ship.

Alice nodded as she studied the picture of the doomed vessel. "Bad news indeed, those poor people," she said quietly, shuddering as she put down the newspaper.

For a moment both women were silent pondering on how it must have felt being on that ship as it went down. Then Alice sat down and began to sip at her tea, noticing that Rose had a strange look on her face and was staring at her intently.

"Changing the subject, Alice. How are you, anything happening in your life?" The corners of Rose's lips turned up into a half smile as she spoke.

"I'm well thank you. My usual self, you know nothing changes in this house, Rose."

"I don't think that's quite true is it? Something has shifted I can see that." Rose unclipped her hat from her head and shook out her fair curls.

Alice's face flushed. She felt under scrutiny from this woman who'd once been so close to her mother and who now over the past months had become her friend as well.

"Whatever it is certainly suits you. Your skin is glowing and you're looking radiant."

"Am I?" Alice was surprised that the happiness was so evident on her face and for a moment found it hard to find the right words. She smiled at Rose and let out a sigh. "You don't miss anything do you?"

Rose shook her head then waited for Alice to enlighten her.

"I've met someone." Alice stopped and looked at Rose seemingly unable to go on.

"She's wants to make a difference as I do..."

"What is it, Alice?" Rose leaned across the table and touched Alice's hand.

Alice's green eyes suddenly looked troubled and she fiddled with her red hair, pulling it this way and that. Her eyes were moist as she struggled to explain. "Her name is Connie and she's very different from Beth. I'm confused. I don't want to lead her on. I'm not sure if my feelings for Beth will ever go away." Alice's dilemma now clouded her face and caused a frown to appear across her forehead.

Rose nibbled at the corner of a biscuit. "What is she like, Alice?"

Alice looked thoughtful as she described her new love. "Connie is like a girl-woman, delicate and small. Looks like she needs protecting from the world. Although from what I've seen she is strong underneath her exterior. I've only met her once, but know already I have feelings for her."

Rose sat back in her chair and regarded Alice thoughtfully. "I think you know you'll always love Beth there's never any question of that. Even now the two of you have an incredible friendship, supporting each other in times of need. But any fool can see she's head over heels in love with that Irishman." Rose studied the blue sleeve of her dress as she spoke. "You deserve some happiness too, Alice. Don't deny yourself just because you think the way you love Beth will never be matched again. There are different kinds of love in this world and we all have to find what works best for us. You'll always have Beth's friendship, so you must settle for that and move on." She lifted her gaze to meet Alice's.

Alice's face flooded with relief. "Oh, Rose, you're so right. You know me so well." She leaned across the table and hugged Rose tightly.

Lizzie's whimpering penetrated the air. Rose got up and walked through to the parlour to check on her. Picking up the baby, she rocked her gently and began to sing a lullaby softly into the infant's hair. Lizzie quietened and Rose carried her back through to the kitchen and picked up her hat from the table.

"Being alone is never easy, Alice," she said, as she juggled holding Lizzie with replacing her hat onto her head. "All too soon love can be snatched away, so you must grab it with both hands. I have no regrets and if I had my time again, I would still have loved your mother with all my heart. Even though, she wasn't free to love me back."

Alice nodded at Rose. "I know." She said smiling, "thank you for understanding," she added getting up to clear away the cups and saucers.

Rose returned Alice's smile. "We need to be getting back now. Don't forget, one step at a time. If it leads to love then embrace it with outstretched arms and enjoy any happiness that comes your way. You will know soon enough if this 'girl-woman' is right for you."

Alice kissed Lizzie goodbye then saw Rose to the door. "I think I'm only just beginning to discover who I am," she said as they stood in the doorway. "I'm grateful to you for helping me find my way."

Rose blinked her long eyelashes then leant over to hug Alice. "I'll always be here for you never forget that. It's the least I can do for Megan."

Alice watched as Rose pushed the perambulator up the path and cooed at Lizzie, who kicked her legs in the air unravelling the carefully laid blanket from her small body. As Alice closed the front door she felt secure in the knowledge that, although she still missed her mother dreadfully, she would always have a friend in Rose.

Chapter *Thirty Five*

THE SAPPHIRE BROOCH

Beth awoke with a start and immediately became aware of perspiration running between her breasts. Blinking quickly in the half light her heart raced, remembering the intense passion of her dream. In the two months since their last meeting she'd often dreamed of Finn, longing for him to appear on her doorstep once again. Only pride stopped her from visiting him, knowing that she could never trade her love for the movement. If only Finn could understand her need to fight alongside countless other women in their quest for a better life.

The stillness in the cottage since Mary and Lizzie's departure, only accentuated Beth's loneliness. She was alarmed to find tears on her cheeks as she got up and pulled back the curtains. Gazing out at the overcast day and the meadow beyond, her thoughts returned to yesterday, when a brave suffragette called Muriel Matters sailed aloft in a cigar shaped balloon. The airship had crossed over London, Wormwood scrubs, Kensington, Westminster and

Tooting dropping thousands of flyers as it went. Beth, along with others, had followed the trail from the ground, cheering and encouraging Miss Matters on and therefore showing the government their resolve.

Beth's body felt heavy and her head throbbed with pain as she dressed. Making her way down the narrow stairs, a sudden sharp knock at the door sent her hopes soaring. But it wasn't Finn who waited on the doorstep. "James, what are you doing here?" Beth's tone of voice even to herself sounded cold as she opened the door and regarded her brother.

James was dressed in riding breeches with his curly dark hair standing in disarray around his head. She looked past him to see his favourite horse Saffron tethered to the gatepost.

"Well that's a nice welcome, Bunty, I must say. I was out for a ride and thought I'd see how you're doing old girl." Amusement danced in James's blue eyes as he studied Beth's dishevelled look. "Aren't you going to invite me in?"

Beth sighed and held the door open wider to allow him to step past her into the parlour. It was some time since she'd seen her sibling, this being only his second visit to the cottage in the past year. The first time he'd called round, Mary had answered the door with Lizzie in her arms and he didn't stay long, feigning another engagement to rush away to. "I was just about to have breakfast. So you can't stay long." Beth said walking through to the small kitchen.

"God you look awful, Sis. Is something the matter?" James followed her, staring at her back as she went about getting herself a slice of bread smeared with jam. When she didn't answer he tried again. "Are you alright, Bunty? You don't seem your normal self."

"James, what is it you want?" Beth swung round and scowled at him. "If its Mary you're looking for she's gone - moved away. And don't go searching for her, because I think you've done enough damage there, don't you?" James's face fell and for a moment Beth felt remorse at her outburst. But this was her selfish brother she was talking to and after all a leopard doesn't change its spots.

"I suppose I deserve that after the way I've behaved in the past." James shifted uneasily from one foot to the other. "I'm trying to make it up with you, Sis."

"What's brought on this change of heart?" Beth was suspicious of her brother's intentions. This wasn't the James she knew.

"I keep hearing about the Suffragette's injured at the rallies. Knowing how involved you are with them..."

"Oh, not you as well!" Beth's hands were on her hips and her brows knitted together. "I'm having enough trouble on that particular issue with Finn."

"Alright, Sis. Calm down, I'm concerned for you that's all." James looked hurt at Beth's outburst and took a step towards her.

Beth backed away suddenly feeling awkward. The years and their differences had put distance between them and she felt unable to reciprocate any affection he was about to show her. In an attempt to change the subject she enquired after their parents.

"Oh they're fine, except Mother is mourning the loss of her Sapphire brooch. Grandfather brought it back for he, I don't know if you remember, from a trip to India?"

Beth nodded. She was well aware that losing the brooch would be very upsetting to their mother for sentimental reasons more than value. "It's obviously long gone now. After the police informed us of Helen's confession that Hugo had been hiding the jewellery here, I've searched the place from top to bottom and found nothing." Beth sat down at the kitchen table.

James shook his head. "Then maybe you're right and it's long gone."

Beth looked thoughtful. "Perhaps we should have another look around but I think it will be fruitless. I've looked everywherc." She stood up, filled the kettle with water and placed it on the hob.

"Who's Finn?" James asked into the silence.

"Finn is the man I was going to marry," she said over her shoulder. Finding the tea caddy empty she went into the pantry to find a new packet.

James could hear Beth moving stuff around in the pantry and impatient for an answer got up and stood in the doorway. "What happened, Bunty? Why aren't you marrying this...Finn?"

Beth swivelled round and bumped into James standing behind her. "Blast!" She said pushing past him to get the kettle and turn off the hob. "We're out of tea-leaves." She sat down and let out a long sigh. Clutching at her stomach Beth felt the familiar knot twist her insides when she thought of Finn. "We can't agree." She began not wanting to tell James anything, "he wants me to leave the movement." She looked towards James who was now inside the pantry. "I would rather not talk about it. Look, James you need to go." Beth wanted James to leave so she could be alone with her thoughts. "Come out of there," she said testily.

"Beth, come in here. I want to show you something." James sounded excited.

Beth got up to find her brother reaching up towards the small outside window in the pantry. "What are you doing, James?"

"Can you get me a chair to stand on? There's a tile loose on this window sill."

Beth did as she was told and watched as James climbed onto the chair and slid the loose red tile out carefully and handed it to Beth. Swiftly he ran his fingers slowly over the brick sand and Beth saw him take hold of something.

"What is it? What have you found?" Beth felt a tiny sliver of excitement bubbling up inside her, surely there couldn't be anything hidden in there.

"Shhh, I don't know yet."

Beth strained her neck to see that James had hold of a piece of wire. He handed her a flat nail and pulled the wire out slightly from the gap between the bricks.

"The nail was holding this piece of wire in place hooking it around the brick, there's string attached to the wire and I can feel some weight on it." James explained. Beginning to pull the string slowly out from between the cavity in the bricks, they both held their breath as out came the end of the string. Tied onto it was a small cloth package. James got down from the chair and put it on the kitchen table. "I think we've found Mother's brooch," he said excitedly looking at Beth whose eyes were wide with surprise. "Do you want to do the honours, Sis?"

Beth closed her fingers around the cloth, undid the knot and out fell the brooch. Its sapphire stone shone in the half light of the kitchen. They both laughed out loud. Beth momentarily forgot her anger towards her brother and spontaneously hugged James patting him vigorously on the back. "Well done, clever brother! Who'd have thought we would find it there." James smiled as she held him away from her. For a moment his expression reminded Beth of bygone days when they were very young and spent the long summer days playing together. His blue eyes searched hers and she saw the need in them reaching out to her. "What's troubling you, James?" She asked quietly aware that something had been reconnected between for the first time in years.

"I know I have no right to ask, but how is Mary and the baby?" James pushed a lock of dark hair from his forehead as he nervously spoke. Sitting down at the table he leaned back in his chair and regarded his sibling.

Beth raised her eyebrows in surprise, she hadn't expected James to ask after the woman he'd so badly wronged. "They're doing fine now, but surely you've no interest in Mary?"

"No of course not, but knowing that she was living here with you... I felt so guilty that after she was dismissed from the house I had cared not a jot for her fate."

Beth sat down and stared at James for signs of amusement, for this change of attitude towards Mary went against his selfish nature. There seemed to be no signs of mirth or merriment in his face. "What on earth's caused this change of heart?"

As if he could read her thoughts James continued. "I'm not jesting with you, Beth." James studied his fingernails as he spoke. "I've been feeling bad about Mary, I shouldn't have taken advantage of her the way I did. Now that I'm in love myself and want to get married, I realise the error of my ways."

As James lifted his head Beth could see his face was full of sadness. Sympathy for her brother welled up inside. "What's the problem doesn't she want to marry you?"

"She wants to marry me very much, but she's not from a rich family. She's the daughter of the Head Gardener."

"You don't mean Ned's daughter, Grace?" James held her gaze and nodded sadly. Despite herself Beth couldn't help laughing. So, she was no longer the black sheep in the family. "Sorry," she said leaning across the table to lay a hand on James's arm, "of course our parents wouldn't approve. Do you truly love her?"

"Yes!" Suddenly James's eyes were full of fire and his face looked animated. "More than life itself, I can't live without her."

Beth sighed and picked up the piece of bread and jam she'd prepared earlier and began to take small bites. "Then, I'm pleased for you," she said between mouthfuls. "I'm sure that if you really love her then it will work out, whatever the odds."

"Beth, you don't understand. I told Mother and Father and they've threatened to cut me off without a penny if I continue to have anything to do with Grace. I'm not like you, I can't live without luxury." James looked around the small kitchen as he spoke.

"In that case she's better off without you." Beth was angry at what she saw as James's lack of courage to stand up to their parents'. "Look, James, it depends how much you want to marry her. If you really love her you would give up the money."

"I admire you for what you've done, Sis, really I do. Tell me...are you happy?"

Beth lifted up the brooch and began wrapping it in the cloth. "Yes I'm happy to be living my own life and the suffragette activities keep me busy." She concentrated on tying the string into a bow as she spoke thus avoiding her brother's gaze.

"What about you and this Finn chap?" James persisted. "Is there any chance for the two of you?"

"I need to forget Finn and move on." Beth bit down on her lower lip and looked at James. "We'll never be able to make it work. He's too stubborn."

James lifted his eyebrows at Beth's words but said nothing.

"Besides he already has another love. Her name is Aisling. She's an old flame from Ireland." Beth put down the brooch. She could feel her headache creeping painfully round her brow.

"I'm sorry, Bunty old girl. If that's the way of things, do you not think an understanding could be reached?" James seemed for once to genuinely want Beth to be happy.

"No, I will not compromise not after fighting so hard for my freedom!" Beth couldn't bear her brothers sympathy and she quickly got up, overturning her chair as she did so and disappeared into the front room.

James found her staring out of the window at the slow drizzle of rain that was soaking the patient horse as she waited for her master to return. "I'd best be going, Beth." He said quietly looking down at the cloth parcel in his hand. "Mother will be so pleased to have this back."

Beth's eyes were full of pain as she turned from the window. "Yes, give Mother my love and, James..." She took him in her arms for the second time that day and holding him away from her she looked into his handsome face. "Money is important of course, we all need it to survive. But love... love is a fragile, precious thing that no amount of money can buy."

Chapter *Thirty Six*

A VISIT TO VIOLET

"He's gone! Don't live here no-more." Mrs. Williams pale eyes were wide and her cheeks flushed as she scowled at the young lady standing on her doorstep.

Beth inhaled deeply and willed herself to stay calm knowing that returning the woman's anger would do nothing to help her find out Finn's whereabouts. "Would you be able to tell me where he's living then?" she said evenly, taking in Finn's former landlady's scarlet painted lips. Her white-blond hair was tightly wound into small curls about her head which, along with the vast amount of pink on her frilly apron, reminded Beth of an over pampered poodle.

"Don't know and don't care. That man's nothin but trouble!" the poodle retorted through narrowed lips as she looked Beth up and down rudely.

Beth shifted awkwardly in the doorway, wishing she were anywhere but standing in front of this rude woman, whose face seemed to be having a battle with itself to tell her what she wanted to know. She lifted her chin and stared back at Mrs Williams. After the past weeks of torment Beth knew she had to find Finn and say goodbye properly, only then could she perhaps move on with her life. Clearly she would have to change tactic with Mrs Williams.

Beth tried to sound concerned. "Have you had a fire, Mrs Williams?" Stepping backwards and looking up towards a charred and blackened window on the second floor, her observation seemed to incense the woman even further.

"Yes you could say that! I weren't best pleased neither, you wouldn't believe what happened, bloody Irish men with their fiery tempers and careless ways. The fire almost burnt the whole place down, it did!" Mrs Williams put her hands on her hips and glared back at Beth coldly.

Beth's eyes widened in disbelief at Mrs Williams words. "Surely...Finn wouldn't have..." feeling her knees begin to give way Beth leaned on the doorway for support. She couldn't believe what this woman was telling her. "Where is he? You're lying I know you are!" She accused loudly. Stilling her shaking body Beth straightened her spine and stared behind Mrs Williams, hoping to see Finn appear with laughter in those sparkling eyes and flaxen curls falling across his face.

At the sound of a raised voice, passers-by began stopping to see what the commotion was at Mrs Williams' lodging house. Beth watched as the other woman's face suddenly changed from that of a snarling dog to a grinning Cheshire cat. "Come in,

Miss Hamilton-Green. Don't stand on the doorstep," she trilled to a surprised Beth as she opened the door wider then led her into the house.

"First of all where's Finn?" Beth demanded of Mrs Williams once they were in the front parlour. Beth's heart was racing but she forced herself to face the other woman. "Also how do you know who I am? I don't remember introducing myself."

Mrs Williams folded her arms across her ample bosom. "Finn's long gone." She said stonily.

A ripple of alarm surged through Beth. "Gone...gone where?"

"As soon as the room is repaired I'll be letting it out again." Mrs Williams replied through pursed lips.

Beth sighed deeply. "You haven't answered my question, Mrs Williams" she said firmly. "Where is Finn?" Receiving only a blank look Beth was frustrated by Mrs Williams's evasiveness and was finding it hard to keep her temper. She leaned towards the other woman and raised her voice. "Just answer the question, please!" she demanded.

A slow smile spread across Mrs Williams painted face. "If you really wanna know..." she paused to inspect her nails as if debating whether their scarlet shade was the right colour. The look on her face told Beth this was of far more importance than answering Beth's question.

Beth drew in her breath and willed herself to be patient with this detestable woman who was obviously enjoying seeing her discomfort.

"Well, Miss Hamilton-Green, me lady." Mrs Williams did a mock bow to Beth her voice thick with sarcasm. "Course I knows who you are, many a bird comes chattering and I keeps me ears open, if you get me drift. And you might learn a bit more if you did the same and not have to ask the likes of me where yer man is." She lifted one brow slowly at Beth, "you lot are all the same, born with a silver spoon in your mouth but you ain't got a clue what's going on."

"Mrs Williams. If you don't tell me now what's happened to Finn I will go to the police." Beth watched Mrs Williams face drop, so there was something she was hiding. "I will tell them all I know," she added.

Alarm flitted across Mrs Williams face. "How do you know about the insurance claim?" She clamped a hand across her face realising too late that Beth was bluffing.

Beth carried on the pretence. "I know everything. As you say people talk, so you'd better start telling me where Finn is."

Mrs Williams face was as cold as steel. "Finn's with Aisling."

Beth felt as if she'd been hit in the stomach and tasted the bile as it rose in her throat. She fought desperately against revealing her inner turmoil to this spiteful woman. "Alright so he's alive and well then," she reinforced, keeping her voice level and trying to sound disinterested in his relationship with Aisling.

"The happy couple are to be married soon." Mrs Williams added, looking pleased with herself, "you'd do well to stay away, let 'em be happy together."

Beth's first instinct was to run as far away as possible from this house where Finn had lived. Away from this woman who was taking pleasure in breaking her heart by telling her that Finn, the man she loved and whom she thought loved her, was soon to be wed to another.

"Mrs Williams." She said pushing back her shoulders and addressing the other woman. "I have no romantic entanglement with Finn, we are merely friends," feeling her eyes burning with unshed tears she ploughed on, "you have at last told me what I needed to know so I will take my leave." Turning her back on Mrs Williams she headed quickly towards the hallway before a tidal wave of grief overwhelmed her.

"If you say so, Miss Stuck-up-Madam," Mrs Williams muttered under her breath as she followed Beth towards the front door, "you should've given him more attention." She shouted at Beth's retreating back, "instead of gallivanting around with them troublesome suffragette women. Maybe 'e wouldn't have been tempted by Aisling then!"

Beth stopped in her tracks and turned slowly around. Stepping back into the doorway she felt her distress turn to anger at the sheer cheek of the woman. At the expression on Beth's face Mrs Williams looked unsure and took a step back.

"What would someone like you..." Beth jabbed a finger at Mrs Williams, "with your cheap looks and over made-up face, know about fighting for justice?" Mrs Williams gasped and lifted a hand towards her rouged cheeks.

"Oh yes, and Finn told me about your tendency to poke your nose into other people's business. If you put a fraction of that energy into helping your fellow women..." Beth felt her voice begin to rise, and realising she was losing control of her tongue stopped herself before she started to sound and act like this vulgar woman.

Shooting Mrs Williams a look of contempt Beth swung around and with a swish of her skirts walked slowly and deliberately out of the door and down the footpath. Keeping her head held high she closed the gate behind her just as Mrs Williams violently slammed the front door. It wasn't until she turned the corner and was out of sight of the lodging house, that she allowed a trickle of hot tears to slide silently down her cheeks.

It took Violet a minute or two to recover from Beth's words, and she stood in the hallway leaned over the small table and peered at her reflection in the mirror.

The face that stared back at her was what she called 'well looked after.' She prided herself on never coming downstairs in the morning without her lipstick on, two layers of powder and one of rouge. After all, you never knew who'd walk through the door on that particular day. The lost love of Violet's life, the man who hadn't made it to the alter, might well return for her she thought nodding to herself.

Holding that glimmer of hope, that one day *he* would come back for her despite not having set eyes on him since the day before their wedding all those years ago, Violet practiced a slightly embarrassed and flirty look just in case. In a tiny corner of Violet, a part she could never reveal to a living soul, a voice spoke to her. The voice told her how all this time he'd regretted his dreadful mistake. She saw him crouching on bended knee saying it was all fine now he was back and he would never stray from her side again.

Letting this tiny spark of hope come to the surface, Violet could feel again the heartache of her loss, the humiliation of standing at the alter waiting in vain for him to arrive. Cupping her breasts in her hands and inspecting herself in the mirror she tried to squash the memory rearing its ugly head. In order for her to survive she had to stop dwelling on the way he'd treated her that fateful day. Of course she'd loved Albert she told herself, but he was a poor substitute for the exciting man she should've wed. "In truth," she addressed the glass, "during our marriage, Albert, you bored me rigid."

Rubbing her finger along the line of lipstick on her lips, which she had carefully applied earlier, Violet moved away from her reflection. Revenge was sweet. "If Aisling was denied Finn then why should that suffragette tart have him?" she asked herself. Now, Aisling like Violet would be marrying a man who was second best. Poor dear Aisling would soon be sailing back to Ireland without the man she cherished, after that disastrous attempt to trap Finn into marriage. Violet smiled to herself and allowed a smug feeling to creep through her body and take rein. She couldn't of course have guaranteed the plan was going to work, after all Aisling didn't have the body of experience that Violet had. She had done her best to advise a friend in need and that was that.

On hearing a couple of her lodgers chatting amicably, Violet brought herself upright as they walked up the garden path. Quickly she whipped her lipstick out of her apron pocket and swiftly dodged back to the mirror to reapply her beauty. With a sticky smile firmly in place she hurriedly opened the door.

Chapter *Thirty Seven*

REGRETS

"Men don't cry, son. That's reserved for the womenfolk, so it is." His father's words spoken while he was a lad rang in Finn's ears. Pressing his fingers against his eyes he exhaled loudly, but he could still feel hot tears squeezing onto his face. Thoughts of his father had plagued him daily the past few days, intermingling with the gaping hole of loneliness left by Beth. Pain clawed at his insides unabated. Silently now, he wept, these past six months had been hell without Beth and his life was empty.

Finn had woken up on the morning of his fourteenth birthday with dread heavy in his heart and sure enough the confrontation wasn't long in coming.

"Well, son," said his father at the breakfast table looking directly at Finn with eyes of steel, "you're a man now, sure you are. With that in mind it's time you joined us..." he indicated towards Finn's brother Shamus, "...on the fishing boats." Excitement had mixed with expectation in his father's heavy-set face as he spoke.

Finn knew his father saw it as Finn's duty to follow in his brother's footsteps and join the family business. But as young as Finn was, he had long ago decided his destiny lay elsewhere. Unlike Shamus, Finn had a restless nature with a yearning for adventure, he was determined not to be stuck in the small fishing village in which he had grown up.

Finn had never found the courage to tell his father how he felt as it was hard to find the right moment, especially in the light of his father's frequent and quick bouts of temper. Finn knew that moment had now arrived, but the words long rehearsed in his head, were stuck firmly in his dry parched throat.

"Well, son, cat got your tongue?" his father's resounding voice boomed across the small kitchen as Finn's stomach tightened.

Knowing it was now or never Finn lifted his head and looked from his mother's worried frown to Shamus's surprised glare. Inhaling deeply he said, "I'm sorry, Father, so I am...but I'm not doing it, I'm just not."

For a split second the atmosphere in the air was as heavy as lead then his father flew into such an intense rage that Finn feared for his life. As he lifted an arm to strike his son, his father's face turned a terrible shade of puce. Finn had squeezed his eyes tightly shut waiting for the strike to land and was holding his arms protectively over his face. That fatal blow never landed, instead his father let out an agonised cry and with a loud thud fell unconscious to the ground.

The stroke made Finn's father into one of the living dead. Unable to move at all down one side of his body, he could only sit in a chair and stare accusingly out of his grotesquely misshapen face. Finn could not bear the bitter twisted glint in his father's eyes and made the agonising decision to leave home. Creeping out in the dead of night he left Shamus to look after his mother and run the family business alone.

However, Finn was never to be rid of the guilt. It had followed him to Dublin where he made a new life and it had clung insistently to him ever since. Most of the time, he was able to bury it deep beneath the layers in his mind, only occasionally it would surface gripping him with its long finger of relentless blame.

Moving over to the window Finn looked down at the street children playing below. His thoughts turned to Aisling and her attempt on New Years Eve to trap him into marriage, encouraged he was sure by that old witch Violet. It had shocked and appalled him the way she'd lied and led him on. Finn realised now how desperate she must have been and couldn't believe his stupidity. He knew what the drink did to a man, having watched his own father turn from a mild tempered individual to a roaring bear with fire inside his belly. Poor Aisling, whom he had known all these years and who'd travelled alone across the seas to find him. What had he done? Drink had mixed with his mind, fuelled his temper and caused him to come close to striking her.

As soon as he set eyes on her ten years ago he had been overawed. She was a couple of years older than him, but a woman of the world. Struck by her shapely bosom, curly brown hair and vibrant smile Finn the young man had been drawn to her. He had hardly heard a note when Aisling began playing the guitar and singing, and was intrigued when she stood with the men afterwards sipping her drink. He'd gone to congratulate her on the way she played and after that they had become close. He was constantly aware that she wanted more from the relationship than he did, but Finn thought now he had never fully appreciated how devoted she was to him.

Finn had always held back knowing he wouldn't be staying in Dublin. Despite this, he was young, her lips tasted good and she was always there for him ready to listen or offer her womanly comforts. A gentle girl, she'd never demanded anything more from him than he could give and leaving had been relatively easy for him. Now, as his heart longed for Beth he realised Aisling had been telling him all along she'd been deeply in love with him.

Finn vowed after that disastrous evening with Aisling never to drink again and so far not a drop had passed his lips. He felt as if he were lower than the dirt under his feet.

Looking back he realised he'd been lucky to escape with his life that night, lying unconscious on the bed while flames licked around the room. One of Violet's burly dock workers must have dragged him out into the street, along with all his belongings depositing him on the pavement outside. He awoke the next day his body aching and sore from sleeping on the ground, bewildered at how he came to be there. Knocking on Violet's door had been a mistake.

"You set fire to the place that's what happened!" She screamed at him slamming the door in his face. Slowly things had come back to him. Aisling lying on the bed half naked, the white hot anger seizing control of his body, the lamp he threw as she escaped through the door. Then oblivion. Finding somewhere else to live had been hard. He'd lived on the streets for several nights until George, one of the bosses at the Thames Ironworks, took pity on him.

Irish like Finn, George had worked his way up by hard graft and dedication. Finn knew George must have noticed the state he was in every day at work and saw the sympathy reflected in the other man's eyes. "Is it a woman's doing?" He'd asked a tight lipped Finn. George had a lot of sympathy in that direction as he had only been married six months before his wife ran off with another man. He'd offered Finn one of his two spare rooms, since he lived alone now in the small terraced house. Finn had accepted, grateful to George for his hospitality. Finn had begun to work hard from early in the morning until late at night and would retreat to his room spending his evenings alone.

George tried to enquire about what had happened but Finn always clammed up not wanting to talk. Until the day Aisling visited him at work. The sight of her walking into the Ironworks certainly turned the men's heads as he'd heard rather than saw her arrival. The men were suddenly silent and a high pitched whistle rang through the air passed from worker to worker as she moved through the Ironworks towards Finn. He stopped what he was doing to find her standing to one side of him dressed in a vibrant red gown and matching hat. A scarlet feather hung at an angle across one eye. His attention was drawn to her protruding bust-line which accentuated her tiny waist. She surely was a sight for a man to behold but he was as usual, untouched by her striking appearance.

Finn straightened his back and for a moment the two surveyed each other. "Aisling, what are you doing here?" he couldn't keep the surprise out of his voice.

"I have come to say good-bye to you, Finn." Her bottom lip quivered as she spoke and her brown eyes looked sad. He was aware of others standing around watching them but George came to his rescue.

"Come with me, you two. See, you don't want to air your business in front of these busy bodies, no you don't back to work, all of you!" He swept his arm out indicating to those gawping at the lady. He then led Finn and Aisling away whilst the men let out a low disgruntled murmur and ambled back to work.

The sparsely furnished room smelt of tobacco and strong tea. It housed just a few wooden chairs around a square table. In the corner was a hob on which sat a well-used and blackened kettle. This was the place the men took their breaks, where comfort took the form of a rolled up cigarette and a cuppa, rejuvenating them for the hours left of their shift. Silence clung to the air. Now they were alone both appeared to be tongue tied.

"So, have you decided to return home?"

Aisling swung round to face him from where she'd been studying an old photograph on the wall, desperation was written across her face. "Yes, unless there's a chance...?" The scarlet feather fluttered in the air as she spoke.

"Not a hope, Aisling. The sooner you realise that the better for us both."

"I'm sorry. It was Violet who suggested I did that to you. If only I could turn back the clock." Aisling hung her head and began to sob.

Finn went to put his arms around her but stopped himself lest the gesture was misconstrued. He held his arms by his sides trying his best to explain. "It doesn't make any difference," he said as Aisling lifted her head. "Oh, of course I was shocked at what you attempted to do, to be sure. But you have to understand, I'm not in love with you anymore." His words fell softly into the air between them and the only sounds were the clanging of the ironworks in progress behind them. It would be so simple he thought. If only he could love this striking looking woman standing before him.

"I see." Aisling wiped her hand across her face and salvaged the last of her pride. "In that case I'll be going. I hope you find what you're looking for, Finn and wish you only happiness."

Finn took a step towards her. "Wait, Aisling..."

Hope darted briefly in her eyes and he instantly regretted his words. "Yes, Finn, what is it?"

"Nothing, just..." he looked awkwardly back at her. "Will you be alright? Are you going home to Patrick?" he asked.

"Yes. I am." A nerve flickered in Aisling's left cheek and the words seemed forced from her lips.

Finn nodded in acknowledgement. "Well then, I wish you both well, so I do. Patrick is a good man and will look after you."

Finn saw Aisling struggling with herself. Before he could pull himself away she had leaned towards him and planted her lips onto his. The kiss was brief and over in an instant. She righted herself and with a swish of her skirts was gone, walking at a fast pace into the yard and out of his life forever. A large part of him was relieved but a tiny section of his heart yearned for what might have been.

A loud knock interrupted his reverie and he looked up to see George standing in the open doorway. "You all right, son?" he said looking slightly ill at ease.

Finn blinked quickly suddenly feeling very tired. "Course I am, George."

"Well, my lad you don't look fine. But then I would look down in the mouth if a woman, the likes of that one..." George looked behind him and indicated at Aisling's retreating back, "walked out on me." George laughed at his own joke until seeing Finn's dark look changed the subject. "The blokes are on their way in for their tea," he said informing Finn of the obvious fact that it was tea break time.

Finn nodded. "That's fine, but right now I need some fresh air." He got up and walked quickly past George towards the yard.

Now, Finn moved away from the window. He could hear George calling him for supper. Tonight he didn't feel able to face one of his friend's unappetising meals despite the rumbling in his stomach. He pulled open the bedroom door and descended the stairs, then grabbing his coat he was out of the front door in an instant and heading for the nearest public house.

Chapter *Thirty Eight*

AISLING'S RETURN

Feeling her stomach lurch Aisling clasped a hand over her mouth and tried not to retch as she made her way slowly up The Mauretania's wooden steps. An observer would have seen this attractive full figured young woman with curly brown hair sway, as she tried not to lose her footing. People may have assumed she was feeling seasick already. For Aisling the sickness had little to do with the sea. On her inward journey all those months ago, it was only excitement she felt at seeing her beloved Finn once again.

Now, she was leaving Finn behind, returning to Ireland and the faithful Patrick, who'd waited patiently for her to return. "What a fool I've been," she thought as she reached the deck.

Other passengers jostled around her full of excited chatter as they too boarded the ship. Aisling hardly noticed the beautiful vessel despite hearing Patrick's words in her head. Once he'd learnt of her plans to return home to him Patrick had boasted in his eagerly written letter to her. "Aisling my love, The Mauretania was built only two years ago just three months after her sister ship, 'The Lusitania.' The two ships were built by Cunard and, Aisling, they are said to be the 'fastest and most luxurious on the Atlantic run. In no time at all you will be back home with me where you belong."

If only Patrick knew how much she dreaded going home knowing that the journey would be even faster only made her feel worse. Her heart was broken and no amount of luxury would make up for that.

Aisling stood on the deck amongst the crowd who were waving frantically to people gathered on the quayside. Next to her a young girl clutched at her mother's skirts and cried. "Daddy! Daddy!" Her mother gathered her up in her arms murmuring words of comfort, "You will see Daddy soon darling," she soothed. The woman, who was slight in build and loaded down with bags, noticed Aisling watching them. Taking her expression as a look of concern she explained. "She's upset, my husband is to follow us to New York as soon as he is able, but she is too little to understand."

Aisling nodded and went to move away reluctant to get embroiled in the woman's problems. Patrick's letter replayed in her head. "Aisling, when you are home we will start a family and..." to her horror she felt her eyes fill with tears and against her will, her body shook with uncontrollable sobs.

All at once the woman had moved to her side. "Oh, my dear, have you left someone behind as well?" Her eyes were full of sympathy as she put down the child and reached out a hand to Aisling.

Aisling shook her head, wiped her face with a handkerchief, then after a moment took a deep breath and lifted her head. "No, I'll be fine, really. Thank you." Somehow she didn't want this stranger to know of her humiliation. Turning away she pushed her way through the crowd, looking for somewhere to sit.

In the darkness the moon shone a shaft of light onto the waves below as they moved slowly beneath the ship. It was a beautiful evening and Aisling watched the occasional couple wandering past her on the almost empty promenade deck. Despite the lateness of the hour she sat on the wooden seat looking out to sea, reluctant to retire to her cabin where she would find the loneliness too much to bear. Out here on the deck she found that the gentle waves calmed her soul and her thoughts could more easily be borne.

"Would she have done anything differently?" She asked herself. Immediately the answer was a resounding "No." Devoted to Finn she would have tried anything, travelled anywhere, if there'd been a chance for their love. But in the end she had to admit defeat. On the train journey to Liverpool that morning she'd had time to think about her life and Finn. She realised now that he'd never really made a commitment to her even in Ireland. "How could I have got it so wrong?" She wondered. "Love is blind." Finn was a wonderful man, but he didn't adore her the way he did Beth. Part of her, although stinging from the realisation that she had really and truly lost him, hoped that one day Beth would return his love.

It had been wrong of her to let Finn carry on thinking she was Beth after he mistook her for the other woman on New Year's Eve. But Aisling couldn't resist it knowing that if they'd made love and she'd become 'with child' Finn would have married her. She knew now it had been a terrible mistake for what sort of marriage would that have been? Seeing Finn's temper that evening, how out of control he was, had frightened her. What kind of woman must this 'Beth' be? Didn't she realise that Finn loved her more than life itself? How could she have let him go? It just didn't make sense to Aisling that a woman could throw away such devotion in order to put all her energies into fighting for women's rights.

Wrapping her shawl around her shoulders Aisling thought about the day after her fight with Finn. Having heard the fire engine the night before, she'd gone to see Violet, never dreaming that it was her friend's house on fire. Violet told her how Finn had thrown an oil lamp at the door after she'd left and how he'd been dragged from his room, he was so drunk. Aisling felt guilty and partly responsible, but Violet hadn't agreed with this telling Aisling she was best off without him and that she'd thrown him out. Luckily she and the other guests had become aware of the fire before it got out of hand. Aisling shuddered as she thought about what Violet had told her. After going upstairs to investigate they had found flames licking around the room and Finn unconscious on the bed.

Aisling gasped as she pictured the scene in her head. Violet had said she had to shout to the other guests and get someone to go and alert the fire brigade. Tears welled in Aisling's eyes as she thought about the way that Violet had described Finn being hauled out onto the streets and told never to darken Violet's door again. It seemed that by the time the fire brigade had turned up, the fire was almost out thanks to Violet's lodgers. Triumphantly Violet had recounted to Aisling how Finn was left lying on the pavement outside, his belongings all around him, to sober on the pavement. "Yes," Aisling corrected herself, "Yes I would change that. Finn hadn't deserved that treatment. He hadn't deliberately scorned her and chosen Beth."

Violet seemed to have forgotten that it was her suggestion that Aisling try to trap Finn into marriage. In some ways relieved, she was glad that she had made one final visit to Finn at The Thames Ironworks. Putting her hand down and gently smoothing her skirt and soothing her aching heart Aisling smiled at her clothes. Her finest dress, the one she'd worn that day to tell Finn she wouldn't go back to Ireland if there was the tiniest chance he could still love her. He'd barely noticed how she looked and at last she'd realised his heart lay elsewhere.

Dear Patrick had never wavered in his loyalty. So proud of her he'd bought Aisling a ticket on The Mauretania to bring her home. "Nothing but the best for you, my love." he'd said, "nothing but the best."

Aisling got up from the bench and stretched. She walked to the side of the ship and leaned over looking into the black waves below.

"Miss? Miss!" A man's concerned voice pierced the night air and she turned to see one of the crew standing behind her. "Miss, it's late, almost midnight. Are you feeling unwell?"

"No, I'm fine thank you." Aisling attempted a smile to alleviate the man's anxiety. Shivering she pulled her shawl closer around her shoulders again as she walked slowly past the crewman, biding him goodnight as she went. Disappearing through the companionway she made her way down the stairway towards her cabin relieved that the rough cargo ship of her inward journey was a ship of the past.

Chapter *Thirty Nine*

DISASTER

"Well, Finn." George faced Finn across the dinner table watching him push his food listlessly around the plate. "You've lived under this roof for six months see and I still don't know what's troubling you." George didn't like to pry it wasn't his way. But today Finn looked worse than ever, the black circles under his eyes were more pronounced and his skin had a greenish tinge. Also George had begun to notice lately how Finn's clothing hung from his body. This wasn't surprising as he hardly ate a morsel and every night came home in a drunken stupor. Somehow, he didn't know how George had to try to help him.

Finn lifted his head and dropped his knife and fork with a clatter glaring back at George. "Fecking shut up, George!" he shouted his eyes full of fire.

George was aware that in the past if Finn held that guarded look in his eyes there was no getting through to him, but perhaps persistence was all it needed he told himself. "Don't talk to me like that...for God's sake man, look at yerself!" Leaping up George grabbed the small mirror hanging on the wall above the sink then shoved it roughly into Finn's face.

Finn stood up abruptly, took hold of the mirror and threw it violently across the room. The sound of the glass smashing against the wooden floor echoed across the kitchen. The two men faced each other. Defiance danced in Finn's eyes but then was quickly replaced by defeat as he sank into his chair and rested his head in his hands.

George sighed, looked sadly down at Finn and then walked across the room to begin clearing up the shattered glass. His next words to Finn were to provide the catalyst that was so sorely needed. "I know..." he murmured slowly, "what it feels like to lose the woman you love." George didn't really know if Finn's troubles were to do with a woman, but the image in his head of the shapely woman visiting Finn at work a few weeks ago sprang to his mind.

"I know, George. I'm sorry about the mirror." Finn sat up and looked across at George where he was crouched on the floor sweeping the glass into a dustpan. "I understand you were only trying to help." Finn's hair stood up in clumps around his face and his eyes were bloodshot and moist.

George turned back to Finn and the muscles in his face tightened. "It doesn't matter about the fecking mirror," he said angrily, "who was that woman... the one who visited you at work a few months back?"

Finn lifted a brow and said simply. "It's not about her, George. You don't understand, so you don't."

"Course I don't understand, because you haven't told me. Now I'm not one to interfere in other people's business but...you look like death most of the time. If only you could see what you're doing to yourself, Finn."

Finn sighed, suddenly feeling guilty for the way he treated George. "I'm sorry so I am." He looked intently back at George with anguished eyes. "I feel mixed up at the moment, but I'm grateful for your generosity. God knows where I would have ended up if you hadn't let me rent the room."

"No trouble, no trouble at all. If the truth be told I like the company. Although I know my cooking's not up to scratch most of the time." George gave Finn a wry smile then sat back down at the table.

"It keeps body and soul together and isn't all bad," lied Finn. For a moment there was silence and George thought that as usual that would be that and he would be none the wiser about why Finn was torturing himself.

Finn laid his hands on the table and stared solemnly down at them. "Her name's Beth and the woman you saw at work was an old flame."

George held his breath feeling the room fill with tension as he waited for Finn to go on. When the silence became unbearable he leaned towards the other man. "You don't have to tell me, Finn. I just thought it might help."

Finn lifted his head and said in a determined voice. "No, let me. I need to get this out. Maybe then I can move on."

George folded his arms across his chest and nodded in acknowledgement.

Finn began telling George at first falteringly, his and Beth's story, outlining her background and how he came to meet her. He described their last meeting and his voice trailed away and he stared sightlessly towards the window. When he'd finished talking he looked at George and saw him staring at him in dismay.

"You mean you walked away from a woman like that purely because she was a suffragette? That's why your so fecking unhappy?"

Finn gazed back at George clearly surprised at his reaction. "What do you mean, man? What would you have done then?"

George placed his elbows on the table and sighed at Finn. "I would have snapped her up, that's what I would have done," he said giving Finn a quizzical look. "She sounds quite a woman. Leaving behind her family's money and all, not like my Doris see. No, Doris was out for all she could get from a man leaving me as soon as she found someone else with more of this." He rubbed his fingers together as he spoke. "Sure, anyone can see that this suffragette business won't last forever not the way they're going, they will get their way and then it'll all be over. And, why shouldn't they? That's what I say." George could see that his words had made Finn feel uneasy as he watched his friend push his hair back from his face and regard him thoughtfully.

"Maybe, you're right, George," said Finn looking totally unconvinced. "But I can't see myself marrying someone who spends all her time getting into scuffles and fights with the police. No I can't."

"Isn't the real truth that her refusal to do as you say makes you unhappy?" George argued.

"Course not." Finn pushed his shoulders back and lifted his head as something akin to indecision flickered across his features.

"To be sure, there's a demonstration going on right now this evening. Did you know?" When Finn didn't answer George added, "outside the House of Commons. It started at Caxton Hall this afternoon. Hardly a square inch could be found between the bodies there were so many people there."

Finn looked taken aback at George's words. "It sounds as if you were there, George."

"That's because I was, Finn." George now had Finn's full attention and began to describe all he'd witnessed that afternoon. "We all followed Mrs Pankhurst and seven of her women as they marched towards the House of Commons. They were escorted by police officers. The new fife and drum band was playing martial music and were an impressive sight I tell you, with their purple uniforms and green sashes." George's eyes sparkled as he recalled every detail.

Finn just stared at George unable to believe his ears. George was now in full flow and lost in his story telling.

"There was an Inspector, stout and red faced, waiting patiently at the door of the Commons for the women's' arrival. I was at the front of the crowd and I saw him pull himself up to his maximum height as they strode towards him, he had an envelope in his hand. Everyone watched as Mrs Pankhurst took the envelope from him taking a moment to look at the contents. She then made an elaborate show of opening it and holding it up to her followers. 'It's a letter from Asquith's private secretary saying that the Prime Minister will not receive the deputation. I will not accept this,' she said, 'we are subjects of the King and have come in the assertion of a right!'"

"I felt the crowd around me grow angry and a murmur passed through the mob. They all began to move forwards towards the police officers who surrounded their leader and the tension in the air was frightening. Mrs Pankhurst turned to Inspector Jarvis and slapped him in the face three times, he took no notice. She then hit him again, at least twice. I could see it was much stronger this time. Another of her ladies knocked off his hat and it was then that the arrests began."

"Men and women started pushing and pulling their way towards St. Stephen's entrance, shouting at the top of their voices," continued George. "The noise was deafening." George took a deep breath. His face had gone quite red while telling his story and he lifted his gaze to meet Finn's intense stare. "I decided to leave, I had a feeling things were going to turn ugly. But I take my hat off to those women they are very brave."

Finn's voice was thick with emotion as he stood up. "I can't believe it, George. I had no idea...that you..." he said jabbing a finger towards George.

"No idea what?" George didn't like Finn's accusing tone." That I was supporting these women? I can't say that's how it happened, son." George got up and turned towards the sink. "I've just heard so much about the suffragettes I thought I'd see for myself what it's all about." As he began the washing up George felt Finn's movements behind him. "Where are you going, Finn?" He said watching Finn rush away. But Finn ignored him and George's answer was the loud slam of the door.

It was nearing eight thirty and beginning towards dusk when Finn arrived at the scene. Wondering how in this disarray he could possibly find Beth, he stood for a moment at the back of the crowd staring at the angry faces. George's words were ringing in his ears, he couldn't wait until the next day to tell her how much he regretted their parting and how he

354

missed her. It seemed so fruitless now for them to have been apart for six whole months. Beth's spirit was one of the things he loved about her and he'd tried to crush it, he'd been such a fool and only hoped he wasn't too late.

Guessing that she would be at the front of the crowd Finn launched into the mob pushing his way towards St. Stephens's entrance. All of a sudden he found himself surrounded by women who were acting like savages, their faces contorted in rage and their arms flailing in the air. Trying to ignore the raw anger that emanated from those around him, Finn kept pushing until he was almost at the front of the crowd. Here his sympathy was instantly aroused at the sight of several police constables being violently assaulted by women. He could hardly believe the fairer sex could be capable of such aggression. He watched one constable grappling with two women at once, minus his hat, which must have been knocked off in the scuffle. Another was being attacked by a suffragette who seemed to have lost all reason and was kicking him hard repeatedly in the shins. Finn winced as he watched, then continued to thrust himself forward as hard as he could, having no idea what he would do when he got there.

In the midst of the chaos a small cluster of protestors with banners were being shoved roughly back into the crowd. Finn noticed their flags going down as they lost their footing. His fear that there would be many injuries at this demonstration forced him to focus on finding Beth and he stared in all directions for a sighting of her. At this moment he noticed a small group of women breaking away from the main mob and stretching his neck above the heads he at last caught a glimpse of Beth's retreating back. For a second he stopped pushing, then deviated off to the side and began to follow them, sliding sideways through the bodies until he found himself at the edge of the melee. As he pursued the women, keeping his eyes focused on Beth in the distance, he realised he wasn't alone and that many of those around him had also noticed the action. They too were heading in the same direction.

Once again he found himself in a crush of bodies hardly able to move. Finn watched as the dozen or so women he'd been following stopped outside several Parliament office windows. Now, completely hemmed in, he found to his alarm that he had lost sight of Beth. The light was now fading and his eyes darted this way and that trying desperately to locate her. Finally he spotted her at the front of the gang with her back to him. He watched helplessly as they all began to take small packages out of their pockets, wrapped in brown paper and tied up with string. They began hurling them at the glass. Everyone watched and cheered the women's actions as shouts went up that the police were coming, and quite suddenly the atmosphere changed. A mob of uniforms were running towards them.

Full of panic for Beth's safety, Finn shouted her name at the top of his voice. He was sure she couldn't have heard above the noise, but she stopped and turned to stare at the faces behind her. It was at that moment while she was distracted that the woman in front of her threw a stone with considerable force. Finn watched powerless as it reached its target. Then almost as if time had slowed, it bounced back and hit Beth square on the temple. Riveted to the spot Finn watched as she fell headlong into the crowd, just as the police reached the protesters. No-one seemed to notice her plight in the chaos that followed.

Using frustration to generate all his strength Finn catapulted himself towards Beth. Finding that he was in the middle of the fighting he desperately searched for Beth aware that every second counted. The falling darkness made finding her more difficult and he tried not to imagine her being trampled underfoot. As he searched frantically in the area where she had fallen, he could feel the hysteria rising in his throat and had to force himself to stay calm.

Finally Finn came upon Beth lying on the ground unconscious and bleeding. He pushed those nearby roughly out of his way and bent towards her still body, his heart thudding against his chest. 'Please don't let her be dead, he prayed.' With trembling hands he moved her hair gently back from her blood soaked face. "I've only just found you again, my love," Finn whispered into her ear while the world whirled on around him, "don't leave me now..." he cajoled lifting her head gently. Letting out a sigh of relief he found she was still breathing. His eyes roamed her body for signs of injury and it was for the first time he noticed her leg. It lay twisted completely in the wrong direction at an odd angle and he was afraid to move her in case he did more damage.

"Stop!" Finn stood up and shouted into the angry mob then grabbed the sleeve of a nearby policeman, who was battling to hold onto a woman he was trying to arrest. Finn met his eye, then looked down at Beth and finally someone realised there'd been a crisis of a different kind in their midst. One of the suffragettes paused in her fighting and Finn found Alice was standing beside him. Her mane of red hair was in disarray about her head, her face anxious. "Finn, what's happened?" She bent down beside the policeman to look at Beth then shocked she stood up quickly. "We must get help she's badly hurt."

"I know. I saw her knocked down!" Finn's breathing was laboured and short and his fists were clenched by his sides. He looked at this woman who surely must take some blame for his stricken Beth lying prostrate at his feet.

Alice had no time to acknowledge the accusation in his eyes. Concern for Beth superseded everything else. "We need an ambulance!" she screamed at the police constable.

"It's on the way, Miss." said the officer standing up and waving his arms at the vehicle in the distance that was trying to manoeuvre its way, in the half-darkness through the dense crowd. "That's if it can get through this mob."

"It will, we'll make sure. Finn, help me to move these people back!" Alice shouted above the noise of the melee.

Numbed by shock Finn watched as Alice took control. Others began to assist and slowly they were able to push their way through the crowd, briefly explaining what had happened to Beth. The police constable was informing the masses that the ambulance, which had been on standby outside St. Stephens's entrance since late that afternoon, needed a pathway to get to through.

Soon the way had been cleared and the ambulance was standing in front of them with its doors wide open. Alice and Finn stood back as Beth was carefully lifted onto the stretcher. Alice leapt into the back of the ambulance. As Finn went to follow her the medic put a hand on his arm, "sorry, Mister only space for one," he said pushing him away and anticipating trouble from this burly young man. Cursing, Finn took a step backwards watching angrily as the vehicle drove away its glaring headlights lighting up the now muted mob. He then turned away and disappeared like lightening back the way he'd come.

Chapter *Forty*

GRACE & NED

Ned slowly stretched his back his face was etched in agony as he stood up and looked across at Grace. "It were a terrible thing." He said his voice was low and filled with emotion. "I won't ever forget the look on the mistress's face." As he spoke Ned's eyes glistened with tears that he quickly wiped away with the back of a grimy hand. He ambled over to the bench and pulling his old straw hat down over his face to protect against the warm rays of the sun; Ned sat down next to his daughter, under the shade of the tree.

Grace ran a hand through her long brown hair and sat back on the bench. "I heard there was an accident. Do you know what happened?"

Ned didn't answer but stared into the middle distance as if she hadn't spoken and thought he could never feel as heartbroken as the day his darling Kitty died. Since hearing of Beth's accident those same intense feelings had returned to haunt him.

Despite the class divide Beth was like a second daughter to him. She had been the only one of the family to try to help him when he lost his wife. When the rest of the family only made sympathetic noises, it was Beth who visited Ned and Grace at the cottage. She offered her condolences in person, not by messenger or wordless gestures. At the time Ned had hardly been able to look at ten year old Grace's face. He shuddered as he reminisced how much like her mother Grace was, and as he sat beside her now he saw how that similarity remained.

Beth had spoken to Grace about Kitty's death helping the young girl to come to terms with it, and when Ned had fallen behind with the gardening, Beth went to her family and pleaded with them to give him time. He'd tried to thank her but she wouldn't have it saying it was her duty as the mistress's daughter. But Ned knew that no such duty existed. He knew that by finding the most sensitive and empowering words, Beth had saved his life by telling him how Kitty would have wanted him to carry on without her. "She would have been proud of you, Ned, for caring for Grace and carrying on with your work." Ned had nodded at her and then she'd said something that had helped him through some of his darkest days. "One day, Ned, you and Kitty will meet again." So for Grace and because of Beth he had lifted his head and faced the world again.

"Da? You look so tired today. Da, can you hear me?" Grace's hazel eyes looked troubled as she studied her father. "Tell me about Beth." She said gently placing a hand on Ned's arm.

Ned refocused on his daughter and shook himself mentally. He'd been thinking about Beth constantly since hearing the bad news. "Oh, Grace. Poor, Beth." Ned stared back at Grace his face filled with anxiety. Last night he'd dreamt Beth was dead.

Grace was shocked at finding her father looking so distraught and watched him remove his straw hat and begin picking at a loose thread as if his life depended on it. "It's all right, Da. Start at the beginning. How do you know about the accident?"

Ned lifted his rheumy eyes to look at Grace. "Me heart was in my mouth when I see them clappers arrive. I knew something truly awful had happened. The master's face was white, frozen with shock when they left. Him and the mistress rushed off in the motor car and the mistress were weeping."

Grace nodded then waited patiently for her father to continue.

Ned took a long breath. Replacing his hat, he stood up and gazed across at the tidy garden. "Bowles called us indoors, he told us, she were in hospital. The accident happened at one of them suffragette meetings." He turned to Grace and his voice waivered as he spoke. "She...Beth... she hasn't woken up yet."

Grace rose from the bench and put her arms around her father burying her head in his shabby shirt. Ned suddenly felt the numbness inside loosen and had the overwhelming desire to weep profusely in his daughter's arms. He pulled Grace from his arms then turned abruptly back towards the garden, where he picked up the spade and began digging.

Grace ran over to Ned. "Da. I'm sure she'll be all right." Her father didn't answer her but carried on intent on the task in hand. "If I hear anything...about Beth, I'll come and tell you."

Ned leaned on his spade then looked up at Grace. "How are things at Catherine and Samuels? They treating you right?" He asked, remembering how he'd been so pleased when Grace had got her position with the middle class couple. "I heard they be into supporting them suffragettes. Is that true, Grace?" When Grace looked sheepish Ned ploughed on driven by strong feelings after recent events. "I don't want you involved." Fury paced through Ned's body replacing the sadness at Beth's plight. "Look where it's got poor Beth! You need to just do your job and keep your nose clean, my girl."

"Da, there's nothing to worry about honestly. I just pass round the scones and tea when they hold meetings at the house. I barely take any notice of what's going on."

A furtive expression flitted across Grace's face ringing alarm bells in Ned's head. "Is there something you're not telling me, Grace?"

"How do you mean, Da?" Grace said innocently. Her father knew her too well and ever since she was a tiny child he could tell when she was hiding something.

"You know wot I mean, daughter." Ned reached across and lifted her chin looking into her eyes. "Just feel you haven't told me something that's all."

Grace shook her head free her from her father's grasp. "There's nothing on my mind. Honestly." Grace hated lying to her father. Despite this she knew he would not approve of the path she was treading. He would not believe it was true love that she held in her hands. Grace would have to wait until their wedding was announced before telling him the truth.

Ned wasn't convinced, but today his thoughts were too focused on Beth and her situation than worrying about what his daughter was getting up to. "What you doing this afternoon then. Have the day off do you?"

Grace looked down and smoothed a hand over her skirt. "I have to work this afternoon. Catherine has one of them meetings we were just talking about," she said kissing her father on his weathered cheek and hugging him tightly. "I must go now. Try not to worry about Beth."

Ned nodded and lifted one gnarled hand to wave at Grace as she hurried off. His thoughts were now focused on his precious daughter. Watching her grow up into a beautiful young woman, without the guidance of a mother, he'd only ever wanted her happiness. Each day he prayed that she'd find a good man to look after her and get married. Smiling now Ned's thoughts went to his son Billy. He remembered well the day he got married to the strong and capable Marianne and had been relieved that his boy was happy. As the grandchildren came along they filled Ned's life with joy.

Ned suspected that the strong willed Billy didn't always get his way with his wife, but he could see that things were good with their young family. He watched Grace until she disappeared into the distance before taking a moment to rub vigorously at a knot in his back. Then picking up the spade he returned to his vegetable patch to continue his digging.

Grace tried to ignore the guilt gnawing away at her as she walked away from her father. She had seen in his eyes that he hadn't believed her, but there was little she could do until their love was announced to the world. Her eyes sparkled with anticipation, hopefully that wouldn't be long in coming. She hurried towards the old secluded summer house which was hidden behind a clump of trees. Excitement surged through her body heating her to the very core and her heart thumped wildly. As she approached the small wooden building, a shadow fell across the window. In an instant the door opened. Grace flew into the open arms of her lover as the image of her father's disapproving frown melted from her mind, and all sensible thought left her body

Chapter *Forty One*

COMA

Leaning on the bed Alice put her head in her hands. Sitting this way for a moment she looked up at Beth and for the umpteenth time that day willed her to wake up. For the best part of four days now she had stayed by her friend's bedside, hoping against hope that she'd soon recover from the injuries she'd sustained outside the House of Commons. So far, not even a flutter of her eyelashes could be detected and Alice was becoming more anxious with each passing day.

"Beth, you must pull through," she whispered into her ear, "please don't give up now. Not after all we've been through together." Alice continued talking as if Beth could hear her, "you have helped me to understand that the love of a friend can be just as precious as that of a lover."

Alice couldn't allow herself to imagine what Beth's reaction would be when she finally awoke and looked into a mirror. She had witnessed the gaping hole in Beth's cheek the day of the accident. Now it was covered in a neat white dressing. Alice could see the whole right side of Beth's face being pulled towards the wound beneath the bandage. Beth's beauty had been taken away and her features looked distorted. Alice shuddered as she was reminded of an advertisement she'd seen for a travelling circus. "The World's Ugliest Man!" it had boasted, showing a picture of the said man. His disfigured face was pulled together to form an unsightly grimace in an attempt at smiling. His pig-like eyes stared out at the world either side of a large bulbous nose.

"Her face will heal in time," the nurse had told Alice the day after the accident. "She was lucky she didn't loose an eye as she fell, banging her head on the pavement." Alice looked at the bed where Beth lay motionless. Then her gaze strayed to Beth's leg which had been badly injured as she lay on the ground unconscious. Now heavily bandaged Beth's leg lay hidden and redundant under a metal cage. The cage was keeping her limb from coming into contact with the heavy blankets and starchy sheets. Alice bit down hard on her lower lip as she remembered the sight of Beth lying sprawled on the ground, her leg lying at an angle her face filled with blood.

The doctor's prognosis echoed repeatedly in Alice's mind. "Beth's leg is so badly broken that even when healed she will have trouble walking without the aid of a stick," he'd told her coldly. She'd noticed the matter of fact way he'd spoken to her and seen the accusing look in his eye. Alice had stared back at the doctor defiantly, knowing that all that didn't matter. Beth was strong and would cope with her injuries especially as Alice would always be there to help and support her friend.

The noise and chaos of an emergency in the ward interrupted Alice's deep thought. It was obviously well past visiting time and as she looked around, she could see Nurses running this way and that and beds being shuffled here and there at an alarming rate. Alice could hear the word 'Scarlet Fever' being whispered by nearby nurses. She'd been told to leave several times but Alice had on each occasion crept back into the ward, convinced that the minute she left, Beth would wake up and need a friendly face at her bedside.

As if in a trance Alice sat alone, unaffected by the cacophony. She began to wonder where Finn had disappeared to. For the last three nights he'd been beside Beth willing her to wake up, appearing after a long day at work and staying until he was told to leave.

Tonight, there was no sign of him. Alice was puzzled by this, judging by his recent overriding concern for his past love. She thought he might return to take his turn next to Beth's sick bed. Alice was secretly pleased that Finn was absent from the Hospital as she wanted her face to be the first one Beth sees when she awoke.

Alice's forehead furrowed. Knowing that once again she might have to share Beth with the handsome Irishman was not a welcome thought. However she had accepted it and come to terms with it. How did Finn feel when he looked upon

Beth? She wondered. To see her once beautiful face changed beyond recognition must have been a terrible shock.

"What are you still doing here? You must leave at once we have an emergency!" Sister Blakely's words interrupted Alice's reverie as she stood next to Alice, hands on hips and a steely look in her eyes.

Alice rose reluctantly from her seated position and took one last look at Beth. "I'm sorry. I was convinced she'd wake up today." She reached out and took hold of Beth's limp hand then bent to kiss her ashen cheek.

The other woman's tone softened. "I understand, but tonight we've had a death from 'Scarlet Fever' and have had to isolate another patient so everyone here is at risk."

Alice, who at that moment cared not a jot for her own safety, turned to go. Gathering up her shawl from the chair, she said. "I'll go home now and return first thing in the morning. If Beth wakes up, tell her I will be back soon." Alice looked intently at the sister and in her eyes was a longing, a pleading, for a glimmer of hope that this would soon be the case.

The sister's face was full of sympathy as she leaned towards Alice and placed a hand on her arm. "Try not to worry, my dear," she said reassuringly. Long reconciled to this desperate look from relatives of the sick, Sister Blakely knew she could give no guarantees to this woman that her friend would survive. She simply nodded her head sympathetically and bid her goodbye. For a moment she watched as Alice walked down the ward, her long red hair swung about her shoulders, thinking what a striking looking woman she was. Then the nurse looked down at the woman's friend and sighed. Would the poor girl really wish to wake up looking the way she did now? Then suddenly aware of the crisis on the ward she turned around quickly and went back to issuing orders to the new recruits.

An hour later, feeling completely exhausted, Julia Morgan who was a young nurse and one of the new recruits, made her way out into the corridor. It was only her second day on the ward and she'd been shouted at constantly for the last few hours. "A couple of minutes silence," she told herself as she stretched her arms across her back in a bid to get rid of the pent-up tension, "wouldn't do anyone any harm and give me a chance to gather my thoughts." she told herself closing her eyes for a second. She leaned against the double doors and rested her aching head back against the wooden surface. Having been on her feet since early that morning it was such a blessed relief to let go for just a moment.

"Nurse... Nurse! Please let me into the ward!"

Startled, Nurse Morgan opened her long lashed eyes and looked straight into the face of one of the handsomest men she'd ever seen. He towered above her, the muscles clenched tightly in his arms and his breathing laboured. Leaning forwards the attractive man bent down and put his hands onto his knees in an attempt to catch his breath. "I've rushed all the way here, so I have," he gasped.

Nurse Morgan waited until the man slowly straightened up. He was absolutely gorgeous and whoever he was looking for was indeed a lucky woman. Looking at her questioningly, he pushed a lock of flaxen hair from his eyes.

"I'm sorry the wards closed," she said firmly, putting her hands out in front of her to indicate that he couldn't go any further. "I have been told that under no circumstances let any visitors in. The ward sister reprimanded me only a short while ago for allowing a red-haired woman to stay on the ward after visiting hours. We are in the middle of an *emergency!*" Nurse Morgan pronounced the word emergency so that the man was under no illusion that it was more than her job was worth to allow him in the ward. He looked stricken at her words but the thought of losing her position made her brave.

"I know it's late, but I got held up at work and couldn't get here sooner. Please tell me, how is Miss. Hamilton-Green?"

Alarm bells rang in Nurse Morgan's head, her mind whirred in several directions. Young and inexperienced, she was too slow to automatically hide the way she was feeling from a patients caring relative.

The man took a step towards her his face full of fear. "What is it, Nurse?"

Nurse Morgan attempted to change her expression but it was too late. In desperation she turned to look through the small glass paned window. Frenzied activity still occurred beyond and it was obvious no-one would have a spare moment to tell this poor man the terrible news. Julia swallowed hard as she looked back at him, trying to ignore the intense look on his face she dipped her head to avoid his gaze. "I'm sorry I have to go back to my duties," she murmured.

"Nurse!" The man's fists were clenched by his sides and his face had gone red. "Tell me what's happened. *Please.*"

The man now had hold of her arm and wouldn't let go. Desperation...his face, melted her heart. Before she knew what she was doing the words flew out of her mouth. "I'm so sorry. She caught the Scarlet Fever you see."

Agony chased itself across the man's features as he tried to read her face, searching her features. "When...? Did she...?" The words seemed stuck in his throat and came out as a dry croak. Nurse Morgan was alarmed to see him cover his eyes and press his fingers into the sockets with such force she thought he surely would go blind.

Backing away she became aware that she shouldn't have told this man anything. However stretched and busy they were, to impart bad news wasn't her place. On the other hand now he knew, perhaps she could offer him some comfort. "I was there when she died," Nurse Morgan said, waiting for him to stop doing that awful thing to his eyes, "it was peaceful at the end. She..." moving towards him she touched his arm, but he didn't appear to hear. He removed his hands from his face and wrapped his arms around his body. Standing this way for a moment, he began swaying slightly from side to side. To her horror, tears spurted from his eyes and he let out a low animal-like moan.

Although riveted to the spot, Nurse Morgan could hear her name being called and through the window she saw the ward sister looking for her. She wished the man would disappear, take his grief somewhere else and not draw attention to her in this way. Despite this she knew she must get help. Pushing her way through the doors she rushed up to the sister but before she could speak the other woman admonished her.

"Where have you been, Nurse Morgan?" Sister Blakely snapped as she approached. "Sister! There's a man outside the ward he was looking for that woman who died."

The ward sister stopped and gaped at the young girl and her tone changed. "The poor man."

Nurse Morgan's thoughts were running amok in her thumping head. She shouldn't have told the man that his wife, that poor Mrs Hamilton had died.

"Nurse Morgan, I trust you didn't tell him anything did you?" Sister Blakely wagged her finger at the young girl.

The ward sister's warning look made sure the young nurse could not tell the truth. "Of course not." The denial was firm and she forced a passive look on her face although her heart was racing.

"I'll go out and see him. You get on with making up that bed at once."

Nurse Morgan watched the sister stride out into the corridor. Almost immediately she returned. "Did you find him, Sister?" She asked knowing already what the answer would be.

"No, he's gone but he'll be back soon." The sister glanced impatiently around. "Nurse Morgan. Didn't I tell you to make up that bed?"

"Yes, Sister." The young nurse replied, putting her head down to continue with the bed-making and attempting to block out the recurring image of the handsome man's grief.

Chapter *Forty Two*

CONFIRMATION

Dizziness engulfed Finn as he teetered on the edge of the hill and the world swirled madly around him. Staring down at the cottage through narrowed eyes he forced his legs to move. He had to find Beth, Beth...he had to know where Beth was.

He forced his mind to focus and struggled to remember. He'd had a dream? Beth had died. But that couldn't be true Finn told himself. He remembered he'd woken and found himself dirty and bedraggled in a quiet backstreet. Looking up he'd seen the grim reaper hovering over Beth's prostrate form. Her face was covered in blood, her leg twisted beneath her lifeless body. A hand, icily cold and clammy as death had taken hold of Finn. His limbs felt as heavy as stone beneath him as he'd struggled to move, like a wild beast caught in a net. Screaming her name he had found that no sound emerged from his dry, parched lips. Blackness had returned. Upon waking he'd heard Beth calling his name. "I'm coming!" he'd told her as he'd staggered to his feet.

Unaware of how the miles were being covered, Finn followed Beth's cries until eventually he had arrived at his destination.

Forcing stillness into his body Finn stopped to listen to the silence in the air. Beth's cries had ceased and the chill of dread shivered coldly through his body. Finn fought against the blind panic gripping him as he lurched forwards, his feet flying beneath him. "Beth...I'm here," he called to her. At last he would find her he told himself as he pushed open the gate. "Beth, where are you?"

Stumbling towards the door and finding it ajar Finn stepped over the threshold just as a sound reached his ears. Heart wrenching sobs filled the air. "Beth..." lunging in through the door he followed the sound of the weeping. Struggling in the half light he attempted to focus on the outline of a girl slumped in a chair. Even in his drunken state, Finn recognised that this girl was not Beth.

"Where's Beth?" he bellowed angrily his eyes flashing with fire. "What have you done with Beth!" Swaying in the doorway and clutching the door frame for support he stared at the distraught girl menacingly.

The girl's head jolted in his direction and she glared at Finn with red swollen eyes. Her fists were clenched against her chest and her face was a mask of fear. Pushing herself further back into the chair she managed to utter a few words from between her trembling lips. "Who... are you...?" she said visibly shaking under his gaze.

When Finn didn't move but stared back at her his face twisted in confusion she asked again. "Who are you?"

Finn was frozen in time. His mind whirled. His face twisted in confusion as his gaze circled the room as if he might find Beth hiding in a corner. The girl took her chance and standing up she reached into the hearth and grabbed the poker from the fireplace. But before she could lift it in self defence, Finn had covered the distance from the doorway and taken hold of her arms with an iron grip. "Where is Beth?" he raged. "Tell me, for the love of Mary, where she is!" The girl didn't appear to hear him. Her terrified face stared back at him as he began shaking her like a rag doll.

Her shrill scream filled the room startling Finn. Temporarily he loosened his grip. "Let go of me now!" she shrieked and pulling herself from his grasp she lifted the poker and struck him hard across the head.

Finn fell to the ground with a sickening thud. The room swirled in all directions as he clutched his head in agony. "Where is she...? Tell me..." he pleaded feeling the fire inside dissipate into thin air.

Staring down at him the frightened girl inhaled deeply and let the poker fall, sounding a deathly toll as it came to rest on the floor. Lifting a hand she wiped her tear stained face. Her own intense pain was so raw that she desperately needed to get rid of this intruder in order to be alone and lick her wounds. "Go away!" she ordered. "There is nothing for you here." Fear was now replaced with a look of resignation as the girl looked into Finn's stricken eyes. "Beth's gone for ever." She said simply.

"Is she...has she, I mean..." Finn began heaving himself up. The girl reached for her discarded weapon. "Please..." his words were slurred but Finn forced them from his lips." She is really dead?" Pain filled Finn's eyes as he focused on the girl and saw the truth written across her grief stricken face.

Tears poured from Finn's eyes as he felt something inside him snap. He could do nothing to stop the outpouring of grief as his body involuntarily curled up into a ball on the floor. Denial filled his lips. "No... Oh, for the love of Mary. No..." Finn's body seemed detached from his mind and he was hardly aware that the horrendous heart wrenching noise filling the room was coming from his own mouth.

The girl observed her attacker and pity filled her mind. The sound of his weeping filled the room. She took a step backwards, her eyes never leaving this terribly sad man who was crying like a baby. For the first time she thought about poor Beth. "It was a terrible accident, yes. Dear God. Poor Beth..." she murmured. Fresh tears were running freely now and she saw her own grief mirrored in the man's face. She sat back down in the chair and sank her head into her hands.

After a few minutes Finn's sobbing subsided. He lifted his numb head and looked across at the girl. A feeling of loss like a bottomless black hole was filling his insides. Suddenly he had to be away from here. He had to go now. Heaving himself up, he took one last look at the girl and fled out the door.

Grace watched from the window as the man staggered up the path and collapsed by the front gate. She could do nothing to help him she told herself he had probably passed out from the drink she had been able to smell on his breath. He frightened her and she was relieved he'd gone back outside. Her own grief was giving her no respite. It was gripping her so tightly that she had no compassion left for others. Bone weary now, she went to the door and twisted the key in the lock. She had to keep him from returning.

Sitting down in the chair Grace leaned her head back and stared up at the ceiling. The hollow feeling in her stomach was making her feel sick. An image of James came into her mind and she once again dissolved into floods of tears. "If only... How am I going to live without...him, I can't go on," she moaned to herself. Desperation filled her body. No amount of justifying James's behaviour could help Grace come to terms with what had happened. Their love affair was over and she couldn't see a way to go on living without him.

Everything was so bleak and empty without him in her life. His own selfishness and lack of courage had brought them to this conclusion. They'd had such wonderful ideas, plans that included them sharing their life together. James had been convinced he could persuade his parents to allow their marriage. Because she was Ned's daughter he thought it would make a difference. Grace believed James would never leave her with or without his parents' money. But he had proved too weak she told herself rocking as if soothing a baby. "You wasn't resilient, my love," she whispered, "unlike your sister, Beth. Not strong enough to leave the money and your family behind."

Grace lifted her head and looked around the room. It was grimy from lack of care. She thought of her Da and sighed. He was so worried about Beth, but was keeping the hope alive that she would get better. That's why he'd asked her to come here today on her one day off and clean, ready for Beth's return. She remembered her words to the distraught man and guilt filled her being. Her father believed that Beth would survive. But she'd just told the intruder that Beth was gone for good, because she'd had to find a way to get him out. Her own agony had overridden the pity she felt for someone she didn't even know.

Thoughts of her father filled Grace's head. His way of coping was to keep busy. That's what she needed to do now. Somehow she would survive James's rejection and carry on with her life. She didn't know how but she would. For now she would fill her days with hard work and learn to live with the agonising pain that losing James had brought. Perhaps in the future the pain would lessen she could only hope that this would be the case. Grace rose from the chair, smoothed down her dark hair and returned to the task of cleaning the cottage ready for Beth's return.

Finn lifted his sore head and tried to focus on his surroundings. The ground felt hard beneath his stiff body and bruised face. His hand felt the rapidly forming bump on his head. "Beth..." he rasped her name against the cold gravel path. Slowly everything came back to him, his search for Beth, the girl in Beth's cottage and the knowledge that she was dead. He forced himself round to look at the cottage in the half light. How long had he lain here? It was now early evening and he could see that the door was tightly shut. Sluggishly he began moving his limbs and forcing himself upright he walked back towards the cottage.

Pushing against the door with all his strength, Finn soon realised it was pointless. The windows were shut and the curtains closed. The girl had obviously gone. He turned around and began to take small painful steps back towards the gate. He felt his body rebel at this physical action and the bile rose in his throat. Stopping to take a breath he wiped his brow then staggered away from the cottage and began the long walk home.

Chapter *Forty Three*

LOST LOVE

Beth's arms were wrapped around Finn and he could feel her lips touching his and her sweet perfume filling his senses. He dissolved into her embrace and for a brief moment he knew again the ecstasy that loving Beth brought. The next moment she wrenched herself roughly away and glared at him with darkened eyes. The blood poured from an open wound on her right cheek as she spat the words into his face. "It's your fault, Finn!" she screamed wildly as her raven hair flew about her head. "All your fault," she repeated.

"No..." Finn surveyed the horrific injuries. "Please, Beth..." He cried, reaching out to touch her and pull her back into the comfort of his arms. Instead his hands touched only thin air as she faded away from his vision. "Beth, come back!" He called panic stricken. Desperately he searched for her. Where she'd been just a moment ago there was nothing but a black void. His shouting must have been loud. As he opened his eyes he saw George towering over him shaking him awake.

"Finn! Wake up, man," frowning down at Finn, George said, "you're having a nightmare, son."

Finn focused on George's face. Realising once again he was only dreaming the reality came flooding back. Beth was dead. A hopeless feeling which gripped him daily began enveloping his body caused him to groan loudly.

George bent over Finn's motionless body and urged him to sit up. "Here, I've got you a cup of tea."

Finn sat up and rubbed at his tired eyes and swung his legs out of bed. His limbs ached from lack of sleep. As far as he was concerned he didn't care at all whether he got up or not. He would rather bury himself back under the covers and stay that way indefinitely. Unrelentingly George plagued him daily and wouldn't give up his nagging. "For the love of Mary, George! Can't you leave me alone?"

Ignoring this remark George handed Finn a steaming cup. "You'll be late for work, Finn and Mrs Munnings is coming in a bit earlier today, so we need to be out of our rooms so that she can clean."

Finn knew George's last sentence was entirely fictional and that this caring and loyal friend was trying to motivate him to get out of bed again. Mrs Munnings was never in the house before ten o'clock to do the cleaning. Finn nodded at George, not trusting himself to reply. Bleakness lurked within him creeping everywhere, and sometimes made him say things that hurt other people.

George clicked the door shut behind him and Finn got out of bed leaving the untouched tea on the small bedside table. He made his way across the room to the window and pulled back the ebony curtains. The street lamp shone through the darkness of the early morning as he stared down at the pavement below. This was a ritual and Finn didn't stop to question why he did this as soon as he awoke. Perhaps in the deepest recesses of his mind he was looking for something. He didn't know what it was. It was almost as if he were checking the world was still here. Checking that other people still lived, still worked and went about their business as usual, despite Finn's life having fallen apart. For him death would be welcome as he no longer had anything worth living for.

Daily as he stood this way, Beth came back to him in such clarity he almost felt her presence. The dream, still fresh in his mind made him shiver. These illusions always began with Beth as she used to be in his arms murmuring words of love. Within seconds she would turn into a screaming anguished fiend who blamed him entirely for her death. "Was he to blame?" He frequently asked himself, feeling responsible for calling out to her at the rally and causing her to lose concentration. If he hadn't done that, "would she still be alive today?" Finn felt the familiar tightness in his chest as the oxygen around him disappeared and he gasped.

Stumbling back towards the bed he lay still for a moment forcing air back into his body. As his breathing returned to normal he knew that today would have to be a turning point. He couldn't go on any longer this way. He desperately needed to find something, anything, which would give him enough inner strength to carry on existing without his beloved Beth.

George spooned the hot food onto Finn's plate. "Would you like more stew?" he asked without pausing for an answer and ignoring the look of indifference on his friend's face. Every day that passed George watched with concern as Finn became more haggard. He hardly ate a thing. This was despite George's best efforts at tempting him with Mrs Munnings cooking. For a large man Finn was beginning to look extremely thin. It pained George to see him suffering in this way. He knew only too well what Finn was going through. His wife Doris hadn't died but she may as well have, for she had left a gaping hole in his life that would never be filled.

Finn rarely spoke at breakfast and in the silence that followed, George thought back to the first night that Finn arrived home in a dishevelled condition four months ago. Finn had been missing for two nights. The night he returned he was out of control and roaring drunk. George could hardly understand his ramblings. It was all he could do to stop Finn from harming himself as he flailed this way this way and that declaring his guilt. George had heard through others about Beth's tragic accident at the

House of Commons, but he'd failed to see how her death could have been Finn's fault.

After all it had been Beth's decision to support the suffragettes and as far as George could see Finn had done everything to discourage her in her crusade. George had to keep watch on Finn all that night. He was afraid Finn would get up and make his way to the Thames as he kept threatening to do. "I want to lose myself in its murky waters." Finn had muttered over and over. George's thoughts had returned to one of his labourers, a man by the name of Jed. His wife had died in childbirth and he hadn't been able to cope with their six other children and a new baby, with no woman to look after them. Jed had sunk into deep despair while trying to hold everything together. When his children were taken into the workhouse, Jed could take no more and had jumped into the freezing waters of the Thames. George refused to let the same thing happen to Finn.

Finn's terrible state that day had brought back bad memories for George. He had felt again the agony he'd experienced the day Doris left. It wrenched at his heart and he remembered how he had blamed himself for not noticing things weren't right between them. He knew though deep down that she had never been happy with him. It had only been a matter of time before someone else laid claim to her affections. Someone with money was what Doris had been looking for. Knowing what a selfish woman Doris was hadn't stopped George's heart breaking in two, the day he arrived home from work to find her note on the kitchen table. George knew the only way to survive this blow was to be determined Doris wasn't going to ruin his life. He'd picked himself up and buried himself in work. Staying all hours, he'd drop into bed each night exhausted with no energy left to think about his loss.

George recalled to himself how Finn was the morning after his drunken escapade. He had displayed an un-natural silence, which in its own way was more worrying. George had attempted to reason with him. "It wasn't your fault, Finn," he'd said. "Beth died doing something she believed in. Nothing to do with you...you tried to stop her from taking part in the ever-increasing violence of the movement." George's words had been met with a cold blank stare. In the days that followed, Finn was struck incapable and unable to get out of bed and George was forced to make excuses for him at work.

The turning point came when George had to give Finn an ultimatum. He could no longer keep the little Victorian house running without Finn's rent. "I will be forced to sell up, so I will." George had said truthfully to a silent Finn, whose eyes held the look of a haunted man. Fortunately the next morning Finn got out of bed and returned to work so George had won one small battle.

These days George hardly heard a word from Finn, apart from the shouting of Beth's name in the middle of the night, or the quiet sobbing seeping from his room in the dead of night. George didn't see him most evenings. Finn's despair had now been replaced by anger. This manifested itself in long bouts of drinking and George heard that Finn had been visiting the local whorehouse.

George pulled himself up from his thoughts realising he had lapsed from attempting to encourage conversation from his tenant. He put down his knife and fork and looked across at Finn. He was as usual pushing the food around his plate and making no attempt to eat. "Finn, what are you doing tonight?" George said the words lightly, "do you fancy a game of cards?" he suggested hoping that for once Finn would take him up on his offer of company.

Finn gave up any pretence at finishing his meal and leaned back in the wooden chair. He sighed deeply and stared intently at George with bloodshot eyes. "No. Thanks for the offer, George. I'm going out tonight."

Pity shone in George's eyes as he regarded this dear friend who had become gaunt, lined and old beyond his years. "Why not stay in tonight?" he urged.

For a moment George saw indecision flicker across Finn's face before a deep frown knitted itself between his brows. Finn stood abruptly, retrieved his coat from the hook on the wall and made his way towards the door.

As he reached the door Finn glanced back at George. "I'm sorry, George. I have to go out, see...just have to..."

George nodded in resignation and resisted the feeling of rejection as he watched Finn disappear through the door. He looked around the small kitchen which now seemed to exude an air of sadness left behind by Finn. Wearily, George lifted himself up from the table and began clearing away the dirty crockery.

Chapter *Forty Four*

BETH'S INJURIES

Beth clamped a hand across her mouth and desperately tried to erase the image looking back at her from the small ornate hand mirror.

"Oh. My. God." she whispered her eyes were wide with shock as she forced herself to look at her face. A purple bruise ran the length of her forehead and there was a small graze over one eye. Slowly she lifted one hand to touch the white dressing covering her right cheek. Instantly it was as if a knife had been plunged into her skin bringing the bile up from her stomach and causing her to retch violently.

"Beth..." Alice rushed from her chair and ran out into the corridor shouting for the nurse who appeared almost instantly.

"No need to raise our voices," the nurse said calmly. She took in the situation and with a swish of her starched uniform disappeared to fetch a bucket, "only to be expected," she elaborated on her return. She began changing the bed. Beth's scream pierced the air as, despite being careful, the nurse accidently touched Beth's injured leg when she began easing the sheets from beneath her.

"I'm so sorry, my dear," the nurse's efficient expression had disappeared and her face softened with sympathy as she finished tucking in the bed. "I will check on you again shortly," she said over her shoulder as she picked up the bucket and left.

Alice's brows were knitted together in a worried frown. She moved to sit next to Beth again and for a moment the two women were silent.

Beth's voice came out as a croak. "How did it happen?" she asked.

Alice got up to pour some water from the jug at the side of the bed. "Do you have any memory of that day?" she said as she helped Beth sit up then handed her the glass of water.

Beth sipped at the liquid and stared beyond Alice as if searching the blank walls for a script of a day long forgotten. "I remember hearing my name being called in the middle of all that chaos," she shook her head then winced at the pain this action caused. Looking intently at Alice her moist eyes lit up. "I saw Finn, it was him that shouted at me wasn't it?"

"I don't know. Was it?" Alice's expression was quizzical. She replaced the glass back onto the table and took hold of Beth's hand. "Why did Finn shout at you? He didn't tell me anything of what happened before your accident."

"I only know that I heard his voice..." Beth lifted a hand and pushed a strand of hair from her eyes, "from behind me," she continued, her eyes lighting a little as if returning to an old familiar novel. "I turned around and saw him." Her face puckered in confusion and she painfully closed her eyes.

Alice looked forlorn as she dipped her head and stared down at the bed. "I should have been with you, maybe I could have prevented this happening."

Beth opened her eyes and reached out clutching at Alice's arm urgently. "Was he really there, Alice? It wasn't all a dream was it?" she said anxiously. When Alice didn't answer Beth became agitated. "Alice! Please tell me..."

"It's all right, Beth. Calm yourself." She looked at Beth's pale and bandaged face. "One of the women threw a stone. It bounced back in your direction, you turned around..." Alice's voice faltered, she felt reluctant to apportion blame for Beth's fall. "You were distracted by something behind you."

"How do you know, Alice? Did you see all this happen?"

"No, I didn't." Alice looked uncomfortable for a moment and drew back from the bed.

"What is it, Alice?" Beth looked alarmed at the expression on her friend's face.

"Finn told me how he was watching you - he said he couldn't reach you in time." Alice looked stricken as she recounted Finn's words. Guilt as heavy as lead, weighed her down as she remembered how she hadn't been there to help Beth.

Tears poured down Beth's cheek as she realised that Finn had come to find her. "Alice, he must have been looking for me," she exclaimed.

Alice blinked at Beth then nodded slowly and reluctantly agreed. "I think he was." When Beth's expression changed to that of joy, the green monster fluttered accusingly in Alice's stomach. Ignoring its urgent call for attention she hurried on. "The stone hit you on the temple and you fell hitting your head hard. That must have caused the concussion." Alice spoke with haste as if rushing to get past and far away from the mention of Finn. "There was a piece of glass found on the ground and we think it may have caused the injury to your cheek."

Beth looked down at the cage beneath the bed covers which housed her damaged limb. Clearly still in shock she spoke weakly again. "They told me about my leg," whispering as if not to make a fuss she added, "it's so painful that any movement is excruciating."

Alice longed to reach across and brush Beth's dark hair from her forehead. Her arms ached to hold Beth in her arms and tenderly comfort her by kissing away her fears. But it was not to be. Mentally shaking herself Alice managed to curb her desires knowing that Beth would not welcome such intimate gestures. Instead she touched Beth's arm gently and looked into her blue eyes, "I'm sure it is painful as it's such a bad break because of the angle you fell."

Beth returned Alice's gaze and tried to smile at her sympathetic expression. She lifted a hand and indicated towards her cheek. "I'm glad I can't see beneath these bandages." Her bottom lip quivered as she spoke. "I've been told it will take a long time to heal and so I fear that will mean many weeks of sitting here in this hospital." Beth raised her chin slightly and there were signs of the old determined look on the good side of her face, "Alice, tell me where is Finn now?"

Alice wasn't sure if it was the smell of disinfectant on the ward or the sudden sound of a woman in a nearby bed crying out in pain. Whatever it was she found it hard to know how to answer Beth. Swallowing hard she struggled to find the right words. "I honestly don't know. He was here for the first three days. He was by your bed willing you to wake up." Alice shook her head then rubbing at her temple regarded Beth. "On the fourth day there was an emergency on this ward and there has been no sign of him that day or since." Seeing Beth's surprised look Alice hurried on. "Of course I would have gone looking for him...if I'd known where he lived." Alice felt the guilt stab at her again as in reality she hadn't given a thought to Finn's whereabouts, being too focused on Beth waking from the coma to care about the Irishman.

"That is strange." Beth lifted herself up onto her elbows in an attempt to quell the sickness she could feel returning in her stomach. "What could have happened to him, Alice?" Alice shook her head and looked mystified, "what emergency did they have on the ward that day?" Beth asked urgently.

"There was an outbreak of Scarlet Fever on the ward." Alice explained. "One woman died and they had to isolate other patients. As for Finn, I am surprised he hasn't been back." Then she added something Beth thought she'd never hear from Alice. "He was very concerned for you." Her voice held an air of reluctance. "It doesn't seem to fit that he would just disappear and not find out how you are getting on." Alice shivered as the green monster stirred within. 'If Finn truly loved Beth then he would be here today,' it whispered.

"Maybe he was afraid of catching the fever." Beth covered her eyes with her hands. "Or it was the sight of my face."

"How could he have seen your face when it was all bandaged up?" Alice tried to be practical and find the words to reassure Beth. "He couldn't have known how your face looks now," she lied, knowing that this wasn't quite true as the bandage didn't cover the whole of Beth's face. Alice had seen the looks of sympathy on the nurses faces as they had dressed Beth's wounds and overheard them talking about her leg which will be left twisted and lame.

"He would have seen how badly disfigured I am. Finn would have been able to tell I'll be left..." Beth covered her mouth with a hand and tried not to retch as the sickness threatened again. "...scarred."

But Alice had seen the love reflected in Finn's expression as he sat next to Beth's bed. "No. I'm sure you're wrong," she said. "I expect he has regrets about your parting."

Beth leaned back and her raven hair stood out stark against the white, starched pillow. "I met Mrs Williams his landlady, when I went to see him about six months ago."

Alice looked surprised but waited for Beth to continue.

"Awful woman. Brassy and common. She enlightened me about Finn and Aisling." Beth lifted her head and Alice saw a tiny spot of blood on her bottom lip. "She told me that Finn had moved out to be with Aisling and that they are to be married soon."

Beth's hand hovered over the dressing on her cheek where Alice caught it and slowly put it back down on the bed covers. "I can hardly believe that, Beth."

"It's true so it seems." Beth caught her breath at the Irish lilt to her speech. "So why did he come looking for me?" She looked down at her fingernails and reflected that, despite her terrible injuries, her hands still looked white and smooth.

"Could he have been there anyway as a protestor?" Alice tried to find an explanation for his presence at the rally.

Beth attempted to smile but her damaged face wouldn't let her. "I don't think so do you? After all the main reason for us going our separate ways was that he's against the cause."

Alice was confused there just didn't seem to be an answer as to why Finn had been at the rally. Although his presence by Beth's bedside could be explained as mere concern for an old friend, his intention was unclear.

Beth let out a long sigh and looked so downcast that Alice attempted to be upbeat. "I saw your mother yesterday," when there was no answer from Beth Alice tried again, "she's coming in to see you later today."

"Is she? Well I know what to expect don't I? Her usual 'I told- you-so' attitude." Beth's eyes flashed with anger.

Alice had never heard her friend sound so negative. "Beth, listen to me. You mustn't feel sorry for yourself. I know it's hard, but you're alive. Remember you still have a life to live, please believe that, as soon as you're on your feet we need you back in the movement." Alice tried hard to sound firm despite her desperate sympathy for Beth.

Beth looked back at her intently and Alice shifted uneasily in her chair at the open envy in the other woman's gaze, when it fell upon her own unaltered face. Alice watched her friend and sensed hostility in Beth's eyes and saw how she was slowly shutting her out.

"I'm tired now, Alice. I think you should leave," Beth said, her voice small as she closed her eyes.

Chapter *Forty Five*

DESPAIR

Beth sat in the wheelchair with her right leg jutting out in front of her feeling frustrated and angry.

"But Alice it's so hard!" Why can't I get up and walk, like everyone else," she raged at herself. Despite many weeks of resting she'd woken up feeling bad, finding that things only got worse as the day went on. The presence of what she'd come to think of as the 'black dog' was sitting by her side and steadfastly refusing to go away. The 'black dog' was not a physical presence she knew, more a bottomless, black void of utter desolation. Beth likened it to being trapped in a long dark tunnel of which there was no hope of escape.

In desperation she'd confided these feelings to Alice recently. Her friend had known something of the kind of hopelessness that Beth was experiencing. "It is only you that can make the 'black dog' disappear, Beth," she'd advised wisely.

Alice looked up from her work then patiently rose from her sewing machine and walked over to her friend. Guiltily Alice was beginning to wish Beth hadn't declined her mother's offer of a temporary home. She knew she should be glad Beth had decided to live with her but the strain was beginning to show. Tension between the two women was running high, especially in the light of Beth's dark moods which were more frequent of late.

"I know, Beth. But you've got to try a bit harder. The doctor said you could start putting your foot down to the ground now if only you would make an effort." Almost immediately Alice regretted the tone and impatience in her voice and hurriedly added. "I'll take you out for a walk later. I just need to finish sewing this garment." Alice gestured towards the window at the late September sunlight streaming in through the curtains. "It's a lovely day."

Beth ran her fingers along the jagged scar on her cheek and bent her head letting the tears pour openly down her cheeks. "I can't go out, Alice."

Alice sighed at her friend. "Of course you can, I've told you before your face is not as noticeable as you think."

This statement much heard from Alice, served only to increase Beth's frustration. "But it's all right for you to say that, Alice. Your face is beautiful, I'm ugly and no-one will want to look at me, either that or everyone will stare rudely... "

"Stop it, Beth. You're not ugly. You are still the same person you always were." Alice had lost count of how many times she'd used these same words, so many times now. She couldn't understand why Beth preferred to wallow in self-pity. Alice didn't like herself for thinking it, but maybe Alice's own tougher upbringing made her more resilient than Beth when faced with life's troubles.

Just in time a knock came at the door. Relieved that a visitor had stopped a row between the two women, which had been brewing for two days, Alice went to see who was calling.

Beth strained to hear who was at the door. Lifting her head she hurriedly wiped the tears from her eyes then twisted uneasily in her chair as if trying to escape. From her position in the back parlour she could hear that Alice sounded happy and greeted whoever had arrived with a cheery voice. The sound of the front door being closed caused her to try to disguise any evidence of weeping as she heard footsteps and laughter as they walked along the hallway towards her. Beth's spirits plummeted even more. Today she didn't want to see anyone. The persistent black dog stirred in the corner of the room.

Alice appeared in the doorway with a small fair haired woman standing beside her. "Beth, I would like you to meet, Connie." Beth shrunk from the introduction expecting Connie to look horrified at her appearance, but there was no such expression on her face. Alice took hold of the woman's arm and guided her towards the wheelchair. As she did so a look passed between them, making Beth suddenly feel like she was the outsider. These two women obviously knew each other well.

Beth mumbled a greeting at Connie and observed her appearance. She was striking looking, small in stature, with fair hair pulled up away from her face as was the fashion. Beth could only guess at her age for she looked young and had a girlish way about her. When she smiled her large blue eyes lit up. Beth tried her best to smile back, but there something about the other woman she couldn't quite put her finger on.

"Connie, would you like tea?" Alice offered her guest.

"I would love a cup of tea, Alice." Connie replied. To Beth's relief Connie followed Alice towards the kitchen. Beth felt left out as she heard them amicably chattering. She was suddenly overcome with a feeling of intense jealousy towards Connie and clenched her fists into her lap.

As they returned from the kitchen carrying cups of steaming tea and still chatting, Beth observed that their conversation was mainly about the movement and its latest news. A strong feeling of misplacement nagged at Beth and she struggled against its iron grip. With a jolt she realised that her expression must have been a picture, because in front of their visitor Alice quite suddenly asked her if she was feeling unwell. Feeling a little embarrassed Beth felt like a child with her hand caught in the biscuit jar.

When she answered Alice, Beth's tone was sharper than she'd intended and even to her ears she sounded indignant. "Of course I am. Why shouldn't I be?" At Beth's words Connie's eyes widened in shock and her expression immediately looked wounded. Beth then realised what it was about the woman she hadn't been able to work out. It was the look of intense vulnerability about her as if she was in need of protection.

Connie quickly fastened her bonnet. Her face now looked guarded and she shot Beth a quick glance then headed towards the door. "I think I'd better be going," she said addressing Alice.

"But you haven't drunk your tea, Connie. Please don't go." Alice was upset at her friend's imminent departure, but the other woman was already out in the hallway and heading towards the front door.

Beth heard the sound of the door being closed then Alice re-appeared her face clouded with anger her green eyes blazing.

"What do you think you are doing, Beth? You are going beyond it all now, how much harder must I try with you? You drove Connie away with your doom and gloom. You have to take a hold on yourself!" Alice paced around the room like a caged animal.

"What do you mean, who is she anyway? I've never seen her at the movement before and yet you seemed to know her well." Beth retorted.

Alice stopped and turned to face Beth. "She's new to the movement so you wouldn't have seen her before. And, as you haven't been for months... although if you tried I'm sure you could start walking again." Alice accused. "I asked her to call round I thought it would do you good to see someone other than me. But clearly...not."

"But, Alice. Who is she?" Beth was puzzled there was something Alice wasn't telling her.

"She is a friend." Alice replied angrily and then composing herself and calming her speech she added, "she's someone I've met recently. Connie is a lovely person and has been through a very hard time." Alice sighed and sat down leaning her chin on her hands and looked across at Beth.

Beth could feel her jealousy flare again blinding her to reason. Even she could hardly believe the words that came from her mouth. "I see. So while I'm sitting here at home unable to go out or meet anyone you're making new friends."

"Beth, for God's sake," Alice looked at her friend with a quizzical look on her face. "You sound jealous."

Overwhelmed by conflicting emotions Beth burst into tears.

Alice softened realising she shouldn't berate her friend for her self-pity. Instead she waited patiently for the sobbing to stop. "I know how hard it is for you, Beth. But you have to move on and begin to get on with your life again."

Beth's eyes were red from crying and she blew her nose hard lifting her chin to gaze at Alice. "I love him, Alice. Now I've lost him." She said sadly.

Beth's reference to Finn surprised Alice. She hadn't spoken his name since that day in hospital. She tried to be philosophical about Beth's broken relationship with the imposing Irishman. "Well, maybe it didn't work out because he wasn't right for you."

Beth's eyes narrowed. "And now, you have Connie." She sneered.

Alice wondered what had happened to the Beth she used to know, she seemed to have been replaced by a bitter and twisted woman. She went over to the window and staring out at the passing traffic decided that honesty was the best policy. "So you noticed," she said quietly.

"Of course I noticed. Why do you think I feel so awful?"

"But, Beth..." Alice faced her friend sensing herself searching within, questioning what had gone before them. "There was never a chance for us, was there, so why the jealousy?"

"I don't know." Beth looked into Alice's emerald green eyes. "I saw something in your expression when you looked at her. I know that feeling, to be deeply in love with someone. I suspect I was jealous of that." Beth sounded uncertain and bit down on her lower lip. "Does Connie feel the same way about you?"

Alice couldn't contain herself and Beth saw her face was aglow and her eyes sparkled as she spoke of her feelings for Connie. "I think so. We've discussed many things including our feelings for each other, although both of us are cautious. Beth, she is so young and vulnerable, only just twenty. She's not ready for a relationship just yet and I have to be sure. Her husband has recently died and the poor girl has suffered at his hands for years."

"I could see that, Alice. Her vulnerability was there in her expression." When Alice merely nodded at Beth with a resigned expression, Beth struggled to find the right words to express her regret. "I shouldn't have behaved that way, Alice...I don't know what came over me. It's not like me to act that way..."

"It doesn't matter, Beth. Forget it. I'm sure Connie will get over it. I'll explain you haven't been feeling yourself lately." Alice replied looking intently back at Beth. "That's true anyway, isn't it?"

Beth dipped her head and rubbed at one eye with the back of her hand. Alice hurried on aware that Beth could so easily slip back into self-pity. "Connie has ambitions to start a women's refuge," she said buoyantly.

Beth lifted her head questioningly. "Really? How? Surely you need money and determination to start up something as challenging as that."

"She's been left some money by her husband." Alice looked at Beth's dismal expression and had a sudden flash of inspiration. "Would you be interested in helping Connie, Beth?"

Beth looked down at her useless leg and sighed. "Oh. No. I can't even put my foot to the floor and walk. How could I become involved in a project like that?"

With a thoughtful expression, Alice nodded as she picked up Mrs P, who'd suddenly appeared by her feet. She stroked the cat's soft fur holding it against her skin for a moment. Then she sat down at her sewing machine, put the material in place and began working on the final hem.

Chapter Forty Six

HELPING OTHERS

"You're going to do what?" Charles's voice was raised and his face flushed with anger as he stood with his back to the window glaring at Beth.

Beth's thoughts went back to the last time she'd stood in this room confronting her father and how she'd felt then. His anger had not deterred her never that, but had instead made her feel unworthy, for he had always ruled all of their lives. Her thoughts went to James, who after being told that if he dared to marry Grace he would be penniless, had given her up. This she'd learned only this morning.

Beth looked at Charles intently before leaning heavily on her stick and bending to sit on the settee. All at once his anger forgotten he came to her aid, taking hold of her arm and attempting to guide her towards the seat.

She pushed him aside and sat down carefully, "I can manage." Once rested, she looked up at him to explain. "Thank you for your concern, Father. But I am quite capable of getting myself organised." Her father took a step backwards and she noticed a fleeting expression akin to respect pass across his face. A warm feeling crept into Beth's body as she realised she no longer cared what he thought or how angry he became, she was her own woman and would always be that way now. Never in her wildest dreams could Beth have known how good this new freedom would feel. Leading her own life and making her own decisions was everything she had ever hoped it would be.

"As I explained, I have made an agreement with another young lady to start a refuge. It won't be a big one as we have only two rooms, three at the most to offer. But it will be enough to help a few of those poor women." A silence filled the air in which she could hear the soft tick of the grandfather clock in the corner of the room. Its rhythmic sound soothed her as she waited for the next tirade of anger from her father who now paced the perimeter of his lair.

Charles stopped and glanced across at his wife, who sat mute in an armchair. Beth expected nothing less from her mother, for she rarely contributed to the conversation when her father was present. However what Charles said next came as such a complete surprise that Beth's eyes opened wide and she wondered if her ears had deceived her.

"You can always come home again." The words were spoken softly and in his eyes Beth saw the pleading for her to accept this offer. For the first time she noticed the slight protruding of her father's once flat belly and the grey hairs on his head. Pity filled her heart for this naive man. After all this time, he expected her to come back and live under his roof. He would no doubt, resume his dominant ways and all because lately her life had taken a bad turn. Her father must think that she needed his protection again. Sadly she knew it would not be protection but only a prison to which she'd return.

"Father," she began, "I could never come back here to live." Compassion dissolved quickly from his face and his eyes once again became two angry slits. Straightening his back and letting out a long sigh he prepared to speak but Beth continued unperturbed. "I've come to ask for help with the finances for the refuge," she held her breath and her fingers as they were apt to do when she was nervous, searched for the scar on her face.

Tracing the line that ran the length of her cheek, Beth knew what the answer would be and wondered why she'd bothered to ask the question. The last time she'd seen both her parents had been when they had visited her in hospital. Despite her injuries the atmosphere had been frosty. Her father had looked uncomfortable and left soon afterwards hinting to her that she'd brought this fate upon herself. At that particular time she hadn't needed to hear those words and after he'd gone she'd wept bitterly in her mother's arms. Later on when leaving the hospital she was to discover that Charles had paid all her medical bills.

A moment passed and when no answer was forthcoming Beth pressed on. "Connie has been left some money by her late husband so we have enough to get started."

"What may I enquire, happened to her husband?" Her father's voice was icy cold.

Beth lifted her head and explained. "He died of a heart attack some months ago."

"No doubt brought on by his wayward wife's antics!"

Her father's self-righteous attitude fuelled Beth's own anger and she struggled to keep it under control. "Her husband treated her very badly." Beth attempted to soften her tone not wanting to bring herself down to his level. "Connie suffered a terrible marriage with a man who was often violent, and she wants to help other women who find themselves in the same situation." Beth glanced across at her mother who was now looking thoughtful.

"Well, I think it's a wonderful thing to do, Beth." Sarah looked straight at her daughter from her place in the corner of the room. "I would like to help, if you'll have me?" Her voice was raised slightly and Beth barely recognised her mother. Her chin jutted forward and she completely ignored the meaningful looks her husband was directing towards her.

Sarah's words enraged Charles so much that his face turned puce and his chest puffed up. He took a large intake of breath and they both waited for him to exhale.

"Over my dead body you will, Sarah!" In an instant Charles was by his wife's side and taking hold of her arm he attempted to pull her up from her seated position.

"Let go of me!" Her mother shouted angrily.

Beth couldn't believe the tussle that was taking place. Her parents were having a fight right in front of her. She stood up uneasily wobbling on her stick and all at once they were both by her side. In their united love for her the argument was forgotten and she shooed them away.

"Stop! I told you before I can manage." No-one spoke for a moment. "Mother, me and Connie would be honoured to have you on board but what about your social standing?"

"I don't care anymore." On hearing this declaration her father huffed loudly and strode from the room slamming the door hard behind him.

Mother and daughter embraced. Beth leaned on the arm of the sofa and took hold of Sarah's shoulders. "You know you can't do this to him don't you?" Sarah's eyes were round with surprise at Beth's words, "he knows no other way. Can't you see it will ruin your lives?" Beth could hardly believe what she was saying but she knew that her father would never change.

"Perhaps you're right." Sarah looked sad as she leaned forward and kissed Beth's cheek then walking across the room to the window she gazed at the gardens beyond. For a moment she said nothing. Then she turned back towards Beth her face animated. "Surely I could help in some way? I will certainly ensure you're given money for the project."

"How Mother, if father does not agree?" Beth was puzzled.

Sarah took hold of her daughter's hand. "I am aware that you have received no allowance since leaving this house and I don't know how you manage to live." She looked down at Beth's brown serviceable gown. "I will do my best to get him to agree to the money you need. Besides if he doesn't agree, I will tell those in our social circle about my involvement in the project. I will no longer go on as before and this is my compromise."

Beth was overwhelmed by her mother's generosity knowing that this small step towards change was a major one for her. "Thank you, Mother. I'm so proud of you."

"No. It's me who is proud. Seeing you today I have become aware of how hard things must have been for you in the past months. How you must have been affected by your injuries." Lifting her hand Sarah stroked Beth's damaged cheek. "You are determined it seems, to improve the lives of women everywhere and that is commendable."

Beth could not let this pass without reference to Alice. "I've had support from a wonderful friend she has been a good teacher."

Sarah nodded, somehow knowing it must be the vibrant red-haired woman that had influenced Beth several years ago. "Tell me is there anyone special in your life?"

The unexpected question surprised Beth for she knew it was a referral to her unmarried state. She shot her mother a quick glance then turned away frowning. "There's no chance for me anymore. The one I love has married another."

"I'm so sorry, my dear. I always thought you would marry but I'm sure James will provide us with an heir. That is, when he weds the girl your father's chosen for him. Never give up though. Someone else may come along." Beth knew her mother's sympathy was sincere.

Beth laughed a shrill noise that sounded hollow even to her own ears and rubbed her damaged leg. "I don't think that will ever be possible not the way I look now. Besides I cannot imagine loving another - not as I've loved him." Her voice wobbled as she spoke and a lone tear snaked its way down her face.

Beth's mother wrapped her arms around her and the two women sat this way for a few moments as the fire crackled in its grate casting long shadows across the room.

Chapter *Forty Seven*

THE REFUGE

Alice knocked lightly on the brightly painted front door and waited. Aware that a baby may be sleeping she tried to be quiet and when there was no answer she peered through the letterbox and gently called to Beth. Immediately the door was flung open and she found herself in Beth's embrace.

"Hello, Alice. Come in." Reunited with her loyal friend a wide smile illuminated Beth's face making her eyes dance merrily.

"Now that you've had a few weeks to settle in I thought I'd call in to see how everything's going." Alice's heart lifted as she glanced around the hallway and then looking back at Beth she was delighted to see how joy had camouflaged the ugly scar on her friend's features. "I must say everything is looking spick and span," she said enthusiastically, running her hands along the cream coloured walls. "This was a dirty grey colour last time I was here," she added returning Beth's smile.

"I know...Oh, Alice. You wouldn't believe it's like a new beginning." Beth's face was radiant. "Connie and I spent ages getting ready and a good few days giving the place a much needed lick of paint before the women arrived," she stopped in mid-sentence and turned to Alice, "now it looks wonderful. Helps lift morale you know." she said conspiratorially. "Know what I mean, Alice?"

"I certainly do, Beth. It seems you've both done a wonderful job." Alice was amazed at how not only did Beth look animated, but that she was hardly leaning on her stick at all as she led her up the hallway. It was a vast change from only two months ago when she'd sat in Alice's back parlour with self-pity clouding her face refusing to move from her wheelchair.

Alice sat at the spotless kitchen table. "Have you got many residents at the moment?" She asked watching Beth hurriedly fill up the kettle and place it on the hob. Beth seemed impatient to arrange the cups and saucers and Alice winced as they clattered together in her friend's haste. "Beth, don't worry. I'm not desperate for a drink. Sit down and tell me your news," she cajoled.

Beth let out a long sigh and sat down carefully opposite Alice. "You're right we don't need tea. I have so much to tell you. As to your question we have several. One poor woman turned up on the doorstep last night and was desperate for help." Beth's face had gone quite pink as she explained to Alice about a young girl by the name of Daisy.

"She's been through so much, Alice. As soon as she knew we could help she was so thankful.

Beth sat back in her chair and smoothed down her dark hair. "Connie is with Daisy at the moment and apparently, if what we've heard is true, she needs to leave home immediately." Jumping at the sound of the kettle boiling, Beth slowly lifted herself up and turned off the hob. "She has a young baby," she continued as she returned to her seat. "Naturally we've said we'll take them both."

"Of course, what choice do you have?" Alice said passionately as she listened to Beth explaining how Daisy had told no-one about her husband's constant abuse. Alice marvelled at what she was hearing. When Beth had first set up the refuge with Connie she was disbelieving that Beth would be capable of helping at all. At that time the task ahead seemed impossible. Alice now realised as she saw how her friend's strength had returned, that this project had been exactly what Beth needed to shake her out of her self-pity.

"Alice. Are you listening to me?"

Beth's voice cut through Alice's thoughts jolting her out of her reverie. "Oh, I'm sorry. I couldn't help thinking..." Alice lifted her head and met Beth's eyes, "how you're so different, I mean, there's been such a change in you, Beth."

Beth smiled at Alice. "I know, Alice. I feel different. Things are so good and I feel more fulfilled than I ever have before."

"I'm so pleased everything has turned out well, I knew you could do it."

Beth leaned forward and took hold of Alice's arm. "When I didn't believe in myself you still had faith in me, Alice. I will never forget that."

Alice felt the emotion prick the back of her eyes and she blinked quickly. "It's you that's achieving this though, Beth. I was happy to help and just seeing the happiness on your face is reward enough."

"Oh and there's something else. It's unbelievable." Beth looked like a child bursting to tell a forbidden secret. "My mother called in this morning."

Alice raised her eyebrows and grinned back at Beth's enthusiasm. "That's a surprise, your mother?"

"She's going to call in often to see how things are going. I can't believe how she's defying my father." Beth's eyes were two round circles of wonder at this revelation.

"Well it must mean things are changing in the Hamilton-Green household." Alice touched her finger to the end of her nose and raised her chin. "Helen, my finest gown is needed, I'm attending a ball." She mimicked bursting into fits of giggles.

Beth's laughter echoed her own. "Oh...Alice, don't." Beth clutched at her sides and for a moment the two women were overcome with mirth.

When they had both recovered Beth sat back and wiped at her moist eyes. "I'm not saying mother's living her life any differently." Beth's expression softened, "but small changes such as visiting me behind my father's back are like climbing a mountain for her."

"Yes, I see. It must be a huge step for her." Alice agreed nodding her head. "Tell me how is it working alongside Connie?"

Beth saw the hidden meaning in Alice's question and in the wary expression on her friend's face. "We get on well. Because of her own experience Connie is able to relate to the women and she's teaching me how to help them." Beth lifted one eyebrow and regarded her friend. "Alice. What is it?"

A smile crept across Alice's face and there was a gleam in her eyes she couldn't hide from Beth. "Things are good. I am...very much in love," her face was warm as she met Beth's eyes but guilt at her new found happiness stabbed at her heart. A cloud passed across Beth's face and her eyes suddenly looked sad, making Alice instantly regret her words. "I'm so sorry. I didn't mean to upset you," she murmured wishing she could restore Beth to her happy state.

"What are you sorry for?" Beth interrupted forcing her expression back into the semblance of a smile which didn't quite reach her eyes.

Alice could see Beth struggling with her grief, the sanctuary may be her saviour but Alice knew that

Beth yearned for her lost love. "That was heartless of me telling you how I'm feeling about Connie." Alice's voice was barely more than a whisper, "I'm sorry that I've found love and you're still alone."

"Don't be silly, Alice. I'm pleased for you as you deserve happiness." Beth hesitated and Alice saw the glint of tears in her eyes quickly followed by a look of resignation on her face.

"Beth, I don't want to upset you further but I have to be honest with you, something isn't right. I really can't understand why Finn disappeared and didn't return. Seems a mystery to me?"

Feeling the ghost of her past chill her spine Beth whispered, "I know why he didn't come back," she ran her fingers along the cruel scar on her once smooth and delicate cheek. "Finn's landlady must have been telling the truth that day I visited."

Alice looked surprised as Beth's explanation confused her. Attacking the rising grief that was appearing to dissolve Beth's new found resilience Alice spoke with a suffragette's passion. "No Beth, whatever my jealous heart may have felt in the past, I cannot believe that. If he was betrothed to Aisling then why did he come to the meeting that day?" Not waiting for an answer Alice fought onwards, "it looked suspiciously like he was looking for you."

Beth shook her head and stared across the room with sightless eyes. "Who knows, maybe he wanted to see me one last time."

"I don't believe that." Alice refused to allow a conniving Irish strumpet to destroy Beth's life and resign her to second best as Beth deserved all that love could offer. She was an extraordinary person with a fragile heart. She took a deep breath and with the courage of her convictions she defied Beth's fears. "If he loved Aisling he would never have tried to see you again," she said firmly.

Beth's eyes were moist but Alice was on a mission now and she refused to allow herself to regret bringing the Irishman into their conversation. Gone was the carefree Beth of a moment ago, now she looked overburdened and downcast as she battled with her dread.

"That woman - Finn's landlady. She seemed angry with me that day claiming that Finn had caused a fire in his room." Beth looked thoughtful. "It's funny when I told her I'd go to the police if she didn't tell me where Finn was, she asked me how I knew about the insurance claim. I expect she's on the fiddle. Anyway I got the feeling she was hiding something else from me about Finn. When I asked if he had been injured she said not really and for a moment I had feared him to be dead..." Beth's words faltered. "To be told that Finn and Aisling were together and that it was my own fault I'd lost him, this was something I hadn't prepared myself to hear."

Beth let out a long sigh and regarded Alice adding. "Also, she seemed to know who I was. I suppose Finn must have talked about me." Fighting the desire to dwell on how things could have been Beth lied, "I'm over him now it's all in the past."

Alice didn't believe that for a moment and knew something was not right about Beth's visit to Finn's former landlady. "Where does this woman live?" She asked.

"The address is Old Castle Street just off Whitechapel High Street. Why do you ask?"

"No reason, just wondered." Alice regarded Beth. "Don't worry I'm not going over there," she said an idea forming in her head, "not if you say Finn no longer lives there."

Beth shot Alice an indifferent look. "Exactly, there would be absolutely no point," she agreed.

Chapter *Forty Eight*

THE TRUTH

Alice took an instant dislike to Mrs Violet Williams from the moment she'd opened the door.

"Yes?" she'd snapped. Violet's red lips smiled at Alice and she patted her coiffured hair into place. "We only have one room to let at the moment and that's for couples only. No lone women staying here, my dear" She looked Alice up and down as a sneer appeared on her heavily powdered face.

Alice's stern tone caused the other woman to stand up straight and glare at her visitor. "I'm not looking for a room, Mrs Williams. We can either discuss this on the doorstep or inside, it's entirely up to you. It's about your insurance claim for the fire in one of your rooms." Alice's words changed Violet's demeanour entirely. Her shoulders stooped and she hurriedly opened the door, while glancing across Alice's shoulder to the street beyond.

"Come in, my dear. Come in." She led Alice through to the front parlour a worried frown had appeared between Violet's brows. "Please sit down." "Are you from the Sun Alliance company?"

Alice perched herself on the end of one of the sofas, although tempted to say yes she didn't think it would get her the information she required. "No, Mrs Williams I'm not."

Violet looked confused. "Well, who are you then?"

"My names Alice Sparks and I'm a friend of Beth Hamilton-Green."

Mrs Williams's eyes became two angry slits and she opened her mouth to speak.

"Before you say anything, you should listen to what I have to say!" Alice glared at the other woman, who folded her arms across her chest, pursed her lips and leaned back in the chair to scrutinise her visitor.

"I know Beth came to see you at the beginning of the year. I also know that you lied to her about Finn." Alice kept her tone stern and defied the other woman the opportunity to interrupt. "I want to know the truth, Mrs Williams. I need to know Finn is and why you told Beth that he was marrying Aisling?"

"Why should I tell you anything? It's none of your business." Violet got up quickly and held the door open waiting for Alice to leave.

Secretly Alice thanked Beth as it was as she had suspected, Mrs Williams was on the fiddle with the insurance company. The gossiping women from the local shop had unintentionally given Alice the rest of the information she needed, that Mrs Williams was being less than truthful with the insurance company and was claiming more money than she was entitled. It seems she was lying about the damage that had occurred in Finn's former bedroom. "If you don't tell me what I want to know believe me, old woman, I'll tell the Sun Alliance the truth about your claim." Alice retorted.

"How...?" Pausing, Mrs Williams's chest puffed up and her face went quite red. "Who told you?"

"It doesn't matter who told me. Although..." Alice hesitated she was quite enjoying the theatricals and assuming a thinking pose continued as if suddenly struck with an idea. "I would choose who you tell your business to more wisely in future. What does matter is that you need to tell me the truth about Finn."

Violet's body seemed to deflate, but competing in dramatics, she sat back down putting a hand to her bosom in order to stop it heaving up and down. Next, she got up and began pacing around the room.

Alice was impatient for an answer from the old witch. "Well? I haven't got all day."

Mrs Williams stopped pacing and leaned against the mantelpiece. Alice could see an expression of defeat on her face reflected in the mirror on the wall. She turned around slowly and pointed a long red finger-nail at Alice.

"Alright then I'll tell you. Finn should not have pursued that 'Beth' woman, he should have left her alone. Aisling was the one that deserved him. She travelled all the way from Ireland to marry him and yet that stupid Irishman still couldn't see how much she loved him. Aisling waited months for him to change his mind but Finn still ignored her. So she was forced to do what she did, she had no choice. He gave her no choice."

Alice sat up straight. "What did she do?"

"Oh nothing really, just attempted to get him to see that she was the woman for him get him to appreciate her curves and comforting embrace."

Alice guessed what Violet was trying to say. "Do you mean she threw herself at him?"

Violet's expression was intense. "You could say that. It didn't work out though cos that Finn's not wot you'd call a normal man. I mean what normal man could resist the likes of Aisling? And he acted like a madman afterwards starting that fire the way he did!" Then, as if she suddenly realised she'd said too much she clamped her lips shut. "I think you'd better go, Miss whatever your name is." Once again she was striding towards the door.

Alice continued to sit firmly on the sofa refusing to move until she'd received the information for which she'd come. "You haven't told me where Finn is yet."

Violet's eyes were full of fire. "I don't know where that no-good Irishman is." Alice stood up and rounded on her, leaning towards the other woman who cowered away. "You know more than you're letting on and if you don't tell me, rest assured, I'll go straight to the Sun Alliance with the information I have on you."

"I only know where he works. It's the Thames Ironworks I have no idea where he's living."

Alice exhaled deeply before roughly pushing past the vile Mrs Williams. Heading for the front door, she knew that was all the information she would get from the old woman, but she hoped it was enough to track down Finn.

The rain shone on the passing Motor Cars and the horses carried their sodden heads high, in order to stop the trickles of wet dripping into the blinkers covering their eyes. As the clouds in the sky began to part, the darkness had started to lighten as sunshine peeked gingerly through their midst. The day promised a brightness to come that did nothing to lift Beth's mood. Her thoughts were far away. She hardly registered the presence of a familiar face smiling at her in the distance. Almost too late, she waved back at the young woman pushing her perambulator along the street and past her window. The woman's smiling face was quite different from the one she'd presented to Beth on her first visit to the refuge. Gone was the bruised and anxious expression. Now she looked healed and happy. Beth was proud of her achievement, although not all her charges had such storybook happy endings.

The tick of the clock on the wall drew her eyes back to the time. Once again Beth glanced up to discover that just a few minutes had passed since she had last looked. As she turned her head away, she caught sight of her reflection in the mirror that hung above the fireplace. Her fingers followed the familiar line of the long jagged scar that ran the length of her cheek. Her head spun and she sat down briskly in the armchair. Leaning backwards, she began furiously rubbing at her eyes in an attempt to erase the image of Finn from her mind.

A sudden knock at the door jolted her out of her reverie and brought to her attention how unusually quiet the house was that morning. This was far from normal for this time of the day. How she wished for the chaos that reigned the day before, at least that way she would have little time to think.

Beth opened the door to find Jane, a smile spread across her face, lighting up her eyes. In the crook of her arm she was cradling a baby who seemed oblivious to the world around him. Jane's body rocked gently backwards and forwards keeping the infant soothed and his eyelids heavy.

"Beth, I came to say thanks for yesterday," she explained.

Beth stepped aside leaning heavily on her walking stick, her leg was being particularly troublesome that day. "Come in, Jane," she said warming to her visitor her gaze lingering on the baby. "Sit by the fire, we don't want little William getting cold." As Jane entered the room Beth felt a warm glow of satisfaction. This young woman had arrived at the refuge only yesterday with her spirits almost completely broken, but with the trauma of the day before behind her, Jane now looked far more relaxed and at ease with the world.

"How are you both this morning?" Beth asked, looking down at William who was now fast asleep in his mother's arms.

"Oh, we are fine, Beth. Thank you and I am so grateful to you for yesterday. I really thought I would never be able to escape but you have changed our lives forever."

"Jane, you know we're not out of the woods yet? He may well come looking for you both again," Beth warned, aware that this poor mother may still be at risk.

"I'm sure he'll think twice about coming back, now he knows I can stand up to his bullying ways." As she spoke Jane's eyes filled with tears and her voice had become a whisper.

Beth strained to hear her words as she took hold of the other woman's free hand and held it tightly.

"For the first time in years, I feel safe from any harm he might do to me or little William." Jane's words were uttered with a determination Beth had not seen within this young lady before.

"I'm glad you're feeling better. Certainly no need to thank me it's all part of my job here." Beth rubbed vigorously at her right leg as she spoke.

"Are you alright, Beth? You don't look yourself this morning."

Beth attempted to smile at Jane but the pain of her leg prevented her doing so. "My leg is not so good today that's all. Also..." she hesitated aware of the mixed emotions she was experiencing, "it's almost Christmas and at this time of the year absent friends are missed so much more," she rushed the last part of the sentence as if tidying away clutter from a messy room.

Jane leaned closer to Beth. "Was this person a close friend, Beth?" she asked softly. The child in her arms stirred then returned to his slumber making a contented snuffling noise as he slept.

Beth tried again to smile but her eyes gave away her agony. She glanced at Jane before pulling herself up from the armchair and slowly approached the window where earlier she had studied the world's business. "No, Jane, just someone from my past." With her head dipped she bit down on her bottom lip and tried hard to control the wave of emotions sweeping through her body. The room around her seem unbalanced and far away. The night before she'd had such a vivid dream in which she and Finn were together again. Awoken with a start she'd found the black dog by her bedside, ready to pounce. It had taken an enormous effort to get out of bed that morning to begin her day.

The soft sound of the baby's breathing filled the room as Jane rocked William gently, his eyelashes fluttered and his tiny mouth smiled fleetingly in his sleep.

Suddenly a loud noise cut through the cloud that surrounded Beth glancing out of the window she saw Alice knocking vigorously on the front door and looking quite agitated.

"Would you like me to answer that, Beth?" Jane offered standing up.

"Yes please, Jane. It's Alice and she looks a bit distressed."

A moment later, Alice burst into the room. Her red hair was in disarray her green eyes full of urgency. "Beth. It's Finn!" She said in a tone of desperation, "he's leaving for America this morning!"

"Leaving...for America....but, Alice, why are you telling me this?" Beth's face was a mask of confusion at Alice's words. "I thought he was in Ireland, with..."

"No. You don't understand." Alice interrupted then stopping to take a break she sat down beside Beth, "he's not with Aisling as Violet told you."

Beth looked askance at Alice's words just as William's cries filled the air.

Jane hurriedly left the room obviously relieved at leaving what was clearly a private conversation.

431

"What on earth do you mean, Alice?"

"Look I haven't got time to explain. I've been to see that awful woman Violet and discovered that she lied to you that day you visited her, as Aisling went back to Ireland months ago." Alice pushed a strand of wayward hair back from her forehead and stared at Beth intently. "I went to see Finn at work, he wasn't there but his boss George said he was on his way to the Port. Quickly, Beth."

"But, Alice, even if he isn't with Aisling anymore he probably won't want to see me." Beth couldn't see why Alice was torturing her this way.

Alice got up and paced the room in exasperation. "Oh, Beth, you don't understand. George told me Finn's spent months and months pining for you," she put her arms around Beth, pulling her close and looking straight into her eyes, "he thinks you're dead...we haven't got time to talk." Alice glanced up at the clock. "If you don't leave soon you'll miss him."

Beth looked at her friend, this woman who loved her and had only her best interests at heart and her expression softened. "Do you think there's a chance?" she asked, her eyes hungry for reassurance like a child asking if the tooth fairy could possibly be real.

"Of course, you must go." Alice handed Beth her walking stick then held the door open as she walked out into the hallway. "Hurry, his ship sails in an hour."

Beth stopped in the hallway, her eyes filled with doubt. "Alice. What about everything here?"

"Don't worry. I will help out until you get back."

Beth attempted a smile which didn't quite reach her eyes then lifting her head she left the house.

Alice watched Beth leave, realising for the first time that she was no longer in love with Beth other than as a very dear friend. She desperately wanted Beth to find the kind of happiness she had managed to find with Connie. "Good luck, Beth. I pray you find him in time," she said softly as the front door clicked shut behind Beth.

Chapter *Forty Nine*

LEAVING

Finn stood by the gangplank waiting and watching. All around him the passengers had boarded the ship, but for a reason he couldn't fathom the defeated Irishman held back. He'd watched as the cranes lifted the heavy bags of sugar onto, *The Marjory*, the waiting ship. Arriving too early he'd felt unable to move from his position, terrified somehow of the moment he would have to go. He had even offered to help with the loading, but this was met by cold stares and threatening looks, as if he'd tried to take the workers' jobs away, instead of just having the need to give his idle hands something to do. Despite it being his decision he was finding it hard to leave his memories of Beth behind.

If he had a good passage with calm waters, Finn would be home with his family this time tomorrow. Finn's father had died many years ago but he would see his dear mother and brother Shamus and his family. After a short stay he would head for America where he would have a new beginning. A part of him wanted to stay in London, but he knew he could no longer bear to be in a city where everywhere reminded him of his lost love.

The thought of never seeing Beth again made his heart burn. He'd tried so hard to erase her from his mind. At least in different surroundings another land, maybe he could start again. He would always love Beth and regret the months they'd spent apart before her death, but this was the only way he could survive the rest of his life without her.

Finn covered his eyes with his hands in a vain attempt to stop the whirling in his head. The sounds of seagulls, men's voices and the clanking of metal against metal appeared to be closing in on him. He tried to focus on the soft lull of the waves as they washed up against ships that waited to sail to far off lands, whilst attempting to fill his mind with thoughts of what the future might hold.

Jack made a point of studying every female that rode in his cab and today was no exception. He'd watched as this one stared out of the window at the passing traffic. She had obviously been beautiful once, but now the jagged scar across her cheek had taken that away. It was a shame, he'd thought as he drove away leaving the forlorn figure behind him.

Beth stood for a moment on the pavement trying to summon the courage to walk towards the noisy bustling port. She let out a long sigh. The taxi journey had relieved the pain in her leg for a while, but now it was back with a vengeance. Her confidence had all but deserted her despite Alice's words of reassurance that Finn still loved her.

She watched the cab driver pull away. Then ignoring the apprehension she felt, Beth pushed herself onwards with all her strength.

This place was a man's world and a lone woman was rarely seen in their territory, especially unaccompanied. She drew attention without having reason to and several males could not help but stare in her direction. Beth's head was held high but beneath her the world wobbled. Her left leg struggled to keep up with the right giving her a slow ungainly gait. Trapped by her disability and desperate to run towards the ship that Finn would be boarding, Beth felt imprisoned by her own body.

Stopping to lean on her stick for a moment, she found herself in the midst of a cluster of people, some were waiting to board a ship whilst others were filtering down the subway to join the queue. These were obviously first class passengers men dressed in suits and the women in fine dresses. Their chatter filled the air but above the noise another sound reached Beth's ears making her pause to listen.

It was the soft silvery trill of a bird singing. Its song reached high into the air. It took her a moment to realise the haunting melody was coming from a gilded cage placed by the feet of a particularly striking looking woman.

The cage was small, gold coloured, and the afternoon sunlight glistened on its thin metal bars. What caught her attention and made her heart lurch was not the ornate encasement but the beautiful bird held captive within. Its feathers were a vibrant shade of yellow that stood out amongst the dull landscape around.

Despite her hurry, Beth couldn't help but stop. The sweet exquisite song lifted Beth's heart. As if the bird had noticed it had an audience, it suddenly stopped the bewitching call and with its beady eye piercing hers, began slowly tapping on the golden bars. Beth had an almost irresistible urge to open the barred cage and release the delicate creature from a life of captivity.

A shrill voice interrupted her thoughts. "Do you like my canary? She's beautiful isn't she? I know this one will be such a good breeder." The woman leaned towards Beth. "When I've chosen her a suitable mate, of course," she added conspiratorially. "Certainly her offspring will be something to show all my friends."

The woman, who had noticed Beth's initial interest, was obviously in the habit of boasting about her possessions. Dressed in red velvet and a feather hat, from under which peeped blonde curls, she was the centre of attention with several men and women clustering around her.

Beth stared blankly at the bragging woman but couldn't take in what she was saying all she could hear was the tap-tap tapping of the bird's beak on its cage. The woman's red painted lips moved up and down making Beth feel quite sick. Her arms gesticulated as she continued to explain to Beth her intentions for her pet. All of a sudden Beth felt overwhelmed by the woman's presence. The noise of a ship's horn soared loud into the air releasing Beth from this entrapment and jolting her back to reality. She needed to hurry if she was to catch Finn. Ignoring the woman and her boasting, she turned away from the waiting crowd and made her way, as fast as her leg would allow, deeper into the port.

The further Beth went into the port the more the noise became deafening. Men were scurrying this way and that shouting orders, their sweat mixed with the dirt and residue of whichever cargo they happened to be handling. The clanking of the cranes swinging high above Beth, made her feel small and insignificant in this dark and forbidding world. She tried to stay out of the men's way but it was hard because she didn't really know in which direction she should be heading, or where Finn's ship was berthed.

Odours filled her nostrils and it was hard to pick out what they were: a mixture of oils, varnish and a chemical smell she couldn't identify. The strongest smell was tobacco. She stopped for a moment to rest her leg, then closed her eyes and breathed in slowly, letting the activity swirl on around her. The deafening noise of barrels being rolled into place cut through her thoughts and her eyes opened quickly as she lifted a handkerchief to her nose and looked around anxiously. Her stomach churned as the smell of tobacco became overpowering.

The line of quays stood before Beth. She stared at the row of ships, some in the process of being loaded and others waiting to be relieved of their heavy cargo. Then incredibly she saw him but he hadn't noticed her yet. Finn was standing by a ship and staring up at her bow where the name *The Marjory* was brightly painted onto her hull. The boat swayed from side to side and the waves were splashing against her sides as she waited for her last passenger to board.

Finn stood with his back to Beth, his legs wide apart and hands on hips. His baggage was set to one side of him. He seemed to be watching the ship about to sail, but making no attempt to board it, not a muscle moved on his body. Beth longed to call out to him but knew that from this distance the wind would carry her voice far away from his hearing. She moved as quickly as her injured leg would allow towards him.

As she got closer Beth shouted at his back. "Finn… Finn!" Suddenly frightened that her arrival was too late, for he seemed not to hear her, Beth watched in horror as he took a step towards the beckoning ship. Forcing all her strength into her leg she pushed her body forwards wincing at the pain this caused, ignoring the warnings whirling in her head that he no longer wanted her. In the blink of an eye he turned towards Beth. Time stood still as their eyes met then he was standing in front of her.

"Beth?" He reached out and tenderly touched her arm. "Is it really you? It can't be...I must be dreaming. I've gone mad, crazy with love for you and now your image has materialized in front of me. Oh. God." Finn slumped forward covering his eyes with his hands.

Beth swayed unsteadily as she felt her walking stick fall from her grasp and land with a clatter next to her foot. "Finn, look. I am alive please...look at me," she attempted to stoop towards him but felt herself begin to lose her balance.

Finn's head jolted up and he put his arms around her. "It is really you, Beth?" he whispered into her hair. His lips found hers and instantly they became lost in each other. The shout of the gangplank being raised startled them from their embrace. "I cannot believe it really I can't." Finn's amber eyes were full of adoration as they gazed into hers. "I thought you were dead. Beth. What...happened?"

The chill of dread shivered down Beth's spine as she suddenly remembered her scars. Dipping her head she attempted to hide from his gaze. "I don't know, Finn," she murmured avoiding his eyes, "as you can see I'm alive and well apart from these battle wounds," her voice broke as she lifted a hand to touch her cheek.

Finn took hold of her chin and lifted up her face. He then bent towards her and kissed her damaged cheek. "It is nothing, A grá, you are still so beautiful," as he whispered the words he ran his fingers softly over her face.

Beth couldn't move or stop the flow of tears. "Oh, Finn," she said between sobs, "you wouldn't believe it but Violet told me you'd married Aisling."

Finn looked askance. "I would never have married her it's always been *you* I love."

"I love you too." Beth said firmly, looking into Finn's eyes. "I saw a bird on the way here it was in a beautiful cage, but it was trapped. I used to feel like that bird," she explained. A quizzical look passed across Finn's face. "I'm trying to make you understand why the suffragette movement is so important to me." Somehow it seemed imperative to Beth that Finn hear what she needed to say.

"It doesn't matter anymore. I just want to be with you forever." Finn tried to reassure her. "I don't care that you support the suffragettes, don't you see?"

At this revelation Beth's smile lit up her face as behind them *The Marjory* began her journey without her last passenger.

Finn held Beth at arm's length and looked into her blue eyes. "I've seen the light now, Beth my love. I understand more about the cause and want to help. Tell me, how can I help?"

Beth could hardly believe this disclosure from Finn it was so much more than she'd thought was possible. She had come to the port hoping for reconciliation with him, but knew that in her heart of hearts if his attitude remained the same their love was still doomed. But here he was not only declaring his undying love for her, but also pledging his support in the fight for the cause. It was far more than she had ever dared hope was possible.

Beth felt the breath catch in her throat. "There will be many ways you can help, Finn. There is still so much to do."

Finn's smile matched Beth's own as they walked arm in arm from the port with their heads bent low discussing a bright future together.

Beth glanced back at the departing ship, which was now sailing off into the distance, and her happiness was at last complete. The beautiful bird that fought long and hard to gain its freedom had finally found happiness beyond its gilded cage.

The Inspiration behind Bird in a Gilded Cage

Whilst in the process of researching an Edwardian piece of clothing, found by the present-day heroine of my recently begun contemporary novel, I found that research led me to look at Edwardian women, how they lived and what was important to them. I began to see how women in that era, were trapped in a world without freedom. A world where men ruled and women were denied even the most basic of rights. One of those rights was the right to vote.

At the turn of the century, two thirds of adult men in the United Kingdom could vote in parliamentary elections, along with convicts, inmates of lunatic asylums and workhouses. Women could not vote, and as a result their interests were inadequately represented in parliament. The suffragettes fought bravely for their right to vote and eventually achieved this when in February 1918, the Government passed an act giving women the vote if they were over the age of 30; and either owned property or rented for at least £5 a year, or were the wife of someone who did. As a result, 8.5 million women became entitled to vote in the General Election of 1918.

It wasn't until 2 July 1928 a law was passed allowing all women over the age of 21 to vote. Some say it is debatable how much effect the suffragette movement had on bringing about changes in voting laws. Others believe the movement's militancy made the Government more intransigent. Others say the 1918 Act was passed as a reward for women's efforts during the war rather than anything the suffragettes did. There is no doubt however, that the suffragettes raised the profile of the issue of women's votes to that of national consideration. They must forever remain in our history books for the way they fought so bravely and for the sacrifices they made along the way.

Acknowledgements

Bird in a Gilded Cage is my first novel and for me it will probably prove to be the hardest, for every new novelist must surely have the same doubts 'will I ever reach the end.' Therefore, I would like to thank my family, Kelly, John and Charlie who endlessly listened to me reading out the chapters as they evolved, and encouraged me to keep writing. Thank you also to my knowledgeable husband Shaun, for helping me with the research.